Praise for *Heart of the Hunter*

A finalist for the 2005 RITA Award in Paranormal Romance!

"Magical. Enchanting. Tina St. John is a true bard of the middle ages, whose stories sizzle with passion and fire. *Heart of the Hunter* begins a series destined for keeper status."
—KINLEY MACGREGOR,
author of *A Dark Champion*

"Enchanting, sensual, and intense . . . Tina St. John delivers stay-up-all-night storytelling at its finest."
—GAELEN FOLEY, author of *One Night of Sin*

"Braedon [the hero] . . . is the kind of strong, charismatic, slightly dangerous hero that will have readers salivating."
—*Publisher's Weekly*

"A vividly detailed setting, bold and adventurous protagonists, and a compelling plot laced with passion, danger, and a bit of mysticism all come together brilliantly in the first in a bewitching new medieval paranormal series by the wonderfully gifted St. John."
—*Booklist*

"4.5 Stars—St. John spins a spellbinding story with freshness, vitality, and strong characters whose riveting adventure makes for a nonstop read. This is St. John at the very top of her form."
—*Romantic Times BOOKclub Magazine*

Other enthralling romances by Tina St. John

LORD OF VENGEANCE
LADY OF VALOR
WHITE LION'S LADY
BLACK LION'S BRIDE
HEART OF THE HUNTER
HEART OF THE FLAME

HEART
OF THE DOVE

A Novel

TINA
ST. JOHN

IVY BOOKS • NEW YORK

An Ivy Books Mass Market Original

Copyright © 2005 by Tina Haack

Published in the United States by Ivy Books, an imprint of The Random House Publishing Group, a division of Random House, Inc., New York.

Ivy Books and colophon are trademarks of Random House, Inc.

ISBN 0-345-45996-2

Cover illustration: Judy York

Printed in the United States of America

www.ballantinebooks.com

OPM   9 8   7 6   5   4   3   2   1

For Celeste, Olivia, and Jasper,
my beautiful nieces and adorable nephew.
Wishing you a world of peace, love, and happiness.

❧ 1 ❧

The Irish Sea, off the coast of England
June, 1275

A HUGE WAVE gathered under coal black skies and rolled with deadly menace toward the side of the ship. It hit much as the dozens that had come before, a fist of crushing force that exploded against the wooden hull, rocking the vessel and spewing a sheet of drenching water over the already sodden deck. The cog lurched heavily under the pummel of the storm, the protesting strain of its joints screeching over the steady clap and roar of thunder.

Randwulf of Greycliff sat apart from the rest of the ship's few passengers on deck, his back pressed against the sheltering wall of the sterncastle, knees drawn up, boot heels braced apart to help steady him for the hurling pitch and swoon of the storm. It had only worsened since their departure from Liverpool's harbor, and showed no sign of reprieve. Three travelers had joined them in the port town when they docked for supplies that morning, two men and a young woman. At first Rand thought they were together, but the man and his wife had since moved off to share the cover of a moth-eaten blanket with five other passengers, all of them shivering, their gazes anxious and wide, holding similar looks of concern for their safe passage.

The man who also boarded in Liverpool seemed no more inclined to mingle with the others than Rand himself. One arm lashed around the railing, he sat less than a dozen paces from Rand on the same side of the deck. Rain pelted his uncovered head and beard, wetting shaggy dark hair to spiky bristles in the sudden flashes of lightning that illuminated the somber community of the vessel.

"You look as miserable as I feel," the man called to him, chuckling wryly. With his free hand, he held something out to Rand. A hammered metal flask glinted in the brief arc of light that broke as another bolt ripped jaggedly overhead. "Irish whiskey. Have some, friend. It will warm you."

Although he had done nothing to warrant mistrust, Rand decided he did not like the man's look. Ignoring the offer, soaked to the marrow of his aching bones, he pulled the dripping hood of his mantle down a bit lower on his forehead and steeled himself to ride out the churning squall.

The weather had been unseasonably harsh since he had set out on this journey more than a fortnight past. His destination, Scotland, was still several days north—easily more if the conditions of the sea did not clear up. And judging from the furious roil of the thick, sooty clouds overhead, he doubted there would be any mercy forthcoming.

In truth, it seemed the farther north he sailed, the more ferocious the ocean's turbulence became. As though God Himself knew of the unholy purpose that drove him, and sought to dissuade him with the unrelenting lash of the elements.

Let Him rage, Rand thought with grim savagery as another gale shouldered the side of the vessel and sent it groaning into a listing starboard plunge. The women on board screamed as the prow dipped sharply and took on more water.

Rand did not so much as flinch where he sat. He refused to cow to the vicious tumble of the waves. Biting rain needled his face as the storm spat and hissed all around him. Let the ocean swell and the winds tear him apart. Not even godly fury would be enough to turn him away from his goal.

Revenge.

It was his sole intent now, all of his hatred focused on one man . . . if that's what the villain he sought truly was. Rand doubted it. Born of flesh and blood, perhaps, but there could be no shred of humanity left in the one called Silas de Mortaine. Not when he commanded a small army of changeling beasts from another world, sentries conjured by some manner of sorcery to aid him in his quest for wealth and power. De Mortaine would stop at nothing, and woe betide any who stood in his way.

Even innocents, for on his order two months past had come the brutal deaths of a woman and child.

Rand's wife and son.

They had been everything to him—life, love, more blessings than were deserving of him, he was certain of that. But they were gone now. With the slayings of fragile, sweet Elspeth and little Tod, Randwulf of Greycliff no longer had anything to live for.

Save to avenge them.

And he would, justice delivered with the slow and agonizing death of the one who took them away from him in a hellish night of fire and screams, and the waking nightmare of their blood spilling before his very eyes.

Rand carried the tool of his vengeance with him on the ship. Its weight knocked against his hip with the roll of the deck, an artifact secured within a leather satchel and concealed beneath the wide fall of his cloak. There was nothing Silas de Mortaine wanted more than the treasure that Rand and his brother-in-arms, Kenrick of Clairmont, had claimed from an abbey church at the crest of Glastonbury Tor three weeks ago.

That treasure—coupled with the final piece Rand was headed for Scotland to find—would be all the lure he would need. De Mortaine was certain to rise to the bait, and when he did, Rand's retribution would be dispatched by ruthless, savaging steel.

He did not expect he would survive to savor his victory. Nor did he delude himself with the notion that he might join his family in the hereafter when his heart was blackened with hatred, his hands soon to be willingly stained with the cold-blooded murder of his enemy. But it mattered naught. Elspeth's and Tod's deaths would not go unmet, even at the price of his very soul.

"For them," he muttered under his breath, the words misting in the rain before the rising howl of the storm swept them away.

The crash of another wave slammed the side of the cog, spraying briny water into his eyes. With the answering lurch of the deck, the young woman from Liverpool gave a sharp cry of distress. She flung her arm out to reach for a small purse that had come loose from her belongings. The tide washed across the deck, carrying the little pouch swiftly toward the edge. Too late to retrieve it, the errant purse rode the pull of the retreating wave right into the sea.

"My mother's brooch was in that bag!" the woman wailed to her husband as he gathered her close to comfort and protect her.

"Best keep a tighter hold on your treasures. Wouldn't you say, friend?"

Above the din of the storm, Rand heard the voice of

the man seated down the deck from him. The query—
and the oddly phrased advice—was directed at Rand,
rather than the couple huddled across the deck. Rand
lifted his head to peer at the stranger through the pelting
rain. Dark eyes stared back at him from under the fall of
a thick forelock, their narrowed, unflinching look too
focused to be mistaken for anything less than cunning.

And now that he considered it, Rand noted with a degree of cool foreboding that the man had at some point
moved closer to him. No longer a dozen paces, but less
than half that distance. Just out of arm's reach.

"I am not your friend," Rand growled in warning,
"and I've a blade at my hip that's itching to convince
you of that fact. I don't like your look, sirrah. I'd advise
you to back off."

The man gave an abrupt shout of laughter. "You advise me, do you?"

"That's right." Beneath his mantle, Rand wrapped his
fingers around the hilt of a dagger sheathed on his belt.
"I won't tell you again."

There was something peculiar about the stranger's
face. Indeed, something peculiar in his very being. The
sheeting rain seemed to distort his features, sharpening
the man's bearded jaw, bulking his dark brow. The eyes
that stared at Rand with such boldness seemed lifeless
and devoid of color now, coldly black. In the scant light,
they took on a feral glint.

Battle instinct clamored an alarm in Rand's gut. He
pressed his spine against the sterncastle wall, feet planted
firmly apart as he prepared to spring into combat mode
in an instant, heedless of the raging weather.

The stranger grabbed the railing of the deck and
hauled himself to his feet. The man chuckled now, his
mouth filled with sharp, bared teeth. "You arrogant,
stupid . . . *human*."

He spat the word, as much a curse as the one Rand hissed when he realized what faced him now.

A bolt of light cut across the blackened sky. Thunder cracked and rolled in ominous fury. Rand ignored the tempest, sluicing water out of his eyes as he rose to confront one of Silas de Mortaine's deadly minions.

"Give me the satchel," the man snarled, his lips curling against the bright slash of his teeth.

"I'll see you dead first—and gladly," Rand told him. He did not wait for the attack to come to him. Preferring to be on the offensive, he made the first move, drawing a dagger from his baldric as he took a step forward.

One of the other passengers across the deck shouted through the driving force of another shuddering, spitting gale. "Sit down, fools! The storm will sweep you over!"

The warning went unheeded, wholly insignificant when one understood the truth of what was at stake here. The storm was brutal, to be sure, but there was a deadlier force at work on the rain-slickened deck of the ship. Rand was not about to let that threat go unmet.

He surged forward, lunging for de Mortaine's man and locking him in a punishing choke hold. The dagger found vulnerable flesh and sank in, tearing a roar of pain and anger from the man's throat. Blood flowed at once, tainting the briny darkness with the stench of rising death. De Mortaine's henchman struggled to reach his own weapon, but Rand's blade drove home again, this time plunging into the heaving barrel chest.

Where Rand anticipated surrender, he felt further resistance from the bearded man. The bleeding bulk of his body seemed to shift in his grasp, rippling with a queer power. Fingers that curled into Rand's back for support grew longer, digging into his flesh with the hard bite of beastly claws.

Everywhere the shapeshifter's body touched him, Rand's skin crawled as though charged with the force of lightning itself. He broke the jolting sensation and delivered another savage strike of his blade.

A lady screamed from somewhere over Rand's shoulder. "He is killing that poor man! Someone do someth—!"

The terrified cry cut short an instant later, when the eyes of the other passengers finally focused on what played out before them. Rand himself saw the feral glow of an animal's eyes staring up at him, the slavering jaw of a wolf drawn open, wet with blood and rain.

The beast he now held roared with otherworldly rage, then swung its massive head down to lock on to Rand's arm.

The jaws clamped hard, pure fire shooting through him as a churning wave careened into the side of the hull. Rand went down on one knee, fighting to hold his ground while he struggled with his assailant. The screams of the other folk on deck rose with the vibrating shock of thunder and lightning clashing high above their heads. Water rushed over the side of the vessel, tipping it into a starboard lurch.

Rand flung his hand out for the railing—and missed it.

His fist closed around empty air. He lost his precarious footing, the wolf falling with him, dragging him down onto the slick planks of the deck. More water sluiced over the side of the ship. Rand saw only the dark form of the shapeshifter beneath him, its bulky weight knocking hard into his legs before the wave caught it. Too late to free himself of the iron jaw still sunk into the flesh of his forearm, Rand's world tilted with the wild lurch of the ship.

More shouts of horror sounded from the passengers,

more screams from the women and wailed prayers that would surely go unanswered.

Pushed by the heavy hand of the wave as it swept the deck, Rand could only gasp a quick breath and prepare himself for the sudden chill plunge as he followed the shapeshifter over the side of the vessel and into the black, roiling sea below. At once, the waves pulled him under. The shapeshifter released his arm, caught in its own struggle to survive as the storm-swept sea engulfed them.

The waves rocked and churned, dragging Rand farther under. He fought the drowning squall, his efforts impeded by the strangling weight of his mantle and clothing. Sinking like a stone, he freed himself of the heavy cloak, letting it drift away on the tide. His boots were sacrificed next. He pulled them off, his lungs straining for air as the cold sea continued to swallow him.

God's love—he was drowning.

He needed air. Rand opened his eyes and saw only darkness, the salt water burning his vision and searing the bloody wound on his arm. Muscles cramping in the cold wetness, he hauled his body through the black distance until his face broke the surface of the water. Rand gulped in great mouthfuls of the rainy night air, choking in his haste to breathe.

Too soon, he was going under once more, raked by the sharp talons of the shifter as it pawed him from beneath the surface of the water. The beast flailed, using Rand's body as a ladder to hoist its heaving girth above the waves. Rand felt his tunic shred, the muscles of his chest and thighs searing as the wolfen claws slashed at him in blind panic.

Before him in the darkness, Rand saw the shifter's form mutate from wolf to man, to wolf again. And all the while, it kept attacking him, its hellish eyes gleaming with murderous intent. Rand kicked it away, giving himself only the briefest opportunity to draw his sword from its sheath on his baldric. His movements were slow, his usual battle-trained agility compromised by the force of the water that closed in on him from all sides. Oblivious to Rand's plan, the shifter splashed and clawed to swim toward him. Rand held the long blade concealed beneath the lightless surface of the water and lunged forward with all he had.

Hard black nails tore at his neck as the wolf and he collided and locked in a deadly embrace. Rand thrust his sword arm through the impeding tide and felt it connect with solid flesh and bone. The shifter screamed, its long jaws dropping open in a howl of inhuman rage. Rand ended the bone-jarring cry with a savage jerk of his wrist, driving the blade home. Blood warmed the cold seawater as the shifter's dead body went limp and slowly sank out of sight.

Treading water, bobbing under the swelling rise and fall of the waves, Rand pivoted to look for the ship. It was gone. He was alone in the storm, adrift and exhausted. His limbs felt leaden in the cold embrace of the sea, his many gashes stinging like fire as he spilled more blood into an already tainted tide.

His only hope was to swim.

But to where?

Naught but darkness surrounded him, miles of open ocean and a tempest that beat down on him in relentless fury. There was no sign of the shore in any direction, only vast emptiness. Rand's head went under, submerged by the pitch of another wave. What clothing remained on him dragged him down, as did his weapon and the priceless cup that bumped solidly against his leg in the satchel slung over his shoulder by its long leather strap.

If he had a prayer of swimming any distance now, he had to lose some of the weight, as much as he could. In haste, Rand stripped off his torn tunic. He let his sword slide out of his grasp, his only means of defense gone in an instant as the hungry sea took it down.

All that remained was the Chalice treasure.

The heavy gold cup with its pair of priceless stones had already proven a significant burden. But he would not release it, not even for the chance to save his own life.

Rand began to swim, commanding his aching arms to motion, kicking his way through one pitching wave to another. The treasure he carried at his hip—the tool of his awaiting vengeance—would go with him to the nearest shore . . . or it would accompany him to a watery end at the bottom of the churning sea.

❧ 2 ❧

SUNSHINE STREAMED THROUGH the thick canopy of
summer foliage, glossy green leaves limned in golden
light as they rustled in the soothing summer breeze. The
morning had dawned in tranquil hues of pinkish rose
and yellow amber, tinting the thin clouds that smudged
the pale blue sky at the outlying edge of the forest grove.
The soft skitter of woodland creatures foraging in the
bramble mingled with the gentle waking of the day,
while above, perched on a sturdy bough of an ancient
sheltering oak, a dove cooed to its snuggling mate.

"And good morrow to the both of you as well,"
replied a young woman who strode the narrow path
through the heart of the woods.

With fingers gloved in supple leather, she lifted the
skirt of her simple ecru bliaut and continued on her way,
her bare feet glistening with the dew that yet covered the
ground from the previous night's storm. It had been a
virulent tempest of crashing thunder and bright, streak-
ing lightning, uncustomary for the time of year, and not
a little terrifying. Her mother had feared for their very
lives, shrieking with each rattling clap of thunder that
shook their humble cottage.

Not so, Serena.

She had been secretly thrilled with the immensity of
the storm. So little of the unusual touched her, here in
the sanctuary of the far-flung forest that had been her

home all the nineteen years of her existence. She was protected here, and while she enjoyed the peace and simplicity of the life she lived with her dear mother, something peculiar had begun to stir within her of late. That stirring urged her toward reckless thoughts—toward wilder shores than the one that stretched in a sandy line on the other side of the woodland grove.

It was toward that familiar beach that Serena wandered now, her thoughts trailing over the routine tasks that awaited her back at the cottage. There were herbs to be cut, a garden to be weeded, linens to be laundered, floors to be swept. . . .

Mundanity, all of it, she reflected with a sigh. Her mother had set her about her morning's duties some time ago, but once Calandra's watchful eyes were turned, Serena had taken the opportunity to stray in search of more interesting diversions. The call of the rolling surf whispered of adventure, and she followed it with eager feet.

Serena emerged from the forest edge and paused, eyes closed as she tipped her face up into the sun and breathed deeply of the crisp, briny air. Her toes sank into the warm brown sand, the smooth grains still damp and packed firm from the rains that had come so feverishly overnight.

Her senses filled with the wide openness of the world before her. The unbound mass of her long dark hair lifted and swirled about her, tickling streamers caught on the breeze, blowing unfettered. She heard the throaty cry of a seabird and opened her eyes to see a snowy white gull sweeping overhead. She delighted in its arcing flight, smiling as it dipped and soared in effortless freedom above the beach. Some score-and-a-few paces ahead of her, the ocean lapped in froth-curled waves, rolling onto the shore in a playful tumble.

Serena strode toward the water with a barely stifled giggle of joy—and abruptly stopped not halfway there.

A large, bulky shape drew her gaze askance, to where a clump of seaweed-strewn debris lay a short distance down the beach, just at the water's edge. She shielded her eyes from the sun's glare with an upraised hand, peering at what looked to be an unfortunate sea creature tossed ashore and unmoving in the sand. Intrigued, saddened for the lifeless beast that likely perished amid the storm, Serena began to approach it, silently intoning a prayer of compassion.

She could not have been more shocked when she glimpsed the pale tones of human flesh shrouded in the dark, twisted strands of water vines. It was a man, she realized at once, her eyes widening as she gaped at thick muscled arms and a bare torso slashed with angry lacerations. Bright red blood trailed from his wounds, and from a cut that had split his dark brow. The thin rivulets gathered and twisted in a small pool of salt water that had accumulated around him. His clothing was common enough—what little remained of it. The man wore only tattered hose and braies, all of him looking battered and forlorn, so alone.

Where had he come from?

Serena pivoted her head to scan the rest of the beach, looking for clues to his origin. If he had been shipwrecked, there was no trace of other victims, nor of the vessel that might have carried him into the storm. The man lay half on his chest, his right shoulder dug into the moist sand, his cheek resting on the beach as if he slept. Seaweed and the spiky fall of his dark brown hair obscured what little she could see of his face. He gripped the strap of a leather satchel in his fist, his knuckles gone white with the ferocity of his hold.

"Whoever you are, I pray you did not suffer in your

final moments," Serena whispered, feeling a wash of sorrow for the man at her feet.

She bent her head in a somber reflection, her gaze narrowing on him. A wave reached for him then, swirling about his legs and gently rocking his motionless body as the tidal rush lapped at him, then receded back into the sea. As his solid bulk shifted, something metallic glinted at the base of his strong neck—a pendant chain, its links seeming far too delicate for a man of his size. Perhaps it would tell her something of who he was, or where he came from.

Curious, Serena retrieved a long stick from nearby and came to stand beside him. Her fingers trembled within the leather encasement of her gloves.

Never lay your hands on one of them. You must never allow yourself so close to a man that he could taint you with his wickedness.

Her mother's warning issued in Serena's head as if Calandra stood at her side. The words were as much a part of her as breathing, cautionary advice she had heard countless times since her birth.

Never touch, child, for their kind will bring you only pain.

Serena caught her lip between her teeth. Surely there was naught to fear from this lifeless stranger. She gripped the stick more firmly, mustering her courage. The sun-bleached length of wood hovered at the man's bulky shoulder, its wavering tip belying her apprehension to put herself so close as to touch this man, even with more than an arm's length of hard oak between them. Serena placed the tip of the stick against his arm and quickly nudged him over.

He rolled gracelessly onto his back, dislodging some of the debris that covered his face and torso. He was handsome in a rugged way, although Serena had been schooled not to give much notice to the face and form of men. This was not the first man she had seen. Once, she had come across a russet-haired youth from the nearby village of Egremont, when she had ventured too near the grove line. The young noble had been in the woods hunting hare; Serena had nearly taken an arrow in her backside as she attempted to escape the stranger's notice. She had learned to be more careful in the time since.

And there could be no comparing the lanky arrogance of the beardless village youth with the hard planes and angles of this man.

Serena came down on her knees in the sand and leaned over his supine body to study this unsettling gift from the sea. A mat of downy hair darkened his chest, but did naught to conceal the slabs of hard muscle beneath. Nestled against his heart lay the golden pendant that had peaked her curiosity. It was a delicate thing, like something her mother would wear. Serena edged closer, wondering if the design might tell her something of the man who wore it, or of the lady for whom it likely had been crafted. She reached out a gloved hand and gingerly lifted the filigree amulet. To her dismay, the tiny links of the chain gave in her loose grasp, breaking away from the man's neck. She caught the memento before it could fall into the sand, and held it tenderly in her gloved palm.

It was made in the shape of a heart, the wiry gold strands woven like a spider's web, and nearly as fragile. Serena brought her free hand to her mouth and used her teeth to strip off her glove. The gold was warm against her fingertips.

The trace heat of the metal jolted her into sudden awareness.

She glanced back at the man, at the fresh blood that yet trickled from his wounds. She frowned, then gasped in startlement as his chest rose with the claiming of a shallow, indrawn breath. At the sound of her surprise, his black lashes lifted, revealing muted hazel eyes. He blinked once, slowly, as though trying to focus.

"Mercy!" she shrieked, leaping to her feet in an instant. She stumbled back on her heels. "You are alive!"

With a groan, he rolled weakly to his side. A ragged, choking sound gathered from his throat as he coughed up a mouthful of seawater.

Serena backed away from him, astonished and filled with mounting, irrational fear.

He was alive.

Absently, she dropped her glove into the damp sand. Her bare fingertips tingled, clutching the pendant she had retrieved from around his neck.

Never touch, came the dire warning in her mind. *Men are wicked and cruel, every last one of them. They can bring you only pain.*

"Help . . ." the man sputtered in a deep, commanding voice. With obvious effort, he lifted his head and met her stricken gaze. "Please . . . help . . . me."

He thrust out his arm to grab for her. Serena yelped, then turned and bolted like a terrified doe. She crashed through the bramble, speeding along the winding forest path, heedless of the briars that snagged her skirts and clawed at her bare feet. She ran in breathless panic, fleeing as fast as she could for the haven of the cottage. Her mother would know what to do. She would know how to help him.

"Mother!" Serena called, her voice sharp, pitched to a frantic level. "Mother, where are you? Come quickly!"

Calandra appeared at once, dashing from around the back of the squat cottage. Her hands wrung the modest apron she wore over her dun-colored bliaut, crumbs of dark earth marring the simple weave. Loose tendrils of her silver-streaked, pale blond hair flew out of their confining plait and fell about the oval of her lineless face. Her expression was one of sudden dread and terror, all of it centered on Serena.

"What is it, child? Are you hurt?"

Serena shook her head. "Nay, not I. But there is a man—he's washed up on the beach!"

Calandra rushed forward to clasp Serena's shoulders. Her fingers clenched tight, almost bruising. "Where is your other glove?"

"I don't know. I . . . I must have dropped it." She winced at the bite of her mother's worried hold. "The man has been injured, Mother. He is bleeding. He begged me to help him."

Some of the color drained from Calandra's already pale cheeks. "He spoke to you? Heaven above, Serena—tell me you did not lay your hands on him!"

"Nay. I would not. You have warned me—"

Calandra's exhaled breath of relief fanned across Serena's brow before she caught her daughter in a fierce embrace. "I have tried to teach you well. All of it was to prepare you for something like this. A stranger, bringing his trouble to our doorstep."

Serena extricated herself from her mother's arms, shaking her head. "He is the one in trouble. He has suffered, Mother, and very nearly drowned. Come, we must help him if we can."

Calandra did not move. Indeed, when Serena pivoted to return to the forest path, her mother caught her by the wrist, halting her before she could take the first step.

"Why do you stand there?" she asked, confused by this queer show of apathy from a woman who had nurtured scores of wounded and sickly animals back to health with less persuasion. Could her fear of men be so deeply rooted that she would not act to aid someone in desperate need of care? "Will you not come with me?"

"I will not," Calandra answered simply. "Nor will I permit you to go to him. You will stay here, and you will put the stranger out of your mind."

Serena stared at her mother as though looking upon a stranger even more foreign than the one now washed ashore on their secluded beach. "But . . . he is injured, perhaps gravely. He's bleeding and suffering. Do you understand? He is weak, and if we do not help him, he is likely to die there."

Calandra's gaze was steady, uncompromising. "Pray he does, my child."

❧ 3 ❧

SERENA LAY ABED that night, unable to sleep for the nagging sting of her conscience. How could she rest knowing that somewhere, out there in the dark, another human being might be breathing his last—or worse, struggling to live, yet suffocating on the incoming tide as it swept ashore and dragged him helplessly back into the sea? Serena frowned into the dark quiet of the small cottage, tossing off the coverlet as she rose to a sitting position in her bed.

On a pallet across the room, her mother's soft snores rasped the slow rhythm of a deep, untroubled slumber.

It hardly seemed fair.

It certainly did not feel right to her that they should do nothing for the stranger now abandoned on the beach.

She still had his pendant. With tender care, Serena retrieved the necklace from beneath her pallet mattress, where she had secretly stowed it that afternoon, concealing it from her mother's disapproving notice. The small gold links of the chain curled serpentine in her open palm, the delicately wrought pendant winking in the starlight that spilled in through the unshuttered window. She had not meant to take it from him, but in her startlement and her haste to get away, the piece had gone with her.

It felt as wrong as stolen goods in her hand. The pendant did not belong to her, and while she had not taken it intentionally, she could not keep it. She had to bring it back to him, regardless of in what woeful state she might find the man down on the beach.

And she had to admit there was a part of her that wanted to know—needed to know—if there might be some slim chance that she could still help the stranger, regardless of her mother's adamant refusal.

Very carefully, mindful to make not even the slightest noise, Serena withdrew from her pallet bed. Her chemise floated about her feet, ghostly white, as silent as her footsteps on the crude floor of the cottage. Less than ten paces and she reached for the latch on the abode's oiled wood door. The rough-hewn panel gave only the faintest creak of protest as she slipped past it.

Serena paused at the threshold, waiting just long enough to see that the sound of her leaving had not disrupted her mother's sleep. Then, with the pendant caught fast in her hand, she stepped out into the moonlit night and headed for the narrow forest track that would lead her to the shore.

The surf rolled in on whitecapped waves, high tide nearly at its fullest. The water stretched almost halfway up the beach, receding from the sand as a glistening blanket of wetness. Serena looked at once down the line of the shore, walking quickly toward the place she had been that day, but she saw nothing. All that remained was sand and surf.

The debris and seaweed—the injured man—all of it was gone.

As if her unexpected discovery that morning had been naught but a troubling dream.

She stood at the edge of the shoreline, her toes immersed in salt water and foam as another wave skated up the beach. Guilt welled bitterly in her throat when she thought of the stranger and how she had denied his plea for help. Was he out there somewhere, drifting lifelessly in the black vastness of the ocean beyond?

If so, then she was an accomplice to his death, as responsible as the storm he had barely survived, and the sea that likely claimed him after all. The knowledge squeezed her heart, useless remorse pressing down upon her as she gazed out at the emptiness of the horizon.

"I'm so sorry," she murmured, the pendant chain dangling limp from her fingertips.

Something knocked lightly against her foot as the wave that surged about her ankles now slid back from shore. It was her errant glove, the one she had dropped in her fright. Serena stooped down to pick it up, her ears ringing with the liquid roar of the sea. Waterlogged, likely ruined from its salty bath, the leather glove dripped a steady patter around her feet. She wrung it out, then turned to go back home.

Something tall and shadowed blocked her path.

"What did you do with it, wench?"

Serena tilted her head up . . . and up some more . . . until she was staring into a night-dark expression of seething rage.

Animosity radiated like fire from the man she had unwillingly left to die on the beach that morning. Serena took a step back in reflex.

"You stole something from me," the stranger growled, his voice a raw, throaty scrape of sound that skittered along her spine. "Damn it, woman! Tell me what you've done with it."

"H-here," she stammered, holding the pendant out before her in her ungloved fingers. "I didn't mean to take it."

A large hand jutted toward her to grab for the necklace. Serena drew her arm back the instant his fingers closed around the chain, relieved that she could command her wits enough to avoid contact with him. His coarse chuckle held no humor.

"So, you're a petty thief as well." The pendant disappeared in his curled fist. "No more games now. Give me the other item you took while I lay bleeding and unconscious at your feet."

"I-I don't know what you mean. I took nothing else from you, I swear it."

He took a step forward, a menacing step that put him much too close to her. Serena retreated a couple of paces, wading backward into the water. Wet sand sucked at her heels as the tide swelled with the incoming rush of another wave, the dark water catching the hem of her long chemise. The fabric twisted about her ankles, nearly tripping her.

"What did you take from this satchel?" he demanded, flinging an empty leather bag at her.

Serena caught it in her arms, confusion swamping her as quickly as the coming tide. "I took nothing out of this. You had the bag when I found you today, but I know naught of what it contained. For all I know, it was empty even at that time."

"Lies!" he bellowed.

His fists were held rigidly at his sides, and in the scant light of the partial moon and scattered stars, something wild flared in his eyes.

It was all the warning she had. In a flash of movement, the stranger lunged for her. Serena cried out, narrowly escaping his swinging grasp. She threw the satchel at his face, hearing the wet leather slap his skin as she pivoted on her heel and dodged his long reach.

All of Calandra's warnings came back to her now, a thousand cautions about the brutal, unfeeling nature of men. What a fool she had been to doubt her mother, even for a moment.

Serena ran out of the water and up onto the beach, but the man was right behind her. His steps were weak, faltering from his exhaustion and the lack of traction in the sand. But still he gained on her, each long-legged stride outpacing two of hers. Suddenly he was on her. A firm, heavy hand landed on her shoulder, throwing her off balance. He spun her around to face him, teeth bared bright white in the darkness, his breath hissing out from between his clenched jaw.

"Why run if you have nothing to hide, eh, girl?"

"Let me go!"

Serena struggled against him, but it was futile. He locked her shoulders in his iron grasp, glaring down at her. Before she could think better of it, she brought up her hands and slapped them against the muscular planes of his chest.

Mother Mary.

She touched him.

Touched him without the protective barrier of her gloves.

Sensation hit her at once, a gale-force wave of emotion. Her palms felt white-hot where they pushed against him, enlivened with the awakening hum of insight. Too stricken to break away, too awash in the power of her gift, Serena could only stand there, frozen, gaping up at his furious countenance while her touch read all the anger and hatred that filled his heart—indeed, his very soul.

Rage.

Destruction.

Bloodshed.

Anguish.

Emptiness.

Vengeance.

Too much pain to bear. Serena's breath went shallow and panting as the blackness of his feelings engulfed her. It ate all of her strength, devouring her like a pestilence, swiftly, thoroughly. Serena felt her legs go weak beneath her. She could not stop the flood of hurt and violence that assailed her in that moment, a chaotic tempest of seething emotion pouring out of him and into her as if it were her own.

"God's blood, what is wrong with you?"

The stranger's words sounded far off and muffled. He shook her, but it only made her sway more on her boneless legs. She could not hold her own weight any longer. She could not think, nor could she form the words to demand that he release her. The Knowing held her in a tighter hold, merciless and unrelenting.

Shadows edged her vision. . . .

The stranger's face blurred before her, and then she felt herself collapse against him.

Rand let out an impatient hiss, forced to catch the woman as she slumped against him in a faint. His fingers closed on slender ribs and warm, soft skin, her feminine curves too thinly covered by the muslin chemise she wore. Small, pert breasts pressed firmly against his bare chest, sending an instant, unwilling spark of awareness through his veins.

Anger flared in its wake.

Fragile maid or nay, this uncaring wench had shown him a heart as cold as stone when she left him to die on the incoming tide. If holding her now should inspire anything in him, it should be mistrust and suspicion. And not a little fury. Gruffly, he drew her away from him, his hands gripping her beneath her limp arms.

"Wake up, girl."

She flinched at the stern command. Her head lolled on her shoulders, but she did not rouse. Her long, straight dark hair fell like a glossy veil to her waist, the mass of ebony silk swinging as Rand tried to jostle the woman to her senses.

"Open your eyes," he ordered her, having no use for helpless female swoons—particularly coming from someone who had refused him much-needed aid while casually stealing him blind. "Wake up, I said. Before I drop you."

It was no idle threat, for while her weight was as slight as a child's, it was more taxing than he cared to credit. His muscles ached from fighting the sea the night before, and his injuries from the shifter's claws now bled anew, freshly opened. He needed food, rest, and care. He needed to find the Chalice treasure that had been safely ensconced in his satchel when he washed ashore.

Hadn't it been?

God's bones, but the ordeal he had endured at sea had left him uncertain of that fact.

He swore he could remember seeing the lumpy form of the bejeweled cup within the satchel as he lay exhausted on the beach. He swore he could feel its weight in the leather bag, the long strap caught tight in his fist, tugging at him with each pull of the lapping waves.

And he swore he knew the presence of a woman—this woman—prodding his motionless body with a stick, her homespun skirts brushing his bare skin as she walked around him, merciless of his suffering, yet morbid in her curiosity. She admitted she had taken Elspeth's pendant from his neck; what would keep her from taking the object of greater value?

With a snarl, he caught the woman around the waist with one arm, then reached down to grab her lifeless hand. He brought her fingers up between their bodies, clasping her in a hard grip as he shook her.

"Damnation, wake! Whatever your game, I have no time for it!"

At last, success.

Her eyes flew wide open, her long-lashed gaze staring up at him, stricken. The delicate bones of her hand jolted in his firm grasp, the tendons of her fingers flexing tight. All of her went rigid in that one instant.

"N-no!" She drew a breath, sharp and shallow. "Release me!"

He held fast. Although his grip on her was unyielding, he did not aim to hurt her. Not unless she forced his hand. Yet despite his efforts to keep from bruising her small hand and wrist, she arched and writhed as though clasped in a vise of burning iron. She cried out, a keening howl of anguish that carried high on the night breeze. If she pretended at the pain to win his sympathy, she would find him an unswaying audience. Still, he had to admit she gave a convincing performance.

Rand's patience held on a threadbare leash. "I warn you, woman, do not trifle with me."

"Please," she begged, her voice raw, almost whimpering childlike. "Let me go. I cannot bear any more. . . ."

Her eyes fixed on his with a piercing, wild intensity. Her pupils seemed huge in the moonlight, as though they had absorbed the darkness around her.

As though her gaze had absorbed far more than that.

The fight seeped out of her, but her queer rigidity remained. Rand thought she might fall into a second swoon, but no sooner did the possibility register than he heard a sudden disturbance of the forest vegetation behind him. There was a banshee scream, then Rand turned to find a white-haired wraith flying at him from out of the woods.

"Unhand her!" The female voice shook with fear and selfless, protective fury. A slim dagger flashed metallic in the moonlight as the woman crashed toward him, prepared to kill. "Take your hands off my child!"

Rand released the younger woman to pivot and face the elder before she had the chance to plunge her wicked little blade into his back. She leaped on him like a mad she-cat, thrashing and snarling, a frenzied blur of flowing white hair and flailing limbs. Her rough homespun gown smelled of cooking herbs, rich earth, and spicy soap—a madwoman, perhaps, but a clean one, and surprisingly agile as well.

Rand kept his focus on the weapon, his combat-trained hands seeking out the threat with greater strength and speed than even this desperate mother determined to protect one of her own. He wrenched the dagger from the woman's grasp and flung her off of him in a heap. She hit the wet sand of the beach not far from where her daughter sat in a mute daze, her legs folded beneath her. Dark hair shielded her downturned face from view; her crossed arms shielded her body, which rocked back and forth in a slow, mindless rhythm.

"Serena! Oh, mercy. What did he do to you?" the woman cried, her attention diverted from Rand only for a moment. Long enough to spy the blood marring her daughter's chemise from where Rand's wounds had touched her. In the dim moonlight, the stains looked near to black, alarming against the stark white muslin. The crone sucked in a throttled moan. Her accusing pale eyes cut toward him again, narrowed with loathing. "What have you done to her—you and your brutish hands!"

She did not wait for his answer, but instead lunged at him, fingers curled into talons. Rand brought her up short in a trice, her own dagger leveled calmly at her throat. She eyed the blade, then registered a note of under-standing as her focus lit on the slash marks that glis-tened slick and red on his bare arms.

"I have done nothing, woman, save to question why I was left to die on this beach today. And why this girl—your daughter, do you say?—thought fit to insult me fur-ther by thieving my belongings while I was too weak to stop her."

A sober look crept into the ice of her gaze. Or per-haps, he guessed, was it guilt?

"She did only what I told her to do. If you wish to punish the hand that did not help you, then take it out on me. Not her. Serena left you on the beach because I told her to. She only obeyed my wishes."

Rand scowled at the chill admission, but he believed the woman told him true. "Is it your custom to be so un-caring to others in need?"

"Our customs are of little concern to you," she an-swered, bolder than was wise when she did not know him, or whom he might serve. "The only thing I care about is the safety of my child. I don't expect a man to understand that."

So, it was his gender alone that earned him such ani-mosity. The woman was wrong about his instincts toward protecting a child—or protecting anyone weaker than himself who could not rise in their own defense—but the crone's barb stung with more accuracy than it should.

"What cold shore is this that breeds such hostile women?" he asked, gesturing to the dense strand of night black forest that edged the long pale stretch of beach. His body ached for a bed, his stomach for a trencher of warm food and strong dark ale. The gashes on his arms and chest needed cleaning before the sand and crusted salt from his prolonged sea bath invited in-fection.

And even more crucial than those immediate physical needs, Rand was determined to recover the piece of the Dragon Chalice that now appeared inexplicably lost to him. Unbelievably lost, he was tempted to think, his gaze straying back to the wary-eyed woman and her peculiar daughter.

"What is this place, I said?" Rand quickly grew tired of waiting on a reply. He flicked a meaningful glance at the blade still gripped and threatening in his right hand. "I would know what town or fief you and your daughter hail from, woman. It is not a difficult question."

"The nearest town is Egremont. It lies inland, half a day north by foot."

The answer came not from the crone before him, but from the strange beauty named Serena. She was calmer now, recovered from her hysteria, although her face still glowed ashen pale as she looked up at Rand.

"And the both of you—where do you live?"

"Here," she replied simply, no guile or venom in her voice.

Rand noted the narrow footpath leading from the forest edge, the only sign of human habitation on the entire stretch of sand and sea. "You and your mother live here, in these woods?"

She nodded her head.

Hunkered down at her side, Serena's mother cast a look at him that seemed on the verge of pleading. "We've a simple life, and wish no trouble from the likes of you."

Rand lowered the dagger with a low-pitched oath.

Half a day to the nearest town. Half a day's walk to the nearest hope of food and shelter was half a day's more strength than he had at present. Half a day's walk would take him that much farther away from this shore,

where, if the Chalice treasure had indeed washed out
with the tide, it might also return.

God's love.

To think he could have lost the cup to the sea after
fighting so hard to keep it!

Rand cursed his own misfortune, scowling as Serena's
mother helped her to her feet. He scrutinized both of
them in turn, the waifish forest nymph and the haughty
hen who clucked and fussed over her as if the young
woman were crafted of breakable glass. Perhaps neither
one was fully sane. They might share an inherited madness, cast out in shame of it, or otherwise forced to live
on their own in this wild wood. They had no man to
look after them, overlord or kin, or Rand surely would
have faced him by now. No, these women were alone.
Like him.

He would have to make do with what meager boon he
had.

"I will needs stay with you for a day or two," he informed the women, his tone inviting no refusal. He
stepped toward them meaningfully, then gestured to the
forest path with his chin. "Show me where you live."

Neither one seemed eager to oblige him, so Rand
reached out his arm. He meant only to turn Serena onto
the beach trail behind her, but before his hand could de-
scend to nudge the young woman forward, her mother
had stepped between them like a shield.

"Very well. We will take you there, as you give us no
choice. You've no need of force."

❧ 4 ❧

THE COTTAGE HAD never seemed so small as it did with the stranger occupying it. He stalked through the cramped space like some barbarian warrior from one of her mother's many tales. Those tales never ended happily, Serena reflected. Not for the maidens who embarked on foolish journeys, nor for the many splendid kingdoms that fell to the battering of steel and brutality delivered by men with hearts as dark as this one's.

He had not seemed so large, so formidable, when he lay unconscious on the beach. But now, as he commandeered her home, half-dressed, bloodied from the savagery he survived at sea, Serena thought him nothing short of terrifying. She kept her distance from him while he perused their meager abode, regret gnawing at her for the fact that her actions had brought him there. A terrible mistake, she feared, to have returned to the beach against her mother's instructions.

Would that she could take it back.

If there was any providence to be claimed in this evening's misfortunate turn, it was that the intruding stranger had washed ashore without the trappings of war. He had no sword on him, no weapon at all, save the small dagger Serena's mother had forfeited to him on the beach. All he wore were tattered breeches and braies, the dark fabric hanging limply from his body.

His chest and arms were bare, his tanned skin crusted with a fine layer of salt and sand.

Firelight from a new blaze on the hearth glittered against his broad shoulders and the sculpted slabs of muscle that banded his torso. For a moment, Serena was transfixed, her gaze rooted on him as the undulating flames of the cook fire played about his bare skin like the kiss of starlight on smooth sand.

It was a queer observation, one that only added to the feeling of how misplaced he was in the cottage, a creature of another place, another world. One she did not wish to understand, she chided herself, looking now to the fresh blood that trickled in thin red streaks from the slash marks he bore on his body and arms.

His dark hair had seemed near to black that morning when it was wet, and again tonight with only the moon to light his features. Now, in the glow of the crackling fire, she could see the chestnut hues of a rich brown, the spiky waves falling thickly around the broad line of his shoulders. His face was grizzled with the shadow of a beard, his cheeks slightly hollow, the bones feral and sharp.

And his eyes . . . like a hawk's keen gaze, the stranger's hazel eyes took in everything around him with a swift, assessing glance.

He was large and commanding, an unsettling creature hewn of muscle and might, whose very air bespoke danger.

Serena could not keep from staring at him.

In part fear, part wary intrigue, her gaze strayed again and again across the small expanse of the cottage to where he paced and inspected, a conquering overlord familiarizing himself with the meager boon of his new territory.

Her hands still trembled from touching him. If she

closed her eyes, she still could feel the power of his tangible rage. His anger lingered within her, an echo of feeling that reverberated deep in her bones, coursing through her veins. Her gift of insight—the Knowing—had shown her such bleakness in his heart, such eager bloodlust in his mind. She had touched him for only an instant, but she had read his soul as surely as if he had spoken the truth of his purpose aloud.

He meant to do murder.

Violence drove him, and woe betide any who stood in his way.

The thought haunted her as she turned to retrieve her last pair of gloves from a clothing casket on the floor near her bed. Kneeling, she took them out, glad for the comfort the soft brown leather would give her, however small.

Before she had a chance to slip the gloves on, she heard the stranger draw near.

"Whose pallet is that one, beneath the window?"

His rumbling voice filled the cottage like a sudden roll of thunder, despite that he spoke in a low tone. Serena spun around and drew herself up off the floor to face him. With a glance, he gestured to the humble bed that lay in disarray, a tangle of coverlet and bolster. Just as Serena had left it when she crept out of it earlier that evening to see what had become of him.

"It is mine," she answered, purposely stepping aside as he crossed the small space of earthen floor toward where she stood.

He grunted, scarcely looking at her. Bending down, he retrieved the thin feather-stuffed bolster, then thrust it into her arms before she could react. "It will do," he pronounced. "You'll have it back in a few days, after I am gone."

"A few days?"

The blurted reply flew off Serena's tongue faster than she could bite it back. Across the sole room of the cottage, her mother cleared her throat, a subtle warning against stirring the stranger's ire. Serena understood the prudence in cooperating with his demands, at least for the time being, but that did not make the situation any easier to accept. She frowned down at the bolster gripped in her tight fingers.

A few days, he'd said. Could he mean to commandeer their home for so long?

Whatever his intention, he gave her no explanation or excuse. With little more than an arched brow in response, he pivoted to face her directly, less than a hand's breadth between them. Serena clutched the bolster against her, a feeble barrier, but the only one she had when the stranger loomed over her so closely.

"I will take this pallet for as long as I need it. And I'll have your ladies' word that no one will know that I am here. Do you understand?"

His look penetrated as deadly sure as his voice. Serena nodded once, unable to tear her gaze away from the stormy threat that lingered in his eyes.

"Good," he said, apparently satisfied, although his tone conveyed that he had expected no refusal. Scowling, he glared down in annoyance at the bloody trails raking his bare arms. "While I eat, I would have you fetch a basin of soapy water and a cloth to clean these scratches."

At the implied order that she should aid him—that she should be made to touch him—Serena shot an anxious look at her mother. Calandra paused, carrying a small black cauldron of stew over to the fireplace.

"I will tend your injuries," she volunteered, giving an abrupt gesture of her head. "Serena, come and mind the pot."

The stranger's eyes had not left her face, Serena noted when she dared a glance back in his direction. More flinty green than brown in this light, his gaze fixed on her in considering silence, watching as she dropped her bolster on the nearest stool and sidled away from him.

Was it rancor at being gainsaid in this small command that she attend him, or was it suspicion over her eager avoidance of him that tightened the stern line of his full mouth?

Serena did not hesitate long enough to guess at it. Hurrying to distance herself from the idea of touching him again, she went to the hearth and took up the task of cooking his sup. Calandra's look of acknowledgment was grim as Serena pulled on her gloves, then reached for the long stirring spoon. Serena mouthed a rueful apology for having unwittingly invited this trouble to their doorstep, but her mother's expression only softened to one of resignation.

"I'll go fetch water for the washbasin. I won't be long," Calandra said, her voice reassuring even if her gaze was not.

Serena nodded. She put the spoon into the pot of warming stew and listened as her mother's footsteps retreated behind her. The cottage door opened, then closed, leaving Serena standing there alone with their unwanted guest.

How she wished she could undo the mistake of finding him. How she yearned for the peace she knew on awaking that morning, before she discovered the rage-filled stranger washed up on her shore. How she regretted the touch that yet reverberated in her bones, the terrible rage that belonged to him before spilling into her the instant her hands pressed against him.

There was no undoing that, to be sure.

The peace she lost today was one she would not know for whatever length of time he stayed.

One she dreaded might never be hers again.

"Your mother and you live here by yourselves, do you?"

His voice jolted her, almost as much as his question. For a moment, Serena contemplated telling him that she had a sire and six strong brothers, all due back to the cottage in a short while, but she did not think it would matter. This man was too shrewd to believe the lie. No doubt he already knew the answer before she said it.

"Yes," she replied, watching her pot instead of looking at him. "It is just the two of us here."

"For how long?"

Serena shrugged, stirring the thick stew. "Forever. At least, as long as I can remember. I had a brother and sister, but both died when I was a child. I never knew them, or my father. He left soon after I was born."

Silence loomed at her back, a measuring quiet that unsettled her more than the deep timbre of his voice. "It must be difficult," he said after a moment, "two women left to fend for themselves."

"We manage. We look after each other. No one bothers us here."

Until now.

The unspoken comment hung in the stifling air of the small cottage room. The stranger went silent again, studying her, and this time Serena could not help glancing over her shoulder toward where he sat. His hawk's gaze was fixed on her, hooded in the undulating warmth of the firelight.

"I've no intention of harming you or your mother."

It was a simple declaration, one that seemed in earnest when she considered the sober look in his eyes. But the

Knowing still skated through her fingers, whispering to her in black, steel-edged tones.

Rage. Annihilation. Vengeance.

"I do not think you came here in peace," she said, anxiously rubbing the palm of one gloved hand against her skirts. The friction did not dispel the current that yet swirled through her like smoke twining in the breeze.

"Only the lowest cur would bring pain on a defenseless woman." He stared at her as he said it, his voice rough with an emotion she could not name, his gaze narrowed and hard. Then he shrugged. "Think what you will. I am here only by sheer wicked luck—and a storm that seemed wont to kill me."

"You were shipwrecked?"

"Tossed overboard by the waves."

"You are bleeding," she said, her eyes straying to the scarlet slashes on his arms and chest and abdomen. The lacerations were angry and welted, uniform trails that had an animal look to them. "You were not the only one lost to the storm."

He hardly acknowledged her concern or his injuries, answering her considering frown with the slightest lift of his brow. "Another passenger was swept over with me. He did not survive."

There was something flatly cold, something matter-of-fact, in the stranger's simple statement.

Merciless, came the hissed whisper of the Knowing. *Relentless. Dangerous.*

"Where were you sailing to?"

"Why do you want to know?"

Serena blinked, taken aback by his frank suspicion. She had never been beyond the boundaries of the forest grove that was her home. She had never talked with anyone except her mother and the animals who inhabited the woods—admittedly, one-sided conversations for the most part. Serena had so many questions and curiosities, but no one willing or able to answer them.

And now here was this man, this interesting creature from a world she knew nothing about. Her fear of him paled a bit beside her curiosity.

It was that desire for contact, her thirst for knowledge of what lay outside her world, that prompted her to question this stranger now, regardless of the wariness his presence caused. Her mother would disapprove of her speaking to him, Serena knew. But Calandra was not here to censure her. The nearest well was no fewer than two hundred paces from the cottage; she would not return for another handful of time.

"I don't mean to pry, but it is a rare thing for us that bloodied, shipwrecked strangers should wash ashore to invade our cottage and demand help from my mother and me," Serena said softly, somewhat meekly, lest the bite of her words incite the fury she knew simmered just below the surface of his steady gaze. "I should think it only natural to ask a few questions. Where you came from, where you were going . . . your name, at the very least."

"I am Randwulf of Grey—" He cut the reply short, and a muted shadow of emotion seemed to creep into his unreadable expression. "Most people call me Rand. That is all you need to know about me, Serena."

Her own name slid off his tongue in a slow drawl, an almost physical caress of sound that sent a wash of inexplicable heat into her face. She pivoted away, turning her attention back to the pot of stew that had now begun to simmer over the fire. He spoke as she gave his meal a vigorous stir with the long-handled spoon.

"I imagine it is also a rare thing that you should have any ale or wine in this place."

Serena heard the creak of the wooden chair as he leaned back in it and spread his long legs out before him. She did not look over her shoulder to confirm the picture her ears gave her of his negligent sprawl behind her. Already this man—Rand, she amended, testing the name in her mind—had disrupted her confidence.

Normally she was a calm person, possessing a level head, steady hands. But since his arrival in the cottage, Serena felt not unlike a stranger to herself, blushing and trembling, awkward and uncertain. She did not like the change he brought to her in such a short while in his presence. The air fairly crackled around him, ripe with a foreign current. Disturbed by a savage intensity.

"We have neither wine nor ale," she told him, "but there is a sage tea left from our sup this afternoon."

"Good enough."

At his reply, Serena abandoned the stew and went to retrieve the pitcher of cooled tea. She brought the vessel to the hearth, intending to place it onto the coals to warm it for him.

"No need for that," he said. "I'm too parched to wait on it. I'll take the brew as it is."

The pitcher in one hand, Serena withdrew a clean tankard from atop the fireplace mantel. She pivoted back toward the table where he waited, and placed the cup down before him. She began to pour, watching the tepid tea swirl into the deep bowl of the tankard.

"What is wrong with your hands?"

Her gaze snapped up at once. Instinct made her pull her gloved hand back before he could think to touch her. Tea sloshed over the scarred wooden planks of the table as she withdrew, the spiced brown liquid puddling and dripping through the slats. Serena exhaled a frustrated puff of breath, hurrying to sop up the spill with a rag that lay nearby.

She could not have been more shocked—nor more starkly terrified—when he reached out to take the cloth from her. His large hand closed over the top of her gloved fingers, too warm, too firm.

"Do you glove them to hide a disfigurement?"

His query barely registered in her mind, as though issuing from within the murkiness of a deep well. She could not answer him, for the Knowing had stirred again, awakened by the sudden contact, even through the barrier of the leather.

Mistrust. Wariness. Something else, too, something harder to read . . .

She heard a splintering crash somewhere close to her, felt the splash of wetness hit her skirts as the pitcher slipped out of her free hand and hit the floor. A curse punctuated the jolt of shattering pottery, but this, too, was a distant sound.

Her senses became entangled in the stranger's reactions, until his emotions were all she knew.

Confusion, concern . . . a small ripple of contempt.

He thought her mad, she realized. He assumed her weak-minded and frail.

He pitied her; the taste of it was bitter in her throat.

"Please," she finally gasped, forcing the words out in a rush. "Let go."

His grasp loosened only slightly, but Serena jerked out of his hold, cradling her hand against her breast.

And all the while, his hard hazel eyes remained fixed on her face.

"God's love, girl. What did you think I would do?"

The cottage door creaked open in that next instant, sparing Serena from answering him. Her mother's eyes lit on her at once, then cut to the large intruder who was standing now, his brows furrowed in annoyance, his stance one of impatience rather than excuse.

"What has happened here?" Calandra demanded. She carried in the bucket of water from the well, looking to the broken pitcher that lay in shards at Serena's feet. "Serena?"

"It slipped out of my grasp," she managed after drawing a few deep, calming breaths. Her head still rang from the touch, but it was dimming quickly, cushioned no doubt by the protection of her gloves. " 'Twas nothing, Mother. Just clumsiness on my part."

The stranger—Randwulf, from a place he would not name—studied her, but did not betray her small lie.

Serena noted the dubious look coming from her mother. Calandra knew as well as she herself that Serena's hands were nothing if not careful, precise. Her touch never erred, for even slight mistakes could bring her too much pain. But things were different this evening. Rand's presence had changed everything. He had upset the balance of the peaceful life they had enjoyed as late as that very morning. Calandra's softening expression said she understood.

In the silence that followed, Serena hastened to clean up the mess she had made. She mopped up the spilled tea, and retrieved the wedges of earthenware from the dampened rushes on the floor while her mother prepared the soaps, salves, and bandages needed to tend Rand's wounds.

Serena finished quickly, then returned to the hearth to mind the cooking.

Behind her, Calandra assembled her supplies on the table, clucking her tongue as she inspected the cuts and bruises on her patient's body. Water trickled into the basin as a cloth was wetted and wrung out. Long moments passed, moments drawn to excruciating length by the silence in the cottage, but then, at last, Calandra proclaimed her work done.

Rand murmured his thanks, but all it won from Serena's mother was a grunt of acknowledgment. Followed by an exclamation of alarm.

"What are you doing?" Calandra shrieked.

Serena threw a glance over her shoulder.

Rand was standing now, his hands working to unfasten the laces that held up his torn, sodden breeches. "I am soaked to the bone, madam. These clothes are naught but rags. If you want me to wear them any longer, they will first need to rinse and dry."

Calandra regarded him narrowly, then submitted to his request. "Very well, take them off. You can don a blanket until your things are fit to wear again."

He nodded with a courtly show of gratitude. His long fingers gripped the waistband of his torn breeches, which were loosened and sagging down over damp, low-slung braies beneath. Bare skin peeked out above the rolled waistband, the bone of his trim hip framing an intriguing play of hard muscle that girded him like tightly knotted ropes at his abdomen. And even more intriguing was the thin track of dark hair that arrowed down from his navel to lower points at which Serena could only guess.

She had not dared look so openly at him when they were alone in the cottage, but now . . .

"Avert your eyes, Serena."

Caught by her mother's stern advice, Serena felt her cheeks flame. Rand's gaze slid to her, unfazed. Almost in challenge. He seemed to think nothing of disrobing before two women he did not know. Perhaps that was simply his way. Perhaps it was the way of all men, base creatures who cared only about themselves, so she had been told all her life.

This man certainly seemed to fit the mold her mother had so often described. He was brutal and demanding, full of arrogance and lacking any care for how his uninvited presence disrupted their simple way of life.

Serena turned away from him to mind her cooking while he continued to undress little more than an arm's length behind her. Her mother left him to his immodest task as well, crossing the room to one of the linen chests. Over the crackle of the hearth fire, Serena heard the soft creak of the casket lid, then the muted riffle of wool as her mother shook out a blanket.

The pot of stew began to bubble on the fire. Serena stirred it, braving another quick sidelong glance over her shoulder. Still standing, Rand had partially turned now, pivoted away from her view.

And he was naked.

His bare back was wide as an ancient oak, solid muscle tapering to a trim waist and lean hips. Firm buttocks, somewhat whiter than the sun-bronzed hue of the rest of him, drew her eye and encouraged appreciation of the rugged strength of his long, sinewy legs. Clutched in his fist and held before him at his waist were the damp breeches and braies. Shadows hinted at the blatant masculinity concealed beneath the fall of heavy, salt-stiffened fabric.

Serena dared a longer look.

He must have sensed her watching him, for he slowly swung his head around to face her. His eyes seemed darker somehow, the deep-set lids hooded as he lifted a brow in lazy acknowledgment of her unseemly stare. His knowing gaze held hers for an overlong moment, piercing her.

"I wager you've given that ample attention, wouldn't you say?" he said, his voice a low drawl that seemed more amused than affronted.

Serena endured the heat of yet another fierce blush,

and stammered to make an excuse. But he only smiled, mockery lifting the corners of his mouth.

"The stew," he said, indicating the pot that was suddenly bubbling and hissing on the fire. "My sup appears to be heated through well enough."

Serena turned away from him at once, her face flaming as hot as the amber coals, which were now smoking and spitting from the stew that boiled over onto the grate.

Rand did not sleep that night, despite the fatigue that pulled at him like a dark tide.

The tea had been cold, the stew burnt and scalding hot, but Rand had partaken of both like a ravenous beggar gone a fortnight without a meal. Now, hours later, he reclined on the pallet near the window, his back against the wall of the cottage, cushioned only by the woolen blanket wrapped about his body. The coverlet's weave was careful, smooth against his bare skin, expertly loomed. Like the pallet beneath him, the blanket smelled of forest flowers and a faintly woodsy spice that pleased his battered senses.

It smelled like home.

Not his, he thought ruefully, denying himself even the meager comfort of reflection, of pleasant memory. He would take no comfort in anything, not yet. He was not deserving, not until his purpose had been met.

Two pairs of wary eyes seemed to concur that he had no right to be there, filling his belly with their food, warming his bones with their fire and hospitality—be those gifts willingly surrendered or nay.

They observed his every move, Serena in particular. She and her mother were seated together on a humble bed at the other side of the cottage's sole room. The women huddled there in silence, Serena, timid, with her gloved hands clasped lightly in her lap. Her mother's arm encircled the delicate line of Serena's shoulders, draping her in a protective embrace.

Rand considered Serena for a moment, not the first time his gaze had settled on the waifish maiden with the night-dark hair and face of ethereal, placid beauty. She was so fine-boned and petite, he had guessed her to be merely a girl at first, scarcely past her first blood. He had been wrong. Beneath the willowy figure and wide, long-lashed gaze, was a woman full grown. Fear haunted her pale eyes.

Fear of him.

For a pained instant, Rand was reminded of the night his own home was raided. The invasion had been swift. The decimation had been thorough. Elspeth's screams would ring forever in his mind, her fear an acid that would forever scald his soul. He had long been her protector, had pledged to always keep her safe, to make her happy.

How deeply he had failed her.

Distantly, Rand noted the weight of a similar anxiety in the air of the cottage. Serena watched him in wary silence, moving not in the least from where she sat on the pallet, as though waiting for him to strike out like the beasts turned loose on Greycliff. She could not know that horror—God's love, no one should—but she looked at him with a gaze that seemed expectant of bloodshed that was certain to come.

Bloodshed to be delivered by his hand.

With a scowl, Rand turned his head and broke the hold of her clear stare without a word. He was in no mood to offer reassurances that would likely not be believed anyway. Nor could he be sure these women were, or would remain, his allies. From what he had seen in recent weeks, there were very few souls, male or female, who could be trusted.

Now that the food and drink had revived him, Rand's mind returned to the unfinished business that still lay ahead of him.

Namely, Silas de Mortaine.

Vengeance parched his mouth when he thought of the ruthless villain who had cost him all he held dear. It was all Rand lived for now—to avenge his slain wife and child. To gut and bleed de Mortaine until every drop had drained from his black heart.

His plan had been simple enough. Armed with part of the Dragon Chalice, the treasure that Silas de Mortaine lived to possess, Rand would lure him out of his well-guarded lair and into the open. It was the only way to get close to his enemy, for he was a formidable man with unlimited connections. De Mortaine's great wealth bought many an ally, corrupted many an honest man. And then there was the matter of his bodyguards, those inhuman sentries born of the same mythical place from which the Dragon Chalice originated—Anavrin.

Rand had already faced several of the shapeshifting minions, most recently the one who attacked him on the storm-wracked ship two nights ago. He knew what they were capable of, had seen their treachery firsthand . . . as had his precious family, in those hellish hours of the raid on Greycliff.

As for the Dragon Chalice and the kingdom from whence it came, Rand knew little, save what his friend Kenrick of Clairmont had told him. For years, Kenrick had studied the legendary treasure through his work for the Templar church. His findings had uncovered the history of the Chalice lore, from its creation on a wizard's forge eons ago, to the properties of four precious gems that were said to ensure the very life of Anavrin itself. Calasaar, Vorimasaar, Serasaar, and Avosaar—the stones of Light, Faith, Peace, and Prosperity—had each glowed like fire in the bowl of the Dragon Chalice.

According to Kenrick's work, this enchanted treasure was stolen from Anavrin centuries past and brought beyond the veil that kept its kingdom secreted from the Outside. The Dragon Chalice was lost to Anavrin, having fallen into the hands—and into the corruptible hearts— of mortal men. But a protective magic enveloped the treasure, and when it left Anavrin, it was immediately rent into four pieces, each containing one of the precious stones. The four parts were said to have scattered into mist, to lay in hidden places across the realm of man.

Silas de Mortaine already held one of those priceless cups, Avosaar, under close watch. Kenrick of Clairmont, along with his sister, Ariana, and Braedon le Chasseur, the man she'd since wed, had also located one of the missing pieces, this one recovered from an island abbey off the coast of France. And just over a fortnight ago, Rand himself had beheld a third, when he and Kenrick had unearthed the piece from within the hilltop chapel at Glastonbury Tor.

Rand had witnessed true magic that day, when the two pieces of the Chalice treasure were united. Drawn together by an unexplainable force, the two parts formed a larger cup bearing Calasaar and Vorimasaar—one half of the Dragon Chalice. It was that priceless jeweled golden vessel that had been in Rand's satchel when he washed overboard in the storm.

Only one of the four Chalice pieces remained to be found. All of Kenrick's sources seemed to point toward a holy site in Scotland, which was where Rand had been heading when the storm blew him off course.

It was said that whoever restored the Dragon Chalice to its original state would have power beyond imagining. Whoever returned the treasure to its rightful place in Anavrin would taste the glory of a life eternal, of prosperity without end.

Rand had no interest in glory or power. He would restore the Chalice only if it meant taking that victory from Silas de Mortaine. The only power he needed was the knowledge that de Mortaine had lost, that he would beg for mercy and breathe his last at Rand's own hand.

If only he had made it to Scotland as he had planned. If only he'd had the chance to merge the last of the Chalice cups with the other he carried with him on the ship, de Mortaine would hardly stand a chance against him. If only he'd held tighter to the satchel, not allowed it to slip away . . .

Now the very tool of his vengeance—perhaps his one chance at getting close to his enemy—was all but lost, washed away on the stormy tide that delivered him to this remote shore.

How could he have been so careless?

He would have died before he let that satchel leave his grasp. God's truth, without the promise of vengeance driving him, all he had was misery. All he had was the bleakness of waking up each day, living with the pain of his loss. And the guilt.

Anger seethed within him suddenly, rejecting the notion that he could fail so soon. The need to crush and destroy tightened every muscle, pulsed with cold fury through his veins. He could not sleep. He could not sit in the confining space of the cottage for another moment. He had to keep moving, or he would lose his grip on the slender thread of his own sanity.

Across the sole room of the abode, Serena and her mother had settled into their pallet. Shadows enveloped

them where they lay, the soft sounds of slumber rasping
in the darkness of the cottage. Rand gathered the blanket about his shoulders and got to his feet. He found his
braies and torn breeches, nearly dried where they had
been spread before the fire. Taking both in his fisted
hand, he quit the place and stepped out into the brisk
night air.

❧ 5 ❧

A DOVE COOED somewhere nearby, waking Serena from a fitful sleep. She had been dreaming unpleasant dreams, struggling against the thin coverlet she shared with her mother on the small pallet near the wall. Calandra yet slept beside her on the down-filled mattress, her back to Serena, her slender shoulder rising with each deep breath she took. Carefully, Serena lifted the blanket and slipped out from beneath it.

It was not quite dawn. Only the palest light sifted in through the window, heavy with gray morning mist. The dove gave another throaty coo from its unseen perch outside, but within the small room of the cottage, all was quiet. Serena pivoted her head slowly, allowing her gaze to scan her surroundings, looking for *him*.

Save for her mother and herself, the cottage was empty.

There was no trace of the stranger who had invaded their home and tormented her sleep. He was gone, as was his clothing, which had been left to dry near the hearth. Randwulf the intruder was nowhere to be seen. A tentative peace settled over her as she took in his absence from the small abode.

Gingerly, Serena rose from the pallet where her mother slept and padded to the cottage window. She raised her gloved hand to push open the wooden shutters, parting them just enough to afford a view of the grounds beyond the cottage. Serena peered out at the muted light of the new morning, searching for movement among the trees or on the forest path. Nothing. The breath she had been holding leaked out of her in a quiet sigh of relief.

Had she dreamed him there last night? It seemed too much to hope, but the simple fact that he was gone now was reason enough to rejoice.

Her cloak hung on a peg on the wall. Serena retrieved it, then wrapped the soft homespun around her shoulders and quickly fastened the knotted riband ties at her neck. She crossed the room and took the water bucket from next to the fireplace, relieved to go about her usual morning routine undisturbed by the presence of a domineering, unwanted guest.

With the empty pail slung over her arm by its leather handle, Serena stepped outside. Her bare foot had scarcely touched the cool earth of the wooded trail before she heard someone approaching from the area of the beach. Purposeful steps, wrathful and brooding. She hesitated, knowing at once who was there, but uncertain what to do. She pivoted to go back inside.

"Serena," he said, not quite a greeting or command. "You are awake early."

When she did not reply, when she stood there unmoving, her eyes shut tight as if to will him away, Rand drew nearer. He stood behind her, so close he could easily place his hand on her shoulder and turn her about to face him did he wish it. Serena pivoted to avoid such an impulse in him, backing no less than two paces out of his reach.

"I thought you had gone," she said, voicing her thoughts aloud.

"Thought or hoped?"

Serena swallowed, staring up into hawkish eyes of unreadable, muted brown. "Both."

One dark brow lifted at her reply, but he said nothing more. In the misty light of dawn, his face seemed less harsh than it had in the shadows of last night's hearth fire. But his bearded jaw had lost none of its steely set, nor had the firm line of his mouth lost any of its grimness. His gaze settled on the bucket Serena clutched before her, then lifted to her in question.

"I was on my way to the well for water," she said, answering the demand that surely would have followed an instant later.

"And your mother?"

"She is yet abed, sleeping."

He glanced to the quiet cottage, as if measuring the truth in her statement. "Very well," he said after a moment. "Fetch your water. You can show me where it is."

Serena drew in a breath, nary a heartbeat away from refusing his order, but she bit back the urge to gainsay him. She wanted no conflict with this dangerous man, and it was clear from his unwavering look that he would not take no for an answer. He stretched out his arm, prompting her to walk ahead and onto the path. Serena complied. She trod the narrow track of earth several paces in front of him, unable to ignore the heavy fall of his feet. He was barefoot like her, but where she stepped carefully, avoiding tender flowers that had crept out from the edge of the forest vegetation to spill onto the path, Rand crushed them underfoot without a care for their destruction.

It rankled her somehow, his arrogant stride and dominating air. Stalking along behind her, he seemed to think she was his to command, that her woods were his domain now, merely because of his presence in them. In just a few hours, one short turning of a day, he had infiltrated her peaceful world like the very storm that had swept him ashore.

"Just how far is this well?" he asked when they had walked a fair distance from the cottage.

Serena answered without turning to face him. "We are nearly there."

She had deliberately taken him on the longer of two different routes. One cut an unmarked, cross-length line through the forest to a pool of clear freshwater—the path only she and her mother knew. This one meandered deep into the thicket, toward a secondary source that flowed from a lesser artery off the main well. The path had gotten less discernible this far into the woods. Behind her, Rand cursed, no doubt in contempt of the overgrown nettles and sharp stones hiding beneath the cover of summer greenery. Serena skirted them all with easy aplomb.

"This way," she said, veering off the trail and down a small incline.

She wasn't nearly as tall as he, and thus the low-hanging branches and prickly bramble was easier for her to avoid. She tried not to take overmuch satisfaction in the idea, navigating her way toward the small well yet obscured from untrained eyes.

She led him to the spot and paused as he glanced down at the thin slab of granite that rested in a bed of forest moss on the ground. The stone was old—ancient, according to her mother, likely first placed here by the original inhabitants of the glade. Hand-carved symbols had long ago faded into illegibility, the artistry eaten away by time and the elements. Serena had always wondered what message might have adorned the lid to the well; even spotted in lichen, the pattern bemused and intrigued her.

Contrarily, Rand gave the beauty of the carvings not even a scant appraisal.

"The water is under here?" he asked, crouching down,

his big hands already gripping the edge of the round slab.

Serena nodded. Without preamble, he removed the lid and set it aside to peer into the deep pocket of crystal-clear water. He bent forward to reach into it with one hand, then retrieved the wooden cup that bobbed on the surface of the well. Water spilled over the edges of the little vessel and down the length of his bare forearm.

"It smells good to drink. Is it safe?"

"Aye," Serena replied, her nose filling with the clean mineral scent of the spring-fed well. "My mother and I drink from this source every day."

He stared at her for a moment, then held the cup out to her. "Then drink."

He was testing her, she was certain of it. He did not credit her word, ready to confront and mistrust, even in this simple matter. But she spoke the truth when she declared the water to be safe. Serena took the dark wood cup from him and brought it to her lips. She was parched after her restless night, and the water was crisp and cool on her tongue. She drained the cup and placed it back in Rand's waiting hand. He smiled, a fleeting look of satisfaction, then dipped the cup back into the well and quenched his own thirst. Three times he filled and emptied it, drinking like he could never fill himself, heedless in his craving.

Serena stared at him mutely, watching rivulets of water spill down his chin and neck, and along the tanned planes of his chest. He wore the pendant around his neck, the heart-shaped knot of gold that had come unclasped when Serena found him on the shore. The precious yellow metal gleamed against his skin, its bright twinkle and delicately wrought pendant so incongruous on a man as hard and rough-hewn as him.

In her mother's fairy stories, Serena recalled, ladies

often presented their champions with tokens of their affection—colorful scarves, ribbons, rings, and bows. She wondered if this golden heart had been a gift from a lady Rand had known. A lady who had held the angry, rage-filled man in high regard—perhaps even loved him? Serena knew little about him, admittedly, but it seemed beyond difficult to imagine this dangerous warrior needing any trifling remembrances as he set off on his adventures . . . or on the ominous mission that consumed him now.

Finally, panting, he'd taken his fill of freshwater. He wiped his forearm across his wet mouth and set down the cup. "Give me your bucket," he commanded her.

Serena did as her told her, setting the container down next to him and backing away to let him begin to fill it.

"I am glad to see that your token was not ruined after all."

He glanced down abruptly, to where the pendant swung against his bare chest. He dismissed her concern with a shrug. "The clasp is weak, but it will hold for now."

"It's lovely."

"It belongs to my wife."

"Oh." Serena weathered a peculiar twinge upon hearing he was wed, a curiosity that battled with abject surprise. He seemed such a remote man, it was difficult to imagine him in the company of others, let alone bound to a lady in wedlock. A lady far out of his reach, when his dread plans had carried him to the northern wilds of the realm. "Does she wait for you somewhere?"

He was quiet for a long moment, drawing water from the well and watching it pour into the bucket before him. "Yes, she awaits me. She and my young son both."

"A child?" Serena replied, warming to him in spite of herself. "How old is he? What is his name?"

"You ask a lot of questions."

"I'm just . . . curious. I don't mean to pry."

"Tod," he said after a moment, as he poured more water into the bucket. He glanced up at her, and Serena detected a note of tender regard in his hazel eyes. "My son's name is Tod. He was six this past winter."

"He must miss you terribly," she said, guessing at the separation that muted some of the warrior's harsh edges when he spoke of his family. "Have you been gone from them a long time?"

"Fifty-eight days." This answer came quickly, as though it sat at the fore of his thoughts. "I fear it will be a lifetime before I see them again."

"I'm sorry," Serena said, uncertain why she felt the need to offer her sympathy, yet unable to hold it back.

He gave her a look that indicated he had no use for gentle words. In truth, the rigid line of his mouth seemed almost contemptuous of kindness, rejecting it with a scowl as he turned back to his work at the well.

"You must have a good familiarity with this place," he said, more statement than question. "How large are these woods?"

"Half a day's walk in any direction, I should guess."

"You don't know for a fact?"

Serena shrugged. "I don't often test the boundaries. My family has lived in this forest for generations, in the very cottage my mother and I share today. There has seldom been cause to·venture past the grove line."

"The grove line?"

"Aye," she said. "A perimeter of stones that was laid by my ancestors to mark the farthest edge of our land."

"And what of the village you mentioned—Egremont? To the north of the woods, you said?"

"That's right. It is the nearest town."

"How big is this Egremont? Who controls it?"

Serena shook her head. "I couldn't say. I do not know much about the place, for I have never been there."

"Never been there?" He exhaled a sharp breath, as though disbelieving. "Not even for supplies?"

"We want for nothing here. There has been no need to leave."

He continued ladling water up from the well to fill the bucket. "You and your mother are peculiar women, Serena." He slanted a measuring look at her. "I can't say I trust that about either one of you."

From what she knew of him thus far, Serena could find little to trust as well, but she stifled the urge to tell him so.

"If you would prefer Egremont to our meager quarters here, I'm certain it would be no trouble to pack up some water and food so you might make the trek post-haste."

He smiled now, a cynical baring of his teeth that said he knew precisely her meaning. "I understand you are eager to be rid of me. And like I told you last night, I will go, Serena, as soon as I am ready. But there also remains the matter of the property I lost on your beach."

At once she recalled his anger from the night before, when he had seized her and demanded to know what she did with an item missing from his satchel. "A cup of some sort?" she asked, trying to push past the blur of confusion his searing touch had caused. "You believe you had a cup in your bag when you washed ashore?"

"I am certain of it." He held her captive in his unwavering gaze, his look boring into her as if to search for deception. "That's why I spent most of the night and this morning scouring the beach, looking to see if the tide might have swept it away, and if it might return."

"It must be very valuable, to be so important to you."

"It is very important. Understand that I won't rest until I find it."

There was a threat lurking in that low-voiced statement, a challenge that seemed just a hairbreadth away from fury. Everything about this man seethed. Serena glanced down and realized she had been slowly backing away from him, fearing he might lash out, provoked or nay.

"I don't know anything about this object you've lost. I swear it."

His reply was as deadly calm as his look. "Pray you don't."

He stood up, and took the filled bucket in hand. "Now show me the other water source in these woods. This well is but a small spring fed from a greater one, is it not?"

Serena gaped at him, but she did not attempt to evade him with falsehoods. "There is a waterfall not far from here," she admitted, not without reluctance, for the cascade and crystalline pool at its base was something of a sacred haven, not meant for outsiders to enjoy, so said Calandra since the time Serena was a little girl. Serena had steered him away from it in coming to this well for water, but she might have known this hawk-eyed knight would not take long to invade every corner of the land she called her home.

"Which way?" he prompted when she was not quick to lead him.

Serena pointed past his beefy shoulder. "It is through there. No path will take us to the falls. We'll have to cut through this way."

At his gesture to begin, she strode forward, uncomfortably aware of his presence too near her as they walked.

Traversing the thick summer foliage of the forest required concentration, for Serena in particular. Uneasy with her hulking companion striding along beside her, she was lost to distraction. Twice she nearly slipped on the leafy undergrowth, and each time Rand reached out to catch her. She was careful not to touch him in reflex, but when her foot became lodged under a sturdy green vine in midstep, she suddenly found herself held upright only by the surety of Rand's strong grip, clamped around the fingers of her left hand.

Irritation, said the Knowing, awakening to read him in that quick instant.

Impatience. Too much time wasted here already. Damn the storm! Damn these unfamiliar surroundings, the weakness of these wounds. Too far from home. Too far from all that matters. Can't go back until it's ended. Blood for blood. Pain for pain. It will be enough.

His thoughts passed through Serena in a fleeting wave of heat and anger, soundless words, though brittle as a shout in her mind. Buffeted by the dark voice of the Knowing, Serena felt a momentary unsteadiness. She calmed herself, willed herself to withstand the blackness of his torment, which raged just beneath the surface of his outward calm.

"This way," she said, guiding him through the lush thicket.

The forest quickly became more dense, the ground more uneven, climbing toward rocky inclines that taxed with each step. Serena looked back to check that Rand was making the trek without difficulty, though why she should concern herself with his well-being she really did not know. His face showed his strain, but he kept easy pace with her despite the fatigue of his injured body. She doubted he would be the sort to give in, even if he were walking up to death's own door.

Relentless. That was how she was coming to think of him in the short time he had been there, intruding on her life with his simmering rage and dominating ways. While it was not a quality she had been taught to admire, Serena could not help feeling a measure of respect for the solidity and resolve of the man. Nor could she help but pity the one he sought to destroy.

Vengeance, hissed the Knowing, reminding her of the darkness that drove this man.

He had washed ashore on thoughts of revenge and murder, but for what ill? He and his family had been wronged, she guessed, recalling the sadness in his voice as he had spoken of them. He had been torn away from them, something Serena herself could not imagine. Her mother was all she had in this world; how dearly she would miss her if she were gone. But to be separated from a child and the one you love . . . she would not hope ever to know that sort of loneliness.

"It is not far now," she said, turning back to reassure him with a sympathetic smile.

He only grunted, a wordless rebuff tossed at her from under a heavy fall of hair that had swung down over his face.

They walked the rest of the way in silence, until the roar of the waterfall drummed out even the thought of conversation. Serena skirted around a sprawling, ancient ash tree, and paused to face him.

"We are here."

He nodded once, then strode past her to enter first, his left hand trailing behind, outstretched as though to hold her back until he had deemed it safe for her to enter. It seemed a protective gesture, one done on instinct more than out of any particular care for her, but Serena waited until he motioned her forward.

As always, her breath was swept away on sight of the place.

White veils of water spilled over the top of a wall of granite that rose, sharp and steep, on the other side of the pool. Overhead, sun rays angled down through the forest canopy, branching golden fingers of light that fragmented in the mist of the falls. Hues of red, orange, yellow, and green mixed with violet and blue, creating an arc of color that dazzled the eye. Beneath the radiant bow was a pool of fresh, crystalline water. Its surface danced with small, rippling waves from the churning white rush of the falls, but Serena knew there was tranquillity and warmth below.

The pool was as clear as a summer sky, and while the bottom was visible from where she and Rand now stood, it was but illusion, for the pool was as fathomless as the ocean itself. Serena had swum it since she was a child, and not for lack of trying had she ever had breath enough to dive down and touch the smooth floor that seemed only an arm's length away at any depth.

"Impressive."

"It is magnificent," Serena corrected, reverent as she feasted her gaze on the wondrous vision of the cascade.

Rand, however, looked only for a moment. He glanced away, his eyes scanning the outlying area of the woods that surrounded them. How could he stand beside such natural beauty and not pause to stare agape, as she did? Serena had seen the falls countless times—nearly once a day for all her life—and never remained unmoved by the sparkling, enigmatic splendor of the place.

There was certain magic here, she believed, but Rand did not see it. How sad for him that he could not, or would not, appreciate something so inherently awe-inspiring as this gift of nature. Scowling now, he pivoted from the edge of the pool and strode away from her. Serena followed him reluctantly, loath to leave the cascade now that they were there. She knew not what drew Rand, but his attention was rooted on the leafy bramble some few yards in the distance.

He got there first, and immediately hunched down to inspect something on the ground. Approaching cautiously, Serena suddenly realized what he had found. Dread coiled in her belly, coupled with a squeezing sense of outrage.

On the ground, concealed by the flora around it, was a neat construction of small rocks, arranged in a sharp arc. At the open end, the top of a springy sapling had been fastened to the earth by a length of strong twine, its small noose and leading line swept over with dirt and a handful of grain.

Rand gestured to the snare. "Do you know what this is?"

"Yes, of course," she said. "It is meant for killing doves. It is a trap."

She brushed past him in a surge of dismay and anger. Kneeling in the undergrowth, she reached for the twine that held the piece in place, intent on dismantling the offensive killing machine.

"Serena. Leave it." Rand did not touch her, but his stern voice made her pause. "There have been others like this one?"

She nodded. "I've found two in the past month, but they were farther out in the woods, closer to the grove line. I took them down—just as I will take this one down."

Rand stepped closer now. "Leave it. Unless you mean to tell the hunters that you and your mother are here."

"These are our woods," she said, defensive even

though a trace of dread wormed into her heart. "The creatures that live here are my friends. We cause no harm to anyone, so I cannot abide harm coming to us. I *won't* abide it."

"Do you think it so simple as that?" Rand shook his head, staring at her with what seemed a mixture of amusement and pity. "These woods belong to the king, as do all such woods in the realm. This trap does not belong to some lowborn poacher. Only a nobleman has leave to hunt such quarry; the lord who placed these traps here did so by his right. If you take them down, you do so at the risk of your own hand, for destroying his property. And you alert any who come to check these snares that a foolish young woman and her mother are squatting on royal lands, stealing the king's God-given bounty each time you take a meal or burn a fire to warm your cottage."

Serena let out a huff of breath and rose to her feet. "Those are your rules—men's rules, not mine."

"Like it or nay, those are the rules of this world. From this evidence here, you had better believe that very world you scorn will soon be standing at your doorstep."

She did not like it at all, but it was hard to refute what Rand was saying. For a long while, she had felt the forest shrinking around her, the grove line seeming less distinct as trees thrust between the stones and the edges of the town beyond spread out, reaching for the woods. This trap was not the first sign she had seen of man, but it was the closest they had come so far. In her heart, though she dreaded it, she knew this would not be the last.

" 'Tis not safe for my mother and me anywhere but here. This is our home. I have lived in this forest all my nineteen summers, my mother even longer, and we have never known any trouble here."

She looked back down at the snare, its deadly spring all but invisible on the ground, the scattered handful of grain inviting any unwitting dove to come and feast. It appeared fully safe, even tempting, so crafty was the man-made trap.

"Leave it," Rand said to her again, as if knowing how badly she wanted to destroy it, whether doing so would betray her to the hunters or not. "Let it be."

She thought of the crude men who would have laid the device, ignorant men, caring naught for the beauty they would destroy. This was but one trap; there had been others, and soon there would be more. Where would it stop, if not here?

"Nay," she said at length. "I cannot simply let it be."

Serena lunged down to ruin the snare, but was halted by the astonishing restraint of Rand's fingers, clamped about her hand. She whirled around to face him, stunned at the unyielding grip.

Stubborn girl.

His face was firm with command. She didn't care. "Let me go."

"Don't let emotion rule you, Serena. You will regret it."

You've no idea what trouble you may invite.

"They have no right to hunt here," she replied, answering his thoughts as much as his command that she cease.

"Hunters come in many forms, Serena. These men are no mean commoners. They serve an overlord, who serves the king. Where men like these want, they take. Do you understand?"

"I do not fear them."

"Then you are a fool. Leave the snare as it is. One hunter's quarry is not worth the price you might be made to pay should you be found raiding his nets."

Such an innocent face, even in anger. Beautiful. Avenging angel of the forest, fierce yet fragile. Any would want you on sight. None would be able to walk away from such spritely sweetness and fire.

Rand held her tighter, taking her by the elbow with his free hand, unaware that he only worsened her dizzy state. The Knowing, ever vigilant, seized on his thoughts at once.

So warm, her skin. So soft . . . precious velvet bathed in sunlight. Fragrant, alive—too much so—such a queer effect she has. Something wise in her touch, something more intriguing than her beauty, more pure than her innocence. Life, to be sure, but something deeper. Leaping, twisting, reaching out. A caress, sweet and embracing, no harm here, only safety, only blessed sanctuary. God's blood, how easy it would be to lose oneself. . . .

"Very well." Serena heard her own voice, so small in the quiet of the glade. She did not wish to be touching him. Certainly she should feel no pleasure in it, not this tingling awareness that worsened with each whisper of his innermost thoughts and emotions. There was danger in his touch, she knew it with every hitching breath she tried to drag into her lungs. She threw him an urgent look, and tried once more to extricate her fingers from his grasp. "I will do nothing, if you just . . ."

Let me go, she thought, but the words did not find their way to her tongue. She was held captive, as neatly as one of her doves, soon to be caught unawares in the trap she could not destroy. Rand stared at her, intense in his silence. Something sparked in his expression, then turned down the corners of his sculpted mouth.

By the Saints, those eyes. A gaze like the ocean—blue-green, deep with secrets, not all of them hers. How deep did that gaze go? Too far. She was pulling him in, stripping him to raw flesh and bone.

"Why do you look at me so?" he asked, something rough in his voice.

Serena tried his grip again, but found it firm around her fingers.

Suspicion.

He did not trust her, true enough, but there was something more than anger in him now, something more than simple irritation with her.

Desire.

Shame.

Fury.

His emotions buffeted her like an engulfing tide. She could not break his hold or his gaze, which narrowed on her dangerously.

Jesu, her eyes compel as a touch, beckoning, physical, and strong. Intruding. Nay, impossible! Madness to think it, yet . . . she is here, peering through thought and feeling, prying open doors better left shut and locked.

Turn away from her. She will see too much. . . .

"What are you doing?" he demanded of her, scowling now. His grip went tighter, almost punishing. "What do you know about me?"

Serena shook her head. "N-nothing."

His anger flared, twisting around to protect him. She felt it as surely as a lash.

"Nothing," he remarked, clearly disbelieving. "Then why do I feel you seek to look through me with the barest glance?"

"I wish to do no such thing," she answered, wholly honest. Serena drew in a breath, trying to tamp down the powerful swell of the Knowing, which was swimming in her head, drowning out all but the swift torment of his feelings. "Why is it you seek so badly to hide?"

In the long moments in which he did not reply, a wildness tightened his expression. Fury seared her fingers. He fumed at her bold question, but he would give her nothing. It saddened her, feeling the desperation with which he struggled to keep his emotions barred and silent. Deadened to all, including himself. All he permitted himself was rage. Everything else lay behind a thick wall of denial and fear.

"You needn't fear me, Rand."

Serena spoke in earnest, needing him to see that truth. He was as good as a stranger to her, but he was hurting in a way she could not fully comprehend, and there was little she could bear less than the suffering of another.

"Fear you?" he scoffed, brittle, as if aiming to wound her in some way.

"You can trust me," she told him, meaning it utterly. "There is no need to hide from me."

For one teetering moment, she felt him weigh the notion. He considered . . . hoped . . . then shut her out with a mocking snarl of laughter.

"You have no idea what you speak of, Serena. I am not one of your woodland creatures in need of rescue." He released her at once, letting go as if her touch scorched him as much as it did her. "This place is too peculiar by far. So, by God, are you, lady."

Paused in the middle of the thick growth of the forest, Serena could only look at him. His touch was gone, his words lost to the gentle sounds of the forest around them, but the whisper of the Knowing still echoed in her ears.

Can't hide from the pain, from what I've done, from what I've lost.

Elspeth.

Serena could feel him clinging to the name, to the memory, even as he pivoted to stride away from her. The

Knowing wrenched her heart as his own, his pain washing over her, his grief a raw wound. His guilt tore at her, a writhing torment she could hardly withstand.

Never forget . . . never forsake the vow.
Never desire another.

Rand stalked away from her, shaken to his core. What the devil had come over him back there? What manner of woman was she, that she seemed able to plumb his mind with a glance?

He did not want to know. Nor did he want to consider the unexpected flare of desire that shot through him when he was holding her hand. It pulsed in him still, warm and alive. Unbidden. He had taken hold of her only to prevent her from ruining the trap and betraying her presence to curious hunters; instead he had been struck by her incredible gaze, by the tender sweetness of her skin.

Lustful.

Ravenous.

Animal.

That was what he had often been called in his wild youth, and, later, in his marriage bed. All were badges he had worn with no particular shame. Having descended from a long, proud line of rogues and scoundrels, it was not in his blood to ignore a beautiful face, but never had he taken what was not freely given. And never had his loyalty strayed once he had wed his lovely Elspeth.

Sweet, sad Elspeth. She had been dead just two months and already her features were fading from his grasp. But not her sorrow. That, he knew, would never dim. Nor would the screams that shattered his ears and rent his heart in the moments before she was killed. She had cursed him, said she hated him for what he'd brought down upon them that night.

He well deserved her scorn. He could not make it right, then or now. As ever, he could not fix matters where Elspeth was concerned. But he could make those who harmed her pay.

And he could not allow himself to be distracted by a queer young woman with sea-deep eyes and a soul that seemed to beckon to him.

God's love, a soul that seemed to know his ugliest truths with a single look, the briefest touch.

He was not sure why he'd let Serena believe his family was alive and awaiting him back home. Safety, perhaps—his own as much as hers. The knowledge of what he was about could only put her in jeopardy, should his enemies come looking for him, as he dearly hoped they would.

More than that, however, he wished to maintain a measure of distance from Serena. Mayhap he wanted to keep the reminder of his mission fresh in his thoughts, foremost, lest he be tempted to let his eye linger too long on the many intriguing riches of the unspoiled forest grove, not the least of which being the lady herself, who championed the creatures of her woods like a stalwart knight sworn to protect her domain.

Peculiar, indeed. And too intriguing by far.

Rand cleared the edge of the trees and found himself on the long strand of pale brown beach. His bare toes sank into the warm sand, a small but soothing comfort after the rough ground of the forest. He breathed in the crisp, briny air, clearing his head with a deep-pulled draft. The tide was low, rolling in slender curls far below the head of the shore. Driftwood, seaweed, and other sundry debris were left in the path of the receded waves. Rand strode down the length of the beach, scanning the empty stretch of sand. Mayhap luck would smile upon

him just a little, and lead him to the missing treasure he
had lost.

Aye, a bit of luck was what he needed sorely. That,
and a quick mend of his injuries, so that he could end
his delay with Serena and her mother, and be on his way
toward the vengeance he so craved.

❧ 6 ❧

FARTHER NORTH ON the same stretch of coastline, low tide delivered something more remarkable than seaweed and ocean debris. An Egremont fisherman hauled in his net, astounded at the weight of his day's catch. His luck on the water had been poor of late; but, he thought, no more. Huffing and straining, he gleefully anticipated the pile of coin he would collect when he sold the fish in town. With one last groan of exertion, he dragged the heavy net up over the side of his fishing skiff, stumbling back onto his rump in the shallow boat.

The fisherman stared at his catch, perplexed.

No mass of silver scales and fins writhed beneath the crosswork weave of the net. Nay, not one fish. Nothing stirred at all in the sodden black lump he had retrieved from the water. The stench hit him at once—foul, putrid. Death gone ripe a couple days. Repulsed yet morbidly intrigued, the fisherman dashed off his cap and held it to his nose. Carefully, he crept toward the center of the skiff for a closer look.

He thought the beast a dog at first, seeing the stiff legs and large black paws jutting out from within the net. But he had never seen a dog so large. A wolf, then, he hazarded to guess, although he could think of no reason an animal such as that would meet its demise in the ocean.

A bloody demise, at that.

Its gut was sliced clean as though by a blade, ragged where the flesh had been nibbled away by sea scavengers and the continuous toss of the tide. The wolf's dark head was massive, its jaws fearsome, frozen in an open-mouthed, animal sneer. And its eyes. By the Saints, its clouded eyes stared open and hellish, like no beast of this earth.

That thought put a cold lump of fear in the fisherman's belly.

He crossed himself in haste, and was a moment away from tossing the corpse back over the side of the boat when he realized it might be of some worth to him after all. He had no fish to sell in town, but he could think of one or two folk who might pay him a farthing to gape at the dead wolf. Mayhap more, if he embellished his tale of discovery with a few lively details over at the tavern.

Rand had managed to keep to himself for the rest of that day and well into the next. He took his meals outside the cottage, preferring not to get comfortable around the table, or to be subjected to more of Serena's probing questions and unsettling observations. He had even slept outside that previous night, and his bruised, muscle-sore back was complaining loudly for it now as he scoured the beach on what was becoming a ritual bordering on obsession.

A light rain had begun not long ago. It misted in a fine sheet of wetness and ankle-deep fog that chilled him despite the reasonable warmth of the June afternoon. He was tired and aching, his fatigued body feeling as abused as it would after a bout of heavy combat or rigorous training. The ocean storm he had battled and nearly lost to that night at sea had taken more out of him than he cared to admit. The raw slashes of the shifter beast's claws yet burned where they had raked over his torso and limbs.

He was likely half beaten already in his private war against Silas de Mortaine. Still, he kept searching the beach, kept looking for any sign of the Chalice treasure.

He had found nothing thus far. It was as though the golden cup had simply vanished from within the satchel he carried ashore. He was beginning to think it might never turn up. Without it, he would have to find an alternative lure for the vengeance he sought. Nothing would be as powerful, for there was nothing the villain wanted more than the four pieces of the Dragon Chalice restored and in his possession.

As soon as he was able—another couple of days, at the most—Rand would have to press on for Scotland, to the chapel where Kenrick of Clairmont believed the last portion of the treasure resided. It was his best chance of getting close to de Mortaine. Close enough to kill.

Rand continued his search of the shoreline, heading up the beach to where the land began to slope upward, a grassy hill that covered an overhang of dark gray rock. The rugged stone jutted out into the water and around, creating a small hollowed cove when the tide was out, as it was now. As he drew closer, he saw someone standing in the curved protection of the rock.

Serena.

She stood calf-deep in the shadowed tidal pool, the hems of her faded red skirt and cream-colored under-gown rucked up, knotted in an attempt to keep them from getting wet. A thick black braid swung over her shoulder as she bent forward to peer into the water around her feet. Some of the glossy strands had come loose in the breeze; they lifted around her head in a feathery riot of ebony silk. Curiously, she was singing. The sweet, dulcet tones of her wordless song drifted toward him, and for a moment, Rand wondered if he had come upon an ocean siren, for the vision she presented was something rare, wise, otherworldly.

She glanced up and spied him on the approach. He felt her aqua gaze cut through the flatness of the overcast day, but she did not hail him. She turned her attention back to the pool in which she waded, all her focus centered there. Carefully, still singing her soothing song, she withdrew a small mass of dark, looping material from where it draped at her hip. Seaweed, he wondered at first, but as he got closer he realized it was human-made, not seaborn. She took the ends of the net in her fingers and held it out before her, displaying it almost ritually, as though presenting the fine woven net to the sea for approval.

Rand said nothing as he came to stand nearby the little cove. He waited outside the shelter of the rock, feeling in that moment as if to intrude would be to tread on sacred ground. He listened to her softly whispered song, then watched as she gently released the net from her grasp. It descended onto the water with a bare sigh of sound, then fell, its web of fine knotted squares engulfed at once by the ocean's lapping waves. At Serena's feet, a school of tiny silver fish darted out to safer waters, making a swift escape. Two other fish, larger ones that would make a hearty meal, remained beneath the delicate weave of the net.

Serena's song was but a hum now, she all but ignoring Rand as she bent to retrieve her catch. She took the ends of the net and brought it together, tenderly drawing the fish out of the water. The net dripped as she carried it toward a basket that waited in the shade of the rocky outcrop, the two fish flapping about, splattering water with their frantic struggles.

"I take it that will be our dinner."

"Yes," she replied, sparing him only the most cursory

glance of acknowledgment. All her focus—all her regret, did he not miss his guess—was reserved for her task at hand.

Solemnity dimmed her usual bright gaze as she withdrew a small dagger from a slender leather sheath on her girdle of braided linen. She sighed, very softly, then removed the gloves from her hands and tucked them into her girdle. The words she whispered were inaudible, but apologetic in tone, as she bent down to catch one of the fish in her other hand. The slippery creature eluded her grasp but did not get far, its silver fins beating air as it flopped on its side within the beached net. Serena drew in her breath and shuddered slightly, staring down at her empty hand. Her reaction seemed an odd mirror to that of her quarry; at Serena's feet, the fish gasped for air, convulsed.

"Let me," Rand said, hunching down to spare her the unpleasantry of the chore.

"Nay." She tried to refuse his offer, frowning now. "This is mine to finish. I want to do it."

But Rand's old instincts to protect a lady from any ill—his code of chivalric honor, rusted and battered, buried deep now—could not permit her to endure the task. And he could see that despite her argument otherwise, this was likely the last thing she wanted to do. Her face was pale with remorse, in spite of the firm set to her jaw. What he glimpsed in her face was not mere squeamishness, but something unreadable. What she felt ran much deeper than missish revulsion for a task she had no doubt done countless times before, based on the skill and ceremony with which she worked her net. But the dread was there, swimming in the cobalt green of her eyes.

"Let me," he said again, and took the knife from her agile fingers.

He finished quickly, cleaning the two fish and sweeping the waste into the sea to feed the rock crabs and other scavengers. He placed the fish in the basket, then rinsed his hands and cleaned the knife in a swirling tidal puddle near his foot. When he rose, he found Serena standing solemnly still next to him. She held her face out toward the sea beyond, eyes closed. The ubiquitous gloves of hers were once more covering her hands, which were clasped before her in prayer.

"What are you doing?"

"Thanking the sea for feeding us. Thanking the fish for letting me take them in my net today."

Rand was tempted to chuckle at the sentimentality of such a notion—the mild blasphemy in crediting any but God the Almighty for such gifts—but it was clear that Serena meant it deeply. No doubt she had been schooled in old ways, pagan ways, forbidden by the church yet practiced quietly by a daring few. Rand's own forebears had been less than pious, wild rogues and scoundrels and wandering gypsies being the more respectable of the lot, so he could find no offense in such elemental worship as that which Serena seemed to practice now.

He gave her the moments of peace she required, and found himself staring thoughtfully out at the vastness of the ocean in silence alongside her. A prayer to any higher power did not seem so out of place in those reverent instants, but he could summon no words of praise or thankfulness for a world that was, for him, so empty and unkind.

Lately, on those rare occasions that he bent his head to pray, he merely begged for time and opportunity, for bloody recompense. In truth, he would have bargained himself to the devil if he thought it might give him an advantage over his enemy. He hadn't totally ruled out that prospect, regardless of its certain damning outcome. He was beyond salvation anyway, and he would walk willingly to his fate when that day came.

Beside him, Serena finished her thoughtful silence. She slowly lifted her head and turned her extraordinary gaze on him.

"All life is precious," she said. He could not help but feel she somehow suspected he could not see as much on his own, and that she pitied him for it. She gestured caringly toward the two fish in her basket. "Even these simple creatures' lives are noble and worthy."

Even yours, her long-lashed eyes seemed to say, holding him in an unblinking, tender regard.

There was a time that Rand would have agreed with her. He had embraced life once, had long been the one with a ready laugh and a giving hand for anyone in need. But no more. He could ill afford joviality or compassion when there was no telling who might be friend or foe. To Rand, everyone was suspect now. Silas de Mortaine's reach was long; his ability to corrupt was unparalleled. And it did not take much to recall the depth of his Anavrin sentries' magic, a witchy glamour that allowed them to shift form in a blink of time, from beast to man and back again—at their most dangerous, they could project the illusion of a familiar, friendly face, the deadliest form of their trickery.

Nay, Rand could never go back to the way things had been. He had seen too much darkness to think he might ever reclaim any part of the life he once knew. He had lost too much to foster that foolish hope. His family was gone. His keep was in ruins, miles behind him. All he could do was keep moving forward, alone.

Serena's voice was a softness that drew him out of his grim reflection. "What is it like . . . out there, where you come from?"

"Bleak," he answered without thinking, hearing the

word tumble from his mouth before he could stop it. A pitiful admission, but there was no saving it now. He held Serena's hopeful gaze and watched it dim with each word he spoke. "Out there is a lot of turmoil and greed and death. Dark things exist in the places I have been. Things you should not wish to know. No one should."

"Surely there is some goodness, too," she said, worry creasing her elegant forehead and reducing her voice to a troubled whisper. "With your family, at least? 'Tis clear you love them. You said you were eager to be with them."

Ah, yes. His half-truth of yesterday, stretching back to trip him up. He dodged it with a considering shrug of his shoulder, turning his gaze to the endless blanket of ocean that rippled out to the horizon, steel gray waves reaching to eternity.

"My family is everything to me," he told her, no lie there, only cold, empty truth. "They are all that is good and pure in this world." A twist of guilt formed in his gut, knotting hard at the recollection of his last hours with his wife. Final moments, wasted on anger and accusations, all of it come too late. "I would give anything to be with my wife and son now."

"Why did you leave them?"

"I had no choice. There are things I need to do—a score I must settle—before I can return home."

"I see," she said, soberly, but Rand knew that she could not possibly understand.

The night of the attack, Silas de Mortaine had taken his life, and left him holding naught but charred rubble and ash. Somewhere, in the midst of that decay, was Rand's honor. There could be no more than a scrap of it to survive, but he would reach for it. He would have it back, one day.

"Your enemy must be a very bad man, to have earned such devoted scorn."

"He has earned a war," Rand answered, not bothering to deny that his vengeance centered on a single name. "I will destroy him, and all who serve him."

"At what cost?"

Rand replied without hesitation. "At any cost."

"If you mean that, Rand," Serena said, her voice calm with clarity and reflection, "then I pity this man you seek. I pity you, too."

"Pity me?" Rand swung his head around to glower at her, scoffing at the notion. "You waste your sentiment, lady. Pity, indeed."

She held his angry gaze, unfazed. "To destroy another is to destroy a part of yourself. I think you know this. I think you feel it already happening in your heart."

"And what do you know of evil?" he demanded, the sudden harsh edge of his tone bouncing hollowly off the rock and water that surrounded them. "What do you know of men's hearts, Serena, who has scarce ventured beyond the grove line of these woods? Tell me, what could you possibly know of my heart?"

She looked away from him now, and down, to where her gloved fingers laced together anxiously before her. "More than I want to," she answered, so quietly he could nary make out her reply.

Rand tore himself away from her strange remark with effort, flicking an impatient glance up at the sky overhead. A cover of gray clouds muted the afternoon sun. A building storm fringed the horizon in dark charcoal shadow, bleak as gathering smoke. The light misting rain that sheened his skin would not long from now become a downpour.

"Rand," Serena said, his name sounding too familiar

on her tongue, too comfortable, even in his present state of irritation. "I did not mean to offend you. If I have—"

"Your dinner waits," he said, abruptly cutting her off. His curtness made him all the more aware of her queer effect on him, his growing awkwardness around her. "Take your things and go on. Head back before the storm comes."

He dried the blade of her little knife on the thigh of his torn hose, then held it out to her along with the basket of cleaned fish. She took both in silence, sheathing the knife and hooking the handle of the basket over her arm. But she made no move to leave.

"What do you wait for, Serena?"

"You," she answered simply. "Will you not join us?"

He looked at her a moment, his will briefly tempted, but, ultimately, denied. "Go on," he said, dismissing her with a mild jerk of his chin. "Save your pity and your meal, lady. I have no need of either."

"Where is he? Do you see him out there, child?"

Peering out a corner of the cottage window, Serena lifted her shoulder in a shrug. "I do not see him, Mother. I suspect he is walking the beach, or learning the lay of the forest."

"Skulking around as if he rules this place," Calandra groused. She stood at the table cutting vegetables. Her fine-boned hands made quick work of her task, the small blade of her knife flashing in the mid-morning light of the room. She cleaved a turnip with overmuch zeal, the staccato thunking of the blade meeting wood punctuating her words. "I do not like this man, Serena. His presence here is a sign, a very bad one. He will bring only trouble to us."

"He said he will not remain here long. Just until he is hale enough to continue on."

Calandra brandished her knife as she spoke. "Aye, and until then, he will consume our food and take our shelter . . . don't think he will stop at that, should he decide there is more here that he might want."

Serena frowned, not entirely certain of her mother's implication yet sensing enough meaning there to cause a knot of worry in her stomach. "He is married, with a young son. He told me so. He adores them, and lives to be home with them again."

Calandra paused in her work at the table, and turned a sober look on Serena. "He is a man, my child. His kind is accustomed to conquest and plunder—it is how they are raised. They take what they need, as we have already seen this man do since his arrival here."

"He has been peaceable enough," Serena argued gently. "True, he has an arrogance about him, a ready combativeness, but I do not think he intends harm toward us."

"There are many kinds of harm, child. You are beautiful, and I have seen his eye stray to you in notice more than it should. Marriage vows make flimsy bonds against a man's lusts."

Serena barely restrained a disbelieving laugh. "Well, you needn't fear he likes what he sees. If he looks upon me, it is with disdain and impatience. Everything I do or say seems only to provoke him."

"Desire needs but a single spark to alight. An innocent heart can fall to cinder in an instant."

The hurt in her mother's eyes, the pain she carried in her heart, had been there as long as Serena could remember. It was, she knew, put there by her father when he had abandoned his wife and the children she bore him—Serena and an older brother and sister, who both died while Serena was just a babe. Her mother never spoke of the man who sired her children, or of the siblings Serena had lost. Of her brother and sister, Serena knew little more than how they perished and that both had been gifted with the Knowing, as Serena was.

Serena was all that was left of Calandra's kin. Death seemed too much for her mother to bear. The past seemed too painful for Calandra to relive, and so she refused to speak of old hurts or the people who had once been a part of her life. It was only in times of distress that Calandra even hinted at what had come before.

Serena crossed the small room and enveloped herself in her mother's waiting embrace. "I'm sorry," she whispered, feeling the squeezing clench of loss as she briefly stroked her gloved fingers across her mother's back. "I'm sorry for bringing this upon us. It is all my fault that he is here to cause you this strain."

"No." Calandra released her and gently withdrew, sparing Serena before the Knowing could awaken fully and bring her any pain. "Do not blame yourself. This day was coming, I should have prepared better."

"Prepared for what?"

Serena stared into her mother's clear blue eyes, marveling at the wisdom there, at the ageless beauty of her face beneath the fall of long silver-white hair. "We cannot stay here, child. Not anymore. He is the first to find us, but there will be more. We have to leave."

"Leave?"

"Aye. We have to run, find someplace to hide before others like him come to the glade."

Serena exhaled sharply, disbelieving what she was hearing. "This is our home. Why would we flee it? How can you even think to abandon all we have here, Mother?"

"You touched him—you looked into his heart. I saw what that did to you, Serena. You may not have told me what acrid thoughts came with the Knowing, but I am your mother. I can guess at the terrible blackness that left you senseless and drained of all strength the night he came here. You cannot tell me that you do not understand the danger this man brings."

No, she could not deny that understanding. The feeling was still with her, although fading, an echo now. Standing there, wanting to assuage her mother's rightful fears, Serena tried to shut out even that lingering trace of Rand's fury and bloodlust. But the Knowing would not obey her whims. It only beat stronger when she sought to deny it, rising up as though summoned instead of accepting the bar she attempted to place before it. Stirring now, the strange gift that was also her curse brought her a deeper awareness, plunging her senses further into the torment of Rand's vengeful heart.

She bore the pain of it, forcing a placid look onto her face for her mother's sake alone.

"I do not think he means to harm us. He is angry, yes, and dangerous. He is consumed with a deadly hatred . . . but his wrath is reserved for someone else."

"For now," Calandra said, her expression grim. "But for how long?"

"We cannot run in fear of the unknown. We cannot leave our home—"

Serena's words were cut short, her plea broken by the sudden crash of the cottage door. The oak panel banged open on its hinges, smashing against the abode's inner wall like a thunderclap. Serena whirled around at the startling disruption. She felt the color drain from her face when her eyes lit on the feral look snapping in Rand's dark eyes.

"Neither of you are going anywhere," he snarled, anger radiating from all around him in almost palpable waves, the dangerous force of it filling the space of the open door. In his fist was a muddied scrap of linen.

He gripped it so fiercely, his knuckles had gone white. "Where is it?"

Somehow, Serena managed to find her voice. "Where is . . . what?"

He stalked inside the cottage, his mouth tight, his gaze lashing her with ferocity. "The cup, damn it! The golden cup that was wrapped in this cloth. I will give you precisely one chance to tell me true, woman."

Serena swallowed hard, her gaze rooted to his as he closed the distance between them.

"One chance," he warned in a voice that was too collected, too lethally schooled to be trusted. Without warning, he smashed his fist down onto the table beside her, instantly shattering any illusion of calm. "Now, damn it. Where the hell is it?"

❧ 7 ❧

Serena's face was ashen as he bore down on her in anger, but she met his accusation with nary a tremor in her voice.

"I've no idea—how many times must I say it? If my mother or I knew anything about this, we'd not keep it from you."

Rand scoffed at her denial. He felt his nostrils flare, his fists tremble with the depth of his rage. Serena flinched as he threw aside the muddied scrap of linen and faced her down, crowding her against the table that neatly barred her from escape. She blinked up at him in wary silence, but she did not cower. Indeed, a certain resolve seemed to find its way into her spine, bringing her up a little straighter.

Her defiance only served to anger him more.

"Tell me, Serena. What have you done with the cup? It did not wash away in the storm as you would have me believe. Do not try to deny it, when the evidence is here in my hand."

"I swear to you, the satchel was empty when I found you on the beach. I've never seen the cup you speak of."

As she spoke, her mother moved ever so subtly from where she stood, her arm reaching out toward the surface of the table. A paring knife rested near a pile of chopped vegetables. Rand kept his gaze on Serena, but he raised one hand and pointed a knowing finger at her mother.

"Madam, I would not. I promise, it would end badly for you."

"Please, hear me out!" Serena interjected, an obvious attempt to draw his ire away from her mother. "I know this cup was of great worth to you—"

"You do not know the half of it," he said, vicious in his tone and careless of it when his blood was boiling, his pulse thundering in his temples. "I told you, lady— one chance. You've spent it."

He pushed her out of his path, none too gently, ignoring her small cry as his hands came down on her shoulders in brief contact. At that scant touch, she drew in a pained breath, no doubt looking to appeal to his mercy with a show of overdone frailty. But Rand had no sympathy in that moment, not when it seemed clear she was deceiving him, even in her reaction to his fleeting touch. He stalked past her, upturning the table. The little knife and vegetables rained onto the floor. Serena said nothing, only watched him with clear eyes, while her mother gasped and fretted, shuffling out of Rand's path to be closer to her daughter.

Rand stepped through the mess he had made, kicking over a stool that sat in his way.

God's blood, but he would tear the place apart, rout out every corner, if it meant recovering the crucial portion of the Dragon Chalice.

"Where is it?" he demanded, to anxious silence at his back. "Where have you put it?"

Where, indeed? There could be many ways to conceal a small treasure like the one he sought: in any of the three clothing and linen coffers; beneath the lumpy pallet or bolster against the far wall; in the bottom of the large urn near the door, recently filled with fresh-cut flowers.

"Is it here?" he asked, heading for the wooden chest nearest him.

When neither woman answered, he squatted down and threw open the casket lid. He dug through the neatly folded stack of homespun bliauts and aprons, tossing all of it to the floor. He found nothing but cloth secreted within the coffer. He stood up, cursed, then stalked to the meager bed where Serena and her mother had slept the nights since his arrival. The pallet mattress was rumpled and uneven. Rand reached out to take the edge of it in hand, then flipped it up to expose the earthen floor beneath.

Dust and a spattering of fine down feathers rose in the disturbed rush of air. But beyond that, nothing.

"We are hiding naught from you!" Serena insisted. "You can turn our home on end but it will make no difference."

"So you say," he bit back acidly.

With a scowl, he went to the door and seized the bunch of flowers from the earthenware urn. Water dripped from the long stems, but there was nothing more contained in the bottom of the vessel.

Damnation.

His patience, thin as it was, had nearly reached its end. He spun around, surprised to find Serena just a few paces away from him.

"Please . . . Rand," she said, as always, the unexpected sound of his name on her tongue giving him slight pause. She dared to take another step toward him now. Her expression was one of openness, yet her arms were crossed protectively over her chest. "We do not have anything of yours. You must believe me."

She sounded so earnest, but the seeming sincerity of

her plea was smashed to bits by the full force of his anger. Without the Dragon Chalice, he had nothing. His plans for vengeance were slipping through his fingers; his pledge to avenge his wife and child was fading with every moment the treasure remained out of his grasp.

"I must take you at your word, then?"

"What more do you need? I've given you only truth since you have been here."

Rand turned away from her unsettling sea green eyes and exhaled an oath. His gaze rooted on a shelf near the fireplace, lined with a row of deep bowls and assorted serving vessels. "I will believe you only after I have searched every last measure of this place to my satisfaction. Until then, lady, keep your lies."

"My daughter does not lie!" As predictable as the tide, Serena's mother rushed to her defense. Wisely leaving the little knife where it lay on the floor, she railed at Rand with snapping eyes and shaking, fisted hands. "She is incapable of speaking untruths! If my daughter tells you she knows not where your trinket is, then that is fact, sirrah."

Rand could scarcely curb the rage that was lashing within him. "Do you think me a fool? She was the one who found me on the beach. It was her face before me when I woke—an instant before she refused me help, then left me to die in the surf."

"Because we knew you were wicked!" Calandra cried. "We knew you would bring your violence to our door!"

Rand spared the old woman and her fervent protests not so much as a glance. He stood before the shelf of crockery, fury seething like a tempest in his blood. Already he had lost precious time—more than two weeks since he had set out from Glastonbury with his dubious prize, and another several days spent recuperating in this remote English forest. De Mortaine and his minions were no doubt getting closer to the last of the Chalice stones while he was crashing about like a blind man, searching for something he might never find.

But he had not lost the cup at sea. He could not have let it go. The memory of clutching the satchel, of sacrificing the weight of his sword for that of the cup in his bag was still fresh in his mind. He *did* have the satchel when he washed ashore, and it was not empty, as Serena would have him believe. The cast-off scrap of linen was proof enough of that.

Nay. If the treasure was indeed lost, then he would have to accept that he'd also lost this fight before it had even begun.

Rand refused to permit the thought.

Elspeth and Tod will not have died for nothing. He had sworn his soul on that pledge. He would not forsake his promise to them without a fight . . . to his last breath, if that was what it took. His fragile wife and innocent child had depended on him, but he had failed them in life.

By nails and blood, he would not fail them in death.

The vow rang in his head, louder than thunder, louder than the sudden crash of earthenware pots and bowls falling onto the hard floor of the cottage as he swept the lot of them off the shelf with one pass of his arm. Vaguely, he heard female screams behind him.

"Stop!" one of them cried. "Why must you destroy our home? We've done you no harm! What do you want from us?"

He heard the fear and distress in the voice, but in his mind—in his heart—he was hearing someone else's pain. Elspeth.

It was her terror that pierced his head. It drove deep inside of him, hot as a brand, a searing wound. He saw thick smoke choking the circular stairwell of his keep.

He felt soot clinging to his throat and lungs, floating ash scorching his vision. His sword was cold steel in his hand. There hadn't been time to dress; the raiders had broken in under the dead of night, setting fire to the small castle and its few outbuildings. They had come on simple orders: retrieve the key, and leave no one at Grey-cliff living.

Garbed in naught but braies, armed with one sword against half a dozen shapeshifting guards, Rand had gone down ready to meet the enemy.

Elspeth had tried to stop him, begging him not to go, not to leave her behind. She had grabbed his arm, wrapped her arms around his neck, sobbing and hysteri-cal with fear and the delirium of the herbs she had con-sumed earlier that day. He had shaken her off with a shouted curse, the last words they would exchange. She pounded his chest then, her small fists thudding against his heart, a furious tattoo that he could feel on his bare skin, even now.

Rand heard the crunch of pottery shards underfoot and immediately snapped back from the ugly remem-brance of the raid on his demesne. Elspeth's terrified face was fading, her hysterical screams—her condemn-ing words to him—now dimming.

But the pounding he felt on his chest was very real. Angry blows delivered by Serena. She was weeping qui-etly, sorrow trailing down her fine-boned cheeks. Her gloved hands slowed their assault on him as if she could lift them no more, as if the intensity of her emotion had drained her of all strength.

"Serena," her mother called from across the room. "Stop, child! You mustn't touch him. You know what it will do to you. . . ."

But it was too late. Rand stared down into a face of such clarity and understanding, it nearly robbed him of his breath. Her crystalline eyes glittered with tears, an outpouring of anguish he instinctively knew—one he felt, inexplicably, that he shared.

"They're dead," she murmured. "Sweet mercy, they slaughtered them both."

"What are you talking about?" Rand demanded, his anger over the missing cup swallowed up by this queer revelation. "What are you saying?"

"Your wife . . . your son, just past his sixth year . . . both of them gone."

Something cold clenched Rand's insides. "How do you know this?"

"Fire," she whispered. "So much smoke. I cannot see them . . . but—oh, mercy!" Her trembling hands came up to frame her face, her gloved fingers covering her ears. Her gaze was queerly unfocused. "They are both screaming. Screaming and crying and then . . . *no.*"

"Cease," he commanded her, stunned and bewildered. "What is this game you play?"

But she would not—or did not—hear him. "It is too quiet now," she said, panic rising in her tight whispering voice. "I cannot hear them anymore . . . cannot see them. . . ."

"Enough." Rand took Serena's shoulders in a bruising grip, astonished beyond comprehension at what he was hearing—words that seemed torn from his own memory, from his own heart. "Damn it, woman! How can you know this? Were you there?" He shook her, trying to find sense in her words, to shake loose the truth of her incredible account of the raid. "How the hell can you know what happened that night?"

"Let her be, I beg you!" It was her mother's voice that answered him, her hands clasped in supplication as she rushed forward and beseeched him to release her daughter. "She cannot hear you—she is too deep in the Know-

ing. Release her, please. You only make it worse with
your touch."

"Nothing left," Serena murmured. Rand's grasp had
loosened only slightly, but she shrank out of it, still
adrift in that unfathomable fog. Her eyes were open,
wide yet unseeing, Rand was certain. She looked straight
at him—verily, straight through him, for he felt the pene-
tration of her sightless gaze like a sorcerer's blade, cleav-
ing his secrets wide open. "They are gone, couldn't save
them. There is nothing left, only ash . . . only pain. . . ."

"God's bones," Rand cursed, disbelieving, yet unable
to deny what he was hearing. "The both of you truly are
bedeviled, aren't you? This is madness—"

"Not madness, but a gift," her mother insisted. "You
couldn't understand. No one would."

"Witchery," he said, latching onto the only explanation that made sense.

The woman's white hair tossed in a cloud of fervent
denial. "No!"

"What else can it be?" Rand replied.

He easily recalled another sorcerer's gift he had
witnessed—that of the shapeshifters, who pledged their
service to Silas de Mortaine. The very beasts that slew
his family amid the smoke and destruction that Serena
had just described. The vision, if that's what it was, still
gripped her. Tears streaked down her face from eyes
that were squeezed shut as if to block the images from
her mind. She was panting, speaking low under her
breath . . . pleading for mercy as Rand himself had done
all those nights ago.

Now he swore, his throat raw with memory relived
through Serena's uncanny understanding.

"A gift," he muttered, staring at the strange beauty
with the power of the devil's own eyes. "If this be a gift,
then Serena must be favored by a dark lord, indeed."

"No!" Her mother held up her hands as if to stay his accusation. "Never say that, I beg you! There is no evil here. To speak such—especially to anyone outside these woods—would be to call for her death. Do you understand? My child is no witch. Never say it!"

She went to her daughter and tried to bring Serena into her embrace, but she was rebuffed. Serena was frantically pulling off her gloves, a look of anguish on her face.

"The blood . . . it is . . . everywhere." With a cry, she threw down the leather that had encased her hands—hands that Rand could not help noticing were not scarred or deformed as he had initially guessed. Her pale, pristine palms and slender fingers were flawless, as tender as a noblewoman's. She stared down at them, clearly horrified by what she saw.

Rand understood, as much as he wanted to deny it. He knew what she saw. God's truth, but he remembered it as if it were only yesterday.

"Their blood is on my hands!" She rubbed at invisible stains, growing panicked and helpless in her distress. "Mercy . . . I cannot . . . it won't come off!"

"See what you have done!" her mother railed at him. "Serena, child, 'tis all right now. Hush . . . let it pass."

But Serena could not be consoled. Her gaze wild, breath heaving, she tore away from her mother's outstretched arms and bolted for the cottage door. She ran out, disappearing into the woods outside.

When her mother moved to follow her, Rand held the woman back with a meaningful glare. "You will stay here, woman. This matter is mine to handle."

He did not wait for argument.

Chasing after Serena, Rand navigated the narrow, winding trail toward the beach, following the tremble of ferns and underbrush that stirred in her wake. He found her there at the end of the path, where the forest left off and the golden sand of the shore stretched on to the sea. Serena was sitting on her knees, rocking back and forth, holding herself in utter silence. Her long dark hair sifted all around her, a veil of black silk that caught the sunlight and fractured it like a thousand dark diamonds. She looked as small as a child, as breakable as glass.

He knew that fragility; he had seen it often enough in Elspeth.

Rand came up slowly, careful not to frighten her despite the misgivings and thundering questions that battered him from all sides. What the hell had possessed her back there in the cottage? The question—nay, the demand—perched on the very tip of his tongue. He only barely held it back.

"Serena. Tell me what this about. It is impossible that you could have been at Greycliff that night. So, how is it you can know what you do about my family?"

He got only silence in reply.

"I will not harm you, but I need to know what happened to you just then. Do you hear me?"

She turned and saw him there, clearly stricken. Her eyes were awash with tears but she seemed too deeply affected to give voice to her sorrow. "No," she groaned. With a cry low in her throat, she put her hands out onto the sand, then pushed to her feet. "Please . . . leave me alone."

Rand let her take only a couple of steps before he was at her side, reaching for her arm. She pulled it away before he could take hold of her.

"Easy," he advised, soothing her as he might a startled mount. "Peace now . . . I only want to talk to you."

The gaze she turned on him was still distant, still glittering with tears. She blinked them away, letting twin tracks skim a wet path down her bloodless cheeks.

"Do not touch me," she whispered, desperation edging her voice as it swam in her wild eyes. A profound anguish reflected from deep within the placid blue-green hue, so wrenching he felt it pierce him where he stood. "I can bear no more of your pain."

"My pain?" Rand shook his head, even though a part of him knew she spoke the truth.

My daughter does not lie! She is incapable of speaking untruths!

That was Serena's mother's claim back in the cottage just a short while ago. Now Rand was beginning to see what she meant. Despite the madness of it, he was only now beginning to understand.

"My pain," he said, letting his hand fall back down to his side. "You know what I feel?"

Serena's chin dipped in a weak nod.

"Impossible," he scoffed. "No one can know that."

His denial seemed to bring her close to reason. She frowned at him, shaking her head. Her face yet lacked normal color, but her gaze was focusing again, coming back from whatever spell had held it.

"I know what you feel, and I have seen the atrocity of what haunts you." When he swore a dubious oath, she went on with more conviction, merciless in her effort to convince him of what she claimed. "I know that your wife—Elspeth—screamed for you to help her in the moment before an assailant's bolt pierced her heart."

"Enough."

Rand did not wish to hear another word, true or not. But Serena would not, or mayhap she could not, stop recounting the brutal facts of that night.

"She fell down the tower stairs, dying, cursing you . . . with your young son in her arms." She paused, watching him too closely, seeing too much. "I know that you survived only for them. That's why you are here, for retribution. You have murder on your mind, and I know that you will let nothing stand between you and your vengeance."

"Jesu," he hissed through a clenched jaw. "You weren't there. You couldn't have been. There is no way you could know—"

"I touched you. I saw what happened. I felt all of it, just as you did." She glanced up at him, her eyes mournful beneath long black lashes spiked with moisture. "I still feel it, as you do now, Rand."

He absorbed her soft confession with no small amount of incredulity. He did not want to think about what happened to Elspeth and Tod when raiders descended on his keep in the dead of night. He did not want to relive the hours of brutality that played out in agonizing detail every time he closed his eyes to sleep.

He did not want to be made to admit any of what he felt since that terrible event, least of all to this woman, who might yet prove to be his enemy.

"How?" he asked at length. "How can you possibly—"

"It is called the Knowing. It comes to me on touch— an instant glimpse into the heart of whomever I lay my hands on."

Those pale, delicate hands were clenched in tight fists now, held rigidly at her sides. She had left her ubiquitous gloves in the cottage, stripped off in the midst of her panicked vision. Their significance was suddenly dawning on Rand.

"Touch causes you distress, and so you keep your hands protected to avoid contact."

"Yes. But there are times when the gloves I wear are of little help against the Knowing."

"As was the case back there, in the cottage? You did not shed them until after you had touched me," Rand said. "You were able to read what I was feeling, even through the leather barrier?"

She nodded. "As I said, there are times when nothing can withstand the Knowing."

"How long have you been like this?"

"How long have I been so afflicted?" Her soft exhale was vaguely wry. "It has always been this way for me. I cannot stop it."

"And your mother, too?"

"Nay. She does not have the touch, but my brother and sister both did. They are dead because of the Knowing."

"This"—Rand hesitated to call it a gift—"this . . . thing you speak of, do you mean to say that it can kill you?"

Serena's expression, while still shadowed by pain, took on a placid acceptance. "If what we experience is too strong, too evil, then yes. The Knowing of it can be deadly. But so are those people who do not understand. They fear. They persecute. They kill."

She held him in her silence, unblinking as she stared up at him.

"What of you, Randwulf of Greycliff?"

That she knew the name of his demesne when he deliberately had not spoken it aloud in the days he had been in her presence did not surprise Rand now. But neither did it give him any measure of comfort to know that this woman had been able to read his thoughts—his deepest pain—so inexplicably. How much could she see? How far did her insight reach in those moments she had laid her hands upon him in the cottage? More to the point, could she wield this skill at will, if it suited her purpose?

Such a skill could be dangerous indeed, should Serena be willing—or persuaded—to turn it against him. Rand's enemies were not above torture, and he had seen first-hand how effectively such tactics could render even a strong warrior into a weakened slave.

"What of me?" he mused aloud, his mind continuing to assess the many risks she might pose to his goals.

"Aye," she said. "I have seen your secrets today, and now you know mine. So, the question is, what will you do? Will you betray me to those beyond the woods, whose fear and misunderstanding could destroy me . . . or will you instead do it yourself?"

"I won't pretend to like all that I am hearing today—God's blood, I can hardly begin to credit any of it—but you have given me no reason to bring you harm, Serena."

She raised her chin slightly, perhaps to better discern his veracity, but it seemed defiant to a degree. "Then you believe me now, that I know nothing about the cup you claim to have brought ashore with you when I found you?"

"I believe you," he said, truthfully, beginning to wonder if mayhap he had lost the treasure at sea after all.

The satchel could have been empty, as she claimed. The cup's linen wrapping simply could have washed ashore like he had. It could have been carried into the woods by an animal, or by a foraging bird. But Serena did not have the missing goblet, nor had she seen it on his person when she came upon him on the beach that day. Of that much, he was certain now. He could only pray that the sea might reject the cup and bring it to him on an incoming tide.

Until then—and until he could figure another weapon to use against Silas de Mortaine—Rand would have to exercise patience, something he had precious little of lately.

"Good. I am glad you are satisfied," Serena said, her frank voice breaking into his thoughts.

"I am," he said, "for now."

She tilted her head in a nod of acknowledgment that was anything but meek, then started to walk past him onto the path.

"Serena. Where are you going?"

Steady sea green eyes met his gaze over her shoulder. "Back to the cottage, to help my mother to clean up the mess you made of our home."

Rand did not stop her, nor did he offer comment as she pivoted back around and set off through the woods.

Serena managed to keep her stride calm, collected. A miracle, for inside she was screaming, shredded by the battery of violent images—by the very real experience of everything Rand had endured the night his home was attacked. She did not know how he could carry so much pain with him every moment of every day. It had been her burden only a few long moments but already it was clawing at her from within, scraping her with talons of grief and anger.

And guilt.

She felt that emotion as strongly as the others, perhaps more so. Rand blamed himself for what had happened to his beloved family. Blame for the raid, and something . . . more. He bore the responsibility of their deaths—Elspeth's in particular, as if her blood stained his own hands. The wracking anguish of it rose up like bitter bile in Serena's throat.

Why had he lied to her about them? He had pretended his wife and child were alive, waiting for him to return home, and all the while he knew they slept in cold graves, buried by his own hands amid the ruin of his sacked keep.

Shame, hissed the Knowing. The cruel whisper sifted through the echoing agony of the torment she now shared with Rand. His shame cut deep, a festering wound.

Serena stumbled, her hand at her heart, trying to hold back the hurt, and a budding dread she was only beginning to understand.

At last she reached the cottage. She heard her mother sweeping up broken pottery, muttering curses for Rand and his barbarous lineage. Serena paused at the door, but could not find the strength to enter just yet.

Something else haunted her from that instant when she had touched Randwulf of Greycliff. In the melee of the raid, through the smoke and swirling ash that stung her eyes even now, with the benefit of distance, Serena had glimpsed something astonishing and utterly terrifying.

She had seen the faces of Greycliff's attackers.

They were not men, but wolves.

Shapeshifters, so said the Knowing.

The word was foreign to her, not something she had ever heard. But she understood its meaning as clearly as Rand did himself. She saw the snapping jaws and thrashing, razor talons as the black-furred beasts lunged at Rand through the smoke. It seemed so unreal—even to her, who had come to accept that there were many unexplainable things in this world, good and evil. This, she knew without doubt, was an evil no one should understand.

But Randwulf of Greycliff had lived it. He had survived it. And like the Knowing told her, he survived for one reason alone: retribution on the man who had unleashed such an unholy terror on innocent people. The very man Rand meant to kill.

Nothing would keep him from that goal, so said the

Knowing, reading the truth from the depths of Rand's embittered heart.

He would not be stopped . . . least of all by a witchy maiden and her devil's gift of sight.

His unspoken words ringing in her ears, her limbs still weak from the darkness of his thoughts, Serena opened the door. She gave her mother soft assurances that all was well, then knelt down beside her to begin picking up the pieces of their old life, most of it lying shattered and upheaved on the floor of the cottage.

❧ 8 ❧

THE MORNING PASSED, and still the lingering pall of the Knowing remained Serena's uneasy companion. To her relief, Rand had busied himself outside the cottage most of the time. He did not apologize for the damage he had wrought in his anger, but then, given all that Serena had been told of man-kind, she had expected no such concession. She had not expected him to fetch water unasked, as he had, when the floor had been cleared of debris and ruined rushes and was then ready for a thorough swabbing. Calandra had accepted the bucket with muttered gratitude, but Rand's gaze had been rooted on Serena, as though he offered this boon, such as it was, to her.

Serena did not want to acknowledge his paltry gift, or his paltry gesture of remorse, but she found it next to impossible to ignore Rand altogether. Particularly when he was a constant presence around the cottage, watching her, waiting for her to reveal herself as the condemnable witch he no doubt thought she was. She could not find a full breath, or think a clear thought, until he had taken his leave of the confining place once more.

She rejoiced in his absence, however short it might be. Surreptitious glances out the cottage window told her that he had departed the yard, likely gone down to the beach to search the sand for further traces of the cup he had lost. Serena only hoped it would keep him occupied the rest of the day. He was having a queer effect on her that had to do with something more than merely the Knowing.

Randwulf of Greycliff was a man of war, all that she had been raised to fear. He was a tortured soul, probably beyond redemption. But yet the Knowing whispered to her in a beckoning hush, urging her to look closer, to reach past Rand's pain to glimpse the man in full. Serena did not dare, not after what she had endured that morning. The echoes of that experience still chilled her to the bone—she did not reckon she could bear any more of his secrets. Surely she could bear no more of his pain.

She worked in a troubled silence, putting the cottage to rights with her mother. One last pottery shard was tossed into a bucket that contained more of the same.

"I'll bring the rubbish out to the garden," she told her mother, eager to finish, but more desirous of the open spaces of the yard outside. She picked up the collected pail of earthenware and debris and carried it to the door. "I think I may take a walk as well."

Calandra paused and looked up from her mopping. "Do not go too far, child."

"Of course, Mother." Serena hesitated only a moment, her hand on the latch as she slowly closed the door on the familiar warning. "I never do."

At the heart of the forest, nestled in a forgotten corner that was shadowed by towering pine and leafy ash, lay the fallen rubble of an ancient chapel. It had never been lavish, only a small pocket shelter of rough-hewn wood taken from its surroundings, and smooth salt-crusted stone, retrieved from the shore by the first of Serena's people who had made the forest their home. They had worshipped here, wed here, seen their children named here, and, eventually, one by one, they had been shriven here and laid to rest.

No markers staked their scattered graves, but in an old leather-bound book secreted in the forgotten chapel, their names had been meticulously recorded down through the ages. It was Serena's only link to her past, and the lives that had come before her own. Generations filled the pages of thinning, yellowed parchment. Too many names for Serena to remember them all, some of them odd and foreign-looking, others common, all of them beautiful to her reverent eyes.

Some days, she sat in the tumbledown sanctuary and paged through the sheaves of lives, wondering where they came from, how they met one another, why some left the forest, and where they might have gone. Why others stayed and stayed and stayed, like her mother. Like Serena herself.

On still other days, such as this, she merely appreciated the solitude of the place, sacred and secluded, sunwarmed stone and aged brown wood. Nothing but stretching trees and open sky where the thatched roof of the nave had long since crumbled to dust.

Serena had been there for hours, seated on the weathered, ivy-laced stone slab of the altar, her arms wrapped tight about her knees. She was weeping, and had been nearly since she arrived there. She could not stop her tears. Her breast heaved with the depth of her sobs, great wracking tremors like naught she had ever known.

She mourned, though not for any of the souls who had once trod this same corner of the woods. She wept for Randwulf of Greycliff. For his wife and child, who had perished so violently. Her sadness was his, drawn by the Knowing, and now a part of her as well.

She did not want this burden. She did not think she could bear it, and knew not how Rand himself was able to cope. His fury was his anchor, of course. She felt that, too, in the rippling cold of the Knowing's wake. Rand's need for retribution was likely all that held him steady when the anguish of what he had endured threatened to sweep him away.

Serena shivered despite the warmth of the day. She willed herself toward more peaceful waters, her heart feeling wrung out and weary. The sun that had been blazing directly above when she arrived at the chapel had since drifted past the open-air ceiling of the nave, heading toward afternoon. She had lingered there too long. If she delayed any longer, her mother would worry.

She dashed at her moist eyes with gloved fingertips and scooted off her altar perch. Fine motes of forest silt eddied about her feet as she stepped across the floor of the nave to the peaked stone portal that had long ago given up its wooden door.

Outside the sanctuary ruin, the woods hummed with sudden activity. Leaves rustled as birds took flight, and above the soft sough of the wind, Serena heard the sure strides of long legs and the heavy crush of a man's feet approaching through the woods.

She pushed her hair from her face and blew out a calming breath, just as Rand's tall shadow reached the chapel threshold. He held a dagger in his hand, close near his body, but poised to strike.

Serena drew back with a gasp.

"What are you doing out here?" he demanded of her, turning the blade away. "What is this place?"

He scowled at her, his gaze narrowing on hers as she took a subtle step away from him. Her sorrow of a moment ago was replaced by sudden awareness of him. He stood too close, overmuch so, when a simple brush of contact would wake the Knowing and send her back into the bleakness of his heart.

"This was our family's chapel, a long time ago," she answered, feeling too crowded in the small space with him now. "I came here because I wanted to be alone."

"You've been crying." His voice held the flat tone of disapproval.

Serena lifted her shoulder in a mild shrug. "I came here to be alone," she said again, all the excuse she would give him when he was towering over her like a thundercloud. "And I was just about to take my leave. My mother will be waiting for me at the cottage."

He took a step inside, not bothering to wait for an invitation.

"You didn't tell me about this place when we walked the forest yesterday."

Serena glanced around at the dusty, ancient nave. "I didn't think it important to you. There is naught of interest here. This chapel can serve you in no way."

"But it can serve to hide a curious dove hunter—as I first thought it might when I approached." Rand's mouth turned down at the corners, a sober line within his dark beard. "I should think you'd be more careful, lady. It may not be wise to venture about alone."

"I suppose I am not accustomed to cowering in the bracken."

"No?" There was an irony in his tone that made her bristle a bit.

"No," she insisted. "And I have no wish to start now."

"Suit yourself," he said as he moved farther into the nave, his bare feet soundless on the earthen floor. Serena watched his fingers skate over the stone altar as he slowly walked the confines of the small chamber, then came around to face her once more. "You should know that I've found more snares today. I counted four of them, but I'm certain there are more."

Serena breathed a dismayed sigh. "Where?"

"Scattered hither and yon, farther out near the grove line." If it was possible, it seemed that a note of true concern edged his deep voice. "They will only come closer, Serena. It is merely a matter of time."

Dread settled heavily on her shoulders, for although she was loath to think it, she knew Rand was right.

"You think we should leave," Serena said, grasping his unspoken advice. "We should simply abandon our home in fear?"

"Mayhap," he replied. "Before you have true cause to fear."

A small burst of wry laughter slipped past her lips. "My mother would have us leave in fear of you, and you would have us leave in fear of what might never come to pass."

She caught the note of surprise in his expression at her blurted admission, but he said nothing of it. "What of you, Serena?"

"What about me?"

"Your mother cannot live forever. When she is gone, and it is only you in that cottage, will you be content, living out your days alone in these woods? Have you never wondered what else is out there?"

"I thought you said there was naught but bleakness and sorrow to be found in the world you know."

"Not at all." He grunted, lifting one chestnut brow. "I may have painted an unfair picture."

"As when you told me your family was alive and awaiting your return to them?"

A stiffness crept into his mien, as if to warn that she was treading on hallowed, forbidden ground. "I never said they lived. They do await me . . . in the hereafter, so you now know, after laying all my secrets bare with your touch this morning."

"You still have secrets. Many, I would guess."

"Is that so?"

Serena nodded, carefully watching his gaze. "You can talk to me, Rand. Tell me what happened the night your family was attacked. I would like to know," she gently urged him. "I think I need to know."

He laughed, a harsh sound that cracked in the silence of the gloomy nave. "I admit, I am somewhat disappointed to hear this. I presumed your Knowing to be a stronger magic, Serena. Did I not bleed enough details to satisfy your questing mind?"

"You held something back," she said, trying not to be pricked by his caustic tone. "And there is no weakness in the Knowing. Your thoughts—all your feelings—were centered on your family in the moment I touched you. 'Tis all you gave me, the anguish of what you endured. That, and . . . traces of what you witnessed that night. I know what I've seen, but I cannot make sense of it."

"My apologies if I left you to wonder." His voice was dark and even, more forboding than any shouted outburst. "Shall I confess every grisly moment of that hellish night? You may wish to sit, gentle lady, for the bloodletting and fire went on for long hours, and it may take me some time to relay it all to your satisfaction."

"Or I could touch you now, and know the truth of it in an instant," Serena replied, a statement of fact more than provocation. "I wager your thoughts on that night are naught but clear now."

His bearded chin went up, gaze narrowed to flinty seriousness. "There are some secrets, Serena, that can kill. This is one of them. Do not make a game of it, for it is deadly real. If you do not trust me, think on what my wife and son suffered in those hours of their murder. That brand of evil is something you'll not want visited on you, or your mother."

She thought his harsh words a threat at first, and worried that she had goaded this dangerous man past his slender leash of civility. But as she looked at him, pinned by the steely coolness of his hard hazel eyes, she realized it was no mere attempt at intimidation.

It was a grim prediction.

The worry she had felt chilled to something even colder under the weight of his penetrating stare.

"What are you involved in, Rand? Who is this man you seek? Why did his raiders attack your keep? What were they looking for? Was it the cup you lost at sea?"

"Enough questions," he said, brusquely dismissing her. "I won't bring you into this any more than I already have."

Rand tucked the dagger beneath the rolled waistband of his tattered hose and gestured for her to follow him.

"If you are recovered, lady, I would have you show me the rest of the area here. I would know every corner of it—down to the last inch. And you will tell me at once if anything appears unusual to you."

"What for?"

"I think it prudent that I know precisely what I will be guarding." At her questioning frown, he went on. "So long as I'm inhabiting this patch of woods, like you, I would prefer no surprises from Egremont's hunting lords, or from anyone else. I need to know every perimeter and potential hiding place in this forest. I doubt I'll find a better guide. We can start at the grove line."

As it seemed he would not be refused, Serena acquiesced.

She led him through the copse of tall trees and grasping bramble, to the nearest place where the old stones began their march through the woods, marking the line she had never breached in all her years.

For a long while, they walked in uneasy silence, following the trail of placed rocks that went on a fair distance into the heart of the woods. More than a century old at the least, the grove line more resembled a row of crooked teeth, some of the stones obvious, others overgrown with age, all but obscured by moss, or displaced by stripling trees that thrust up between their careful settings.

"These old stones are the labor of my kin, the first ones to come here and make the woods their home," Serena said, feeling a bit awkward to be making conversation with a man who, not a few hours ago, had been intent on sacking her home in his rage, and had now declared himself a guardian of these woods.

But the day had been nothing short of extraordinary, and deep within her, the Knowing stirred just to be near him, reminding her that whether she willed it or nay, part of this fearsome warrior now lived in her.

"Come this way," she said once they reached the outer curve of the grove line. "I will show you where I found the first traps."

Quiet fell upon them once more, the only sounds those of chirping, flitting birds, and the occasional scuttle of a fleeing rabbit or field mouse, eager to be out of the range of tramping human feet. It was music Serena dearly loved, the happy chatter of animals, the soft soughing of the wind rustling the canopy of leaves overhead, the distant, rumbling crash of waves echoing from the shore to the east.

The concert of soothing forest sounds almost made it easy to ignore the pang of alarm that was ringing in her head, warning of the danger of encroaching hunters, and the other, less blatant danger that now strode beside her, commanding her time as he had all else that once was hers and her mother's alone.

Their guardian, indeed.

Serena did not want to credit that she and her mother needed his kind of protection, but she could not deny that the life they had enjoyed for so long was slowly eroding. Randwulf of Greycliff was only the latest harbinger of the change to come. The hunters' snares were another. The outside world was closing in. Soon there would be more strangers in these woods, more threats to the peace that had been hers all her life.

She accepted Rand's presence with not a little resignation, but subjugation was one thing she could not abide. Serena slowed her pace beside him, then stopped.

"What is it?" he asked. "Why do you pause?"

"There is something that needs to be said between us, here and now. You should understand that there will be terms if you are to stay here."

"Go on," he said, a measured timbre to his voice.

Serena squared her shoulders, facing him on the path. "You need to know that I will not be made a prisoner in my own home."

His shoulders lifted in a vague shrug. "I am not your keeper."

As a reassurance, his statement gave only the smallest comfort. "I won't be made to serve you—me or my mother," she added, needing him to know where she stood. "We will give you the food and shelter you require, but we do so of our own will, not because you demand it. You cannot bully us or seek to cow us into doing your bidding."

"Ah." He inclined his head in mild acknowledgment. "I regret my outburst in the cottage today. I was in the wrong, it seems, and I have no desire to abuse your hospitality, Serena."

He looked at her as her name slid off his tongue, warm as a caress, and in an instant Serena saw herself reflected back in his gaze. She saw her own eyes, wide and wary, filled with something that looked alarmingly like . . . hope.

She could not deny that a strange bond had linked her to this tormented man, formed by the power of her Knowing. She knew what he was about. She knew his pain. She knew he lived to stain his hands with the blood of another man. She knew all of this, yet here she was, standing not an arm's length from him in the middle of an empty forest, demanding his consideration.

She was pressing him for compromise, asking him for acceptance, and it terrified her.

"Anything more, Serena?"

"Yes," she said, breaking his gaze when the intensity of it proved too much. "I would have your word that you will leave as soon as you are able. As soon as you have whatever it is you need to continue with your . . . quest, will you then go, and leave us in peace?"

"I will not linger a moment longer than is needed." He put two fingers over the center of his chest, where she knew his heart beat with the burdensome pain of loss and unmet fury. "I give you my oath, lady. My business is elsewhere. I will not stay."

"Good," she said, with a sense of comfortable finality. "Then we are settled."

"We are," he said, his voice quiet, but firm with an equal resolve.

Serena nodded once, unable to meet the eyes that watched her so unwaveringly.

"Very well, then."

Something quirked at the edge of his mouth, the corner of his lip edging up ever so slightly, into what she was tempted to call a smile. He vexed her, this dark stranger with the wounded heart and penetrating eyes. He unsettled her like nothing she had known before.

But she had won a victory here today. She had presented new terms of his stay, and he had agreed. Looking up at him, his face halved in sunlight and shadow from the trees around them, Serena felt a moment of triumph.

She would not fear him anymore. In truth, she did not fear him.

Nay, far worse was the budding feeling that was growing in her since the moment her touch had laid bare his secret pain. What she felt now was compassion. A tender seed of empathy, of a need to understand and comfort, had begun to take root and unfurl within her heart.

Something deeper than Knowing told her this was what she should fear the most: caring, even a little bit, for a man like Randwulf of Greycliff.

"This way," she said, knotting her hands in her skirts, all of a sudden uncertain what to do with them. Striding briskly past him, Serena set off on the path once more and continued with the unnerving tour of her woodland domain.

❧ 9 ❧

Rand's requested tour of the outlying forest had taken the better part of the afternoon. To his amazement, he found the time had passed quickly in Serena's presence, almost pleasantly. He had followed her through the endless maze of dense greenery, pausing to observe and listen as she pointed out their water and food sources, and the locations where she had discovered more hunters' snares in the past few weeks. She had shown him the grove line perimeter of the woods, a meandering collection of rocks and brick that separated her domain from that of the outside.

The delineation between her world and the other was clear, despite the fact that time and forest vegetation had obscured some areas of the ankle-high wall of stone. Rand could not help notice that even in casual movement, Serena had dared not so much as place her foot beyond that ancient demarcation.

But her gaze had not been so easily contained.

She had looked out past the edge of her neatly secluded world, eyes wide open, lit with a longing she hardly bothered to hide. Rand had caught himself musing over what her reaction might be to a bustling town, or the hearty ruckus of a castle hall at feast time.

He had pictured her laughing, amazed and excited by all she had been missing, and for one stunning moment, he had wanted to be the one to bring that world to her.

Ridiculous, of course. Reckless and selfish as well, for he was a poor choice as an escort when the path before and behind him was riddled with enemies. Keeping company with him, whether it be within the solitude of the forest grove or anywhere else, could prove deadly. In helping him, sheltering him in their home, Serena and her mother could be yet more unwitting victims of the war that waged over the Dragon Chalice, and that was a price Rand would not allow them to pay.

It was a thought that troubled him even now, after they had returned to the cottage and Serena had left him to go inside and help her mother prepare the evening's sup.

Rand occupied himself with a further search of the beach, agitated by impatience and the nagging ache of his injuries. He was healing, but not fast enough for his liking. Each moment he spent with her brought added temptation. Each aqua glance pulled him toward a gentle drowning, a sensual demise he was all too willing to embrace.

Irritated by his own weakness, Rand picked up a staff of pale, knotted driftwood and began an angry stalking of the shoreline. He stabbed at washed-up debris, and dragged the long stick through the muck of the receding waves in but another futile attempt to recover his errant treasure.

When he turned back and reached the place he had started, he found Serena standing at the edge of the beach, the shade of the forest bathing her in cool shadow. She stepped out into the late-afternoon sunlight when he saw her, her gloved hands clasped loosely before her.

"I didn't mean to disturb you."

"You have not."

"You've been out here for a long while. Have you found anything?"

"No." Rand rubbed his palm over the dark beard at his jaw, then pivoted to glance out to sea. "I've recovered nothing more than the scrap of cloth I found in the bracken this morn."

"I'm sorry," Serena said with sincerity. "I could help you look for the cup you lost . . . that is, if you'd like."

Rand said nothing as he turned back to regard her, feeling himself grow very still in Serena's presence. Simply by being there, she drew his senses to alert, commanded every fragment of his attention. He attempted to dismiss her with a shrug.

"There is no need to assist me, Serena. The problem is mine. I can manage it on my own."

"Of course," she replied softly. "I just thought I would offer—"

"Well, don't."

He thought she would take his gruff reply for the dismissal it was and leave, but she did not. She remained where she was, tilting her head to regard him in frank curiosity.

"Rand, I realize that we did not begin on the best of terms, but after today I thought . . . I hoped . . . that we might start over—on peaceful ground."

Every combat instinct in him warned that to agree to peace with Serena would merely begin a new kind of battle, one he would have to fight within himself, with his own desire. Already she was affecting him, despite his resistance and the knowledge that he could only hurt her in the end. But harder still was the thought of refuting her innocent gesture of faith. He could not break her tender gaze, any more than he could smash the hope that lit her aqua eyes.

"Peace," he said, practically growling the word. "I have not known it for a long while. I'm not sure I would know to recognize it, if you want the truth."

"Look around you," she said, gesturing to the deep green of the forest, the golden ribbon of sand, and the blue water beyond. "There is naught but peace here. Won't you permit yourself any part of it?"

He stared at her, wanting nothing more than to refuse her. But her shy smile caused a queer tightness in his chest. Her welcoming innocence cleaved his foolish tongue to the roof of his mouth.

"Come and join us for sup in the cottage, Rand. I've already set a place for you at the table. You must be hungry."

He was. His stomach was empty, and his body sorely needed a rest and a warm meal. Reluctantly, with a cocked brow and a gallant tilt of his head, Rand admitted defeat to the lady's will and followed her to the cottage.

Once inside, he was glad to leave obstinance at the door. He was immediately wreathed in the aromatic scents of baked bread and warm honeyed mead. A fire crackled on the hearth, golden and welcoming. The table had been set with three waiting bowls. Serena's mother tended the cooking. She eyed Rand and her daughter for a disapproving moment as they entered, but made no remark.

Rand approached the table, then paused, confused. Situated near the seat he was to occupy rested a pair of leather cross-strap boots. Folded neatly over the back of the chair was a plain tunic of russet-dyed linen and faded fawn-colored hose.

Rand had neither the eye or the interest for courtly fashion, but even he could see that the attire, although in good repair, left something to be desired. The boots, which looked to be about his size, were outmoded by decades at the least, with leather shin bindings and battered hardware that had gone a bit rusty from the salty sea air. The tunic and hose were equally dated and common; rough woven fabric, well worn. But functional, all of it, and far better than the scant, shredded rags left from his washing ashore.

"What is this?"

"Clothes," Serena said, "for you."

She was smiling at him, offering him this gift like an olive branch to seal the new terms of his stay. Rand bristled at the kindness, but it would be good to have boots again, and clothes for travel, for he would soon be on the march. He reached for the tunic, then stopped himself.

"What's wrong?" Serena asked. She picked up the long shirt and held it up before him to measure its fit with her eye. "These were my father's clothes. We've had them a while, but they were stored in a chest, safe from moths or other damage."

Her father's clothes? From the cut of them, Rand would have guessed they had belonged to her grandfather, perhaps even that man's father.

"I never knew him," Serena added, "but he was a big man, like you, tall and broad-shouldered. Was he not so, Mother?"

Serena's voice was hopeful. Across the room, the old woman said nothing, merely stared at the pair of them with a look somewhere between regret and loathing. For what was not the first time, Rand was struck with the strangeness of these women, of this solitary life they lived in the heart of the forest, away from all but each other. Serena, so open and innocent and kind; her mother, aged beyond her outward years by bitterness and mistrust of anyone, save her daughter.

Rand wished to be beholden to neither of them. He needed only himself, and the fury that sustained him. Already he found the days easing into one another in this place. He was there by chance, delayed only long enough that he could heal. He needed no kindness from them. He wanted none of their consideration, however small.

Although the thought of clean, intact attire—even ancient garb like this—was a boon he could well use, Rand shook his head. "I cannot take these."

"I told you as much," Calandra scoffed, finding her voice at last.

Serena cocked her chin, studying him like a curiosity she did not quite understand. "You won't accept them? Why?"

"He is a man," Calandra said tonelessly. "No gift is ever enough to satisfy. A man would rather take that which he desires than have it freely given."

Rand slanted a dark look at the haughty old woman whose bitterness seemed to pour off her in waves. "I don't want your charity."

"Why not?" Serena asked with frank innocence. "You need it."

He did need it, truly. He could hardly think to walk any distance without a decent covering for his feet. What's more, should he venture to town regardless of that fact, he had no coin with which to buy clothing once he arrived. He had no weapon, no horse . . . nothing. Silas de Mortaine had stripped him of all he loved; fate had taken the rest.

Yet here was Serena offering him food and clothing and shelter, without reservation or expectation.

"We've no need of these things," she said. "Take them, Rand."

He supposed it was only practical to take the garb Serena now held out to him, awaiting his decision. He would be a fool not to take anything that might help bring him closer to his imminent rendezvous with de Mortaine and the vengeance he so desired. God knew,

he needed any advantage he could get, even something
as basic as this.

Rand reached out, and slowly accepted the tunic from
Serena's gloved fingers.

"Thank you," he murmured, and was rewarded with
her smile.

"You are welcome."

He fisted his hand in the rough weave of the russet
homespun, feeling a scowl crease his brow as he realized
the mistake he had just made. With her open smile and
guileless ways, Serena offered him so much more than
she could possibly know. More, certainly, than just a wary
peace and a meager collection of secondhand clothes.
She offered him hope, and that might verily be the most
dangerous gift he could accept from another human
being.

From across the small space of the cottage, Calandra
watched joy spread over Serena's face as Randwulf of
Greycliff accepted the old tunic and hose. She had never
seen the girl so animated, so radiant.

It broke Calandra's heart to see it now.

She did not crave Serena's unhappiness, but she knew
it would come. Calandra knew it as surely as she knew her
own foolish heart. She was watching her own past mistakes play out anew in Serena—history repeating, as it
so often did.

There was little she could do to save her child from
the hurt that was certain to come. She had done what
she could to shelter her, to educate her in the wicked
ways of men, but she had not expected this. For all her
care and worry, Calandra never could have predicted
that a man like Randwulf of Greycliff would wash up
on their shore. In all her endless nightmares, she never

could have imagined that her worst fear would come to roost after all these years.

Fate, she thought ruefully. There was, evidently, no outrunning it.

The wheels were in motion, and it was too late to stop what was destined to come.

Calandra had done all she could to protect Serena; now the girl's fate was her own to decide.

❧ 10 ❧

THERE WAS SOMETHING peculiar in this quiet stretch of English forest, Rand decided, on watch that night outside the cottage. He had taken a seat on a fallen log, reclining as best he could against a thick-trunked, bracing oak that rose, like the scores of others around it, some indeterminable distance into the moonlit night sky. A pearly mist had rolled in from the beach around midnight, from his guess. It had dissipated little in the hours since. The moist air clung to his skin like a shroud, salted his lips like tears. Past the forest edge, beyond his vision, the tide threw itself ashore with a mournful rumble, a hollow, empty sound that seemed to echo somewhere deep within him.

Rand scoffed inwardly at his moroseness. Useless self-pity. He'd never indulged in it before; he would not permit it a place in his heart now.

A subtle movement alerted him to stirring nearby. He looked up, saw the door to the cottage slowly open. Serena stepped out from the dark wedge of space. At first she did not see him at his post within the trees. He had deliberately hidden himself amid the darkness of the woods, more interested in keeping a clear view of the abode and outlying grounds than allowing himself to be seen by any outsider who might approach.

Now he sat in the cover of his position, watching Serena peer about nervously as she closed the cottage door behind her. She turned her head to the left and her gaze found him through the trees. Her hands were not gloved; one delicate fist glowed pale as milk where it clutched her mantle together at her neck. She gave him a look and nodded almost imperceptibly—shy, but not startled, neither offering excuse or seeking permission— before she stepped away from the little cottage and headed onto the forest path.

Rand merely watched her go, guessing that personal necessity called her outside in these thin hours before dawn. She disappeared into the forest, the hem of her long cloak disturbing the low-lying sea mist as it floated over the feathery ferns and dewy greenery that huddled close to the earth like a living carpet.

This was a peculiar place indeed, Rand thought again, as all traces of Serena vanished into the swirling fog and deep, enveloping woods. She was a peculiar woman, a curiosity he had no wish to explore, despite how readily his mind turned to her in idle moments. She was an odd- ity of nature, her strange ability an abomination, surely— a witch's trick—although it was difficult to condemn her outright when it seemed she had naught but light and guileless innocence in her heart.

Since his waterlogged arrival on the beach, when he first glimpsed her extraordinary beauty, Rand had looked for cause to mistrust her. He sought reasons to dislike her, to push her away from him as inconsequential, nothing more than a harbor—safe or otherwise—in which to wait out his next move. Now that he had dis- covered the incredible secret of her peculiar ways, he had ample cause to mistrust and dislike and dismiss.

Yet from all he had seen of Serena, he could not summon any measure of contempt for her. Despite the affliction of her knowing touch, she was no monster. Contrarily, she appeared as goodness and peace in fleshly

form . . . but that did not make him look at her with
anything less than earthly male appreciation. It did not
keep him from wanting.

Rand hissed an oath into the darkness of the woods.

He had to get out of this place, and soon. It was beginning to play games with his mind, and on more than
one level, none agreeable in the least.

He cursed the injuries that had grounded him here,
though thankfully he was well on the mend and getting
stronger all the time. He was well enough to move on if
he pushed himself—and he would—but there was still
the matter of the Chalice treasure. Without it, he was
crippled in his fight against Silas de Mortaine. He could
lure the villain out, of course, but then what?

Without the protective magic of the cup's two stones,
Calasaar and Vorimasaar, Rand would be waging war
with no weapons. His vengeance would be a jest, a mere
annoyance to a man with de Mortaine's power. He dared
not trust the cup he had lost in the storm—wherever it
might have landed—would remain out of Silas's hands
for long. Rand had witnessed too much evil, too much
dark sorcery, to content himself with the idea that anything could ever stop de Mortaine from claiming the
Dragon Chalice in full. Once the four pieces were recovered, the treasure restored and whole, there would be
nothing strong enough of this world to check the deadly
ambition of Silas de Mortaine.

Rand's closest friend, Kenrick of Clairmont, had himself been on a mission to prevent the Dragon Chalice
from falling into de Mortaine's hands. He had spent
years studying the legend of the treasure and its mystical
origins, and had entrusted Rand to keep a secret key—a
metal seal that would open a hidden vault leading to one
of the Chalice stones. Rand had hidden the seal at Greycliff. When the shapeshifting raiders spilled into his keep

with fire and unsheathed steel, it was that bit of precious metal they sought. And they had found it, though not until Rand's wife and child lay bleeding and dead in his hall. Not until they had beaten him to unconsciousness and left him to die along with his family.

He wished he had perished with them, then as now. He wished he could take it back—those hellish hours, the impotence of his vow that he would keep them safe. He had failed them in the most basic way, a trained knight skilled in battle, pridefully unmatched on the field, yet unable to shield his defenseless wife and child in their moment of need.

Which brought his thoughts sharply back to Serena.

She had been gone a long while.

Too long, warned his conscience.

There was no sign of stirring in the woods, naught to indicate that Serena was on her way back to the cottage as she should be by now. Only silence beneath the roar of the sea beyond, and a stillness that chilled Rand where he sat.

God's blood, if the hunters from Egremont had returned—or worse . . .

A pang of alarm stabbed him, fierce and quick, too protective, though he hardly gave himself time to consider the feeling. Without a sound, Rand leaped off the log and trained his eye on the surrounding forest. He saw nothing, heard nothing.

Nothing, save the rising thud of his own pulse when he thought of Serena alone in the shadowed woods, helpless should she meet with harm.

"Damnation," he swore, cutting through the pillars of pine and oak and ash that blocked his easy course toward the path she had taken.

He sped into the forest, torn between the stealth of silence and the need to call out to her, to assess where she was, and in what condition. Pine needles crunched under his boots as he hurried deeper into the grove. The mist obscured much of the area, whisking him unwillingly back to a night when it was smoke, not fog, that blinded him, impeding his vision as he fought off intruders and was forced to listen to his wife's anguished cries.

Those frantic moments bubbled just below the surface now, raw memories spurring him on as though they were real, as though he lived the moment in truth.

"Elspeth!"

He heard her name ring in his ears, soft syllables exhaled almost as prayer. It was his own voice, his own breath huffing out of his lungs in futile rage as the dark trunks of trees whisked past him. He was alone on the path; she had not gone this way. He veered away from the narrow trail and ran down into the bracken. The mist tangled around his ankles, smoky tendrils that churned upward, reaching for him. Was he going mad?

He called to her again, and this time heard an answer—faint, still distant, all but overridden by a great pounding roar of water coming from deep within the forest.

"Rand? . . . Is someone there?"

This was all wrong—somehow, even through the disorienting panic that gripped him, he knew that. It was not smoke before him, but harmless sea mist; not the soot-blackened walls of his keep scraping his arms as he careened past them, but the rough bark of towering, ancient trees. Not Elspeth's voice calling out now, but another.

Rand's head was spinning, but he ran faster, dodging the forest's many obstacles. The din of rushing water was louder now, like the guttural clamor of beastly taunts, sadistic laughter. He headed straight toward the noise, vaulting over a large rock, slapping aside the low branches that clawed for him as he dashed by.

"Elspeth!" he shouted, praying to God she was all right, that he would reach her before they hurt her.

Through the silhouetted canopy of leaves, he saw the speeding falls of a woodland cascade. This was the roar he heard, the liquid plunge of the waterfall. Moonlight spilled over the veil of white, casting it in a shade of ethereal blue. At the base of the churning waters was a pool, its rippling surface spangled as though littered with countless scores of twinkling stars.

She was there, at the pool's nearest edge, having just come out of the water not an instant before he arrived. Her gaze was wide with alarm, her body nude and glistening. Time seemed to slow, distance falling away as his eyes registered reality.

Serena.

Not Elspeth.

He glimpsed only the briefest flash of smooth white skin—long legs, delicate hips, a slender torso curving beneath tantalizingly perfect breasts—before she reached for her cloak and quickly covered herself from his view. Water dripped from the ends of her unbound hair. Rivulets gilded in silver moonlight slid down her legs and onto her fine-boned, bare feet, making small puddles on the flat slab of rock on which she stood. She clutched the edges of her mantle tight with both hands, one between her breasts, the other at her midsection, but it was a futile gesture come too late. Her naked form was seared into his memory.

Serena.

Not his wife.

And she was not in any danger at all, but enjoying a private bath—until he had crashed through the trees like a madman, shouting his dead wife's name. Now Serena stared at him in anxious silence, as if uncertain what to say.

"What is it?" she asked him at last, but Rand could not speak.

She picked up her discarded chemise, having had no time to don it beneath her mantle. Holding the folded gown against her, she walked toward him, unafraid. Unaware of the tumult of feelings assailing him in that moment.

"I heard you call out for . . ." Her gaze was soft as her voice trailed off, no doubt to spare him the humiliation of explaining his frantic arrival. "Rand? Is anything . . . wrong?"

Aye, he answered to himself alone. Something was certainly wrong.

Forgetting the imagined peril that brought him there, or the ghostlike memories that haunted him since the night his keep was attacked, to his mind there could be nothing more wrong than the intensity of what he felt upon seeing Serena before him as she was now.

His body reacted swiftly, all that was male and animal in him waking at once to the tempting picture Serena presented, her dark hair twisted in wet silken ropes, her face glowing pale as milk, her curves tantalizingly apparent, torturously naked, beneath the paltry cover of her mantle. Rand's heart pounded heavily, stamping out the confusion that brought him to the pool and replacing it with a hunger he had no right to feel.

"I came out here to bathe," Serena said, rushing to explain herself and seeming uncomfortable with the weight of his silence. "I didn't think I needed to ask— that is, I thought we agreed yesterday that you would not impose . . ."

She did not finish. Perhaps she sensed that he was not demanding her excuses.

He should turn around and leave at once, he knew that. Propriety demanded it, even if Serena, for all her

sheltered innocence, did not. Secluded from the hungry
appetites of men for all the years she had spent in the
haven of these woods, she could not possibly fathom
the depth to which his thoughts had presently sunk. All
the more reason why he should not linger there, every
particle of his being awakened to a swift, unwanted, and
feverish desire.

"Rand?"

She stepped away from the cascade's pool, and he was
tormented further by the sight of her bare legs peeking
out from the slice of fabric with each gliding movement.
The evening mist enveloped her in gossamer white as she
drew nearer to where he stood, too innocent to know
she should fear him.

Rand took a breath, and his senses filled with the
scent of her: clean, warm, womanly. Her face gleamed,
her wet sable hair glowing blue-black where the moonlight kissed her pate. She was a vision unlike any he had
ever seen, a sweet angel, annointed by enchanted waters.

God's love, but this was a potent siren he beheld, to be
able to rouse this deep a hunger when his heart ached so
keenly for another.

Or should.

She must have registered the danger in his hooded
look, his tense silence, for at last she stilled. Drew back,
an almost imperceptible retreat. Not nearly enough for
his peace of mind; only an arm's length separated her
from him. Her lips were slightly parted, her breath stirring the haze of moist salt air. At the base of her throat,
her pulse beat quickly now, her bosom rising shallowly
beneath the small fist that held her mantle together.

She swallowed, and he could almost scent her wariness. "I'd better go back. . . ."

Less than three small paces brought her up beside him
where he blocked her way out of the glade. He should

have moved aside. She should not have paused there at
his shoulder.

Rand turned his head toward her, hungered beyond
reason. Wrong or nay—honor too flimsy to hold him—
he reached out to her. A cool lock of glossy wet hair
curled around his finger.

Serena drew in a breath. She went rigid beside him,
but she did not pull away. Rand stroked that tendril of
damp silk, let it coil around his hand. Water spiked her
eyelashes, framing her unblinking gaze. Color danced
on her cheeks now, a soft blush muting the nymph-
like white of her skin. Her lips seemed dark as berries,
glistening after her tongue nervously darted out to wet
them.

Rand's body clenched with need.

He wanted to kiss her.

The thought hit him like a blow to the gut. An unbidden wave of possessiveness swept over him. He felt his
grip go a little firmer on the curled strand of black silk
he yet held captive in his hand. He was on the very edge
of control, breathing hard, impulse commanding him
past reason, past shame. He pivoted toward her, and
with his free hand reached out to stroke the moonlit perfection of her face.

God help me, he thought, as his fingers lit on her face.

It was wrong to want this, so wrong, when his wife
was only a couple months cold in her grave.

Elspeth deserved more than this.

Serena gasped, eyes wide as she flinched away from
him. It was a subtle withdrawal, but one he could not
mistake, even in his current state. He let her go at once.

Ah, yes, he thought with wry understanding. His un-
welcome, painful touch. Her fear of that would save her
where he could not summon honor enough to do so
himself. Her brow creased slightly, confusion flashing in

her eyes the instant before her long lashes swept down to conceal them.

Finally, almost too late, Rand found his voice. He could manage only one word.

"Go."

He turned away from her then, while he had the small window of strength to do so. Soft footsteps crunched the blanket of forest greenery beside him. He would not look to make sure she was leaving; he did not trust himself that far. Serena's pace was hesitant as she passed him. Then she was running, her retreat fading away as the roar of the falls filled the empty night.

Rand was alone once more.

He told himself he was relieved.

❧ 11 ❧

SHE HARDLY SAW him at all in the two days that had passed since their encounter at the cascade pool. Serena tried to stay out of Rand's way, busying herself with work about the cottage, throwing herself into any available distraction in the hope that she would soon forget those intense few moments that had passed between them in the moonlit grotto of the cascade.

She had not forgotten.

Nor did she believe she ever could forget the burning look in Rand's eyes, the way his gaze took in every inch of her as she stood before him, dripping from her bath. She should have been shamed, perhaps. He had seen her in full, she was certain of it. And seeing her thus—even in the scant moments before she had rushed to cover herself—had brought a change in his eyes, in his entire mien.

Nay, she would never forget that look. It was burned into her, as surely as the ever-present voice of Knowing. She would never forget the feel of Rand's fingers catching a loose strand of her hair, holding her motionless with nary a bit of coercion. The memory of his fleeting caress of her cheek would stay with her always.

She had wanted him to touch her. Serena knew it in that instant, as she knew it still, when her face flushed with heat just to think on the notion. She had wanted Randwulf of Greycliff to place his hands on her, and she on him, and that was dangerous thinking, indeed. All the worse, when he had come to her with the name of another woman on his lips.

His beloved wife, Elspeth.

His dead wife, Serena reminded herself, not sure why she should feel a pang of irritation for a woman she had never known. She should pity the lady who had been robbed of her life so cruelly.

She did, but pity paled when she thought of what Elspeth's death had so clearly done to Rand. Serena did not wish to think on what that said about herself, but she could not deny her disappointment when Rand had suddenly realized his mistake—that she was peculiar Serena of the grove, not his lost ladylove—and gruffly ordered her out of his sight.

It confused her, this queer tumble of feelings Rand bred in her. Part of her wanted to understand it better, but another part—the part that was schooled for years on her mother's woeful advisements against trusting a man—knew this was a feeling she should not explore.

And so Serena had decided to put Rand out of her mind as best she could. She would not think on him, or the demons that haunted him, nor how his presence was affecting her life. She would not dwell on tender touches or longing meant for another woman.

Soon enough he would be gone. His injuries were healing, and every day he gained more of his strength. His vengeance drew him as nothing else could, and there would be no holding him once he was ready to leave. If she was clever, she would pretend he did not exist. She should be more than eager to help him recover and go on his way.

He had not been the most approachable person when he first arrived in her private domain; however, now he seemed unwilling to speak to her at all, unable to look at her without turning away in distaste. He spent his days stalking the beach for the treasure he had lost, and his nights sleeping out beneath the stars. She supposed his mind was on his vengeance, but part of her wondered if she had somehow driven him into his brooding solitude.

Not that she should care how he felt about anything, but Serena did.

And it was not merely the connecting bond of the Knowing that made her feel this way.

Serena looked at Randwulf of Greycliff and saw a hurt that would not mend with any amount of retribution. Perhaps nothing would mend him. Perhaps he knew that himself, but sought his revenge regardless of its outcome. If that was so, then caring the least bit about him was foolhardy indeed, for he knowingly courted his own death.

With a huff of resignation, Serena quit the cottage and set about her day's duties.

Outside the small abode, strung between the sturdy boughs of two ash trees, was a suspended line used for drying laundered garments. This morning the braided length of rope sagged under the weight of three washed blankets. Serena had cleaned them the day before, along with a swatch of soft linen fabric she thought would suit to replace Rand's last application of bandages.

The white linen had been one of her childhood chemises, an easy sacrifice, since she did not expect she would ever have a use for small garments like that. Particularly if she lived the rest of her days in these secluded woods. A husband and family seemed a far-off dream to her, as unattainable as the moon and stars. Her mother needed her more, and it was selfish of her to yearn for impossible things.

Rand's presence had not helped to curb her curiosity about the world beyond the grove line. Despite his assertion that it was a dangerous place outside these woods, Serena wished to see it for herself. The stirring wildness that had been niggling her in the weeks and months before his arrival had only deepened.

"Impossible," she chided herself softly as she reached up and removed the first blanket from the line.

Draping it over her arm, she moved to the next one. As she freed it, a sea breeze blew in from down the shore path, catching the end of the blanket and pulling it from her grasp. The fabric billowed and went sailing off the line, dropping in a graceful heap at her feet.

"God's blood," she muttered, using one of Rand's own favored curses as she bent to retrieve the blanket from where it had fallen. Brown pine needles and forest dust clung to the clean weave, sullying her work of the day before. She shook it out, grumbling another oath under her breath as the debris floated around her in a cloud.

"Such foul language," remarked a deep, familiar voice from somewhere just out of her sight. "Had I known you'd be so easily corrupted, lady, I might have minded my tongue a bit more around you."

Serena grasped the last of the blankets and jerked it from the line, revealing Rand's position on the other side of the yard. He was seated on a fallen log, his gaze fixed on something he was carving out of a small piece of wood. His fingers were careful, precise, not at all what she would have expected from a man bred to wield a deadly sword for a living. He glanced up idly and met her gaze.

"I didn't realize anyone was out here," she said, her eyes connecting with his. As ever, the sight of him put an odd tremble in her pulse, made her stand a little straighter before him. She drew herself up, holding the blanket in a drape over her arm. "What's that you're making?"

"Nothing." As if belatedly realizing what he was doing, Rand tossed down the half-carved chunk of wood and rose to his feet. "Actually, I was just about to leave."

"You don't have to—"

"The tide will be going out," he said, evidently yet determined to escape her. "I should go down and search the beach one more time."

Serena could not harness her small sigh of exasperation. "You have searched it a dozen times and there has been no trace of your cup. It's gone, Rand. You must give it up before the want of what you've lost destroys you."

Although she did not say it, she could see in Rand's hard expression that he knew she did not speak merely of missing objects. A long moment dragged by while he stood there, regarding her with a look somewhere between anger and resignation. "What I must do is my own to decide."

Serena looked away, occupying herself with her task at hand. She set the blankets down on a small patch of grass, then retrieved the chemise from the line. "Your bandages should be freshened today," she told him, happy to change the subject. "Will you cut this for me? It will make four strips if you rend it lengthwise."

When he did not refuse, she walked the fabric over to him. He set down his dagger and stripped off the tunic Serena had given him a few days before. Shining golden bright against the sinewed contours of his chest was the pendant that once belonged to his beloved wife. Serena averted her gaze, looking instead to the bandages that covered his wounded arms and torso. There were only trace amounts of stain bleeding through.

He was healing well, and soon would have no need to

remain with them any longer. The thought gave her a mixed sense of relief and regret.

"Four strips," Serena said again, handing him her old garment.

"It looks too well kept to ruin on me." He held it up, and Serena marveled at how small the child's chemise looked in his big hands. "Was it yours?"

"A long time ago," she replied. "I have no use for it now. It is little better than a rag."

He accepted the gift with a look of doubt, then sat back on his log seat and ran his dagger through the fabric in a clean slash of movement. The fine linen ripped easily, soon quartered as she had directed and resting in strips over Rand's muscular thigh.

While Serena went back and began folding the blankets into neat bundles, Rand removed his old bandages. The ones on his arms went first, unveiling the vicious slash marks that raked across both limbs. He discarded the soiled bindings beside him on the ground, then began to loosen the bandage that crisscrossed his torso. This proved more difficult than the others. His chest was broad and the strips of linen wrapped round and round the bulk of him.

More than once, he dropped the tail of the bandage and had to bend to retrieve it. Although she doubted he would accept, Serena was a hairbreadth from offering her help when he finally freed the last length of the binding.

As the soiled linen fell away, so did the pendant chain around his neck. The faulty link seemed determined not to hold; the delicate chain swung down, severed and dangling against his chest. Rand caught the pendant before it could fall.

"We could tie a bit of thread through the links to help it hold," Serena offered, watching as he held the errant charm in his open palm. "I have some inside, if you'd like me to fetch it."

"No," he said. "No. It has been mended too many times already. I don't reckon anything will hold it together now."

For a long while, he said nothing, just stared at the glint of delicately wrought gold in his hand. His gaze was far off; his voice, once he spoke, was reflective. "I gave this to Elspeth the day of our betrothal. She said she'd never had anything so fine."

"It's beautiful," Serena agreed. Although her heart pinched at the mention of his wife, she prayed he would tell her more, sensing his pain might be easier to bear if he shared some of it with her now. "She must have loved you very much."

Rand gave a slight shrug of his shoulder. "Our match was orchestrated by our families, but not for a lack of determined campaigning on my part. I first saw Elspeth when I was fostering at another castle. My friend, Kenrick of Clairmont, introduced us." The barest shadow of a grin quirked at his mouth. "I think he regretted his hand in our meeting, but if he did, he said naught to me. She was stunning and sweetly shy. Her father was a landed knight, not a wealthy man, but with her beauty and biddable nature, Elspeth could have had her pick of suitors."

"She chose you."

Again the dismissive shrug, but now a wry gleam had crept into his eyes. "I wager I can be rather persuasive when needed."

Serena believed that without a doubt. "When did you marry?"

"It would have been seven years next spring."

Seven years past, Serena was just a girl of twelve—the very girl who had worn the rended chemise and knew not a single care. How easily she could recall joyful long days spent dancing about the forest and the shore, playing make-believe, dreaming a child's vivid dreams under the boundless canopy of the sky. A world away, Rand-wulf of Greycliff had been pledging his heart to another, making plans for a future that was not to be.

How different their lives had begun. How different they remained, except she feared that Rand was still making plans for a doomed future—one that would end at the cost of his own life.

"I love her," he said, an edge of vehemence in his tone. "I loved her like no other before her."

Serena glanced to him and saw the ferocity of his expression, his features so stark as he said it—as if he needed to convince her of his feelings for his dead wife. She believed him, even as she marveled at the idea that any woman might have so completely captured his steely heart. "My mother says it is rare that a man would wed for love. You must have been fortunate in your match, indeed."

"Aye, well," he said, little more than a grunt. "It doesn't matter now."

He set the pendant down beside him on the log bench, his thoughts seeming to follow his distant gaze. Serena could only guess where his memories were taking him, and seeing the haunted look in his eyes, she could not help but wonder how often his thoughts returned to the night of the attack on Greycliff.

"Rand," she said finally. "The other morning, at the cascade pool . . . I have been meaning to ask you . . ."

It took him a moment to reply, and when he did, there was a threatening calmness in his voice. "What of it?"

"Well, 'tis just something that's been troubling me, and I have not been sure how to ask you about it," she said, hedging a bit now that she had broached the matter. He gave her no indication that he wanted her to ask him anything. If at all, his expression had only darkened, his very demeanor becoming still as stone, and equally cool. Serena rushed on, before she lacked the courage to continue. "When you came through the woods, you seemed . . . upset. You . . . were calling her name. When you crashed into the waterfall clearing, you seemed almost wild, as if you were lost in a terrible dream."

A quiet moment stretched to maddening silence while she waited for him to acknowledge his strange behavior that morning. From the look in his eyes she wondered if he thought she might mean to confront him about another unsettling event of that poolside encounter, the unbidden caress that haunted her still.

Rand held her in a hard stare, then, at last, released his breath on a ripe, black oath.

"I must have frightened you," he said. "My apologies."

Serena was not about to let him elude her with his easy disregard. "I wasn't frightened. I was just concerned. About you."

"Well, don't be. As you can see, I am recovered."

"What happened? Why were you calling out for Elspeth?"

He chuckled. "Nineteen years you've been alone with your mother in these woods? My God, how you must have driven her mad with your endless questions. I almost feel sorry for the woman."

"How often do you relive the night of the raid on Greycliff, Rand?"

He glared at her, unmoving, then he ran a hand over his bearded jaw. "Often enough, if you must know."

"Every night?" she prompted. "More than that?"

He lifted his shoulders in a shrug. "From time to time. Occasionally I get . . . confused. I see the raid like it is happening all over again. I can taste the smoke, and hear my wife's cries. It is nothing," he said, with brusque dispassion, "merely an annoyance that I'm sure will pass one day."

Serena hoped it would, for it was clear that the man who robbed Rand of his home and family the night of the attack had also robbed him of his peace of mind.

"You've endured so much, Rand. I should think it only natural to grieve for your family."

He scoffed. "There will be time for grieving once I have my vengeance."

The way he said it—the unwavering rigidity of his statement—gave Serena pause. "You have not allowed yourself to mourn them?"

"For what good," he answered harshly. "It will not change what has occurred. It will not bring them back."

Serena closed her eyes, absorbing this revelation. He would not permit himself to mourn his wife and child until he had claimed his revenge. "No. It won't bring them back," she said, gently now, seeing him in a clearer, starker light. "But you are still here, and no one should keep so much hurt inside."

He did not respond. He would not so much as look at her now. Instead he reached for the bandage and began to anchor the tail of the linen to his arm.

Serena sat beside him in quiet observation. Just thinking on the details of the raid was enough to choke her heart with sorrow. She vividly recalled her own reaction to the pain she had drawn from Rand the day he learned of her Knowing and she of his suffering. She had wept most of the day in her chapel sanctuary, and then again in her bed that night, weeping uncontrollably, until her body felt drained, her heart numb with exhaustion.

She had mourned Rand's loss as her own. It seemed

impossible to her that he could bear the same anguish in stoic silence.

How cruel his warrior's honor was, that it would hold him so rigidly. So far apart from feeling, from living.

Serena wanted to console him in some way, yet she knew he would not have that. If he would not grieve, he surely would not accept any measure of her sympathy. He was a hard man; by his own choosing now, a solitary man. He needed no one, or had convinced himself as much.

Yet her heart still broke for him, and for the family and home that he had lost. It seemed so strange, how just a few days ago he had been merely a lost soul stranded on her shore and now she knew his deepest pain. Now he had become something more to her . . . but what?

The Knowing had forged a bond between them—unwanted, surely, but unbreakable now that it was made. No matter how long Rand stayed before his vengeance drew him away from the forest, no matter how far it took him, Serena would carry part of him with her for the rest of her days. And if his quest should claim his life, she believed with all her heart that she would feel that as well, and she would mourn him.

"Let me do that for you," she said, scooting over to him when she could take no more of his fumbling with the bandage.

He glanced to her gloved hands and shook his head. "There is no need. I can manage. I know that touch gives you pain."

"I'll be fine," she insisted, reaching for the linen.

"I would rather you didn't."

Serena ignored his protests and began to unwrap his binding. "You've made it too loose. You see? It won't hold."

"It will hold well enough."

"You need two hands. Let me help you—"

"God's blood, Serena!" His voice harsh, he tore the bandage out of her hands. "I don't want your help. Do you understand?"

She flinched, as stunned as if she had been physically struck. Rand looked at her for a long moment, his mouth held tight, his hazel eyes snapping with barely restrained fury.

"I don't want your help," he growled. "I don't need your questions or your concern, either. Go. Leave me alone. That is all I want from you."

Serena swallowed a sudden lump of hurt that had lodged in her throat. Hot tears stung the backs of her eyes but she refused to let them fall.

"I'm sorry," she whispered past her thick tongue. "I'm sorry."

Before she could humiliate herself further, she spun around and fled into the cottage.

❧ 12 ❧

THE CHILL OF the cascade pool gripped him in a bracing, well-needed jolt of clarity. Rand had stripped bare, discarding his clothes and bandages on the slab of rock at the pool's edge. The bindings had proven impossible to manage himself, as Serena had informed him before he so harshly drove her away. Rand had fought with the strips of rent linen for a while after she had left him at the cottage, then finally gave up in defeat.

But it was more than frustration with himself over his inability to tend his own injuries that sent him into the forest in a black mood. It was his maddening reaction to Serena that gave him the most concern. He was unaccustomed to losing control, in any situation. His ire when stoked was rarely, if ever, misplaced. It was entirely unlike him to be so gruff with a woman. For certain, Elspeth would have dissolved into a month of inconsolable hysterics if he had barked at her as he had Serena when she only wanted to help him.

Serena had kept her chin high, but he'd seen the shock in her eyes at his outburst, the hurt, and it bothered him to know that he had put it there. And so unfairly, besides.

The truth was, he did not think he could have withstood the temptation of Serena's hands on him—not in any way. He could not reconcile the desire he felt for her. She was too innocent, too sweet. Despite the inner strength he saw in her, Serena's heart was fragile, and untried. He did not want to be the one to break it. Already he was hurting her, he was certain.

Each time she tried to get close to him and he pushed her away, something in her bright gaze dimmed. But he could afford no entanglements, least of all with a sheltered maiden who tempted him with every winsome smile. When she was near him, he burned with unbidden need. She was sweet and honest and pure. She was unusual as well, but her peculiarities were becoming less strange than endearing; for each one he noted, he wanted to learn more.

And her beauty . . . well, if ever he had glimpsed a woodland nymph conjured by magic to bewitch men with a single look, it was Serena of the grove. From her ebony hair and seafoam eyes, to the graceful perfection of her womanly form, Serena enchanted him.

For all his protestations of devotion to Elspeth, his heart—and indeed, his body—seemed intent to prove him false whenever Serena was near. He could not credit that it was mere lust, for he'd known enough earthly pleasure in this life that he need not slake himself on sheltered innocents. A woman like Serena, so vulnerable and untainted, was the very last woman he should find appealing. Yet he had never before been so affected.

Not even by the one woman he loved enough to take as his wife.

Rand plunged below the surface of the water once more, an icy penance for his lack of honor when it came to his vow to Elspeth, and his vexing desire for Serena.

He worked his limbs with ruthless fervor, ignoring the burn of his wounds as he swam to the far side of the crystalline pool. He needed his strength. He needed to

put his mind on Silas de Mortaine and the confrontation
that awaited him outside the haven of these woods. He
needed to focus on the vengeance that burned in his very
soul, demanding the death of his enemy and all who
served him.

And yet, when he broke the surface to take a lung-
ful of air, it was Serena that commanded his thoughts.
He saw her there, between the trees, heading into the
woods. Her dark hair swung in a glossy train down her
back, her faded bliaut lifted above her feet as she tra-
versed a tricky path into the woods.

At first he thought her an illusion, the woodland
nymph playing tricks on his mind as ever, but she was
real. She had not seen him beneath the surface of the
cascade pool; she strode deeper into the thicket, a basket
hung over her arm.

Rand came out of the pool without hailing her. He sat
on the wet shelf of granite, telling himself he should
merely let her go, that she was not his concern. But even
as he thought it, he was putting on his clothes, hastily
donning his boots, intent to give her the apology she
was due.

Her mother had been correct about Randwulf of Greycliff on one point at least; Serena would be wise to put
him out of her mind. After his harsh outburst earlier
that day, it was clear to her that Rand held little regard
for her. He was dangerous, like a wild animal who'd
been viciously injured and now would lash out to bite
any foolish hand that came too close.

The only peace Serena knew she would find was deep
in the forest. With a basket slung over her arm, she
made her way into the woods, heading for a clutch of
wild berry bushes that grew midway between the falls
and the ancient chapel.

She had not quite reached the place when a niggle of alarm tickled her spine. There was a slight, sudden commotion in the trees—birds taking wing—but then, another sound. A sharp *snap*, then a worrisome rustle of movement on the ground some short distance from where she stood. Leaves and twigs kicked up in a little storm of disruption. The mad flutter of beating wings slapping the earth seemed the only noise in a glade that had gone deathly silent.

Serena's heart lurched.

A dove was snared in one of the hunters' terrible traps. No doubt startled by her sudden appearance, the bird had been newly caught just as she approached. It flailed in a panic, pale gray wings beating furiously, stirring up dust and forest debris as the poor creature fought to free itself from the tight noose of the spring. Its struggle would only speed its demise. Each crazed leap and twist worsened its capture.

"Oh, no. *No*."

Serena tossed down her basket. She ran to the snare in desperation, hesitating not a moment even though Rand had warned her away from disturbing what was a nobleman's rightful property. She did not care whose law she broke, or whose wrath she might invite. She could not stand by and let the hapless bird die before her eyes.

Serena whispered soothing words as she neared the tripped snare. She crouched down, cooing softly, shushing reassurances, but the dove would not calm. Its obsidian eyes, like glossy beads of jet, reflected her worried expression as she reached out to catch the bird in her gloved hands. Perceiving her an added threat, the dove flapped vigorously, chest heaving, heart pounding visibly in its downy breast.

"Hush now, hush. Be still," Serena begged it, working carefully lest she damage its fragile wings.

The snare's twine noose was wound tightly about the dove's neck. In its struggle, one pink leg had been caught up in the line as well, trapped against its body and bent at a painful angle. Still the dove fought for its life, not trusting Serena to save it when death was already closing in, choking off precious air.

"Peace now," she whispered, trying to soothe it in any way she could. "It's all right. I'll not hurt you."

Her gloves were a hindrance. The bird was so slight, naught but struggling fluff in her hands, she could not subdue it. She tried to maneuver it into a firm hold and failed—once, again—each time worsening the dove's panic and causing it to further strangle itself in the snare. She had no choice but to try another tack. Holding the snare's twine to create a bit of slack, Serena let go of the bird and with her teeth stripped off one of her gloves. The other went next, in similar fashion.

Her grasp was more sure now, but each brush of the dove's body against her hands sent a jolt of alarm screaming through her. She felt it all—the panic, the desperation, the choking fear of not being able to breathe for the abrading lash that closed the bird's throat.

"Please," she gasped, working through the Knowing to catch the dove and attempt to loosen the noose from its fragile neck. "Please . . . you must stop fighting me."

Behind her, Serena heard someone approaching through the bracken, heavy footsteps, a purposeful stride. Panic held her too frantic to see if this was a new danger closing in. She struggled to free the dove from the line, but the knots were ruthless, too gnarled even for her small fingers to work loose.

"No," she cried, desperate as the bird's heart grew faint against her fingertips.

Death was twisting like a screw, the Knowing of it clutching at her with cold, dark resignation. She had to fight where the dove would soon be incapable. Her lungs were constricting, her mind blurring with exhaustion. She knew she would not perish here herself, even if the dove did, but her heart felt every pained beat of its pulse, and her soul wept, as ever, with the suffering of another living creature.

From around her shoulder, a strong arm appeared. "Hold it still, Serena. Steady."

The deep, commanding voice was utter calm amid the chaos, a welcome presence she felt rumble through her as Rand came around and crouched down next to her.

"Its foot is caught—there," he said, coaching her in a collected, measured way that seemed so out of place for him, yet so needed by her in that moment. "Just try to maintain a firm grip on the bird. Aye, like that, Serena."

She obeyed his direction, too exhausted to question his intent. But even had she full grasp of her wits, there would be no need to doubt him. She trusted Rand, she realized in those frantic instants. He was there, and she was glad for it. She knew that he would help her.

Almost as quickly as the thought passed through her mind, Rand had freed the dove from the choke hold of the snare. The twine, which had been taut and abrading, giving no mercy, now lay severed in two, sliced cleanly by Rand's sure skill with the dagger he yet held in his fisted hand. He set the blade down, and together Serena and he worked to disentangle the dove from the slack line.

Once loosed, the bird flopped out of arm's reach, stunned, but free. It huddled very still on its feet, breathing rapidly, then with a whistling beat of its wings, flew off, deep into the cover of the forest.

Serena slumped down to sit numbly on the ground. She watched the gray dove vanish, a heavy sort of daze clinging to her, the Knowing having not yet begun to subside. The bird was near death in its fright; her own heart battered around in her chest in like frenzy, echoing the panic that had been shared between the dove and her in those moments of desperate struggle.

Slowly, dully, she realized how close Rand was to her in that small square of space.

Hunkered down before her, he held his jaw clenched tight. He scowled, watching her in a queer, studying way. Her senses yet clamoring within her, Serena grew flustered, impatient, under the intensity of his look.

"Do not—" Her emotions were chaos, making speech difficult. She gulped in a breath of needed air and tried again. "Do not chide me for destroying some hunter's cruel trap . . ."

"I would not," he said, answering before she could summon strength enough to finish.

". . . or condemn me for sparing a creature that belongs to no man—be he a king or commoner."

"Serena. I will not," he said again, then glanced to her bare hands, held like broken wings in her lap. "Are you hurt?"

She gave a small shake of her head.

"You're pale as frost," he remarked, and reached out to gather aside a lock of dark hair that had fallen into her face in the struggle.

Serena was too drained to back away from the contact. She glanced up, meeting his gaze, and he likely saw at once how truly affected she was. She could not sweep away the tear that escaped her eye, but he did. He looked down at the moisture glistening on his tanned fingertip, and his scowl went deeper with understanding.

"Jesu. You felt that dove's fear. Your touch—*the Knowing*—you felt the dove's pain, did you not?"

"I felt it dying," she said, her heart only now beginning to slow, her breath only now beginning to steady.

"The Knowing is that powerful for you? Your ability to touch another's thoughts and feelings—it does not end with humankind alone?"

"No."

"God's blood. What kind of curse do you suffer?"

Serena's senses were calming at last. She blinked slowly, taking a deep breath now that she could breathe, her chest unencumbered by distress and pain. "It is only a curse if I choose to treat it as one. It is all I've known, for all my life. It is just . . . the way of things for me."

Her gloves lay discarded in the dust and disturbed leaves. Rand retrieved them, and held them out to her. "You shouldn't have taken these off."

"I had to. I could not work the snare loose with them on."

She reached out to take the gloves, but his grasp suddenly went firmer, refusing to release them to her.

"The other day, when I came upon you fishing in the cove. You had taken off your gloves then as well."

"Had I?" she asked, well aware of the fact, yet taken aback that he had noticed.

"Aye, lady, you had. It was a deliberate thing you did, removing your gloves to take the fish in your bare hands as you set about to kill and clean them." He blew out a short breath, an incredulous-sounding oath. "Why would you do that, if you can feel what others do—even a creature like that dove, like those fish?"

When she did not immediately answer, he bent toward her, not moving to touch her again, yet his look compelling her to meet his gaze. "Serena. Why?"

"Because I owed them that much," she replied, seeing no cause to evade him, even if he would think her crazed or a fool. "Every life is precious—"

"Even these simple creatures'," he said, finishing the very declaration she had made to him that day at the cove.

She could not feign her surprise that he had paid so close attention, nor could she deny that it warmed her in some inexplicable way to know that he had not merely disregarded her then, as she had assumed by his gruff dismissal of her.

"If I am to take something as precious as the life of another living thing," she said, "particularly if I do so in order to sustain myself, then I must do so with my eyes, and my heart, fully open to the act. It seems only humane. To my mind, it is only just that I bear some of the cost."

She waited for his reaction, some twitch of mockery or scorn. His face told her nothing, his jaw held tight, his eyes holding hers in a gaze that was as dark and unreadable as a coming storm.

"Your warring ways must scoff at that. Do you think me flawed in some way, that I would feel as I do?"

"No," he answered.

"Weak-hearted, then?"

"No, Serena. I see no weakness when I look at you. Not now." He was regarding her with a strange light in his gaze. He shook his head, exhaled a small oath. "I had thought it was your mother protecting you out here in these woods. Now I am beginning to see that is not the way of it at all."

His dark brows pinched, ever so slightly, over watchful, enigmatic eyes. He brought his hand up and gently traced the slope of her cheek, curving his fingers around the sensitive skin below her ear.

"You are the one with the strength, Serena. She thinks she must look after you, but it is you who truly protects her."

She dared not think he praised her, but there was a wonder in his voice—a respect—that warmed her as much as it confused her. "What are you doing, Rand?"

"Apologizing. But I'm not doing it very well."

"Do not trouble yourself. I was at fault. You needn't say a thing." She pushed herself to her feet.

"Serena." He was next to her in no time at all, blocking her easy path away from him. His hazel eyes were dark with concern, his forehead creased with a frown. "Please, hear me out. I have been unfair to you. My behavior could have only confused you—"

"I've never been more confused in my life," Serena admitted. "You've unsettled everything since you arrived on that beach. In coming here, you have changed it all."

"I am sorry," he said, contrite.

Serena gave a toss of her head. "I don't want your apology. I want to know what you think, what you feel."

"Nay, lady," he said, a sure denial, even though his voice held no rancor. "Your gift of Knowing has told you all of that. You know what I think and what I feel, whether I will it or not. You know more about me than you want to, so you said just the other day."

"I mean about me, Rand. I don't know how you feel about me. I don't know if you pity me, or despise me, or if you feel anything at all. More than once when we have been together, you have looked at me as if—"

"Have I wanted to kiss you—is that what you wish to know?" he interrupted, harshly now, sparing her from blurting out any more of her addled thinking. His voice

was low, pitched deeper than the shadows of the surrounding thicket, darker than a storm. "Do you tempt
me, mayhap? Do I think on you more than I should—in
ways I have no right considering?"

Although she had hoped that he would open up to
her, Serena felt her face warm under his sudden direct-
ness, the slightly predatory growl of his words.

"You want to know if it is desire I feel when I am near
you—as I was that morning at the waterfall pool . . . or
any other time I am with you?" His gaze was penetrating, relentless as it held hers. He stepped closer to her
now, his stance and mien all but daring her not to run.
"Are these the questions you would have me answer for
you, or have you other, more specific curiosities that
need be sated?"

Something threatening had sparked to life in his eyes,
a glint of warning she knew she should heed. Instead she
held her ground, not so much as flinching as Rand drew
nearer now, so close she could feel the warmth of his
body reaching out to her.

"Now you're mocking me," she told him, stung in a
peculiar way.

A knot of tangled emotion rose from deep within her
breast, up to her throat, choking her voice. She began to
turn away from him, but the heat of his fingers at her
wrist halted her. Unexpected, almost tender, his hand
brushed hers.

Regret, whispered the Knowing.

*Don't wish to cause hurt. Should not have permitted
things to go so far.*

Serena paused, her hand caught in his now. With the
smallest coaxing, Rand drew her back to him, his careful grasp sending a wave of sensation through her fingertips, her palm, up the length of her arm . . . all the way
to her heart.

"Serena."

She lifted her eyes to meet his gaze, uncertain, her humiliation fading under the power of his touch. Rand's fingers laced between hers, held her fast. Palm to palm, his dark emotions filled her senses, his passion wrapping around her like silken ropes. She felt herself drifting toward him, into the large shadow he cast in the sun-drenched green of the forest.

"Whatever I may feel for you—it doesn't matter," he told her, harsh words belied only by the tenderness of his deep velvet voice. "Know that it will not matter. It cannot. All that matters to me is vengeance. There is nothing else."

Their hands were still joined. All the while he spoke his hard, cutting words, the Knowing thrummed stronger. It rose with the force of his barely contained anger, howling for the pain he suffered, and his frustration at not yet having claimed his revenge.

But behind his simmering gaze was a deep blackness that pulled at her. A yawning oblivion, what she saw there seemed so fathomless. So tired and lonely. Staring into his eyes, listening to the ruthless hiss of the Knowing, Serena weathered a buffeting rush of anguish. His emptiness enveloped her in shades of coal gray and umber, desolate color, chilly isolation. He was drowning in it, nearly lost and too damaged to reach out.

So Serena reached out to him instead.

With her free hand, she brought her fingers up to his face, settling just the tips against his cheek. He went very still, watching her in a threatening silence. Serena was undaunted. She stroked the line of his bearded jaw, and his strong brow, wishing she could absorb some of his hurt with her touch.

A mistake.

The thought was not hers, but Rand's, seething through her fingertips and into the whispered voice of the Knowing.

She continued her brazen exploration, letting her fingers trail down the solid column of his neck, to the powerful line of his shoulders. He said nothing, despite the jump of his muscles as she caressed him, her hands questing to learn the breadth of his shoulder, the astounding strength harnessed in the granite bulk of his upper arm.

There will be no turning back.

Serena gazed up at him, and the words she would have spoken—a soft denial, a breathless plea—were captured in the sudden press of his mouth on hers.

She knew not what to make of it at first. His lips brushed her own, a nudging trace of movement, gentle tease of contact. His lips were softer than she would have guessed, like a warm, woodland breeze. His dark beard was a curious roughness against her chin and cheek, a delightful abrasion that tickled like a cat's tongue. She could taste the mineral crispness of fresh water in his kiss. Not long ago, he had been in the pool below the falls; his hair was still damp, his scent a mingled pleasure of clean skin and cool pine air. He drew a breath and took some of Serena's from her, then fed it back to her on a low hum of sound as the pressure of his mouth on hers grew more intense.

Strong fingers splayed the base of her skull, drawing her closer. She knew not what to do, and so she gave herself over to him completely, allowing him to guide her. She had never been kissed. She had never imagined anything so wondrous strange and heady as the sensation of Rand's lips on hers. There was something elemental and dangerous in its allure, something that curled around her senses, beckoning her deeper.

Although she longed to absorb every detail of the moment, Serena could only release all thought and feel. She closed her eyes and surrendered herself to the bliss of Rand's exquisite mouth. Never had she imagined such powerful yearning, such incredible heat. She clung to him without any measure of fear, not for Rand, and not for the Knowing, which whipped around her senses like streamers of boundless color and light.

Her gift had never felt so alive. Never so immense. It sighed and danced and sparkled.

In that moment, that sweet, stunning moment, Serena felt every particle of her being awaken as though roused from an eternity of listless slumber. How delicious it was to kiss him, to taste him. How wonderfully maddening to feel his hands in her hair, caressing the back of her head with long, strong fingers, teasing the tender skin of her nape. She reveled in the press of his body on hers, the firm strength of his arms holding her, the hard muscularity of his thigh subtly wedging into place between her legs.

Serena could not have dreamed such intimacy. To be so near Rand, holding him, kissing him, left every previous moment she had lived smashed to obliteration. It left her wanting more of something she could not define, or put into words. She merely wanted . . . more.

As though he knew her hunger, Rand suddenly went rigid. He drew away from her mouth with a snarled curse.

"Damn you," he whispered thickly. His hands were still caught in her hair, still stroking her, holding her as his heart pounded against her like a drum. "Damn you, Serena of the grove."

His eyes never left hers, not even for an instant. She was held transfixed by the seriousness of his gaze, the

utter truth that he made no effort to conceal. It was
the same heated look she had seen the other morning
at the cascade pool, the same dark sensuality, save that
now he did not look at her and speak another woman's
name, but her own.

"You want to know how I feel about you? I wager
you have your answer now."

Aye, she guessed she did. He desired her. Perhaps she
should be shamed by this knowledge. He seemed to
think so. But she could summon no inkling of regret or
chagrin for what his kiss told her.

"I should not have done this," Rand muttered, a
roughness to his words.

"It's all right. I liked it. You don't have to stop—"

"Aye, Serena. I do." He moved away from her. His
voice was curt, rasping as though provoked near to
anger, but still he kept his hands on her, his fingers tenderly caressing her face. "I do have to stop. It will only
lead to disaster. I cannot let that happen, do you understand?"

She didn't understand. She did not know what was
happening between them, nor did she understand why
they should stop something that felt so good, so right.

"You don't like kissing me?" she asked, forcing the
words past her tingling lips.

"Sweetest heart," he whispered, "would that were the
case."

"Then, what? If I am doing something wrong, you
can tell me."

He smiled ruefully, meeting her gaze with a look of
discomfort. "You are doing nothing wrong. The problem is mine. If I am near you, I want to kiss you. If I kiss
you, Serena, I will want to touch you. And if I touch
you . . ."

His hands drifted away from her, leaving a cool void where the warmth of his caress had been.

Rand shook his head, scowling. "It is impossible."

"Because your heart belongs to someone else?"

His brow furrowed with a deeper look of torment. "Because I have nothing to offer you, my lady. And I cannot stay. As soon as I am able—"

"I know," she said, nodding as she stared down at her clasped hands. "I know. Your quest to avenge your family will not wait. I know this. I understand. But does that mean we cannot be friends so long as you are here?"

"Friends," he replied, whispering the word as he might express a jest. "Is that how you see us?"

"How do you see us, Rand?"

She waited in quiet dread, for his answer took a long moment to come.

"I don't know," he said at last. "I only know I don't want to hurt you. I would shield you from that."

"I need no such care," Serena insisted. She felt a sudden flare of resentment—for him and his wish to protect her from himself, and for the sheltered life she lived. It was stifling, all of it, and she was nearly choking on it. "My decisions are my own to make. I am tired of forever being told to be careful, to not venture beyond my bounds for fear of the unknown. I am not afraid to live, or to feel. And I'm not afraid of you, Rand."

He did not appear pleased to hear it, scowling darkly at her. But his touch was tender when he reached out and stroked the line of her cheek once again. His thumb traced lightly over her lips, making her yearn all the more for another kiss.

"No, you're not afraid," he said, slowly shaking his

head at her. "But if you were to touch me now, your Knowing would tell you that you should be."

He gestured toward the meandering track that would lead them back to the cottage. "This way, my lady. Before I am tempted to stay any longer and let you shred the last scrap of my dubious honor."

❧ 13 ❧

Silas de Mortaine had lived long enough to know that there were but two things that could ensure the loyalty of another man: greed and fear. He preferred to deal in the latter. So when one of his sentries arrived that night with troubling news from the north, Silas was swift to act.

"You're certain it was one of ours?"

The outrider nodded his shaggy dark head, the sweat of his urgent race back to camp still sticky on his swarthy skin and reeking. "Aye, my lord. I saw him with mine own eyes. I know my own kind, and this one was dead nigh on a sennight by the look of him. A fisherman had him on display outside a tavern in Egremont. Charging two farthing to come and have a look, he was."

"This is unfortunate," Silas replied, seething beneath his calm tone. He had lost many such sentries in his quest for the Dragon Chalice. There were few remaining, just these half dozen among him, now that his spy in Liverpool was dead. "I don't like it."

"Nor did I," answered the shifter guard. His smile was feral and sharp beneath his beard. "But the bastard won't be collecting anything more."

"Oh?" Silas queried mildly. "How so?"

The shifter made an animal noise in the back of its throat, smugly satisfied. "I gutted the sot before I left town to bring you the news."

"You might have brought him with you instead," Silas replied. "This fisherman might have had answers I could use, information that could have proven beneficial to me. Did you consider that?"

He leveled a scathing look on the huge man, unfazed by the knowledge that this brawny sentry could, in a blink, change himself into a deadly shifter beast. No harm would come to Silas de Mortaine. With the aid of the Dragon Chalice, he had harnessed his own dark magic, and he had long ago given up his mortal fears. All those assembled in the lavish camp tent knew this, and their anxious silence now only fed Silas's confidence in his own power.

Still, he found it was prudent to offer occasional reminders of his might. It was good to tighten the yoke of his control, lest anyone in his ranks forget who it was they served.

"I questioned him," the big guard said, breaking in on Silas's quiet judgment. The shifter's eyes darted to some of the others of his kind. No one offered a word of defense. "The man knew nothing. Said he pulled the body up in his nets—a drowned wolf, that was all. He knew not what he had, nor did he know anything about the Chalice."

Silas steepled his fingers at his chin and gave a low growl of contemplation. Despite his man's assurances, Silas was furious that he'd been denied the chance to question the fisherman himself. There was a price to be paid for failure, and well was that fact known among Silas's retinue.

He rose from his chair to stand before the sentry, who tried very hard not to look as Silas withdrew a jewel-handled sword from a bossed sheath on his hip. "Everyone here knows how I despise disappointments."

The large tent had gone utterly silent. No one seemed to dare breathe, testimony enough to Silas's statement.

He pursed his lips as he lifted the magnificent blade, idly caressing the razor edge of polished steel. "I loathe incompetence."

"I have not failed you," said the shifter, prideful even when he had to know he would not escape the night unscathed. "All of us from Anavrin—every guard assembled before you—is here to see the Dragon Chalice restored. We serve our kingdom, and he who sent us through the veil to this Outside realm of man—"

"Nay," Silas snapped, shaking his head. "You serve me. This is my world, and when I bring the Chalice back to Anavrin in my hands, that kingdom will be mine as well. Make no mistake, any of you. Only the loyal will have a place in my court. Only the dutiful will serve me. All others will be put to the sword."

On that pledge, Silas let the tip of the blade slowly come to rest on the earthen floor of the tent. It bit into the space between the elongated toes of his fashionable silk shoes and the shifter's road-dusted boots.

"Kneel before me," he commanded the Anavrin guard. When he did not show suitable respect, Silas's mood grew more foul. "Kneel, cur! Beg my pardon for your failing today, and for the offense you give me by your very presence."

The shifter snarled as his knee slowly bent, and he took an obeisant position as commanded. "Forgive me, my lord. I am your servant, of course."

Silas could see the resentment glittering in the hard black eyes as the guard's shaggy head dipped into a bow. No doubt, everyone else had seen it as well.

The thought sent a flare of hatred burning through his veins. With the shifter kneeling before him in false fealty,

Silas carefully sheathed his weapon. Steel was too merciful here.

"Les Nantres," he murmured, summoning his shrewdest lieutenant from out of the ranks. "Bring me Avosaar."

At that, the shifter's head jerked up. He knew what he had wrought, and Silas enjoyed the next few moments, ripe as they were with delicious fear, as the shifter began to beg in earnest.

"Sire, forgive me. I've meant only to serve you as best I can. If I have failed you in any way . . ."

Silas ignored the feeble plea. To his mind, the shifter had been dead the moment he strode into the tent with news from Egremont. Nothing would have persuaded him to spare the fool, then or now.

"Here it is. Avosaar," les Nantres said from beside him, hardly bothering to mask his revulsion for what was to come.

Silas turned to admire the stunning beauty of this piece of the Dragon Chalice. Avosaar, Stone of Prosperity, glowed as verdant as summer itself, clutched within the talons of a golden, winged serpent. Endless bounty was the cup's gift, but not for this Anavrin shifter.

Not for any shifter. To touch the Dragon Chalice, in whole or in part, was, for them, instant—and excruciating—death. Silas had demonstrated this law on another occasion not so long ago, when a foolish female of their race attempted to steal Avosaar from him. Silas had forced her to hold the cup, then watched gleefully as she met her just demise.

"Do you know what happens when shifter skin gets too close to Chalice gold?" he mused, holding the cup out before him as he approached the kneeling guard.

"P-please," he sputtered, glancing anxiously from

Silas to the terrible beauty of the gleaming goblet. "My lord, please . . ."

The shifter's clansmen did not rise to his aid, despite their number. What would be the point in it? What Silas wanted, he claimed. There was none to gainsay him; in the end, he would outlast them all.

Already Silas could see beads of perspiration forming on the heavy brow, a flush of discomfort in the swarthy face. He strode closer, nearly touching the shifter now. Ugly blisters began to rise on the thick neck and on the hairy backs of the beast's hands. The shifter began to cough, his lungs surely baking. And still Silas drew closer, prolonging the suffering.

"You can end it," he offered. "Just reach out your hand."

The shifter would not budge. Mayhap he thought he could survive the torture. Mayhap he thought this show of strength would earn him some scrap of mercy. But this was not strength to Silas's way of thinking. It was weakness, fear of death.

"Jesu." The oath came from les Nantres, somewhere behind Silas now. "Be done with it, man."

Silas knew not whether the bold knight spoke to him or the shifter, but in that next instant, the Anavrin guard surrendered. With a howl that shook the tent, the shifter thrust out both hands and grasped the golden bowl of the Chalice treasure. Flames erupted as though breathed from the mouth of a dragon in truth. Raging orange fire engulfed the shifter, incinerating him on contact.

Silas stepped back, shielding his eyes against the swift conflagration. It was over too quickly for his liking. All that remained was cinder and smoke. One more Anavrin sentry than he wished to forfeit, but the example had to be made.

With a casual flick of his hand, Silas motioned some

of the observing guards to come forth and dispense of the smoldering ashes of their comrade while he retrieved Avosaar from the pyre. He cradled the treasure to his chest, marveling at the warmth that yet thrummed in it, the vibration of power he held at his command.

"Shall I assemble a party and ride north to see what I can find?"

Draec les Nantres turned a flat stare on him from his position near the tent's entrance. The flames of two flanking torches threw stark light on the mercenary's ebony hair and striking features. Eyes as green as a serpent and as brittle as priceless emerald held Silas's gaze unflinching. Too bold. There was a kingly air about the man, even when it seemed he had gone several nights without sleep. Dark circles smudged the bronze skin beneath his eyes, and did he not mistake it, the lean face and angular jaw held a trace of gauntness, although none would ever look upon Draec les Nantres and call him weak. Troubled, perhaps; haunted, no doubt. But never weak. Silas de Mortaine suffered no weakness in his ranks.

"No," he answered after a long moment's consideration. "I think I should prefer to ride along this time. Unless you have cause to wish I stay behind?"

"Not at all, my lord."

Les Nantres's reply was immediate and utterly devoid of expression. Silas did not trust it. More and more, he was beginning to doubt the man's allegiance.

"How long do you expect it will take to make the trip?" Silas asked him.

"A sennight, I would guess, if we travel light and ride hard."

"I want to be there in no more than six days' time," Silas announced. "We'll leave on the morrow."

Les Nantres inclined his head. "As you wish, my lord."

Silas waited until les Nantres was several paces out of earshot, then he beckoned one of his consorts to him with a crook of his finger. She came up off a pile of furs and cushions and glided toward him with practiced feline grace, half dressed, like the four others who awaited his every carnal whim.

"Go, see to him—whatever he wishes of you."

The whore nodded enthusiastically.

"Work him well. Once he's asleep, search his quarters."

"But, my lord," she said, uncertainty in her voice, "that one ne'er sleeps. And he permits none to stay with him all night. He'll toss me out."

"Convince him to let you stay," Silas instructed. "Do not leave him until he sleeps, however long that might be. You will search his things, and report back to me anything you find."

She nodded again, slowly this time, a note of wariness dimming her jaded gaze.

"Do not fail," he warned.

Silas de Mortaine smiled a threatening smile, and watched the woman's fear deepen to stark understanding. In that moment, she was as loyal as a hound staring at the whip in hand.

She would obey.

They always did.

It rained that evening, a fierce downpour that dashed Rand's plan to sleep another night outdoors, and away from the close confines of the cottage. After the kiss he and Serena had shared that day, Rand did not relish the idea of spending another several hours in her company. It was pure torture to watch her moving about the cot-

tage, helping her mother prepare the supper meal of fish
Rand had caught that afternoon, her cheeks flushing
sweetly every time her eyes chanced to meet his.

They ate in virtual silence, the three of them, Calandra brooding into her fish soup, her slim shoulders
slumped as though weighted down with a hundred-
stone burden. Serena attempted conversation, but Rand
was no good in making idle chatter across the table from
her. Not when his body yet thrummed with hot need.

After they finished the meal, which Rand could not
even recall eating, Serena cleared the table and her
mother took up a chair beside the hearth fire. Rand
stoked the small blaze and added more wood, all the
while his attention straying to Serena across the small
abode. More than once, Calandra's shrewd gaze flicked
to him, but she said nothing, contemplative in her silence.

"Mother," Serena called as she set the last cup in place
on its shelf. "Will you tell us one of your tales to pass the
time?"

Calandra pulled her blanket a bit higher on her lap,
eyeing Rand as he stood up from the fire and offered
Serena the remaining chair. "Not tonight, child. I am
weary. You know them all—some better than I. You tell
one instead."

Rand watched, fairly charmed, as Serena tilted her
head and pondered which story she wanted to recite.
She settled on a tale of fantastical proportions, about a
withering golden kingdom that needed a hero to save it
from doom. It was clear she loved the story, for she told
it with great excitement and wonder, her tone switching
animatedly from the dread whisper of dragons and daring battles, to the dreamy sighs reserved for feats of mar-
velous heroics that won the hero his princess's devoted
heart.

When she was finished and proclaimed the end of the tale, Serena grew shy, looking to Rand for reaction. She turned a quick glance toward her mother, who had fallen into a soft slumber in her chair. "I don't tell them as well as she does. I hope I didn't bore you."

"Not at all." Rand smiled at her. "It was very good. The way you told it, 'twould make a fine song. I can almost hear it set to music in my head as we speak."

"Truly? Sing it for me."

"No," he scoffed lightly. "I am no bard."

"Do you think I'll laugh?" she prodded, her gaze going bright in the flickering glow of the fire. "Does so fearsome a warrior cower at so simple a task?"

"Aye," he replied, but he was half tempted to rise to her challenge. "And I'd not want to wake your mother—or all the hounds from Egremont to Liverpool."

Serena laughed softly, but the sound was enough to stir Calandra a bit. Still snuffling and asleep, the older woman shifted in her chair and lost part of her coverlet. Serena was up at once to adjust it. She tucked her in with caring hands, then pivoted to come back to her own seat next to Rand at the fire.

As she neared, he was unable to resist the urge to touch her—if briefly.

He reached up and their fingers brushed. She stilled, frozen where she stood beside him. He traced her warm palm, filled with a need so strong he nearly grasped her tight and pulled her down into his lap. It would be so easy, all he wanted to do in that moment.

Serena trembled, letting out a shaky breath of air. She was touching him as well, and her Knowing would not mistake the force of his desire.

She looked down at him, her dusky lips parted and moist. She did not refuse him, though well she should have. She remained there, her fingers curled around his,

her lithe body mere inches from him. Naught but a few
fragile moments from being drawn down atop him, and
her sleeping mother be damned.

Her aqua eyes were a deep ocean blue now, calling to
the storm that was rising within him. Rand caressed his
finger along the delicate bones of her wrist. Her pulse
was pounding, her skin warm as fire.

Deny me, he thought fiercely. *Pull away, I beg you.*

She would not, although he could see that in her
Knowing, she understood his torment. She, too, was
lost, holding on to him with like intensity.

It was only the sudden *pop* of a sapling log on the
hearth that saved him. The sharp sound echoed in the
cottage like a thunderclap. Rand released Serena's hand
at once, though not without a keen reluctance.

He looked away, shamed by his need for her. But Serena would not permit it. She touched his shoulder as she
turned to take her chair by the fire. It was a sweet brush
of her fingertips, but even that enflamed him further, and
Rand sank into a deeper pit of misery.

They sat together, not daring to touch again, watching
the fire slowly fade. When it was time, Rand took the
pallet that was Serena's before his arrival, and she took
her mother's, little more than an arm's length away from
him.

They lay on their sides, facing each other through the
dark, neither one of them expecting to find much rest
that night.

❧ 14 ❧

HER WORLD WAS steadily shrinking. Or perhaps it was just that when Rand was around, the sun and sky, the trees and flowers—all the splendor of her once vast and intriguing world—seemed naught but a spectacular backdrop for the man who inhabited Serena's every waking thought.

He invaded her dreams as well.

In the few hours' sleep she had managed the night before, she relived the thrill of Rand's intense gaze as she told her feeble tale by the fire. She relived his impulsive touch as well, when he boldly took her hand while her mother slept only a few feet away. She had wanted so badly to kiss him. She truly would have, a thought that put a shamed heat in her cheeks just to recall it now.

All the while they lay across from each other in the darkened cottage, Serena had yearned to be in his arms. To know his kiss once more.

He had denied her that as the night spun on toward morning, but in her dreams, there was no space or circumstance to separate them, and she was his.

She looked at him now, striding along beside her as they headed into the forest the next morning, and it took all her effort not to allow her hand to brush his. Instead she held fast to her berry basket and marched through the bramble toward the knot of bushes that hung heavy with fruit. She had yet to gather the whortleberries for her mother's favorite tart, a task inadvertently thwarted by Serena's rescue of the snared dove the day before, and prevented by rains until now.

"Calandra arose early this morn," Rand commented as they navigated the dewy greenery of the woods. "Where did she go?"

"To worship, I expect. She has a favored niche in the forest that is hers alone. She goes there every morning to pray and reflect."

Rand grunted in acknowledgment as they arrived at their destination. A small brook trickled in front of them, originating at the falls and ambling past rock and trees to disappear deep into the grove. The berry bushes were nestled into an elbow of that little stream, which created a fertile patch of ground for the dark beads of fruit that clustered in abundance in the bushes.

"I may be at this a while," she told Rand, setting down her basket and watching as he strode to the edge of the brook and stared out into the woods beyond. "I'm sure there is no danger here. You don't have to stay with me."

He crouched down, catching a handful of water in his hand. He drank some, then spread the rest over his face. "I'm where I want to be," he said, regarding her over his shoulder only briefly before sluicing another handful of water over his bearded jaw and into his tousled dark hair.

She dared not think he would choose to be with her, but a hopeful part of her quickened with elation. Serena knelt in the soft moss below the berry bushes and began to pluck the ripe fruit into her basket.

She could not keep from slanting quick looks in his direction, curious now, as he withdrew the dagger from the belt at his hip and cleaned it in the stream. He looked at his reflection in the water, studying each side of his face. Then he brought the blade up to his cheek.

"What are you doing?" Serena asked, alarmed and confused.

"I am removing my beard."

She dropped back onto her heels to regard him fully. "Why would you do that?"

"Because in a couple of days, I will be going to Egremont," he said, pausing to face her now. "If trouble lurks in town, I'd rather it not come looking for me before I am ready to meet it on my own terms. Few know my face without these whiskers. My enemies, in particular."

"You're leaving, then?" She forced a casualness to her query that she didn't fully feel.

"Yes. Soon," he said. "I need supplies, a weapon that will serve me better in combat than this small blade. With any luck, I'll also find a boat in Egremont willing to take me on to Scotland."

"Scotland?" Serena asked, wondering at the unfamiliar name and his purpose in going there. "Is this place— Scotland—far from here?"

He shrugged, then bent down to wet his face again. "Not more than a fortnight, I expect. Faster to go up the coast than travel overland, especially on foot."

Serena noted the subtle stiffness of his movements. His wounds were improving but not yet healed. "Are you sure you are hale enough to make the trip?"

"I'll make it," he said, water dripping from his bearded jaw as he slanted a determined glance at her.

That brief, steely glance said it all: he would drag himself to Scotland regardless of his fitness, for the thirst for vengeance would wait no longer to be sated. "This place you wish to reach—this is where you were heading when you wrecked in the storm?"

He was silent a moment, then gave her a curt nod.

"Does your enemy await you there?"

"He might. My hope is to get there before he does." Rand smoothed the flat of the dagger's blade over the top of his thigh, then lifted the edge to his cheek. "It is my only hope."

Serena watched him scrape the dagger down along the side of his face, from the base of his ear to halfway down the corded column of his neck. The dark whiskers gathered on the blade, clearing a path of bare skin beneath. He sluiced off the blade, rinsed it, then raised it again, using his reflection in the stream as a visual guide.

"Why did this man kill your family, Rand?"

The knife skidded ever so slightly against his cheek, drawing a thin line of blood. Rand hardly reacted. He righted the blade's angle and slid it down the remainder of its path, shaving clean another patch of his tawny skin. The crimson tendril snaked a tiny rivulet along the slope of his face. Serena stared at that elongating stain as silence stretched to awkward lengths.

At last, although he did not look at her, Rand spoke. "He wanted something I possessed—something of great worth, which I pledged to a friend that I would guard with my life."

"The cup you lost," Serena guessed.

"Nay, but a key that would have led him to it."

"You didn't give it to him?"

"I had made a vow," he said, not quite an answer, his voice deadly quiet. "I was bound by my word."

Too calmly, he tilted his chin and began to shave the other side of his face. The glistening blade of the dagger scraped downward in unerring motion. Rand drew water from the rushing trickle of the brook, wetting what was left of his beard. He paused then, his head hung low between his shoulders in heavy reflection.

"In the end, it mattered for naught what I did. The raiders who came to my keep that night had no intention of letting any of us live. Their orders were plain to me as soon as they arrived and the fires began."

Serena closed her eyes, feeling the emotion of that terrible, smoke-drenched night race through her on the merciless current of the Knowing.

"I'm sorry," she whispered.

Her heart ached for him. She wanted to reach out to Rand in that moment, but cowardice stilled her hand. She dared not absorb any more of his pain, but more than that even, she feared he would rebuff her sympathy as he had her every other attempt at understanding and friendship.

"There are days," he said, harshly now, "when I pray this existence I am left with is but a dream. I should have perished that night along with my wife and child and the servants who depended on me to protect them. It isn't right that I am here now, save to deliver my own justice to the man responsible for so much destruction."

"You have more worth than that, Rand. Don't you know that? I am certain there is more for you than just this vengeance that drives you."

"Jesu." He looked up now and chuckled around an oath that held little bite. "Do you seek to save every godforsaken creature that washes up on your shore, Serena?"

There was a jesting humor in his voice, but Serena sat back, stung. It was too hard to hold his mocking gaze, so she dropped hers at once, feigning a sudden, total interest in her work. She carefully plucked the berries and set them into her basket. At the brook, water raced and sloshed as he continued with his shaving. She heard the blade rasp over his skin several more times, then silence as he set down his dagger and dried his face with the hem of his tunic.

"Well," he said, "what do you think?"

Reluctantly, she dragged her gaze up to where he stood before her, wanting to tell him she thought him a disagreeable oaf, a stubborn churl. Instead she gaped, taken aback with surprise.

"You look . . . very different." She frowned, shaking her head. "At a distance, I might not even recognize you."

He grinned, running his hand over his smooth, beardless jaw. "That is the idea."

Serena could not resist a closer look. She set aside her basket and stood up, approaching him with open curiosity. The angular cut of his cheeks was more pronounced without the dark whiskers, as was the stern line of his jaw. His face was lean, unforgiving, striking. He had a dimple in his chin, she noted with a half-contained smile. She wanted very badly to touch him, and see if his skin would be soft beneath the beard that had hidden him all this time. And now that it was gone, his eyes were ever more intense, piercing beneath the deep brown slashes of his brows.

"You have a nice face," she proclaimed, too struck by him to hold back her praise.

He grunted, and the barest trace of a crooked smile tugged at the corner of his mouth. "Elspeth used to say I looked too fierce without my whiskers. My jaw was too strong for her liking. Too grim, so she'd tell me."

To her chagrin, a pang of jealousy bit her, returned again, like the irritation of a burr that she could not quite pluck away. She crossed her arms over her breasts and gave a little shrug. " 'Tis a nice face. Handsome, I would say."

"Truly?"

"Aye," she said, endeavoring to say it with as little conviction as she could muster.

She turned away from him to hide her sudden blush.

"Handsome," he repeated, seeming slightly bemused, but rather pleased with himself.

"That is what I said." Serena turned away from him, retreating to her task of collecting more fruit. When she was settled on the ground once more, she paused and threw him a considering look over her shoulder. "Although I cannot be sure, of course. I've no one to compare you to."

He had upset her again.

He thought to tease her about her stubborn opinion that there was something in him worth saving, but he saw at once that his jest carried an unintended barb. He should have apologized, and meant to still, but she seemed intent to ignore him now. He should be relieved for that small mercy, but instead it left him frustrated and feeling very much a boor. Just being with Serena was making him question himself, his goals . . . everything.

And she thought him handsome.

She likely thought him a charmless brute as well. Perhaps it was a mistake to accompany her out to pick berries this morning. After the torturous night he'd spent with her in the cottage, being with her again, alone, was unwise on many levels.

Soon it would not matter, for he spoke the truth when he said he would be leaving the grove for Egremont in a few days. He had to, before he let things spiral out of control with Serena.

Rand strode away from the thin stream and settled himself on the ground nearby. Serena, meanwhile, worked in silence, her graceful fingers choosing the most succulent fruit for her basket. She hardly wore her gloves any longer, not even around him. He smiled, seeing the purple stains gather on her pale skin as her basket filled. One particularly juicy berry crushed in her tender grasp. She gave a little cry of dismay, then popped the ruined berry into her mouth and sucked the juice from her fingertips.

Rand nearly growled in hunger, though it was not the whortleberries that he craved.

He looked away in frustration, eager for something else to focus on. He found a small branch of old wood beside him in the thicket. The scant patches of dew-moistened bark came off in his hands, baring a smooth piece of oak. Rand took his dagger to it and began carving in idle distraction.

For a long while, there was just the sound of the stream racing by, the soft rustle of the berry bushes, and the rhythmic slice of the blade against the wood. Finally Serena sat back with a sigh.

"That should be enough," she said, lifting the filled basket onto her lap.

She started to get up, but before she could, Rand approached her and hunkered down beside her. He held out his hand to her, his fingers curled into a fist. Serena gave him a dubious look.

"For you," he said, then opened his hand and presented the finished carving to her in the cradle of his palm.

"Oh!" Serena set down her basket, then took the little dove into her hands. She admired it from every angle, gazing upon it like the finest prize she had ever seen. "You made this? Look at the detail, the way its head is tucked toward its wing—why, I can even see the delicate lines of each feather!"

"Do you like it?"

"Yes," she exclaimed. "It's beautiful, Rand. Thank you. I adore it."

He shrugged, uncomfortable with her praise despite that he had sought it. He grew reflective, seeing her joy at his meager creation. "I've lost count of how many such figures I've made over the years. The first was a little horse for Tod. I carved it the night he was born—it was all that kept me from tearing apart the keep while I was waiting the hours for his arrival. As he grew older, I made more for him. My son had a king's menagerie of wooden creatures, knights, and castles by the time he was old enough to walk."

Serena laughed then, and shook her head.

"What is it?"

"Nothing. I just . . ." She glanced down at the little figurine in her palm, her smile not quite hidden behind the fall of her dark hair. "You surprise me, that's all."

Rand found himself warming to her, a smile tugging at his lips as well. "Why do I surprise you?"

"That you would have the patience, the care," she said, then looked up at him at last. "Your hands are so large, so able with a weapon, I would not have thought . . ."

"Ah. You would have thought me suited only for warring, is that it, my lady?"

She shrugged.

"These hands are battered," he admitted, turning up his callused palms, "but they can be tender. With you, they would be most tender. And they have many skills that might surprise you, my lady."

Her blush spread a certain heat through him as it pinkened her cheeks. It emboldened him, that sweet rosy tint and shy smile. He brought his hand up slowly, and touched the deepening shade of her blush.

"They can, for example, strum the strings of a lute in song."

Serena smiled, a note of confusion in her gaze. "A lute?"

"You've never seen one," he surmised, dismayed that she had never known the joy of troubadours entertaining in a bustling feast hall. "The lute is a musical instrument made of polished hollow wood. 'Tis shaped like a pear, but with a long goose neck and strings stretched so tightly down it that when you strum them, like this—" with his thumb, he gently stroked the velvet softness of her cheek "—they sing the most beautiful music."

"You can play this thing—a lute?"

"Aye, and quite well, I should say."

"And you sing?"

He shrugged. "A bit."

"You lied to me last night," she exclaimed, laughing through her outrage.

"I do not claim to be any good, and it was no lie that I might injure your ears if I tried it now. But I once had an interest. When I was a boy, I often thought I would rather strum music than take up the sword."

"Did you?" Serena's eyes widened in surprise.

"I didn't dare tell my sire, of course. We came from a long line of knights and sundry other war-bred scoundrels. My father was a good man, but he would have had my arse if he knew I spent as much time composing my chansons as I did practicing at combat."

Serena laughed. "Your secret is safe with me."

Rand smiled back at her, unguarded and relaxed in her company. It was a strange feeling. He hadn't known such easy contentment in his marriage, not even in the early days. Elspeth swung so readily between giddiness and melancholy, he never knew what to expect at any given moment. He was forever on alert, without peace.

"What is it?" Serena asked, her placid eyes holding him in tender regard.

She was a balm to his very soul, this innocent wood nymph with the sorceress's touch. Her beauty framed by the verdant splendor of the forest, Serena enchanted him. Very carefully, barely permitting his fingers to skate atop the perfection of her lily-fair skin, Rand caressed her pretty face. With a wordless sigh, she turned her cheek into his palm, kissing him there, welcoming him without a word.

Her response was always so open, so giving. Gazing into her eyes, it would be easy to wish he never had to leave her, that he never had to leave this peaceful slice of Eden on England's northern shore.

"I have tried to keep my distance, Serena, but you draw me close every time." Rand smoothed the pad of his thumb along the gentle line of her jaw. "And these hands are too rough for such innocence."

"No," she whispered, her lips moving warm and sweet against his fingers.

She nuzzled his palm, and every sinew in Rand's body tensed with need. He held himself as still as stone, his gaze downcast, unwilling to look at her and see the desire he feared would be there in her eyes. He wanted her more than he had a right, and he did not know how much longer he could keep himself in check.

Lost, he thought.

If she did not turn him away now, he would be lost.

Serena's tender hand came up to cup his shaven cheek. Her touch enflamed him. He groaned, and tried to pull away.

"No," she said, just a breath of sound in the stillness that surrounded them. "Don't try to protect me. I am strong—you said so yourself, remember?"

He looked up then, too late to heed his own advice.

She was smiling at him, her lush pink mouth a supple curve that tempted him to taste it, her ocean blue gaze both innocent and wise.

"If you are lost to this, Rand, so am I."

She smoothed her fingers along his bare jaw as if committing the feel of him to memory. She touched his lips, and Rand could not contain his growling need.

"Serena," he said, a warning, a curse. A plea. "Damn it, Serena."

Rand speared his fingers through her unbound hair, catching her nape in his palm. Their lips met tenderly at first, then swiftly burned into something fierce and urgent.

He needed to feel her body against his. With his hand at her back to guide her, Rand eased her down onto the pad of moss beneath them. The basket of berries tipped, and soon the scent of sweet nectar mingled with the heat of mounting desire.

Rand found one of the succulent fruits and placed it between his teeth. He bent down with the offering, feeding Serena from his lips. The berry crushed amid their kiss, rich as wine and just as heady. Serena sucked on her half and swallowed it. Rand's breath caught in his throat. He had never seen anything as tempting as the sight of her plump lips stained deep red and glistening with juice. A small droplet slid from the corner of her mouth. Rand caught it with his tongue, then claimed her in a deeper kiss.

Her body moved beneath him in a tantalizing squirm of motion. Her breasts pressed into his chest, firm and ripe as any forbidden fruit, making him yearn to touch them. Her slim belly arched into him as he trailed kisses from her sweet mouth to her velvety throat. She groaned a wordless cry of pleasure when his tongue teased the hollow of her neck and shoulder. He nipped her lightly, spurred by the feel of her hips cradling his pelvis, lifting up to meet him in innocent enthusiasm.

He had to touch her.

Bringing his hand up between them, he cupped her breast, kneading the perfect mound. Through the simple weave of her bliaut and chemise, her nipple rose like a pearl. He rolled the tight nub against his palm, squeezing her fullness, mad with the need to taste her.

"Yes," she panted, her spine arching beneath him, offering herself to him so openly he nearly shook with passion. "Rand, yes . . ."

Her entreaty was a sigh against his mouth, no reservation, just sweet, sensual invitation.

He wanted her. God, but had he ever wanted anything—or anyone—so much?

He knew the answer, just as surely as he knew the fevered response of his body to hers. His arousal beat like thunder through his veins, hardening him to the point of breaking. Pressed against her softness, her thighs having sometime parted beneath him, Rand ached to bury himself inside her.

"No," he muttered, hardly able to summon the thought, let alone the will to voice his denial. "Serena . . . God . . . no."

Rand broke away from kissing her and gazed down at her in torment. Her lips were parted, her neck flushed. She said nothing, merely looked up at him in wordless anguish, her nipples erect beneath her bodice, breasts heaving with every panting breath she took.

Rand bent down and kissed her brow, her nose, her chin. He could not so much as look at her sweet, welcoming mouth.

"What are you doing to me," he murmured, dropping his head to her chest. "Why does it have to be you? Why now?"

"Shh. It's all right."

She was stroking his back, soothing sweeps of her hands across his spine and shoulders. Her breathing slowed, calming as she merely held him in the cool shade of the forest. Beside them, the stream gurgled merrily. Birds flitted in the trees overhead. It was sweet how she held him, demanding nothing of him, lulling him toward peace with her gentling demeanor.

This was a new bliss, another he did not recognize from the life he knew before Serena. He felt cared for, and relaxed.

He felt . . . content.

After a long moment, Serena raised her head and peered at his tunic sleeve.

"You've got berry stains all over you," she pointed out, yet a little breathless. She brought her hand up to cover her smile. "You're an utter mess."

"And you as well," he said, eyeing her with considerably less amusement. He moved off of her and got to his feet, then offered her his hand to help her rise. "Your mother will assume the worst—and she won't be far off the mark."

Serena waved away his concern. "I have a plan. Come with me!"

Despite his herculean show of control, he was still tense with desire, still dangerous in his need. He had stopped just short of disaster, and although he wanted to take her back to the cottage while he had the strength of will to do so, Serena was already moving. She took his hand in hers before he could argue, and led him on a mad jaunt through the forest. Rand heard the rush of the falls up ahead. Serena looked back at him, laughing, her eyes bright with mischief.

"Come on, faster!" she cried, pulling him easily along.

The sun shone down on the white rush of the cascade, making it glow like a beacon as the forest gave way to the clearing of the falls. Arcs of light broke in the rising mist, shattering in an explosion of dancing color as the water poured into the pool at the base of the steep cascade.

And in the midst of it all, framed by light and nature and the breathtaking beauty of a moment stolen from a fairy story, was Serena. Her black hair caught in the breeze off the water, lifting around her like a tempest of ebony silk. Her face was flushed, her lips yet berry-stained and lush from kissing him. Her aqua eyes dazzled above all else, shining to shame the brightest jewel.

"Come with me, Rand!"

She was backing away from him, smiling as she edged nearer to the pool. He didn't think a swim together would be wise.

"Don't think," she said, her Knowing touch light on his hand. "Just feel."

She let go and turned to face the crystalline pool behind her. Then she dived in, clothes and all, vanishing beneath the surface of the water.

Rand glanced around him at the empty woods. From within the rolling mist of the falls, he heard Serena laughing, calling to him through the roar of the water. Her carefree jubilation overtook him. With a shout of laughter raw in his throat, Rand bounded for the edge and dove in after her.

❧ 15 ❧

THE NOONTIDE SUN was warm and bright, beating down on the smooth granite of the pool's edge. Rand lay on his back, his eyes closed against the stark light above. His clothes were merely damp on his body under the soothing heat of the sun's rays. Serena sat beside him on the rocks, bracing her arms behind her. She idly swung her bare feet in the water, dangling them over the lip of the cascade pool.

"A good plan, was it not?" she asked, and Rand opened one eye to see her gazing down at him, smiling. "Our clothes are clean, and I daresay you actually look to be relaxed."

Rand groaned despite his agreement. "We're wet as seals."

And Serena looked entirely too beguiling with her face glowing in the sunshine, her black hair spread around her like ribbons, and her plain-spun bliaut drying like a second skin against her curves.

But he was relaxed with her, he realized. He had laughed with her beneath the falls, lost himself in crystalline waters and the sparkling joy in Serena's eyes. Even while his desire for her still burned, unquenched, he knew a certain peace. There was a pleasant calm about him, and it had everything to do with the pure, caring heart of the woman seated next to him.

He felt safe and warm, something he had not known

since the raid on Greycliff keep. Perhaps longer still. It seemed a betrayal of his soul—his honor—to feel so free now. His wife and child were gone. Until that score was settled, he had no right to claim even a moment of this simple bliss.

"You're thinking about home," Serena said quietly.

It was her intuition that read him now, not the Knowing, for she was not touching him at all. She merely looked at him and saw that his thoughts were drifting back to the life he once knew. Rand made no effort to deny it; for their short time together, he believed that Serena understood him better than anyone ever had.

"Tell me what happened, Rand." Serena pulled her feet from the water and carefully settled herself a bit closer to him on the rocky ledge of the pool. She reached out to him, her fingers tender as she combed them through his damp hair. "It's all right. You can talk to me. Tell me what happened."

For a long while, Rand was unable to form words to recount the horror of his last day at Greycliff. The hell had started before the raid, in truth, when he realized his marriage—and the life he had been living—was over.

"There was a healer," he said at last. "She was new to the neighboring village by a year or thus. She was strange and solitary, but learned. She came to our keep with her baskets of herbs, and quickly befriended Elspeth."

He blew out a sigh, glancing up at Serena.

"My wife was not a well woman. She had . . . ailments. Most of them unseen, things only she could understand. This healer, Haven, called on her often with sundry brews and linaments. The day of the raid on Greycliff, while I was away from the keep on estate matters, Haven had given Elspeth a potion of mandrake and pennyroyal."

Serena frowned. "Those herbs are powerful strong. Too much could kill."

"Aye," Rand agreed. "Elspeth had consumed half of the pouch by the time I returned home that evening."

"Mercy," Serena gasped. "Had the woman not warned her that it could do harm as well as heal?"

Rand's chuckle grated his ears, so raw yet was the shame of what had greeted him upon his arrival home that night. "Elspeth knew well the danger in the brew. She procured it purposely, and took it all by choice. She would have taken more, had I not returned when I did."

"You saved her," Serena suggested, hopeful.

"No. That was something I never could do for her, not before, and most certainly not that night. We argued, both said terrible things. And then the attack occurred, and none of it seemed to matter anyway."

For a long while, Serena said nothing. She just looked at him, passing no judgment, showing no pity, simply waiting for him to tell her more. And Rand wanted to tell her more, he realized in astonishment. He needed to tell someone—all of it. He needed to tell Serena, knowing she would be the one person he could trust to see the depth of his wound and not mock him for a fool, not condemn him for his failure as a husband and a man.

Serena's clear gaze held him aloft when he felt himself sinking into self-loathing, like an ocean blue wave cradling his beaten body, his dying heart.

"My wife," he said, finally, "could not bear to endure her life any longer. I could not make her happy. In truth, so she told me that very night, by loving her I had only made it worse. Elspeth was with child again—our child, just a few weeks in her womb—and she feared the babe was eating away her soul."

"Was it true?" Serena asked, a stricken look on her innocent face. "Can a babe possibly—"

"Nay," Rand answered, tersely certain. "A babe can do no such harm. Elspeth's melancholy was the demon that consumed her soul . . . and, slowly, her mind. She felt more deeply than most, but unpredictably; giddy with joy for an instant, then morbid with despair the next. I never knew what moved her. She never let me that close."

"But still you loved her."

"I did," he admitted, hoping it would not hurt Serena to hear him say it, in light of the intimacy he now shared with her.

What he felt for Serena was a separate thing from the bond he'd had with his wife, and while he was not immediately prepared to give it a name, his feeling for Serena was real and deepening . . . more powerful than it should be. Rand met the gaze watching him tenderly in the sunlight. Tranquil peace shone back at him, a sanctuary he never thought to find. Ironic that he should discover it now, when his life was pledged to unholy purpose. A quest that would, inevitably, necessarily, take him far away from Serena and the idyl he was beginning to know when he was in her company.

"I loved her," he said, "but Elspeth and I had grown distant after our son's birth. Before that, even, though I was slow to see it. She had always been vulnerable to illness and headaches, which worsened every year. Nothing seemed to help, least of all anything I could give her. While she retreated into herself, I retreated into my duties about the keep. I knew she was unhappy but I did not fully grasp the extent—not until her last act of defeat, when she swallowed those deadly herbs. Elspeth would have killed herself, and our child, to be free of her pain."

"That wasn't fair of her," Serena said, judging at last, a note of defensiveness lacing the sweet hush of her voice. "Life is filled with equal measure of joy and pain. To deny either is to deny the full experience of living."

As she spoke, she reached across to him and took his hand in hers. Even this, the careful touch of her, was a gift of utter acceptance and trust. Her bare fingers twined with his own, and he knew she could feel all that he did now, the Knowing absorbing his anger and shame, the useless futility that had dogged him in those final years of his marriage. The cutting sharpness of the realization that his wife—a woman he had vowed to cherish and protect, and had done his best to do so—preferred the endless night of death over another day of life with him.

"No," Serena said, tenderly denying his unspoken pain. "What she did is her own. You were not to blame, Rand. I will never believe that, nor should you."

"She was dying even before the keep was attacked," he said, recalling the fits of coughing that had seized her as they quarreled, those lung-shredding whoops, the whiteness of her face as she took to their bed and demanded he leave her to die in peace. "The raiders set the place ablaze as they arrived. When I heard the ruckus, smelled the sudden stench of smoke, I grabbed my weapon and flew out of our chamber. Elspeth was delirious by then. She came after me, despite my order that she stay put. She had Tod with her—Jesu, how terrified he was, crying, clinging to her as smoke poured up from the keep below. In her weakened state, she was scarcely able to hold him."

Serena squeezed his hand, the slightest pressure, communicating warmth and sympathy for the difficulty with which he recounted the horror of that night.

"There was little I could do. The raiders were already

inside. They threatened me, four of them striking out with fists and torches and swords. Enough to wound, degrade, but not kill. They needed me alive, so I could talk. I was keeping something they needed—the whole reason they were there."

"Rand, these raiders . . ." Serena gave a little shudder as she gazed down at their joined hands. "They weren't normal men, were they? I glimpsed them when I touched you in the cottage, but I didn't understand. They were . . . inhuman somehow."

Too late to hide the incredible truth of what befell him at Greycliff the night of the raid, Rand nodded his head. "Shapeshifters," he admitted, all but hissing the word. "They are neither man nor beast, but a slippery meeting of the two. They are treacherous and deadly in their ability to change forms at will."

"Wolves," Serena whispered. "They came to Greycliff as wolves."

"Aye. And it was another such beast that followed me onto the ship at Liverpool. He attacked me on the deck. It was raining; we were swept overboard. The bastard gave me these cuts before I rent his innards and let him bleed out in the tide."

"All for the cup you carried with you that day?"

"All for that," Rand answered. "When the shifters came to Greycliff, they came in search of a key I'd been given by a friend of mine, Kenrick of Clairmont. I had accepted the responsibility for its safekeeping, and vowed to Kenrick that I'd not let it fall into enemy hands. But then the shifters threatened my family. They held my wife and son in the sights of their crossbows, trapped them in the tower stairwell."

"Oh, Rand." Serena stroked his fingers with her free hand. "You couldn't let them be harmed. No promise is worth the lives of your family."

"Elspeth was already lost to the potion she drank. But my son." An oath slipped past his gritted teeth. "My little son was innocent in all of this. And he was crying, screaming for me to make them go away—to make the bad men go away."

"So you surrendered this thing you had sworn to keep for your friend."

"I did, to my shame." He had broken his honor and his word that night, but it had all been for naught. "I took them to the hiding place, gave them the seal . . . and retched a moment later, as a wild shot was fired, fatally striking Elspeth. She fell lifeless, tumbled down the hard stone steps—with Tod yet clutched in her arms."

"Merciful heaven," Serena whispered, reverent, pained. "That poor child."

"He died instantly. I went mad. I slew several of the shifter beasts in my rage, and wounded another—the one who had led the rest of her kind to Greycliff while she spied for the villain behind all of this evil and destruction."

"The healer—Haven?" Serena asked, no doubt hearing the name skate through his own heart in a mixture of bewilderment and slowly subsiding contempt. "She was there, too?"

"Aye. She was herself a shifter—or rather, is still," he corrected.

"You do not hate her."

Rand shook his head, then shrugged. "I don't know. I had wanted to kill her. I turned her own blade on her that night when I realized she had betrayed us. All along she had been betraying us, or so I believed. It wasn't until later—weeks later, when I next saw her, that I was made to reconsider."

"What happened?"

"The unimaginable," he replied, still bewildered by

the events of those astonishing days that followed the raid. "Nothing could have shocked me more than seeing this same woman in the company of my closest friend, Kenrick of Clairmont, after I thought her dead at the end of a blade the night of the attack."

Serena's gaze went wide with surprise. "She survived?"

"Thanks to Kenrick, who came to Greycliff unaware we had been attacked some time before. He found Haven wandering the ruins in a state of senselessness, gravely injured. It seemed logical enough that she had been present at the raid—the apparent sole survivor. Needing to know what had happened to the secret he had left in my keeping, Kenrick brought Haven home with him to his castle, where she was mended and taken in as his ward."

"They had no idea who she was, or what she had done?"

"No. Neither did she, for that matter. Wound fever had scorched her memory."

Serena shook her head, clearly amazed. "Where were you that you could not warn your friend of the enemy he harbored?"

"After the smoke of the raid at Greycliff had settled, and I awoke to find myself yet breathing when my family—my life—was gone, I let it seem that I, too, had perished in the attack. I set three graves in the yard, then left Greycliff for good. I sought out Kenrick, of course, and that is when I realized that Haven was living under his roof." Rand gave a wry chuckle, thinking back on all that had occurred. "I tried to warn Kenrick, once I knew, but it was already too late."

Serena's expression fell into dread. "Did she . . . hurt your friend in some way?"

"Yes, and no. While she recuperated, unaware of her own past, Haven and Kenrick fell in love."

"Nay!" she cried, as aghast as he first had been at the idea.

"Oh, aye," Rand said, tracing the fine bones of Serena's hand. "I could scarce believe it myself, but it was true."

"What about her role in the attack on Greycliff? Did that count for nothing to your friend?"

"It mattered very much to him, but Haven swore she had not called the raid. She came initially to observe the keep and report back to the villain who commanded her, but then she came to know Elspeth and Tod. She came to care about them, emotions forbidden in one of her kind. It changed her, and put her in danger as well. The shifters who came to attack Greycliff had come for Haven as well. I had not known that at the time. It took much convincing for me to believe it when she recounted the tale to Kenrick and me."

"But you do believe it. You have accepted her, because your friend loves her."

Rand glanced at the perceptive aqua eyes that knew him so well, even unaided by the gift that could read him with a touch. "I believe her, yes. In the end, it was Haven who spared both Kenrick and me from certain death at the hands of her shifter clan. I have accepted that she and Kenrick are meant to be together."

"You've forgiven her," Serena assured him. "In time, mayhap you will even be able to forgive yourself."

He wasn't so sure about that, but Rand brought her fingertips to his mouth and placed a warm kiss against them. Her soft skin teased his lips, her clean scent a balm that could wash away all his dark thoughts and haunted past. Unable to stop himself, Rand leaned down and kissed her. Her lips were honey-sweet and tender, opening so easily for him. He broke away with a soft oath.

"You'd better go back to the cottage."

"Must I?"

"Aye," he growled, "the sooner, the better. You've a basket of crushed berries to retrieve, and if I recall, a tart to make for our sup tonight."

Her eyes twinkled playfully, her answering smile anything but compliant. "True, but I would rather stay out here a while longer."

"Up," he ordered, rising to his feet and pulling her alongside him. He pointed in the direction of the woods. "Go."

"What about you?"

"I'll be along."

She hesitated now, eyeing him with mild suspicion. A flicker of concern dimmed her bright gaze. "Are you all right?"

He nodded, then gave her a stern look. "Go, lady. We've tarried here overlong. I have things to attend as well."

For a moment, she merely waited there. She started to reach out to him, but he casually drew back from her reach. Her hand dropped slowly to her side, and she began a slow retreat back into the dense greenery of the grove.

He did not return to the cottage that afternoon, or even that night. Serena ate a quiet meal with her mother, then lay awake on her pallet as the evening stretched toward midnight. The little dove Rand had carved for her sat on the sill of the cottage window, a sweet reminder of the wondrous day they had spent together . . . and the amazing passion he had awakened in her with his berry-drenched kisses near the stream, then again at the falls.

She had saved him a piece of the whortleberry tart from supper. She had waited all day to see him again, but now she began to fear he might never return.

He had opened up to her at the cascade pool, telling her about his marriage and the terrible attack on his home. She had felt his misery as he recounted it all, and she had noted the haunted look in his eyes as he abruptly sent her back home. His pain was clear. He did not think he deserved happiness so long as his enemy still breathed and his family's deaths went unavenged. His wounds were still so raw.

And now, she wondered . . .

Serena sat up in her bed. Had he gone? Would he leave her without a word of farewell?

She did not think he would, not after the tenderness he had shown her that day, but she had to know.

Pulling on her cloak, Serena rose from her pallet and quietly slipped out the cottage door. She padded across the moon-shadowed space of the small yard, and out into the woods beyond. She followed her senses, her heart, bare feet trodding carefully through the cool undergrowth of the forest. There was no path on this side of the woods, only a carpet of old conifer needles and tender, flowering greenery that huddled close to the earth. Serena weaved her way silently through the maze of tall trees, pliant saplings, and forest ferns, letting the cool night air embrace her. High above the canopy, the full moon glowed milky white, threaded with shadowy, tendril clouds.

Her path was indirect, unhurried. Each step brought a dread that she might find the forest empty, that she had lost Rand to his vengeance. Night sounds greeted her: rustling ferns and ivy at her feet, roosting birds shifting curiously above her head as she passed. Farther in this direction was the cascade pool; she knew it even before the muffled thunder of rushing water met her ears.

Serena arrived there quietly, her approach masked by the majestic roar of the place.

Darkness clung to everything.

And there, draped in shadow, solitary beneath the indigo night sky, was Rand. He was seated on the flat crag of rock at the edge of the pool where she had left him that day. His hunched silhouette was haloed by the silvery blue veil of the falls before him. His back was to her as she took a hesitant step forward. He was so still, so quiet.

Oh, Rand.

She did not speak, merely approached him carefully, uncertain if she should disturb his solitude. She knew a moment of true fear, for he seemed so remote. Closed off from everything around him, sitting there in the dark. Serena feared she might encounter his bristly anger. He might snarl at her as he had at other times, like a wounded animal seeking to drive away those who might sense his slightest weakness. Even after their newborn intimacy of that day, he might yet send her away, rejecting her presence as he had so frequently rejected most of her other attempts at kindness.

But then she spied the faintest tremor in his strong back, and her own misgivings faded to inconsequence. His stillness seemed too tightly held. He breathed, but it was a ragged expansion of his lungs, the swell of an emotion that seemed bottled up and fighting to break free. His head was hung low on his broad shoulders, his chin tucked down to his chest, his arms braced on updrawn knees.

Another few tender paces and she was within arm's reach of him. She paused, there at his back, too terrified to do anything but stand there, her heart breaking for him.

Sweet, solitary man.

His shoulders rocked with grief, but the only sound in the clearing was that of the crashing falls, unbroken, relentless.

So alone. So terribly alone.

Serena stretched out her hand, and gently laid her bare fingers across the span of solid muscle at his shoulder. Rand did not flinch or draw away. Nay, for a long moment he reacted not at all to her unannounced, lingering touch.

Serena lived his sorrow in an instant, feeling the pain of his loss travel through the heart of her open palm to the heart of her self, her very soul.

He turned then, slowly pivoting his head to face her. Trails of wetness glistened in the cool light of the falls, tracing twin lines from the corners of his pain-filled eyes, down his cheeks, into the shadow of the beard that once covered his jaw.

"Serena," he said, a rough hush of sound. An entreaty, for he held out his arm, still sitting, perhaps unable to do anything more in that moment, and welcomed her into his embrace.

Serena stepped into the circle of his arms. She wrapped her arms around his shoulders, holding him against her under the fall of her cloak. His cheek pressed into her belly, the glossy tousled darkness of his head nestled just below her heart. She stroked his hair, petting him, weathering the force of his pent-up feelings as they flooded into her, inky black, an ocean storm of fury, pain, and regret.

"I know," she whispered, leaning forward to kiss the top of his head.

His hair was soft against her lips, his arms tight around her, needful.

"Serena . . ."

Her name was an apology that rasped past his lips, his voice thick but steady, warm against her breast.

She quietly hushed him, for there was no need for pardon. She understood now, his flares of unprovoked anger, his abrupt dismissal of her that afternoon. She understood now his need to push her away from him while the door to his past was, at last, beginning to close. She could not bear to feel his regret heaped atop the grief that was just now, finally, breaking.

Sweet Mary. He had held it for so long, the hurt of loss in his heart, fiercely reined. Denied. But no longer. Serena held him, demanding nothing, wishing only that the ache she shared through Knowing could somehow lessen his pain.

But it could not. Her gift was not that strong. No magic could absorb so deep a wound.

"I know," Serena murmured, holding him closer, pressing her lips into the windblown silk of his hair. She would hold him thus all night if he needed. She would share his grief until it was fully spent. "I know, Rand. It's all right, you don't have to say anything."

❧ 16 ❧

THEY DID NOT speak of that night in the day and a half that had passed. Rand's demeanor, while far from lighthearted, had grown less burdened. Serena was glad for that, but there was yet a reticence in him, a distance she seemed unable to bridge.

His wounds were all but healed. He built his strength swimming in the cascade pool and training with a length of heavy wood in absence of a sword. He prepared for battle, and Serena knew in the pit of her heavy heart that soon he would be leaving.

She stood gazing out the window of the cottage, her fingers toying with the little wooden dove that perched on the sill, her thoughts trailing back over the precious moments she and Rand had shared.

She wished they had more time. She wished, just once, they could share a few hours together where she was not Serena of the grove, and he was not Randwulf the avenging lord of Greycliff. She wanted to see the world he belonged to, and know if she might ever be a part of it.

Just once, she yearned to see him look upon her in wonder and see her as the woman she felt she was inside, not the sheltered cottage maiden in drab homespun. For him, she yearned to be a princess, exotic and dazzling, like the ones in her mother's fairy stories.

She wished, recklessly and foolishly, that he would forget his dangerous plans and stay with her always.

Her gaze strayed to one of the clothing chests near her pallet. She went to it, and knelt on the floor before the old wardrobe chest. The lid creaked open as she lifted it, then began to remove the first few layers of folded garments. The simple homespun gowns had been wrought by her own hand, none of them beautiful, despite their careful weave and occasional, modest embroidery. She had been proud of each one when she'd made them, but now they all seemed drab and unremarkable. Serena set them aside. There was another gown in the chest, and it was this special one she sought now.

It rested at the bottom of the wooden coffer, hidden like a precious relic, for that it was.

She removed the last of the homespun, revealing the exquisite sheen of cerulean silk shot with gold thread. Delicate gemstone beading circled the fitted sleeves and heart-shaped cut of the bodice, sparkling like stars. Very carefully, marveling at its rare quality, Serena lifted the gown and brought it into the light. She rose, letting the long skirts unfurl before her, smiling as they danced in the small breeze from the cottage window.

The fabric was as light as air in her hands, its color shifting from pale blue to green to pearl. It was all the shades of the ocean and the sky together, a fantasy that spoke of magical times, and of the elegant lady who had once worn it—whomever that ancient relative might have been.

Serena had often asked her mother about the gown's owner, but the lady's name was long forgotten. Calandra knew only a few generations-old stories of her life among a royal court ages ago. A princess, so Calandra had told her, who lived an enchanted life in a faraway land. Love had called her away from her kingdom home, but soon proved a mistake she could not reclaim. Heart-break followed not long after, and it was here in these remote woods that the princess had begun a new life. A simpler life, as Serena and Calandra led themselves.

Although the gown was astonishingly beautiful, Serena had never worn it. She had never felt worthy of it, never felt it right to risk sullying such finery merely to sate her own vanity.

Entranced by the gossamer perfection of the garment, she hardly noticed the cottage door opening across the room. Inexplicably, a pang of guilt washed over her when she turned her head and met her mother's look of displeasure.

"What are you doing with that?" Calandra asked, stepping inside and slowly closing the door behind her.

Serena shrugged. "I just . . . I suppose I just wanted to look at it."

Calandra edged toward her, something wistful in her voice. "It's hardly aged in all this time. Not even a single pearl out of place. Remarkable, considering how old it truly is."

"Do you ever wonder what her life might have been like before she settled here?" Serena held the gown to her waist with one arm and swayed, so very tempted to don it herself, if only to indulge in its splendor for just a moment. "Do you imagine she lived in a large castle?"

"Yes. I suppose it was," Calandra answered. "Her brother was king of a great realm. I expect the castle she lived in was immense, with tall battlements to overlook the vastness of the land."

Serena nodded, picturing soaring white towers and endless green hills. And within the glittering walls of the fortress was the lady who once wore the exquisite cerulean bliaut. "How incredible she must have been, so beautiful in this gown. No wonder the man fell in love with her on sight."

"His love was false," Calandra said, a flatness creeping into her tone. She came closer and gently withdrew the precious silk from Serena's hands. "And she was careless. If this gown is good for anything, it should be a reminder that her foolish mistakes must not be repeated. Would that any of the women of our line might take that lesson to heart."

Calandra gathered up the diaphanous skirts and neatly folded the gown. "Mayhap that is too much to hope for," she remarked, replacing the lovely garment in the coffer.

Serena watched her sober movements with a knot of sympathy, aware that her mother bore a private pain. Calandra had loved and lost, too. She would not discuss it, save to say that her heart had been broken and she abandoned by a man who claimed to care for her. Understanding the fear Calandra must harbor for her only remaining child, Serena felt a twitch of guilt. "I am careful, Mother."

"Are you?"

Calandra viewed her askance, her blue gaze serious, almost sad. The casket lid closed with a hollow *thump*.

"I am," Serena insisted.

Calandra said nothing, merely withdrew to the other side of the cottage, her back to Serena. She retrieved a broom from its corner resting place and began a vigorous sweep of the cottage floor.

"What is it?" Serena asked. Uncomfortable with the gap that was spreading between them, she approached her mother. "You have been acting strangely for days. Longer than that, I think. Since Rand arrived here."

More silence. Her mother's mouth was tight as she worked, raking the broom over the floor with a fervor that edged toward violence. When it seemed she was intent on ignoring her, Serena reached out, stilling her mother's hand with her own.

"Tell me. What troubles you? Is it something I have done? Is it Rand?"

Finally, Calandra spoke. "What are you doing with him, Serena? Have you any idea?"

"We are friends, that's all."

Calandra gave a slow, sad shake of her head. "I was awake the other night, when you crept out into the dark like a wraith. To look for him, of course. You were gone nearly till dawn, doing what, I fear to guess."

"I did go to find Rand, but we merely talked—"

"You have never lied to me, in all your life, Serena."

"I do not lie to you now."

Calandra withdrew her hand from Serena's loose grasp. She stood up, brushing at the pressed folds of her plain skirts. "You don't know what you're doing, child."

Serena heard the note of disapproval in her mother's tone, the way she did not ask the question so much as issue an accusation. "Nothing happened."

Calandra grunted. "Do you think me blind to such things? I see how flustered you become around him. I see it now, in the high color of your cheeks. I realize you are young, and you likely think me an old fool, but mark me, Serena. I was young once, too. I have made your mistakes . . . and lived to regret them."

"I have done naught to regret, Mother."

"You are taking overmuch interest in this man," Calandra argued. "You are showing him too much kindness when he does not deserve it."

"You know nothing about him, save your own baseless suspicions. Rand did not ask to be marooned here," Serena said, coming to his defense. "He's offered us his protection for the time being. He has given me his friendship, and his trust. Is it wrong to show him a bit of kindness in return?"

"We don't need his brand of protection. We don't need anything he has to offer. You remember that, child."

"I'm not a child." Serena said it softly, but when her mother glanced up at her in reproach, Serena held her gaze. "Next spring I shall be twenty. I am not a child."

"No," Calandra replied, almost sadly. "You're not. That makes this situation all the more worrisome to me. I don't like how he looks at you, Serena. Nor you him. He is a danger in ways you cannot fathom. Every day that he stays here, he puts us in greater risk."

"Greater risk of what? He is but one man."

"He will bring others. If he does not invite them, his business here will bring them sniffing around like so many hounds. Something must be done."

Serena considered the hunters' snares she had been finding in the woods the past couple of months. She had not told her mother for fear it would alarm her unnecessarily. The truth was, the townsfolk were already becoming curious, venturing farther outside Egremont's borders. The sanctuary she and her mother enjoyed could not last. Their secluded haven was already shrinking, and it had nothing at all to do with the arrival of Randwulf of Greycliff.

"Something must be done," Calandra repeated. She looked squarely at Serena, utter gravity in her expression. "About him, Serena. Before 'tis too late."

A twinge of confusion—of disbelief—crept into Serena's chest. "What are you saying?"

"I thought I could leave you to make your own decisions, but I cannot. I will not stand by and watch another man destroy all I love. I was a fool once—I will not be so blind again. Nor will I watch you make the same mistakes I made."

"Mother." Serena took Calandra's hand between her fingers and felt the dull throb of fear, of rising desperation. "Dearest Mama," she said, hoping to soothe her. "I know you worry. You want to protect me—you always have. But you must remember, I have seen into his heart. There is good in him. The Knowing never lies."

"Aye, the Knowing." Calandra withdrew from her light hold. "He has seen it work, he has felt its power. How long do you think it will take him before he decides to use your gift for his own gain?"

"Use it in what way? What can the Knowing do for him?"

"If he sees a means, he will not hesitate. And then what will he do with you once he's done and you prove inconvenient to him?"

Serena shook her head, dismissing the worry altogether. "Rand is not a peaceful man, but he will not harm us. I trust him—"

"Trust?" Calandra fairly choked on the word, throwing up her hands. "Little fool! You are too naive to understand what you are saying."

"He is not what you think. I would stake my life on it."

"Do not be stupid, Serena!"

The chiding tone jolted her, scraped her heart. Her mother had never been so harsh with her, not even when Serena was a careless, curious child, always finding one manner of trouble or another. This depth of anger was wholly new. Serena had never seen this side of her mother. It bespoke desperation, and that frightened her more than anything.

"This is not about him," Serena said, wanting to understand. "Tell me. What are you really afraid of, Mother?"

Calandra was still fuming, shaking with emotion. "His kind knows only conquest and greed. He will use you, Serena. And when he has taken all he can of you, he will toss you away like yesterday's rubbish."

"Like Father did to you?"

The slap Calandra delivered was well deserved, but Serena still stood in shock. Calandra herself looked stunned at her outburst. She let out a broken gasp, her hand yet hovering beside Serena's face.

"You see what he is doing to us already?" she cried. "He is tearing us apart!"

Serena's cheek burned with the heat of her mother's anger. She tasted blood in her mouth. She'd cut her lip on her teeth, but the pain of it paled next to the hurt of knowing that a chasm had suddenly opened between her and her mother. Perhaps an unbreachable one.

She did not know this woman before her now. The shrillness of her voice was so foreign, the violence of her hand that of a sudden stranger. They had never argued— not like this. Her mother had never lashed out at her; Serena never would have dreamed her capable. Astonished, horrified, she brought her fingers up to the stinging bite of her mother's blow.

"Serena," Calandra gasped. "Oh, my child!"

Hot tears welled in Serena's eyes, blurring Calandra's pale features into watery obscurity.

"Serena, please—forgive me! I did not mean to hurt you!"

She did not wait to hear more.

Pivoting on her heel, Serena fled for the sanctuary of the woods.

Serena wiped at the moisture dampening her cheeks, bewildered and stricken. Her skirts snagged on twigs and rough bramble, but she ran heedless, heading deep into the grove.

In that moment, she wished that she could simply run forever.

She sought out the ruined chapel at the heart of the forest, craving its peace and solitude like never before. She saw it ahead of her through the trees. The little stone structure drew her like a beacon. Breath hitching, Serena swallowed a final sob and pushed her hair back from her face as she ran toward the one place that was hers alone.

Before she could reach it, a large figure stepped from the cover of the trees and into her path. Booted feet stood braced apart in the bracken, leather cross-straps wrapped about strong calves encased in light tan hose. Broad shoulders blocked all light, but Serena knew their familiar line. She knew the ruggedly handsome face, and the deep, rough voice that hissed an oath of concern.

Rand.

Serena drew to an abrupt halt, her breast heaving from emotion and her teary flight into the woods.

"Serena—God's love," he said, frowning as he stared at her through the shadows of the forest. "Are you all right?"

She nodded her head, but did not trust herself to speak.

"You're sure?" He came forward, peering at her as if he feared she was injured. His gaze settled on hers and his jaw went visibly tighter. "You've been crying. What has happened?"

"Nothing," she said, her whispered reply choked by the tears she had shed. " 'Tis nothing. I am fine."

He advanced closer to where she stood, stopping just short of reaching out to her. She craved his embrace, but he held his hands fisted at his sides as if to keep from touching her. "Did someone hurt you? By the Rood, if someone from the village has come here—"

"No, nothing like that." Serena felt foolish, allowing him to see her so distressed, but it was too late to hide it from him even if she had wanted to. She glanced down, avoiding his keen gaze. "My mother and I . . . we had an argument just now."

"Ah, I see." She could feel some of the tension in him ease at once. "I wager it happens between mothers and daughters sometimes."

"Not us. We have never fought before, not like this." Serena looked up at him. "We quarreled about you."

"Me," he said. His scowl returned, furrowing hard on his brow. "Ah, Christ. This is no good. I have no wish to come between you and your mother."

He pivoted away and stalked toward the ruined chapel behind him. Serena hesitated, watching his deliberate stride, then she was following him, her footsteps careful, uncertain.

"She says you are only using me—that you will discard me without a care if it serves you to do so. But I don't believe her."

He turned around, a flinty look in his eyes. "She is only trying to do what is best for you. She is your mother, she loves you."

"What about you, Rand?" She felt the true question, the one that had been burning in her mind for days, dance its way to the tip of her tongue. She gazed up at him, refusing to let his hard, stubborn stare drive her off. "What is it you feel about me?"

When he did not answer immediately, Serena reached out for him. She stroked the backs of her fingers along his shaven cheek, feeling his rumble of warning curl up from his throat. His hazel eyes were fierce in that instant, but not with anger. She caressed his face, then let her hand glide down to rest above his heart.

"You care for me," she said, even as he grasped her wrist and took her Knowing touch away. "I know you do. Why won't you say it?"

"Because there is no point in it, Serena."

"No point in feeling, or in admitting that you can?"

"There is no point in either," he said, more gently now. He let his hands drift down to her shoulders, then he firmly set her away from him. "Not when I am leaving for Egremont on the morrow."

Although she had suspected as much, Serena's soaring heart plummeted to her feet on collapsed wings. "Tomorrow—so soon."

"I cannot delay any longer. My plans await, and I only give my enemy the advantage if I do not act now that I am able."

"You are hardly strong enough for travel," she pointed out, feeling a terrible desperation at the idea he was actually leaving. "Egremont is a half-day's walk at least, over difficult terrain. Why, from the grove line looking north there is naught but steep hills and sharp ravines—"

He cupped her cheek in his palm, smoothing his thumb across her trembling lips. "I will manage."

Moments stretched to agonizing lengths as Rand held her gaze in thoughtful silence. Serena wanted to plead with him to stay, but she knew he would not. His vengeance was all that mattered to him—had he not told her so, more than once? She knew nothing would hold him once he was ready to resume his journey.

But she had hoped. . . .

"Take me with you." The words slipped from between her lips before she could bite them back. She said it softly, but once uttered, the thought was set in her mind. "Take me with you to Egremont, Rand."

"Take you?" he echoed, disbelief lacing his deep voice. "I cannot do that, Serena. You wouldn't want me to, not really."

"I do," she insisted. "You must."

He frowned and drew away from her slightly. "You only ask this because you are angered with your mother. I expect I have only confused you further these past several days."

Serena exhaled a sharp sigh. "I am not angry or confused. I ask you this because I know that what you've said about my life in these woods is true. I knew it before, although I did not wish to see it. The day is coming when this patch of forest will no longer be safe for my mother and me."

She glanced around at the trees she knew so well, the unseen paths through the bracken, the shaded alcoves that could so easily hide trespassing hunters and other dangers from the outside. Once it had been curiosity that made her yearn to leave the grove. Now it was necessity, and a growing instinct that her sanctuary home was already breached and vanishing before her eyes.

"You've said yourself, Rand, that I cannot stay here forever. Nor can I hope that others will stay out."

"Going to town with me is not the best solution."

"It is," Serena said resolutely. "I need to know what lies beyond the grove line, because after you are gone, I must be prepared to take my mother away from here and make a new life for us somewhere else. Mayhap I will have to make that life without her."

Rand was staring at her dubiously, but he did not deny her outright.

"Take me with you to Egremont. If you care anything

for me, then give me this one boon, Rand. I can go alone, and I will, but I'd rather go with you."

"I don't like it," he growled. "Neither will your mother."

That much was true. Serena was loath to consider how her mother would react to this decision. But it had to be. "She will understand. She'll have to, for my mind is made up."

That next morning, Rand waited outside the cottage while Serena said her farewells to her mother. He listened for raised voices or tearful pleas for Serena to stay, but there was only quiet in the tiny abode. A pall of resignation settled over the place, punctuated by the slow opening of the door.

Serena came out first, with her mother trailing a pace behind her, stoic and unreadable. Serena paused to give her mother a tight embrace. Calandra returned it, her arms lingering even after Serena drew away. Serena would be gone only a day or two at most, but the look in the elder woman's eyes said she feared her daughter would never return.

"No harm will come to her while she is with me," Rand told the white-haired woman. "I will guard her with my life. I give you my vow, Serena will be safe."

Calandra made no reply. With a defeated look in her daughter's direction, she then turned and disappeared back into the cottage in utter silence and closed the door.

❧ 17 ❧

THE TOWN OF Egremont held a charter for a mid-week market, which was fully under way when Rand and Serena entered on the main road into the square. Walking along at his side, her eyes wide with wonder, her gloved hands held clutched together before her, Serena gaped in unabashed delight at the dizzying spectacle of the town and its folk.

Carts filled with vegetables, flowers, and complaining livestock lined the square from the street's wide entryway to the small stone church at its heart. The aromas of roasting meat and fresh bread mingled on a pleasant breeze that blew up from the River Ehen, which cut a generous path through Egremont's southern end.

There were hundreds of people gathered for the market, some dressed in colorful silks, others wearing fur and bossed leather as though garbed for a tourney feast more than a simple country fair. But these wealthy nobles were but a few of the folk strolling the street and bargaining for food and wares. Minor lords and free men were the ones who comprised the bulk of the market's patrons. They mobbed the rows of carts and stalls, haggling in earnest, the confusion of raised voices a wordless din of racket in the street.

Rand guided Serena through the mass of churning bodies, noting her careful composure, and the protective way she held her gloved hands close to her body. There was a note of fear in her wide eyes, but it was amazement that danced in her eager expression.

" 'Tis so loud," she remarked, nearly having to shout to make herself heard above the cacophony. "And so full of people! Do they all live here in Egremont?"

Rand shook his head. He had noticed the insignia of more than one noble house, and from the dress of a few, he guessed them to be travelers in from other parts of the realm.

"Not all," he answered, taking her elbow and smoothly leading her away from a pit where a cockfight had drawn a number of bloodthirsty spectators.

No one paid him any mind as he weaved through the knot of onlookers. For anyone chancing to note them, he and the plain-garbed beauty at his side were all but unremarkable. Arriving in town with no mount beneath him, no weapon strapped to his hip, Rand could have been taken for a pilgrim or a pauper, so long as no one looked close enough to see the battle-ready glint in his warrior gaze as he glanced about the busy market. His commoner's attire of aged tunic, ill-fitting hose, and worn boots were no hindrance. It was better to blend in with the rest of the simple folk in the bustling square than to call attention to himself and Serena. More beneficial to his cause to watch from the shadows of the street than to parade about like one of the strutting, raucous knights he used to be.

A group of such men had just rode into the main thoroughfare, the five of them coming from the direction of a hill road that led down from a castle perched above the town. They wore red and silver, colors matching the pennant that flew atop the castle's highest tower, their surcoats stitched with three argent bars of crimson, their lord's heraldic emblem. Laughing, trading shouted jests with one another over the pound of their horses' hooves, the knights cantered past Rand and Serena in a cloud of yellow dust. One of them, a lanky youth who looked not a year past his dubbing, swept up his visor and tossed an arrogant sneer to the townsfolk as they rushed to get out of the way of the knights' approach.

The lad had a hook nose and snaggled front teeth, and all the prideful idiocy of his tender age. Brandishing a polished length of steel that had likely never tasted another's blood, he whooped a drunken war cry.

"Stand aside, ye beggarly cottars! Lord Thomas de Moulton's garrison is in need of strong ale and willing wenches!"

One of the other knights chuckled over his shoulder at his foolish companion. " 'Tis ale and wenches for you today, Eldrich. Tomorrow 'twill be vomit in your throat and a piss pot in your arms!"

The retinue passed in a loud clatter of gear and good humor, oblivious to all but their own immediate wants. Serena shrank closer to Rand, her gloved fingers clutching his arm in an anxious hold while the group of marketgoers moved off to resume their business. The knights, meanwhile, had dismounted at the alehouse, and disappeared inside.

"Is that what it was like for you onetime?" she asked as they fell into step among the crowd. "Was it laughter and friendship and ale and wenches for Sir Randwulf of Greycliff?"

He smiled, recalling his own arrogant youth. "It was much the same. But it was a long time ago that I earned my spurs as a knight—before Greycliff came into my holding with my father's passing. I was no less a fool than those simple men, however. Glad for my sword and a good long day of riding, provided it ended with a tankard of fine drink in my hand."

"And a willing wench as well?" she prodded, teasing him with a sideways glance as she strolled along beside him.

He gave a shrug and grinned back at her. "That, too."

They passed the busiest section of the market square, and moved toward the stalls that offered metals of both precious and practical uses. Rand paused before a portly vendor whose jowly neck was ringed with gold chains. Spread out before the merchant and displayed on the table atop a swatch of linen was a collection of smooth polished gemstones in hues of smoky brown, richest green, and pale yellow. Beside them, sparkling gold rings and chains of varying thickness glittered in the afternoon sun.

Serena gasped as her eyes lit on the precious jewelry and stones. "Rand, look at these! Have you ever seen anything so beautiful?"

The vendor gave Rand an enterprising smile, clearly pleased with Serena's open admiration of his wares and likely already counting his profits.

She started to comment further on the collection of baubles, but as she looked to Rand, her gaze dipped and she saw that he held Elspeth's pendant in his hand. Her expression was questioning, rather sad. She gave a small shake of her head.

"Rand, you can't mean to sell it."

"It's all right," he said, fisting the gold chain and fili-greed heart in his palm. "I am ready to part with it. I need coin for passage to Scotland, and a sword if I can find a good one at a fair price."

He turned to the man in the vendor's stall. "A fine collection," he said, then placed Elspeth's pendant on the table. "Have you any interest in adding this piece to it?"

The merchant stroked his pink cheeks, his thin mouth turned down as he lifted the necklace to inspect it. He did not appear overly impressed.

"The chain is broken, but it's gold, as is the pendant."

A disinterested grunt was the only immediate response from behind the table. Finally, the man blew out a sigh that reeked of garlic and shook his head. He let the pendant slide off the ends of his stubby fingers onto the linen-covered table. "Fifteen shillings."

Rand bit back the oath that rose to his lips. "Too low. I paid more than that years ago when I bought it in London."

"Aye, well, this isn't London," the vendor informed him with a smug look.

Rand considered snatching the pendant back. He also considered grabbing the fat little man by his velvet overtunic and shaking loose from his jangling purses what the necklace was truly worth. But he needed whatever he could get, and so he held his tongue and his bruising temper.

Beside him, he saw Serena fidget, but knew not what she was doing until her ungloved hand reached out to clamp lightly on the seller's hairy wrist. The man looked down, frowning at the unseemly contact, but Serena's smile was sweetly innocent, and it took only an instant for his expression to relax into a leering male appreciation.

"This pendant is exquisite. Surely 'tis worth a bit more than what you've offered?"

He sputtered, now looking to Rand in reproach. "What manner of man allows a woman to bargain on his behalf?"

"This one," Rand replied, watching Serena's gaze sharpen with the Knowing. "How much is it worth?"

"Twenty shillings," the vendor answered tersely. He wrenched his wrist out of Serena's easy hold, rubbing his skin where her fingers had gripped him. "I'll not pay a farthing more than that."

"He can get thirty-five when he takes his wares to Liverpool next month," Serena advised Rand as she slyly turned away from the table and slipped her glove back on.

"I'll take no less than thirty-three," Rand told him. "Or mayhap I should try my luck in Liverpool. No doubt I would get fairer treatment there."

"What—" The man muttered something foul under his breath, eyeing Serena narrowly as she casually stepped away to peruse a different stall of goods. He dropped a purse heavy with coin on the table and yanked it open, counting out a sum. He slammed the silver down and glowered at Rand. "Very well. Thirty-three it is. Take it and be gone."

"My thanks," Rand said, retrieving his money and saluting the grousing vendor with a courtly bow of his head.

When he caught up to Serena, she was smiling with total satisfaction.

"That was rather foolish of you, my lady."

She waved him off, unconcerned. "I just wanted to help you."

"Well, do not."

She turned to him now, a serious look in her eyes. "I'd like to help you, Rand."

"What do you mean?"

"I was able to get you the coin you needed. Mayhap the Knowing can be useful to you in some other way."

"No." He shook his head. "No, don't even think it,

Serena. I've already involved you too far—all the worse, now that I've brought you here to Egremont. I will not let you be a part of this. Not in any way."

"I am a part of it." She lifted her hand and placed it against his cheek. The leather was cool and soft on his skin, her gaze tender but determined. "I'm a part of it, because I care what happens to you. Don't you see that?"

He was about to argue that he would not permit her to help him specifically because he cared about her as well, but then a coarse shout brought his head up at once.

"My God! Someone help me—ah, Christ!"

The panicked cry sounded from somewhere nearby, followed by a shriek of pure terror. Something about it cut straight through to Rand's marrow, raising his hackles in dread.

"Stay here," he ordered Serena, moving her to the side of an overflowing flower cart near the edge of the street, out of the milling crowd. He took her slim shoulders in his hands, holding her firmly. "Wait for me, do you understand? Do not move!"

She swallowed hard, nodded her head in compliance.

Rand took off at once. Some of the townsfolk had begun to rush toward the scene as well. He shoved through the center of them, his battle instincts on alert. He rounded the alehouse, which dumped him into the head of a narrow alleyway. A young knight stood before him, panting, clearly frightened out of his wits. It was the snaggle-toothed lad he'd seen riding into the town square a short while ago. His companions must have just arrived to his aid as well, for he was rushing to explain his alarm and taking a good beating for his cry of panic.

"Well, what was it, lad—a man or a wolf?"

"Aye, Eldrich! 'Tis not hard to tell the two apart, after all—even in yer drunken state!"

" 'Twas a wolf that attacked me!" he insisted.

One of the older knights calmed the others with a low whistle. "This is a town full of people, lad. Would no one notice a beast such as you say traipsing through the streets in broad daylight?"

"I know what I saw, Gervaise! I was taking a piss, an' when I turned around, the man who'd been sleeping right there"—he pointed to a shadowed corner of the alley—"was gone, and a beast was standing there as you are now. 'Cept, he was slavering and growling, not gaping at me like ye fools."

The knights traded glances, then burst into chortling laughter. "Have another tankard, Eldrich. Mayhap you'll see a dragon next time you come out to water the alley."

"I'm telling ye the truth, ye addled sots! I chased it off with my sword—the beast would've killed me for certes, had I not given him a taste of my blade!"

"Aye, of course he would've," gibed another of the men. "Come along, then, our great beastmaster. Ye can buy us each a cup back inside and tell us all about it."

The group of knights moved on, but Eldrich stayed for a moment, looking up at the dozen faces that now watched him in a mixture of disbelief and guarded scorn. One old woman braved a snort of laughter under her breath before her husband led her away. Soon the others left, too, and it was just Rand and the young knight standing in the empty alleyway.

"I'm not lying," Eldrich said with sullen conviction. "I'm not so drunk that I don't know what I saw."

"I believe you."

He glanced up, surprise flashing in his drink-glazed eyes. "Ye do?"

Rand nodded. "This wolf—was it black-furred, immense?"

"Aye!" Eldrich confirmed. "As big as you, I wager. Nay, bigger!"

"Which way did it go?"

"I cannot say. It ran off when I yelled for help. I went after it—to the end of the building there—but when I looked, there was no sign of it in either direction."

Rand understood at once, knowing it was part of the beast's skill that he could hide in plain sight, vanishing into a crowd in nary a blink of movement. God's love, but it might have passed Serena and him in the street not a moment ago.

"And you injured it, you said?"

At this the knight puffed out his chest. "I am one of Lord Thomas de Moulton's knights, sirrah, a proud defender of Castle Egremont. I am expertly trained with my weapon, and my aim is true. That beast will not survive the night—wherever it may have fled to."

Rand doubted the prediction, but he said nothing to dampen the youth's pride, ale-soaked as it was. He had greater concerns at present. His thoughts were already speeding toward a dread that had naught to do with the stripling knight before him.

The wolf sighting in town was a bad sign, for the large black animal that Eldrich described was no mere rogue predator, venturing into human terrain. It was no animal at all, leastwise not in the sense that fools like Eldrich would understand. Animals such as these were none that naturally trod this earth. Rand had seen the like himself—at Greycliff the night of the attack, and on the ship that would have carried him to Scotland. And he knew the nature of the beasts well enough to be certain that where there was one, there would undoubtedly soon be more.

"I've a mind to go after it and finish the bloody mongrel off. I wager I'd look as fine as any lord, riding into battle with a wolfskin cloak around my shoulders," boasted Eldrich, flashing his crooked leer as he sheathed his weapon. He sniffed arrogantly as he brushed past Rand without another word, heading back into the alehouse to join his companions.

As for Rand, more and more he was regretting his decision to let Serena accompany him to Egremont. If Silas de Mortaine's shapeshifter sentries were in the area, then they had to be on the trail of the Dragon Chalice as well. Their villainous overlord could not be far behind them.

Rand headed back for the street, his muscles taut, his step brisk with purpose.

Serena was waiting where he had left her, standing bravely near the cart of flowers while the press of the market crowd ebbed and flowed around her. Rand walked up to her in haste, taking her hand in his to lead her away from curious ears.

"What is it?" Serena looked up at him, likely reading the dread in his eyes. "What has happened?"

"Shifter," Rand told her, speaking the word at little more than a whisper.

Although her gaze widened in sudden fear, she maintained her calm. "Here? In Egremont?"

Rand gave her a sober nod. "It nearly killed one of those knights at the alehouse when he provoked it unawares."

"Mother Mary." Her face went pale as frost. "Did you see it yourself?"

"Nay. The beast has fled, but I do not wager it's gone

far. The streets are not secure, my lady. They will be less so once evening falls."

He pulled the small pouch of coins from out of his boot.

"Come, Serena. I don't want you out here any longer. Let us find safe quarters for the night."

✲ 18 ✲

"WON'T YOU HAVE some of this with me?" Serena asked, after they had found a room and a meal at one of Egremont's small inns. "This—mutton, did you call it?—is delicious."

Rand only grunted, shaking his head.

There was no table in their small quarters, only a bed with a fur coverlet and one thin bolster. A squat wooden stool comprised the rest of the furnishings, which was where Rand had seated himself since their arrival. But if the lodgings were sparse, the tavern's food more than compensated. Serena sat on the edge of the bed's hard-packed down mattress, enjoying the warm meal of roasted meat and boiled vegetables. Rand had procured a flagon of wine, too, which Serena found to be a curious drink—too potent at first, then mellowing with each further sip she took from her cup.

"There's plenty to eat for both of us," she told him, concerned that he seemed so tense and preoccupied. So distant. "You should have something, Rand."

He held a cup of wine in both hands, his shoulders hunched, elbows braced on his spread knees. For long moments, from nearly the time he sat down, Rand merely stared into the battered tin cup, his face drawn in dark contemplation.

They had not spoken of the danger they had narrowly avoided in town that day, but it was plain that Rand's thoughts were fixed on his enemies and the confrontation that seemed to be drawing ever closer, even as they sat together in the candlelit peace of the modest inn.

"Tomorrow," he said, speaking at last, "as soon as it is light, I'll take you back to the grove."

"There is no need," she told him, knowing that had not been part of their agreement. "I know the way now. I can make it back home on my own."

"I will take you," he insisted, and the look in his eyes was steely with determination.

"What about Scotland?"

"It will have to wait."

"But if that knight in the market square truly saw what he said he did—a shifter—then the man you seek cannot be far behind. Isn't that so?"

He did not confirm it, but Serena knew it was true. She knew that it was this troubling fact that had put the grimness in Rand's mood. He lifted his cup and downed the wine in one gulp. Then he rose from the stool and stalked over to the bed, pouring himself another serving of the rich claret.

"Rand." When he set the flagon down, Serena reached out to him, placing her hand lightly over his. "Tell me what this is about—all of it. If this man commands these beasts, these shapeshifters, then what does that make him?"

"A monster," Rand answered, and from the stark tone of his voice, Serena knew he spoke in utter honesty now. He took a drink of his wine, then leveled a grave look on her before stepping away to lean his shoulder against the timber wall of the chamber. "I don't even know if he's human. Certainly if ever he was, there is naught left in him that's truly alive anymore."

Serena weathered a shudder as she considered the sort of creature that was Rand's enemy. She knew so little of villainy, had no true examples of evil outside of that which lived in dark fairy tales. She could hardly guess at the diabolical purpose that might drive someone—man or monster—to wreak so much destruction and pain. "What is it about the treasure you carried with you that makes this man crave it so? Why should a cup be worth so much?"

Rand's chuckle was hollow, almost brittle. "It is not the cup so much as it is the power that resides within it."

"What kind of power?"

"Wealth. Strength. The security that comes in knowing there is nothing beyond your grasp, and that none exists who could rise and stand against you. Immortality, my lady. That is the Dragon Chalice's greatest promise."

"Dragon Chalice?" Serena tilted her head, feeling a mix of confusion and mild incredulity at the mention of the name. "The Dragon Chalice isn't real," she said, carefully now, for Rand was staring at her most peculiarly. " 'Tis a fanciful tale—my mother used to tell me about the mythical treasure when I was a little girl."

"You know of the treasure?"

"I know the story—that of an enchanted Chalice bearing four magic gemstones in its bowl."

"What more do you know?" Rand asked, a certain hesitance in his voice. "Have you seen the Chalice?"

"Nay, of course not," Serena replied, shaking her head. "No one has. 'Tis myth, that's all."

Rand was utter seriousness now. "Tell me the tale as you have heard it, Serena."

"Very well."

She proceeded to recite the story that had long been one of her favorites. She explained how the Dragon Chalice was stolen from a glorious kingdom by an evil warrior. How that kingdom's magic had broken the enchanted goblet into four smaller cups, each bearing one precious stone imbued with otherworldly power. A sorcerer's spell then scattered the Dragon Chalice across the mortal realm, where the pieces lie in wait, even now, for a noble soul to restore the Chalice and bring the lost kingdom back to glory. She told him of the dread prophecy, which proclaimed that if the treasure was returned by trickery, or in the hands of a man unworthy of its power, the lost kingdom would face an eternity of enslavement by a great and terrible dragon.

When she finished, Rand's brow was knit above the intensity of his gaze. "Jesu."

" 'Twas one of my favorite stories," Serena added, but seeing his grim expression was making it difficult to cling to the idea that the Dragon Chalice tale was pure myth. "My mother said it has long been known to our kin. The story has been passed through the generations for many years."

"Whatever your mother told you, it is no fairy story, Serena. I have seen the Dragon Chalice—or part of it, at the least. It is real, so is its power. And so are the villains who seek it for their own gain."

Serena swallowed a bitter sip of wine, supposing, just for a moment, that what Rand was telling her now was true. "What about you? You're after the Chalice as well. What will you do with it?"

"Destroy it, if I must. Anything to keep it from the clutches of Silas de Mortaine."

Familiar yet distant, the name flitted through Serena's mind like a hint of brewing storm. "The man who ordered the attack of Greycliff?"

"Aye. The monster who called for me and my family to be slaughtered in our beds by his changeling beasts. He is also the man who took my friend Kenrick of Clairmont prisoner because of his study of the Chalice."

"Kenrick is your friend who gave his heart to the shifter, Haven."

"The very one. Kenrick had discovered much about the treasure in his work for the church some years ago. He recorded his findings in a series of ledgers, not aware that it was de Mortaine who commissioned them. When Kenrick realized who he was inadvertently serving, he took steps to hide his work. Some he kept near him at his castle home; one crucial piece—something no one knew existed—was entrusted to me."

"The object that the shifters sought when they raided Greycliff," Serena said, understanding now.

Rand nodded. "A metal seal that would act as a key in unlocking one of the four Chalice pieces, once its location was found. We had no time to search, for not long after Kenrick gave me the seal, he was captured by de Mortaine and held hostage."

"For how long?"

"Six months, more or less. De Mortaine ransomed him to his family, demanding Kenrick's findings pertaining to the Dragon Chalice. Kenrick's sister, Ariana, all he had left after their father passed while Kenrick was away, was given the charge of delivering the information to de Mortaine."

"And did she do this?" Serena asked, curling her legs beneath her on the bed. She took a drink of her wine, needing its warmth for the anxious chill that was growing inside her. "Did Ariana surrender Kenrick's findings to this man?"

"Not all. She allied herself with a mercenary called the Hunter, and together they cleverly freed Kenrick from his captivity." Rand chuckled a bit, as though recalling the details. "That, however, is a long tale in itself, and one better saved for another time."

Serena watched him for a long moment, unmoving,

gripped with a sudden sorrow. A fear clung to her as she gazed at Rand and understood the day was coming that they would part forever.

"Rand," she whispered, "if, as you intend, you do confront this man—this Silas de Mortaine—will you . . . do you think you can defeat him?"

"If I had the piece of the Chalice I lost in the storm, perhaps. If I had that and the piece Kenrick has told me likely rests in a chapel in Scotland, then it is possible that I could defeat de Mortaine."

"And if you have none of that power to aid you, will you still seek him out?"

Rand turned his gaze to the wobbling flame of the candles. There was determination in his eyes, but also a note of flat acceptance. "He must be stopped, Serena. He is evil, and I have made a vow. Not only to the memory of Elspeth and Tod, but to Kenrick as well. My honor demands this of me. Silas de Mortaine must pay for what he has done."

"Even at the cost of your own life?"

He looked at her now, and nodded gravely. "Even then."

She wanted to curse his bloody honor, but could form no words. She wanted to beg him to abandon his plan, but she knew there was nothing to hold him back.

Not even her love, for that was what she felt for him.

The sweet ache, the tender thrill just to be near him, could be nothing less than love. And the misery in knowing he did not feel the same for her—perhaps never could—bred a desperation in her to cling to him even tighter, especially when she knew he would soon be leaving her.

But she loved him more than that. Enough to accept that she could not keep him, no matter how dearly she wanted to beg him to return with her to the cottage on the morrow and live the rest of his days at her side. His honor would not permit that. He would take her back to the grove, but then he would leave to carry out his plans.

Serena turned away from him and his rigid principles—his honor, which would get him killed sooner than later—and stretched out on the bed. She pressed her cheek into the bolster, determined not to think of what lay ahead of Rand in his damnable quest for revenge.

"You must be tired," he said, misreading her sudden sulkiness. "I'll leave the food here beside the bed, should you want anything more."

She heard the soft scrape of the wooden tray on the floor.

"Sleep well, Serena," he whispered, and stung her further by gifting her with a chaste kiss to her temple.

He did not stretch out beside her, even to be practical and share the meager warmth. He walked away, his feet padding quietly on the floor. There was a short puff of breath across the small room, and then the lights were extinguished.

The bed remained cold. The space beside her was empty, the room dark, and too soon morning would come.

She could not sleep.

Serena tossed in the bed, restless in the unfamiliar surroundings, and her senses too attuned to the fact that Rand was awake in the room as well. Finally she sat up on the mattress.

"What is it?" he asked her, his muscular bulk leaning up against the wall beside the bed.

Serena pushed her hair out of her face and held her hand out to him in the dark. "Come up here. There is no point in you trying to sleep on the floor when the bed is large enough for both of us."

"I'm not trying to sleep."

"What are you doing?"

"Thinking. And watching you."

She slipped out from beneath the fur coverlet and moved to the edge of the bed where he sat on the floor. He was still dressed, but his tunic was unlaced at the throat, and his boots rested nearby.

"Come up here with me."

For a long moment, he did not move or speak.

"Rand. Sit with me." She held her hand out to him once more, fingers bare and outstretched. "Lie down with me."

His voice was rough in the dark. "I think that would be a mistake."

"Why?"

"It could lead to more."

"I am not afraid."

He exhaled a tortured-sounding laugh, but then he was moving, slowly coming to his feet beside the bed. He peered at her through the gloom of the lightless chamber; his touch was gentle as he smoothed away an errant tendril of her hair. "Are you truly so fearless, Serena of the grove?"

"I think so," she answered, smiling as his warm fingers curled around hers. She drew him back with her on the bed. "Isn't this better than the floor?"

He didn't say anything. He was gazing at her in a sort of potent silence. Poised over her, his weight braced on one hand, he merely looked at her and Serena felt a strumming warmth begin to pool from somewhere deep inside of her. The quiet anticipation of something more to come stretched out to agony, but then Rand dipped his head and kissed her.

Serena drifted into his kiss with abandon, wrapping her arms about his neck and eagerly parting her lips to him when his tongue pressed for entry. His mouth was sweet heaven on hers, hot and demanding, and just a bit wild. He kissed her until she was breathless, then caught her head in his hands and kissed her some more.

"Come, then," he murmured against her mouth. "Lie back with me."

He took her by the wrist, and eased back on the furs, smoothly guiding her toward him. He moved to lace his fingers through hers, bringing her hand down against his chest. Serena stiffened with an instinctual resistance. She drew her fingers back, fisting them against her breast. She could not touch him. For all her bravado about not being afraid, she was suddenly terrified. She was afraid to shatter these perfect moments they were sharing.

"What's wrong?"

Serena gazed down at him, her tongue thick behind her teeth.

"Have I hurt you somehow? Are you all right?"

She swallowed hard, forced herself to speak. "I am not her, Rand."

His scowl deepened. He sat back slightly, giving her a small measure of space.

"I'm not Elspeth. I need to know that you know that. I'm not her, no matter how you might wish it—"

"God's love." He raked a hand through his hair, tousling the dark chestnut waves. "Is that what you think? That I look at you and wish you were someone else?"

"Elspeth," she said again, needing to put the name out there even though it pained her to allow her ghost into the room, into this exquisite, torturous moment. "I am not her, Rand. I need to hear you say that you know this. That you accept me. Just . . . me."

"Serena, I have never—"

"Yes, you have," she whispered. "You have compared me to her in many ways. And that early morning, when you came upon me at the falls, you called her name."

"Ah, that." He gave her a remorseful look. "I explained that to you—my disorientation, feeling like I was reliving the night of the raid. It meant nothing. Once I saw you, I knew where I was. I knew who you were."

Serena gave a sad little shake of her head. "You reached out to me, but it was her name on your lips, her name in your touch. I felt it. The Knowing never lies."

"It is you, Serena. Now, as it was that day." His expression became grim, solemn. "Have you any idea how I've had to fight my feelings for you? I have, from the moment I first opened my eyes on that beach and saw you gazing down at me. I didn't want to be attracted to you, Serena. I didn't want to feel anything—not for anyone—until this thing I must do is done. I never wanted to drag you into this."

When she would have inched away from him, he caught her hand in his and held it, firmly yet with a tenderness that made her ache. He brought her back to him, guiding her fingers to the open neckline of his tunic. He placed her open palm against his chest. His heart thudded, strong and warm beneath her fingertips.

"The Knowing never lies," he said, repeating her own words now. "Touch me, and know that it is you I want. It is you I desire, Serena of the grove." He shook his head slowly. "Though why that pleases you I shall never understand."

Serena reveled in the beating warmth of his skin, the crisp hairs on his chest tickling her palm. Very slowly, the Knowing stretched and awakened, showing her the keen pleasure he felt as he reclined in the nest of furs,

watching her stroke the muscular slabs of his chest, the
coiling hunger that gripped him as her fingertips teased
the flat buds of his nipples into small, tight pebbles.

She needed no gift of touch to understand the heated
look in his eyes. It burned through her, simmering embers that sparked in his dark gaze and seemed to settle
someplace deep inside of her, where she was boneless
and needful, where she was melting.

He was holding himself back, she realized. Like men-
tal chains holding him down, he lashed his need for her
with a seething restraint, finding a greater pleasure in
her slow exploration of his body. Serena learned the
contours of every sinewed inch of his broad shoulders,
his strong chest, and his ridged belly. She braved to venture farther down, to where the loose waistband of his
braies met the lacings of his hose.

Rand groaned as her fingertips slid beneath the fabric,
caressing his skin, which twitched under her careful,
tentative discovery. He was both soft and hard, patient
and demanding in his silent observation of her. Serena
delighted in his contrasts, and in the burning, hooded
look in his eyes. That look deepened as she slid her hand
across the uppermost line of his slim pelvis. She drew
in a little breath as she brushed the velvet tip of his
manhood, which stretched greedily toward her questing
fingers. Surprised, curious, she returned to it, and delicately traced its thick, bulbous cap. From its very tip, it
wept a silky bead of warmth, slicking her fingers as she
marveled at its astonishing form.

"Serena," Rand murmured, a feral sound that made
her pause.

He sat up a bit straighter on the bed and dragged her
to him for a kiss. Somehow, as he plundered her mouth
and stirred her toward a mindlessness she could only
surrender to, he stripped off his clothes. He was naked

before her, glorious in his nudity. Serena's mouth went dry looking upon him, he was so magnificent.

"Now you," he said, roughly whispering the words below her ear as he kissed her some more.

With patient, trembling hands, he undressed her. Serena knew no uncertainty, no shame, as he slowly bared her body to his smoldering, hooded gaze. Her simple bliaut fell away to the floor, then her pale chemise.

"Beauty," Rand named her, drawing back to look at her fully. "My God, Serena. You are so exquisite. My woodland nymph."

She smiled, feeling her lips curve under his praising words and the fierce, hungry look in his eyes. He lifted her hand to his mouth and placed a kiss in her palm. He pressed her down beneath him, resting her back onto the plush warmth of the fur. His mouth was hot on her breast, his tongue laving her in rapturous sensuality.

Where he touched her body, his large hands skimming down along her ribs, to her abdomen, to the crisp thatch of curls between her legs, Serena dissolved in mindless delight. She squirmed against him, quaking and sighing as he now took his time exploring her. More than once, his strong fingers drifted to the dampening cleft between her thighs. Each time he stroked her more boldly, until she felt him delve between her slick folds, and deeper still, the tip of his finger breaching that most sacred part of her.

His name was a shaky gasp on her lips. "Oh, God," she whispered, shocked and so very delirious with pleasure as he teased her with his wicked touch. "Rand . . . yes."

He went deeper, and she could not hold back her cry. She knew not what he was doing to her, or how he knew just where she needed him the most, but eagerly she let him play her as he wanted, surrendering to him completely.

"Touch me," he commanded her between fevered kisses. He guided her to the stiff rod that pressed so deliciously against her belly. "I want to feel your hands on me."

Serena obliged him gladly, taking his length in her hand and stroking him as he moved her over him in a teaching rhythm. Soon he was aiding her, thrusting into her grasp, his breath soughing harshly at her ear.

"I need to be in you."

She understood what he wanted. The part of her that would take him within was urging her toward the same thing, throbbing with want for him. Serena could not voice her need, but she lifted up and kissed him, her hand bringing his sex down between her legs.

"When we join," he whispered, his voice thick, breaking off in a curse. "Oh, sweetest heart, I cannot do this without hurting you. If the pain is too great—"

"Shh, I'm not afraid." Serena shook her head, cradling his face in her hands. She lifted up to kiss him, delighting in the heated mesh of their lips, and lower, the dizzying torment of their bodies pressed so intimately together. "There is no pain when I am touching you," she murmured against his mouth. "I am not afraid of this, Rand. I've never wanted anything more."

His answering growl rumbled through her body. He bent his head and kissed her deeply, sucking her lip between his teeth, penetrating her mouth with his tongue. He curled his arms beneath her shoulders, holding her against him, a firm, possessive imprisonment that she hoped never to escape. With his knee, he edged her thighs farther apart, until his pelvis settled fully between them, his sex like a thick length of fire-warmed steel nestling in her moist cleft.

Serena thought she would perish for the astonishing sensation of his shaft caressing her with fluid motion, teasing without entering, the smooth, liquid slide stoking a flame within her very core. She moved with him, needing more, delirious with the sweet, deep ache he bred in her.

Rand broke their kiss and stared down at her, his eyes dark as midnight. His clean-shaven jaw was taut, clenched; the corded muscles in his neck bulging with the rigidity that seemed to engulf him. He dipped his head down once more, nipping her mouth, then bent lower, suckling her breast.

And all the while, he rocked against her, his hard length slipping between her folds until her sex was weeping for him. Serena gasped his name, her spine arched, her fingers clutching at him, needing him closer. He lifted his head, letting her tight nipple slip from between his softly abrading teeth.

The Knowing lashed at her like a tempest, drawing Rand's emotion with little resistance. He did not fight it, but fed it, she realized, all his desire for her dousing her in wave after wave of heat and hunger. He wanted to show her everything, to open her eyes to the world, and to the passion that ran so wild within him.

"Show me," she whispered, panting now, willing to beg him. "Please, show me."

All for you, said the Knowing.

"Only you," said Rand, holding her gaze with an intensity that robbed her breath.

He shifted, and now that hard, demanding part of him was poised like an arrow at the mouth of her womb. He gave a nudge of his hips, seating the blunt tip of him, and then he pushed, watching her eyes as the pressure built and her body prepared to accept his.

"Yes," she sighed. "Rand . . . yes . . ."

He thrust forward, and filled her with a fullness that defied description. Heat spread from her most feminine core, to her heart . . . all the way to her soul. Not pain, but a sharpness of her senses, a sudden awakening. An elemental wisdom.

The Knowing, for all of its unyielding hold on her, was strangely silent now, as though shamed mute by the force of this new feeling.

Rand began to move within her, slowly at first, easing her into his rhythm. Back and forth, thrusting and withdrawing, filling and denying. Serena was lost to the bliss of his lovemaking. She held on to him in near-weeping need, clinging to him and praying for no end to this magical night. A wondrous fluidity began to swirl within her as he rocked above her, the hard length of him creating a wondrous friction that both eased and aroused her. It caught her like a leaf in a funnel of water, spinning and weightless.

Serena rode the feeling, which engulfed her more with Rand's every masterful thrust. She could not hold it, for the power of this thing he gave her was too wild. It broke free like a wave, roaring over, engulfing her even as it lifted her, carrying her up . . . up, toward a blissful disintegration. She cried out in wonder, and a joy so pure it made her want to weep. She did, her tears spilling down her temples and into her hair.

"God," Rand panted now, increasing his urgency, his manhood seeming to grow bolder, harder, with his every plunging stroke.

Serena only crested higher, lost in another wave of sensation. Rand's body was hard as granite beneath her hands. His hips pumped deeper, once, again, again . . . then again, deeper still. He held this last one, throwing back his head and giving a guttural shout as a tremor shook him. Serena held him tight against her, marveling

❧ 19 ❧

THE SUN CLIMBED toward noontide as Rand and Serena paused to rest and break their fast on the way back from Egremont the next day. He watched her nibble on the brown bread and roasted meat he had bought for them on their way out of town, knowing that if he possessed even a scrap of honor, he should be regretting the night before.

He wasn't regretting it. He was savoring the memory of their lovemaking, recalling the ecstasy of Serena's hands on him, her lips on him . . . and the shattering pleasure of being sheathed within the heat of her soft, welcoming body. They had made love twice more last night at the inn; their joining seemed only to create a greater hunger, where it should have sated.

Rand wanted her again, still. He had wanted her from the moment he first opened his eyes that morn, but he held himself in check. Serena was new to passion, and he did not want to push her tender body past what she could bear. But his desire for her was fierce, helped none at all by the becoming picture she made as she sat atop a moss-cushioned boulder, surrounded in sunlight spangles and the fetching glow of a woman well pleasured. Her long ebony hair was yet damp from the quick bath they had taken in the River Ehen outside town. It draped about her like a cloak, so dark against her faded bliaut, her ravens-wing pate shining in the midday sun.

at the sudden, filling heat that poured out of him and into the heart of her womb.

"My God," he swore, collapsing atop her and nestling his face into her neck. "Why did you let me do this? Why didn't you turn me away?"

He sounded so weary, so needful. Serena wrapped her arms around him, and stroked his sweat-sheened back with loving hands.

"Why did you let me take this from you tonight?"

"You didn't take it, Rand." She pressed a kiss to his silky dark hair. "Tonight was yours. I think this night was yours from the moment the tide first washed you up onto my beach."

Serena smiled at him as she passed Rand the wineskin. "I nearly hated to leave Egremont this morning. Would that we could have stayed at the inn for another sennight."

"Just another night alone might well have been the death of me," he teased. "Although I cannot think of a more pleasing way to go."

Rand took the skin from her fingers and lifted the claret to his mouth. He had a long, quenching drink, but was thirsty for the wine-kissed sheen that glossed Serena's lips. He passed it back to her, every nerve and sinew already stirring with need of her.

Their fingers brushed in contact, hers ungloved and warm, his twitching with the urge to catch her hand, to ease her down off her seat of speckled granite and into his waiting arms. A blanket of tiny blossoms spread out beneath the boulder like a fragrant carpet of white and gold. It would make a fine backdrop for her beautiful, naked, supine body, he thought with too little shame. In a heartbeat, he was already picturing her there as he covered her, as he took her once again.

Control, he cautioned himself, to small avail.

The forest was quiet save the twittering of birds high above, and the gentle rustle of green summer leaves all around them. They had made good progress back from town, and there had been no hint of danger on their heels. They would be back at the cottage in a couple of short hours . . . too soon, when Serena's ocean-colored gaze was dancing with warmth and invitation.

With her hair sifting down around her arms, her pale skin as clear as milk but for the pink roses of her sudden blush, Serena looked every bit the sweet woodland nymph. Nay, he thought an instant later. Not a nymph, but a royal forest queen, seated atop her throne and gifting her consort with a private look of seduction. Looking at her now, his pulse thrummed hard with the memory of her lovely body arching and writhing beneath him in carnal release. In that moment, Rand wanted nothing more than to lay her down in the blanket of tiny white and gold blossoms at their feet and ravish her completely.

He swallowed on a throat suddenly gone dry. "Perhaps we'd better move on now."

Serena smiled, her Knowing touch lingering on his fingers. "If you were to pull me into your arms and make love to me again, right there among the flowers, you should know that I'd not say a word against it. A forest queen would never refuse the desires of her dearest consort, no matter how wicked they might be."

Rand chuckled. "Can I keep no secrets from your witch's gift, my lady?"

"None," she replied, ruthless in her power over him.

He laughed lightly, but his intentions were dark with sensual intrigue. "In that case, my willing queen, mayhap we'll start up here on your throne, before I lay you down in your bed of woodland blossoms."

Her eager servant, Rand smoothed his hands beneath her skirts, baring her to his gaze. He bowed over her, then kissed a solemn homage up her slender calves and satiny thighs, to the sweetest petals he would ever know.

"As my royal duty," he whispered, sipping at her with his tongue and lips, delighting in her every breathless gasp, "I don't think I shall stop until you are weeping from pleasure."

"Oh, yes," she whispered, her voice catching on a sigh. "As your queen, I command it."

And so Rand happily obliged.

All her praying had been for naught. Calandra realized the truth of it the instant she spied Serena returning

through the woods from Egremont. She and the man—
the Outsider, Randwulf of Greycliff—walked together
along the forest's narrow path toward the cottage.

It surprised her to see him coming back when it had
not been in his plan to do so. It dismayed her, for she
had thought that in taking Serena to see the town, he
would, at least, be gone. Calandra wondered at his mo-
tive. Did he return to search once more for the treasure
he claimed was his? Had he decided Serena could prove
a useful tool to him, as Calandra suspected he eventually
would? Or was it something . . . other?

Serena's hair was unbound, dancing around her on
the breeze. Her hands were ungloved, including the one
that was slipped so easily into his. They talked in familiar cadence, hushed voices and flashing smiles. Calandra
inched back into a wedge of shade, silent with dread.

They did not see her watching. Newly come from her
morning at prayer within the woods, she had heard the
soft murmur of voices. She knew it was them, and
paused behind a thicket of hemlock, all her breath sucked
out of her. All her hopes of keeping this last of her kin
safe were dashed in an instant. Serena was lost to the
world outside the grove now; Calandra knew it for
certes. This man had corrupted her with his false kind-
nesses and empty friendship.

But that was not all.

As Calandra peered through the bracken, she saw
Rand bend to kiss Serena full on the mouth. He had
something in his other hand—a sprig of tiny yellow
flowers, which he smilingly tucked behind her ear.
Serena's blush told all. Her willing kiss, her intimate
manner with him . . .

Calandra turned away at once, stricken.

She had failed the child terribly. She had tried to protect her from this, just as she had tried to protect the others from making her same mistakes.

They never listened.

They never learned.

And in the end, one by one, the Outside world had killed them all.

Calandra retreated before Serena and Rand could draw near enough to discern her presence. Perhaps there was a way to make him leave for good. Perhaps there was one last thing she could do to ensure Serena did not suffer anything further in letting herself care for this warring man.

It was likely the only way.

She should have done it from the very beginning, after it was clear the man who washed ashore would not perish there as she had hoped.

With desperation dogging each step, Calandra set her feet onto another path, which led deep into the other side of the forest.

❧ 20 ❧

HE HAD INTENDED to leave once he knew Serena was safely escorted home from Egremont, but somehow a few hours became a day and then a night, and then another morning. Rand could not credit his reluctance to leave as simple lust for Serena, although he had that in ample supply. She occupied his thoughts, and he could not recall a time when he had ever felt so . . . at peace. He enjoyed her companionship, her easy nature, her intriguing way of seeing life.

He enjoyed her passion as well, for never had he known a more responsive, giving lover.

In the day that they had been returned from Egremont, Rand conspired to spend his every spare moment with her, manufacturing reasons why he should accompany Serena through her daily work about the cottage and in the grove. He told himself that his concern was purely protective, that he meant to keep her near so he could keep her safe. While that was true, he had to admit his motives were not entirely so honorable.

After that first taste of intimacy in Egremont, and on the way back, Rand's desire for her had become insatiable. But this hunger was itself part of his newfound peace with Serena; the smoldering need in his body, the yearning in his heart, while consuming, had brought him to life once more.

He could not keep from glancing at her now, where

she stood in the shaded overhang of the fishing cove, observing his attempts to net their supper. He was an able hunter on land with bow and arrow, but this was proving embarrassing. Serena had made it look so effortless, almost artful, the way she had cast the net out over the tidal pool. Each time Rand tried, the fish darted out in all directions, eluding him.

"You don't have to do this," Serena called from behind him, her back pressed against the darkened rock of the sheltering crag.

"What manner of provider am I if I cannot feed my lady a decent sup?"

He let fly the net, then cursed roundly as his quarry evaded him once more.

Serena laughed. "You might try singing to them instead. If you ask the fish nicely, they might come to you."

"You have your methods," he grumbled, "and I have mine."

"Aye," she agreed, too easily. "Mine work, and yours, well . . ."

Rand shot her a wry look over his shoulder, then turned and flung the net out once more, aiming for a clustered school of fish that had just gathered nearby. As expected, not one remained as he pulled the sodden net in. But he was not about to admit defeat. His failures only made him more determined to triumph. As he hauled in the empty net, Rand had spotted a fat ocean trout nibbling on a patch of seaweed not far from where he stood.

"As my method is proving inadequate, perhaps another is in order," he said, lifting a brow in Serena's direction. With the net bunched in one hand, he reached down with the other and grabbed the dagger from his belt.

"Wait!" Serena called. "Do not—"

He probably wouldn't have released the blade, but Serena launched herself at him and it was all he could do to catch her from knocking them both into the water. He was chuckling, and it took but a moment for her to realize he had only meant to tease her.

"Oh!" she exclaimed, smiling as he brought the net around her waist and pulled her up against him.

"Mayhap my methods are not so lacking after all," he said, holding her firmly to his body. "Who needs supper when there is a delectable siren in one's net?"

She giggled, not even trying to escape him. "You are getting me all wet."

Rand grinned. "Oh, I do hope so."

He bent toward her and kissed her, feeling her breath rush in and out as the tide lapped around them in the granite alcove. Rand caught her mass of dark hair in his hands and let it spill between his fingers, an ebony cascade. He rained a string of kisses along her throat, and down, to the heaven of her bosom. Serena drew in a gasp as his hand closed around one perfect breast. He smoothed his thumb over the nubby peak that rose through her simple gown, teasing it to a pearly bead before moving on to give equal attention to the other.

Serena's hands were on him as well, not the least shy, slipping beneath his tunic to the bare skin that ached for her touch. She caressed him, inching up his shirt to give her mouth access. Rand jerked with a fierce need as she sank down to her knees in the wet sand and her lips brushed over his chest. She pushed his tunic up, and Rand took it from her, stripping it off and tossing it out of the way. Serena licked him, then took the flat disk of his nipple between her teeth. She suckled him and nipped him, coaxing the bud to hardness as another part of him clenched with like response.

God's love, but he wanted her lips all over him.

She drew back, lifting her Knowing gaze to meet his eyes.

"Yes," she whispered, a single breath that fanned across his bare abdomen as she leaned forward and placed her mouth to the knotted muscles above the waist of his trews.

With unerring fingers, she loosened the ties and let the fabric go slack at his hips. She kissed him lower, down along the tender skin of his groin, and Rand moaned with keen, tormented pleasure.

More.

He didn't know if he said it aloud or merely gasped it in his mind, but Serena and her Knowing touch heard his plea. She freed him of the last of his clothing, smoothing her hands down the length of his thighs, and to his calves. He wanted her so badly, her touch alone nearly dropped him to his knees before her. Serena's fingers dragged back up his legs, slowing as they climbed. The first touch of her hand on his aching flesh jolted through him. She closed her fingers around his girth, stroking his shaft.

Ah, God. Yes . . . more.

She bent forward and tenderly kissed the base of his sex. Her throaty moan, her warm breath, bred carnal heat in him, coiling tight in his gut. Serena moved up his length, her mouth wet and hot, a slow, wicked torture. She reached the crest and her kiss became more ardent. She sucked him into her mouth, her tongue a velvet softness that drove him mad with desire. Rand speared his fingers through her hair, catching the back of her head in his palms.

Deeper. Don't stop touching me.

Serena fulfilled his unspoken demands, wrapping her lips around his manhood as she continued to stroke and caress his fevered flesh. She took him deeper into her sweet mouth, deeper than he would have dreamed. Rand gasped as his arousal surged harder, straining for release. When he teetered at the very edge of sanity, he somehow drew the strength to pull away. He had no words, only a feral growl to tell her he could take no more without bringing her with him. Serena's lips were glistening like dew-kissed berries as she slowly came up. She kept stroking him, sliding up and down the slick length of him.

"I didn't want to stop," she whispered, husky and shameless in her enjoyment of him.

Rand pulled her up to him and kissed her deeply, plundering her mouth with his tongue. He removed her bliaut and chemise, tossing them up to drier ground in the tidal cove.

"My God," he rasped. He was shaking. "Do you know how much I want you?"

She did not answer, save to meet his lips in a decidedly possessive claiming. It stunned him to feel so much power in so delicate a woman. But where Serena was delicate, she was also as deep and vital as the ocean that bordered her woodland realm. Rand gave in to her whim, letting her show him what she needed.

He knew her body now, understood her responses that told him how she wanted him to love her. Serena kissed him as fiercely as a gathering storm. She was liquid in his arms, her aqua gaze darkened to indigo, she every bit the siren as she took his hands in hers and urged him down onto the tidal bed at their feet.

She lay back in the firm, wet sand, resplendent as the small waves rolled up around her. Rand spread her legs, feasting his gaze on every decadent inch of her. He knelt between her knees and bowed over her in worship. The fine down curls at the juncture of her thighs tickled his shaven jaw. He blew them softly, pleased at the spray of gooseflesh that rose in the wake of his attention. He kissed her there, tenderly, a tease and no more, reveling in the wetness that played so silkily against the tip of his tongue.

Serena arched up as he delved within the plump petals of her sex. She cried out when he found the swollen nub at their core and took it between his lips. She was writhing even before he slipped one finger inside her, her body clenching around him, quaking with each deep stroke of his hand and tongue. Only when her climax began did he rise to cover her with his body, bringing her legs up and sheathing himself in one full, penetrating thrust.

Serena came around him like a tempest, savage and wanton, weeping his name as her body seized him in wave after wave of release. Rand moved with her, a fevered rhythm that echoed in the cavernous overhang of the cove. His climax ripped out of him on a roar of completion, leaving him trembling and so blissfully drained. He gathered her close, kissing her lips, her chin, her brow. She was panting beneath him, clinging to him as his weight pressed her down into the soft bed of the tidal pool.

Rand did not know how long they lay there, holding each other and listening to the ocean roll around them. He knew only the feel of Serena's body against his, the scent of her hair as it danced on the incoming waves, the sight of her beautiful face gazing up at him in contented bliss. He could have stayed there forever.

"Tell me what you're thinking."

Although her hands skimmed lightly over his back, her gaze wise with Knowing, Serena smiled up at him and gently urged him to speak what was in his heart.

"I would hear it from your lips," she said, raising herself up from their bed of warm sand to kiss him. "Talk to me, Rand."

He gazed down at her, marveling as always at the feeling of sanctuary he knew in her arms. "I am thinking how at ease I am with you. From the time I was a boy, I was trained for war. It has been the basis of my life: a sword at my hip, a battle cry in my throat, blood on my hands. Even my marriage was a combat more often than not. I have known little peace in my life, Serena. Until now."

"I thought I knew peace," she said, her fingers tracing up along his shoulder, into his hair. "I thought I knew a great many things before you arrived to waken me to all that I was missing."

Rand moaned as she subtly arched beneath him, seating his manhood more fully within her. "It has been my great pleasure rousing you from your slumber, sweet nymph." He was roused as well. He bent his head, kissed the tip of her nose as he greeted her teasing with a slow, deep thrust of his hips. "You make me wish that I could show you everything in this world. All that I have seen, all the places I have been and hope one day yet to go."

"Where would you take me?" Serena asked, eagerness shining in her eyes.

"Across this ocean, to another one where the sun lights the water to the precise shade of your eyes. I would take you to the king's own court in London, where I'd dress you in fine silks and jewels, and we would dine on exotic dishes and rich French wine. I'd like to show you Scotland someday, too. You would enjoy the highlands, I think. Or mayhap I would rather keep you all to myself. We could sail wherever the winds take us, with no borders and no obligations hemming us in. . . ."

He was rambling, caught up in the moment. He let his words drift off like the vapor they were. Naught but a pretty dream, all of it. And like a dream, impossible to grasp and hold on to, no matter how badly they both might wish it could be theirs. Serena yearned to venture beyond the grove line that had hemmed her in for so long, but she would never leave her mother alone to fend for herself; Calandra was her responsibility, her only kin.

As for Rand, he could make no plans beyond the one that would lead him to Silas de Mortaine. No corner of the world—regardless how distant—would be safe for any living being if he allowed the Dragon Chalice to fall into that villain's hands.

Serena caressed his face with a gentle hand, smoothing her fingers along his jaw, which was clenched tight and tense. "I know," she whispered. "But it is a pretty dream."

❧ 21 ❧

SERENA SIGHED, COMING out of her sleep in a languorous daze. She rolled onto her back and let the dawn pour over her through the open window of the cottage. She had been dreaming of sunny skies and blue water, dazzling castle feasts . . . and Rand. Lazily, she pushed herself up from the pallet, tossing back the chaotic mass of her hair. Her sleep-bleary gaze lit on something strange in the window—a parade of small carvings, lined up in a row on the casement.

She leaped up to examine them, smiling at once when she realized what they were.

Doves.

Rand had made her a family of small wooden doves to accompany the first he had given her at the berry bushes several days before. The largest of these new treasures was scarcely bigger than her thumb, but all of them carved with exquisite care. Beaming at the sweetness of his gift, Serena touched each gracefully bowed head, each feathered wing tucked cozily against the plump curve of the doves' bodies.

Oh, Rand, she thought, her heart squeezed with warm affection for the man who had brought so much joy into her life, so unexpectedly. With her mother sleeping in her pallet nearby, Serena padded across the cottage and slipped out to find him.

The cottage yard was empty and quiet. He was not

there. The beach, more likely, Serena thought, and with an eager smile on her lips, she ventured onto the path that led to the shore. Halfway down, she spied him. He was standing on the sand, facing the sea. His dark hair riffled in the ocean breeze, the chestnut waves breaking at the collar of a midnight blue cloak she did not recall he had.

Where had he gotten that?

Serena felt a momentary twitch of alarm, but then he turned his head slightly to the side and she saw the profile of his brow and proud aquiline nose, familiar features of the face she so adored.

"If you think you must continue to woo me with presents, I feel it only fair to tell you that I am already devoted to you, well and truly."

The dark slash brow arched in interest, and Rand slowly turned to face her.

"The figures are precious, Rand. I—"

"Well, well. Aren't you lovely, fresh from slumber?"

It seemed a queer thing for him to say, but that was not what made her stop short on the path. He smiled at her. It might have warmed her to see it, save for one troubling detail.

"Your beard," she murmured, not at all sure she said it aloud, for the sudden clanging of confusion and panic that was rising in her head. "Rand . . . ?"

The vision before her raised a hand and stroked the dark whiskers that covered his cheeks and jaw. It made no sense. How could this be? His face should be cleanshaven, as it was the last time she saw him—mere hours ago.

"Does it displease you, lovely? Come here, and let me show you how gentle I can be with it."

Serena took a fearful step back as the man—this man

who seemed to be Rand but was not Rand—began to
advance on her.

"Who are you?"

He leered now, baring overlong teeth befitting more
an animal than a human. The hilt of a large and deadly
sword gleamed above a bossed leather sheath at his hip.
"Me? Why, surely you know me. Don't be afraid, lovely.
I am Randwulf, lord of Greycliff—"

"No," she said, retreating another pace. "No, you're
not him. You are something . . . other."

The beast chuckled, and the illusion of Rand's face
slipped. Serena glimpsed a hideousness beneath the trick:
yellow eyes glowing around elongated pupils, sharp features, wolfish jaw. "You are harboring the man, and he
holds something that does not belong to him."

The shifter advanced, his heavy boots mutating into
bristly black paws. Thick talons curled into the sand of
the beach as he took a step toward her. Serena faltered,
but she dared not take her eyes off the approaching
menace to gauge her chances of escape.

"I don't know what you're talking about," she said,
stalling as she inched another backward pace. Her heart
battered about in her breast, panic gripping her. "There
is nothing here that you want."

"The cup," growled the beast. "Two pieces of the
Dragon Chalice—Calasaar and Vorimasaar—fused as
one. Greycliff has it, and I know it is here."

One hand behind her to feel her way to the path, Serena shook her head. "No. You're wrong. Rand did have
it once, but he lost it at sea. There was a storm . . . the
cup is gone."

"You lie. The Chalice is here. I can smell it," he
snarled, "as surely as I smell your fear, wench."

Cool leaves brushed her fingertips. From the texture
of the lacy ferns at her back, she knew the path was but

a two-pace at most to her right. She edged nearer, all her muscles tensed for flight.

The shifter must have sensed her purpose, for all at once, it lunged.

Serena screamed, pivoting a hairbreadth too late to elude its grasp. She fell flat, her belly hitting the earthen track of the path, her lungs crushing with the impact. She scrambled forward on pure fright. She kicked and thrashed her legs, feeling the drag of claws at her ankle. The shifter wrenched her backward, but Serena kept up her fight. She freed her leg from his clutches, but then just as quickly, he had her by the hem of her chemise. Talon-tipped fingers curled into the old homespun, shredding it to ribbons.

Serena screamed again, terrified, frantic to get away. "No! Let me go!"

Instinct commanded her where her experience in fighting was nil. She flipped over, tearing loose part of her ruined skirt as the shifter's grip scrabbled for better purchase. Her legs pumping artlessly, she aimed for his snarling face. No longer Rand, but a grotesque merge of coarse human and feral wolf, the shifter slavered over her. Serena bucked, aiming her heel for the lengthening snout of the beast. She kicked hard, teeth gritted in fury, and felt the jarring impact as hard bone and desperate force connected with the vulnerable target of his nose.

There was a sickening *crunch*. Blood splattered her in a rain of sticky warmth. The shifter howled and reared back.

"Agh! You bitch!"

In that instant of reaction, Serena jumped to her feet and set off at a dead run. She heard him leap after her, his gait heavy on the path, his bulky frame sweeping past the overgrown foliage on either side.

Every instinct told Serena to head for the cottage, to

the safety of stone and wood and a door that could be barred against attack. But her mother was there, and she could not bring this evil down on her, too. Instead, Serena veered off the path and plunged deeper into the grove. The shifter followed. She knew not where she would go, or how she would escape.

Rand, her mind screamed.

Oh, God. Rand, please help me!

The scream rang through the forest, pure terror shattering the calm of the morning. Rand's head snapped up where he crouched before one of the woodland wells. The cup of water he'd drawn a moment ago now dropped from his fingers with a dull splash. He vaulted to his feet.

Serena.

He knew it at once, and his blood froze to ice in his veins.

She screamed again and what was ice turned swiftly to a molten rage.

He was running then, tearing through the bracken. On instinct, his hand flew to his hip to find his sword. There was no sword, only the paltry dagger sheathed on his belt. He took it in hand as he cleared an old tree stump and turned down toward the beach, from where Serena's screams had issued.

Pray God she was all right.

The path would take too long for him to reach her. Low-hanging branches lashed his face and arms as he left the trail and plunged into the thicket. He paid no heed to the whiplike burn of his skin. His head was clanging with alarm and the brutal, steel resolve that accompanied him into every battle.

But this was different.

This was Serena, and when he thought of her meeting

with harm, some of the cold logic that served him so
well in combat incinerated with his every furious step.

He heard a rustle of movement fast approaching up
ahead. Rand turned toward it, his gaze homing in on a
flash of pale fabric through the tight network of leaves
and branches.

"Serena!"

She did not hear him through her fear. She was coming straight for him now. She hadn't seen him yet, kept
turning to look behind her, to where a dark shape
dogged her steps. Immense, loping in great strides, her
pursuer was gaining ground fast.

The big man gave a snarl—unearthly, guttural—and
Rand knew at once what he was about to face.

"Serena, this way!"

"Rand!"

Her wild gaze found him at last and locked on. She
ran faster, as though seeing him gave her a final burst of
needed strength. She was panting, her face devoid of
color when she came to within arm's reach of him. Acting swiftly, Rand moved her behind him and put himself
into the direct path of the shifter.

"Get out of here!" he shouted to Serena as she stumbled to the ground at his back. "Go now!"

There was no time to waste, no time to make use of
his drawn dagger. The instant he swiveled his head to
face their assailant, the shifter was upon him. Half-
changed, the man-beast leaped, latching onto Rand's
shoulders with clawed fingers and unnatural might. It
drove him down at once, the both of them dropping to
the ground in a roiling heap.

The shifter gnashed his teeth beneath a savagely bent
and bleeding nose, moving in to land a bite on Rand's
arm. He avoided it narrowly, then railed back and sent
his fist into the man's jaw. The beast shook off the blow,

rolling with Rand as it struggled to take advantage. Rand punched it again, aiming for its already broken nose.

He still held the dagger in his other hand. Rand gripped it tightly, ready to plunge it into the shifter's back while they fought on the ground. But had no chance. With a roar, the man rolled off of him and sprang to his feet. His sword came out of its sheath with a metallic *hiss*.

"Come on," he jeered. His elongated teeth were bloodied, and he motioned Rand forward with one huge, black-taloned hand. "Let us finish it, human."

They began to circle, each daring the other to make the first move. De Mortaine's guard gave an arrogant jab at the air, taunting him with the advantageous reach of the broadsword. Rand hardly flinched at the overture, but behind him some distance, he heard Serena's sharp indrawn breath.

In the moment his attention faltered, the shifter made his move.

He swung his blade down hard, and it was all Rand could do to avoid the killing strike. He twisted around and came up with the dagger, slashing it across the man's thick forearm. The shifter hissed and brought his sword down again. Another narrow miss of his flesh, but this time the blade knocked Rand's dagger out of his hand.

"Now, this will be amusing," the shifter said, stepping on the dagger that lay out of Rand's reach.

Their fight began in earnest, unfairly matched as it was. Rand could only dodge strikes and wait for opportunity, all the while dreading what might happen to Serena and her mother if he failed here. The shifter took great delight in his upper hand. Each swing of his sword was meant to kill, and as Rand continued to elude him, his fury began to show in his wolfish features.

Rand worked to draw the beast away from the dagger. It was his only chance, save wrestling the sword away from the hulking mercenary. He ducked another furious strike, then found his opening. With the butt of his shoulder leading, Rand plowed into the shifter's girth, sending him in a backward sprawl into the thicket.

His eyes followed the shifter's sword. The beast's arm was thrown up, the blade crashing through a patch of flowering white hemlock. With a battle cry seething on his lips, Rand smashed his fist into the shifter's face. He reached for the sword, hauling it out of the shifter's dazed grasp. He rose up, blade deadly vertical, clenched in both hands.

"To hell with you and the rest of your kind," he growled, then plunged the sword straight through the shifter's heart.

The beast spasmed under the punishing blade. Its hideous face shimmered darkly, fading from wolf to man to something that was neither. Its yellow eyes filled with black, the pupils widening as death swiftly dragged it down. It hissed a final breath, at last going still.

Rand backed off with a curse, rising to his feet. With one booted foot on the shifter's body, he pulled the sword free.

"Rand," Serena gasped from behind him. "Oh, God. Rand . . . I've never been so afraid!"

She ran to him at once, wrapping her arms around his waist. Rand was too tense to enjoy her embrace. It was enough that she was unhurt. He might have lost her so easily today; the thought made him shake with anger and not a little fear.

Idly he noted moisture on his face, itching and sticky. He wiped it with impatience. His fingers came away stained crimson with the shifter's blood. He stared at his hands, then let his gaze trail over the carnage he had wrought in his storm of fury.

"This," he said finally, miserable as he brought the sword up before him, "is what I am. Do you understand now? It is what I must do, until every last one of these beasts—and the man who commands them—is purged from existence."

She did not reply, but there was a bleak acknowledgment in her upturned gaze. "You're bleeding," she said, reaching up to wipe at a burning cut at his shoulder. "Come, Rand. Let me take care of you now."

❧ 22 ❧

"**Y**OU'RE ALL RIGHT?" Rand asked, his own bleeding wholly ignored, while Serena prepared a cleansing bowl and cloths with which to tend his fresh injuries. "When I think of that animal's hands on you—"

"I am fine," Serena assured him for the third time since they had settled in at the cottage. "I'll admit I am still shaken, but that is all. You are the one in need of care. Now, sit."

He obeyed her, dropping onto the stool she had placed near the hearth. Serena put her hands into the bowl of warm, herbed water and wrung out a strip of clean linen. Gingerly, she swabbed at the lacerations that raked his arm. They bore the same look as the ones Rand carried when he washed ashore in the storm: four lines bleeding from the strike of thick, wolflike talons. Those older wounds had been more than these and worse, but they were healed now; these new ones cut Serena deeper, for Rand had willingly taken them in the act of saving her life.

His skin was warm in her open palm, and as she touched him, the Knowing seethed with the echoes of his fury, still thrumming from the shifter attack. Serena soothed him with light strokes of the cloth, and a rain of grateful kisses to the strong hands that spared her that day. Rand lifted her chin on the edge of his fist.

"If I should live a hundred years, I will never under-stand what I did to deserve such tender care, my lady."

Serena sat up, smoothing her fingers over his creased brow. She brushed aside the thick chestnut waves that hung into his hazel eyes. "You came here, that is all you did. You came here, I touched you, and I fell in love."

"Love?" He slowly pulled from her loose grasp. He drew back slightly, an unreadable look in his gaze. But then he glanced down at once, shaking his head. "Ser-ena, you give me too much. I am honored, but . . ."

Her heart gave a sudden lurch. She held her hands in her lap, fearful to touch him again, now, after she had so heedlessly confessed her feelings. But she was unaccus-tomed to holding back what she felt, perhaps all the more now that Rand had awakened her to so many wondrous feelings. "I only tell you because 'tis true. I am not looking for you to say you feel likewise."

But she yearned to hear the words, despite the strength she tried to project.

"Sweetest heart," he said, so gently she closed her eyes in fear of what was to come. "I do care for you, deeply. More than I should."

"But you are leaving."

"Yes." The word was softly spoken, final. "I will leave tomorrow, at first light."

Serena nodded. She had needed no telling touch to know that she was losing him for certes this time. She had been awaiting this very eventuality since they had returned from Egremont, anticipating it with a keen dread that was nothing compared to the actuality of hearing him say it now.

"Serena," he said, "these past days—all the time I've spent with you here in the grove—have been unlike any I have known. But this thing I must do will not just go away because I will it to. Silas de Mortaine will not just go away. He grows stronger, and after what occurred today, it won't be long before he knows about you."

"That shifter who attacked me today wanted to know where you had hidden the piece of the Chalice you carried with you the night you washed ashore. I told him it was lost, but he didn't believe me. That's when he came at me."

"Jesu. You see, this is why I must finish this, before I put you and your mother in any greater danger."

Finally, she looked up at him. "What will you do?"

"Go to Scotland. Search for Serasaar, the last piece of the Chalice. I will have to face de Mortaine, with or without it."

Serena could hardly bear to think of that day. She knew naught of the man, but she had seen his evil through the Knowing, and now, today, through the dark magic by which his shifter guards served him. "You must survive," she told him, stern in her desperation. "You must, so that you can come back to me when this is over."

"I would not ask you to wait, Serena."

"I know," she said, smiling sadly up at him. "You would not ask it of me, but I will wait . . . for as long as it takes. So you must not fail, Rand. You cannot leave me waiting forever."

As he beheld her, his gaze darkened in the scant glow of the hearth fire. He came forward, splaying his fingers through the hair at her nape and bringing her close for his kiss. Serena lost herself to the sensual heat of his lips, craving him so deeply she ached with need. She could not bear the idea of parting—not now, and not tomorrow morn.

"Oh, Rand," she breathed against his neck as he held her in the circle of his arms. "I don't want to let you go."

He squeezed her tighter, and the Knowing pulsed with

a storm of misery and desire. At the faint sound of footsteps outside the cottage, Rand's every muscle tensed. "Someone comes," he whispered, already preparing for further battle.

But it was only Calandra. The door creaked open as she entered, her sullen presence halting their intimate conversation at once.

"What has happened?" Calandra asked, looking to the basin and ointments in Serena's lap. "Has there been trouble?"

"There was," Serena answered gently. "Someone came here today—a bad man. Rand protected me. He saved my life."

If possible, Calandra's skin blanched to a whiter shade. "What is this about? What bad man do you speak of? Where is he now?"

"He is gone, Mother. Thanks to Rand. I will tell you all in a moment."

"I should go back out," Rand interjected, speaking to Serena in a low tone. He stood up, a warrior once more and already on the move. "The body should not be left as it is, and another check of the woods would be prudent. I suspect the one today came alone, but I want no surprises." He picked up the shifter's sword and strapped it to his waist. "At least I have this now."

Serena gave Rand a regretful look as she inspected her work on his fresh wounds one last time. "Be careful."

"Always," he said, cupping her face in his palm.

On impulse, she rose up and embraced him, tilting her lips near his ear. "The woodland chapel," she whispered in a rush. "Meet me there tonight. I know you must leave tomorrow, and I won't try to hold you back. But I cannot say farewell to you like this. The chapel," she said again. "Let me have one more night."

Although he said nothing, the look in his eyes was certain. Serena nodded to him, and slowly backed out of his arms.

"Tonight," she mouthed silently, already missing him as she watched him turn and stride out the cottage door.

Calandra appeared so frail. Even against the fall of her long silver-white hair, her skin held meager color. Her blue eyes held little of their usual luster, and her smooth oval face was drawn down with tension. She had only feigned at eating her afternoon sup, and now she sat before the fire in her favorite chair, staring into the embers in a disturbingly prolonged silence.

No doubt the shock of what Serena had told her of that morning's events had taken something of a toll, although Calandra had not reacted as Serena might have imagined. There were no hysterics. No panicked fretting, though if ever she had cause to be anxious about dangers from outside the cottage grove, surely the real and horrific news of what had transpired that morning was enough. But Calandra had accepted the report of the shapeshifter with an almost resigned calm once she was assured that Serena had not been harmed. Not that Serena was completely surprised at her apparent acceptance.

The existence of magic was something Calandra had never tried to dispute. The gift of Knowing ran deep in Serena's kin; her mother embraced what simpler folk might condemn as cursed witchery. What Serena saw that day was dark magic indeed. And despite Calandra's schooled reaction, Serena worried for her.

Calandra had not been herself for some time, in truth, since that first night Rand had commandeered their cottage. She had expected the worst then, calling him a dangerous man who would only bring them harm. Today Serena saw true danger, and survived it only due to Rand.

She shuddered just to think on the changeling beast who might have slain them all just a few hours ago. She prayed they would not see the like again. She dared not imagine how vile and deadly Silas de Mortaine must be to hold power over the shifters who were at his command. To order the deaths of so many for the want of a mythical prize, he would need be black-hearted evil through and through, himself a monster.

His name chased through Serena's mind like a wraith . . . Silas de Mortaine.

Something about it troubled her. She knew not why, but ever since Rand spoke the name of his enemy, Serena had known a certain niggling familiarity. She had tried to excuse it, but each day that passed seemed to embed it deeper.

Serena glanced to Calandra's weary form near the fire. She poured her a cup of warm sage tea and brought it over. "Take this, Mother. You seem so . . . tired. I am concerned about you."

"You needn't be," Calandra answered, her voice strangely distant. "I am hale as ever, I promise you. I'll not be perishing anytime soon, my dear."

She accepted the tea with a wan smile, then sat back and sipped it in silence.

Serena watched for a while, then gazed into the fire as well, her own thoughts drifting. "Rand is leaving tomorrow," she said. Her voice sounded small, even in the quiet of the cottage. "I'm afraid for him, Mother. This man he intends to meet . . . he is evil. I think he will kill Rand."

"Men are always seeking to kill one another," Calandra replied coolly. "It is simply their nature to make war on one another. And if you look closely, you will see that there is evil in all of them."

"Not like this. This man—Silas de Mortaine—can

have no soul to do what he has done, to Rand and to others who dare to cross him. He has murdered innocents, women and children. He is mad, I think. Worse than that, if these changeling beasts are his to command. Rand says he seeks an ancient treasure . . . the Dragon Chalice."

Calandra had gone quite still. She pivoted her head to look at Serena. "That's impossible."

"I told Rand the same thing when he first mentioned it to me in Egremont. That the Dragon Chalice is merely a myth. He knew the tale as well, Mother. He says the Chalice is real."

"And you believe him?"

Serena thought about it for a moment, then nodded her head. "Yes. I do believe him. Especially after what I've seen today. Rand says that this man, Silas de Mortaine, has already claimed one piece of the four—the one bearing the jewel Avosaar, Stone of Prosperity. The cup Rand lost in the storm bore two others, Calasaar and Vorimasaar."

"Light and Faith," Calandra murmured, naming the fabled Chalice stones.

Serena remembered them, too, for the tale of the Dragon Chalice had long been one of her favorites when she was a girl. "Only one cup remains hidden now. The one bearing Serasaar, Stone of Peace. Rand is certain he'll find it in a chapel in Scotland, but only if he arrives before de Mortaine can seize it first. If he does not thwart this evil man . . ." She could hardly finish the thought, let alone speak it. "Either way, I am terrified that I shall never see Rand again."

Calandra turned a strangely sad look on her. "You have known him but a short while. Can you love him so much, Serena?"

"Aye. Mother, I do. I think I fell in love with him the moment I saw him."

Calandra closed her eyes, as if accepting this proved too much for her.

"I know you won't understand," Serena went on, "but he means all to me. I would do anything for him."

Calandra drew back, turning her face away from Serena to stare into the dwindling fire. She sighed heavily. It was a broken sound, as though choked by tears. "I need rest, child. Please, speak to me no more of these things. I don't want to think on them anymore."

Quietly, Serena got up and took the cooled cup of tea from her mother's weak grasp. She pulled the coverlet up around Calandra's shoulders, then busied herself with tidying the cottage.

Once her mother was asleep, Serena went to the clothing chest beside her pallet bed. She opened the coffer and searched through the folded garments until her fingers brushed airy silk and tiny pearl beads.

Tonight, forbidden or nay, she would wear the gown.

She wanted to feel beautiful for Rand—like a woman he might meet in an elegant castle court, not the plain-garbed girl from the cottage in the grove. Tonight she would show him that she could fit into his world, and that her world was his. She wanted him to see that they could have the splendor of both, if he would only return to be with her.

And when he left her in the morning to pursue his dangerous quest, she wanted him to go with her touch still warm on his skin, the passion of their lovemaking still roaring in his heart, as it would be in hers until the day he came back to her.

❧ 23 ❧

How little the place had changed. Silas de Mortaine could not recall the last time he had been to Egremont—decades, at least. Perhaps longer than that; it was hard to recall precisely. To think he had been born not far from this northern berg, which had at one time seemed so significant and vast. A jest, when he thought of all the places he had been in the years since. All the things he had seen, all the pleasures he had tasted.

To be here now seemed a circle coming to completion. Ironic, he mused, for he was hardly the prodigal returning for acceptance, or, even more laughably, redemption. Everyone he knew in his brash youth was gone. There were none here to remember the ambitious knight who came from naught but who knew, without a moment's doubt, that he was destined for great things. No one had believed him then.

How wrong they were, he thought with dark satisfaction.

From atop the strutting white steed that bore him into Egremont's square, Silas de Mortaine had never felt more deserving of worship and awe. With his retinue of shapeshifter guards at his sides and the golden Avosaar cup lying cushioned in a latched box secured to his mount, he had never felt more powerful. But soon, he would.

The Dragon Chalice was his by rights. He would have

the treasure in whole, if he had to raze every building and slay every last man, woman, and child to get it.

He glanced around in contempt at the busy town center, which seemed full to bursting with all manner of folk. It held an almost festival appearance, with fine-dressed nobles mingling among the commoners, and gaudy streamers decorating much of the square.

Silas motioned to Draec les Nantres, who himself seemed to sit his mount in knowing arrogance, a look of mild disdain in his unsettling green eyes.

"Take two of the guards and see what's going on. If Greycliff is here, it will be next to impossible to find him in all this . . . humanity."

"We'll find him," les Nantres assured him.

He chose two of the shifters and the three set off on foot through the churning crowds.

Silas de Mortaine watched them disappear, wondering how long Draec les Nantres intended to wait before he moved to betray him for the Chalice.

Rand buried the shifter's body deep in the forest, and in the hours since, his patrol of the woods had yielded no trace of further danger. That, however, was only a matter of time.

He wondered how the shifter had tracked him to the cottage. Their senses when it came to the Dragon Chalice were fine-tuned; Kenrick had told him how they could scent the treasure from a great distance, their Anavrin blood tied to it by some brand of magic mortal men would likely never comprehend. And as he pondered that fact, he thought back on what Serena had said, that the shifter told her he knew part of the treasure was near.

Could it be?

He had combed the shoreline and outlying areas of

272 TINA ST. JOHN

the forest every day without fail and found nothing. Since he had arrived, he had walked each step of every hour with an eye to his surroundings, hoping, but it had been futile. God's blood, but he had all but sacked Serena's home in search of the cup and come up empty-handed. She and her mother insisted they knew nothing of it, and he was finally beginning to accept that he had lost the crucial half of the treasure to the violent storm and the sea.

But now . . .

Now, after what occurred today, he was besieged with a sudden feeling of doubt. Suspicion settled cold in his gut.

Had they deceived him? Had he been a fool to trust Serena and her mother at their word?

He did not credit that Serena would betray him—not after what they had shared together, not even before. She was guileless and innocent, the purest heart he would ever know. Calandra was a different matter entirely. She was crafty and secretive, and she had made no effort to conceal her disdain for him.

The woman harbored an instant loathing of all men, and he had fared no better under her sharp, condemning eyes. The more he thought on it, the more he questioned her actions—from the very day he arrived. And the more certain he became that Serena's mother had been something less than forthcoming.

Serena strewed a handful of tiny blossoms across the threshold to the woodland chapel, then paused there, tilting her head to assess her work. She was pleased. The ruined little space of tumbling stone and ancient timber was transformed to something fantastical, like something from out of a fairy story.

Candles of precious beeswax, taken from her personal

belongings at the cottage, burned from various places
in the chapel's nave and at the altar. The small flames
danced gracefully, warming the chamber with an inviting glow and the scent of sweet honey. Across the floor,
scattered from the open doorway to the heart of the little church, was a thin carpet of delicate flowers—tiny
white and gold petals like the ones that cushioned them
when Rand had made love to her on the return from
Egremont. A bowl of red berries sat near the altar, which
was made cozy with a nest consisting of a blanket, her
cloak, and a small down bolster.

It was perfect, Serena decided.

She tried not to think about the fact that Rand was
leaving. Instead she buoyed herself with the anticipation
of spending the night in his arms, and the desperate
hope that this evening would not be good-bye, but a
temporary farewell.

Smoothing her palms over the airy silk of her gown,
Serena padded to the altar and seated herself on the
blankets to await her beloved's arrival.

The cottage was still, but for the soft flicker of a candle
within. Fuming, Rand stalked to the door and opened it
into the quiet space. Calandra was seated in the near-
darkness, looking very small and pensive in her chair
beside the cold hearth. She turned to regard him as he
entered, his breath rasping from his run and from the
anger that swirled like a serpent in his gut.

"You lied," he said, a simple charge that said all.

Calandra blinked slowly. She made no attempt to
deny the accusation, or to pretend even momentary confusion. When she spoke, her voice was clear and steady
with resolve. "I had no choice. My child comes first,
above all else."

Rand stalked in, slamming the door behind him.

"Woman, you have no idea what you dally in here. This is beyond you. It is a deadly game you'll dearly wish you hadn't begun."

She laughed at that, a sober exhalation of her breath that seemed more regret than amusement. "I know what I have done," she replied. "I have long tried to make it right."

Rand scowled at her cryptic statement, having no patience for further diversions. Each wasted moment invited Silas de Mortaine to narrow in on his victory. And in the meantime, his shifter sentries were closing in on this very corner of the woods.

"What did you do with it, Calandra?" Rand's boots thudded harshly as he crossed the small space and approached her. When she appeared unfazed, uncooperative, he braced his hands on her slender shoulders and forced her to look him full in the face. "The cup I carried with me in my bag when I washed ashore on that beach down there. What have you done with it?"

"Did you know that the legend of the Dragon Chalice first began in this wild northern shire?" Calandra's blue gaze held his with an intensity he'd not seen in her before. "A penniless knight claimed he'd stolen it from a mythical kingdom, aided by a foolish princess who unwittingly put the treasure in his hands. It was said that magic rent the jeweled Chalice in quarters, leaving four smaller cups, each holding one precious, powerful stone in its bowl and a gilded dragon wrapped about its stem. The cup I found on you when you washed up on our beach matched the tales precisely."

"You stole it from me. You need to give it back, Calandra."

"Yes," she said, agreeing easily. "It is time I let it go. You saved Serena's life today. For that, I am truly grateful. I will give it to you, but I do not surrender the cup without condition."

Rand inclined his head in acknowledgment. "Name it. I must have that cup, Calandra."

"Of course, you must." Her thin smile was rather sad, as if she knew he would say as much, yet hoped for something other. "I will take you to it, but once you have it, I need your vow that you will leave."

"That was already my plan. I mean to head out on the morrow."

Calandra shook her head. "Tonight, without delay."

He thought instantly of Serena, doubtless waiting for him at the little chapel even now. He would hurt her if he did not go to her as she wanted. He would break her heart if he left her without a word.

"Tonight," Calandra said, firmly now, a starkness in her sharp blue gaze. "Understand I do this for her, not you. I have tried to keep her safe from harm all her life. I couldn't bear it if this evil were to touch her now."

"I feel likewise, madam. I would protect Serena with my life."

"So you say. If that be the case, then you will have no trouble doing as I request. You'll leave her, and not come back. Not ever."

Rand grappled with the impossible choice she forced on him, knowing that if he cared for Serena—if he loved her even a little—he had to take the Chalice and its black-hearted pursuers as far away from her as he could. And if Calandra's terms were cruel, only Serena's death at the hands of Silas de Mortaine would be worse.

"Very well," he said at last, forcing the words past his tongue. "Take me to it."

❧ 24 ❧

SHE MUST HAVE dozed. Serena woke with a start, confused to realize the night had passed while she was waiting for Rand in the forest chapel. He had not come. Her heart forced the thought away, but her mind accepted the fact with harsh clarity.

Rand had not been here at all.

The small beeswax candles she had lit to welcome him were long burned out and cold. The scattering of flowers she had dripped in a path from the chapel threshold to the nave were now wilted and lifeless. And she, the biggest jest of all, sat atop the chapel altar in the silk gown she was forbidden to wear, waiting, still hoping that Rand would come through the open door at any moment.

But it was morning; well past first light, the time when Rand intended to depart.

And he had not come.

The thought put a pain in her heart. She unfolded her legs, letting them swing down over the edge of the stone. There was a chill in the morning air, an overcast pall thinning the light from the open roof of the nave. Serena pulled her mantle around her shoulders and slid off the altar.

Why had he stayed away? Why would he reject her like this?

Could he have left her as well?

She prayed he had not. Perhaps he had not gone at all, and something had kept him from their rendezvous. Now pain merged with worry.

What if something was wrong? What if he had met with danger in his last search of the woods—if Silas de Mortaine and his minions had somehow found their way into the forest?

Serena fastened the ribbon ties of her cloak, then quickly padded across the floor of the chapel. As she neared the door, her bare foot struck something hard. It stopped her with a gasp, drawing her attention down. There, half obscured by dislodged bricks and dust, was the record of her family's line. The thick, leather-bound tome had been moved from its place at the altar, as if to be concealed.

She bent and picked it up.

The compulsion to pause there and read it was strong, almost an unspoken command.

She did not want to open the book now, she realized, feeling a certain dread begin to coil in her stomach. And yet she carried the ledger into better light, sinking down onto her knees in the drooping blossoms that littered the nave's earthen floor.

She had to look inside.

She had to know.

Serena's hands were trembling as she flipped open the book of records. She turned the first few pages of parchment, scanning the entries with her heart in her throat. None matched the one she sought. Too recent, all of these, and yet it was unfathomable that the name she needed to see could be any older. She passed each generation, her pulse frantic now that she was reaching the end of the tome. Only three pages remained, the oldest of them all.

Impossible . . .

Still scanning, still hoping with all her might that she was wrong, Serena turned the last of the brittle parchment ledgers and read the final entry.

Nothing.

She sat back and the breath she had been holding left her in a rush.

It wasn't there after all.

But then something odd caught her eye as she began to close the book. A page was missing from the back, the last page. It had been torn out at the binding—recently, for there were yet small fibers of parchment trapped against the cracked leather of the back cover.

"I should have burned the whole thing years ago."

Serena threw a glance over her shoulder and found her mother standing in the doorway of the chapel.

"What have you done?" Serena closed the book and rose to face her mother. "Tell me. Mother, what have you done?"

"I never should have let you play in here as a child, but I thought, what was the harm? For certes, it was wrong to teach you to read those names. I never dreamed it would come to this."

"Mother, please," Serena said, never more terrified in her life. "There is a page missing from this book. You tore it out. Why? What did it contain?"

"I had to keep a record, you see. The years kept spinning away. I didn't want to forget anyone, not even him." Calandra's blue gaze was dully distant. "I lost so many people I loved. One by one, time and this Outsiders' world took them all. But it left me."

"Whose name is missing from this book?" Serena demanded. "I need to hear you say it."

"I was a foolish girl. I had so much to be grateful for—the love of my family, the peace of my home. I wanted for naught, yet I could not stop wondering what lay beyond the boundaries of my little realm." She sighed, her voice wistful. "I had never seen a mortal man before. Certainly I never knew one in so much pain, or in such dire need of aid. It was forbidden to interact with them in any way. The veil that separated our worlds was fragile, and to breach it for any reason was to invite an irreversible danger. But I was young, and he was handsome and golden, and when I called to him through the falls, he could hear me."

Serena swallowed hard, for this tale was familiar, save that now she was hearing it related in disturbingly intimate terms—with a reality that chilled her to her marrow.

"He was gravely injured, bleeding terribly. He was dying. Nothing could have saved him in his world, but in mine there was hope."

"The Dragon Chalice?" Serena asked, unable to summon more than a whisper. "Mother, it was you, in the tale? The Anavrin princess who fed the Outsider from the sacred cup?"

"I couldn't let him die. I loved him instantly. He said he loved me, too. He would have said anything for me to help him. And he did."

"You gave him immortality," Serena said. "You gave him life, and he stole the Dragon Chalice from your kingdom."

"I could not call it back. The mistake was too great. I realized that the instant we crossed the falls and I saw that he had the Chalice under his arm. It was too late then."

"No," Serena murmured, rejecting all she had heard, for it was too incredible to believe. "How can this be? That tale is ancient—hundreds of years old."

"Yes, it is. By mortal years, at least as old as that."

"You couldn't have been there—you are my mother!"

Calandra slowly shook her head. "Your mother died not long after you were born, of mortal disease. Mortal steel claimed your brother's life when Outsiders learned of his Knowing. Your sister, gifted likewise, pledged her heart to a man who grew to despise her for it, and mortal heartache made her take her own life. But you, Serena . . . you would be different, I vowed. I would keep you safe, sheltered away from any who could hurt you. I have raised you, Serena, as I have been left to raise all of my children's children. Many generations of them. But you are the last. You are so precious to me; you are all that remains of our line in this Outsiders' world."

Serena glanced down at her bare hands, for the first time in her life despising them, and their unwanted gift of Knowing. "I am cursed," she murmured, realizing it now. The words caught in her throat, raw and hurtful. "I am an abomination."

"No." Calandra stared at her fiercely. "You are extraordinary—by this world's standards, and by those of Anavrin. The Knowing is rare, even where I've come from, Serena. Only a few of my line are gifted with such clarity and truth. In Anavrin you would be honored like few others."

Serena could not muster a bit of care for how she would be seen anywhere but in this world, her world, where her heart belonged wholly to Rand. In this world, she was losing all that mattered: her past falling away as lies, her present a tangle of confusion and pain, her future never more uncertain. And still there were questions that begged answers, no matter how terrible they might be.

"What about the man," Serena asked, numb with the shock of all Calandra was revealing. "What became of the man you spared, and who took the Dragon Chalice from Anavrin that day? To believe the legend, the drink you gave him granted him immortality. He still lives, as you do?"

For a long moment, Calandra said nothing. "He lives. And after all these years—all these mortal centuries that have passed since the day my carelessness cursed Anavrin and myself—he still seeks to claim the Dragon Chalice for his own."

"Oh, sweet mercy." Although she could not deny her recent suspicions, Serena's heart dropped to her feet. "Silas de Mortaine. That's why the name is familiar to me. You wrote it in this book. The first entry you recorded—the start of our family line—began with his name! I am his kin?"

"You are nothing like him, Serena. None of my children have shared any part of his evil, despite the taint of his blood. Do not condemn yourself for what he is."

"And Rand?" Serena could scarcely command her voice for the reeling of her emotions. "You are the reason he did not come to me last night as he promised. What did you tell him? Did you drive him away by telling him who we are—who I am bound to by blood?"

Calandra shook her head. "He doesn't know this, child. All he needed to know was that he could have part of the Chalice. That's all he wanted, the piece he lost when he washed up on our shore."

"The Chalice—but how? Did he recover it after all? Where did he find . . . ?"

Serena's voice trailed off as her thoughts began to settle on the truth. Suddenly it was all making sense to her—Calandra's instant fear and hatred of Rand, and her orders that Serena leave him to die on the beach rather than give him aid; Rand's insistence that the jeweled cup he carried with him through the storm had been with him the day he washed up.

"You found him first, before I did. You saw him

washed up on shore that morning, and you found the cup in his satchel. You took it and left him to die. You knew what it was. You've had it all this time!"

"We knew nothing about him, child. All I knew was that he carried part of the Chalice, and that alone made him dangerous to us. It is best that he is gone. He was danger, every moment he remained here."

"You don't know anything about him," Serena cried, never feeling so lost as she did just then. She rose, and began to cross the gloomy nave to the doorway. "I love him. Rand is a good man—the one honest thing in my life, I am realizing."

Calandra's hand was firm on her wrist, halting Serena when she would have quit the chapel in her state of distress.

"Can you be so sure?" Her ageless voice took on a flinty edge. "I offered him the treasure he lost on one condition: that he never see you again. I gave him that choice, and he is gone. Men will always choose the Chalice over anything else, child. That is its cruelest power. I regret that I did not take steps to show you that before now."

Serena lifted the cool fingers from about her arm, and in an instant of Knowing, she understood that all her mother—all this woman who had pretended to be her mother—had told her just now was true.

"Don't go," Calandra pleaded. "You're all I have. I need you here, with me."

Serena exhaled a sharp breath, denying her with a look. "Rand needs me more. If there is anything I can do to help him defeat Silas de Mortaine, I mean to do it."

❧ 25 ❧

EGREMONT HAD SEEMED immense and crowded the day Rand had taken her there, but when Serena arrived on her own, exhausted and emotionally drained, the town had swelled to impossible size. Everywhere she looked, she saw people and horses and fine wooden conveyances bearing pennants and streamers. Several couples garbed in gay-colored silks had paused to converse beneath a shady tree, while children in like hues dashed about together in mad excitement, chattering and laughing, paying no heed to where they were going. One of them, a lad with freckled cheeks and sandy brown hair, trailed behind a group of larger boys. His eyes trained on his friends, he crashed against Serena's legs. She caught him on reflex, her hands clasping his little shoulders.

—always leave me out I can play too wish I was bigger like Peter one day I'll show them wait for me let go got to catch up—

The Knowing arrowed through her at once, all of the boy's thoughts filling her mind as he turned startled brown eyes up at her. Serena jolted back. In her haste to leave the woods, she had forgotten her gloves. She released him instantly, pulling her bare hands back against her body, shielding them beneath the folds of her mantle.

"Peter! Kip! Wait for me!"

The imp darted off without a word of pardon. Rubbing the tingle from her palms, Serena watched him chase after his friends and disappear into the thick churn of the crowd. She pivoted back toward the sea of humanity that choked the streets and knew a feeling of uncertainty.

How was she ever to find Rand in the midst of so many people? He could be anywhere. In the crowd, near the docks, already aboard a boat bound for Scotland. She had to be sure. She had to find him, and that would mean she would need to wade through the heart of the crowd, she realized with dismay. And there was little time to waste.

Serena girded herself in determination and walked into the center of the square. Although she kept her hands close to her person, it was impossible not to brush against people as she passed. She was jostled and bumped; here and there, her fingers grazed someone and the Knowing whispered of secrets and mundanity alike.

A young woman, smiling up at the homely-faced man at her side: *he doesn't suspect he cannot I've been so careful and he loves his brother too much to guess—*

A guard posted near one of the elaborate wheel-houses: *should have taken the south road would've been here hours ago and my arse would not be yapping pray God they've a pallet for me and not the floor—*

A wealthy-looking matron, sweat dripping into the folds of her neck as she fanned herself with her bejeweled hand: *such a gathering so very pleased I wore the lavender sendal I wonder if they'll serve peacock or swan when will we be admitted to the castle I am wilting in this sun—*

Serena was panting as she cleared the bulk of the crowd. Her ears rang with a din of voices, a jumble of detached thoughts. She started to dash between another group of laughing travelers, but just then someone came out of a tavern and stepped directly into her path.

"I speak confidently when I say that Baron de Moulton would be well pleased—nay, honored—to have someone of your esteem at his table, my lord."

"Indeed," murmured a smooth, unflattered voice.

It was he—the first man onto the street and the one the taverner fawned after—that Serena collided with in that instant. Head down, she glimpsed only a gleaming black boot and the swirl of an embroidered white mantle before she bumped directly into him.

"Watch your step, clumsy girl!" cried the shrill little man as the one in white and gold halted in offended silence. "My lord, she has made you drop one of your gloves. Don't just stand there, chit—pick it up for Lord de Mortaine!"

Serena froze, every fiber of her being swiftly gone to ice at the mention of the man's name. She dared not glance up and see his wicked face, instead stared dumbly at the spotless boots and agitating hem of his mantle as it caught in the scant breeze.

Her inability to move put a note of hysteria in the small man's voice. "Anon, girl! Retrieve it at once!"

And through it all, Silas de Mortaine said nothing. But she felt him watching her. Mother Mary, but she felt his ruthless eyes cutting right through to her heart, razor sharp, merciless, eyes that had willfully enjoyed so much evil and destruction.

At last, Serena found the strength to move. She slowly dipped down and retrieved the pale leather glove, then rose with it in her hand. Her dark hair fell around her face, shielding her from full view. Serena hid behind it willingly. She could not bear to lift her head and look at him full in the face, too stricken to manage it when she was trembling before him like a leaf.

The taverner took her fear as deference, and clucked his pleasure. "That's more like it, clumsy fool. You have my deep pardon, Lord de Mortaine."

"I would rather have your absence," growled the man who had ordered the deaths of so many for so much less cause.

He reached out a lineless, elegant hand to Serena in expectation.

Summoning every ounce of courage she possessed, Serena handed him the soft hide glove, purposely allowing their fingers to brush for the barest instant. Heat not unlike a purgatory flame licked her skin where de Mortaine's touch made contact. Serena weathered the pain of it, Knowing a sudden lashing of acid evil and the ugly twist of a beastlike heart that thudded within the man's ageless body. Above the rumble of his general wickedness, de Mortaine's thoughts pervaded her mind:

—*delectable mouth the things I'd have it do peculiar though have I seen her before a hundred years ago perhaps something familiar there should remember but no matter have one of the men fetch her for me this evening yes will own this whole town once the Chalice is mine soon yes very soon now look up little dove let your master see you*—

Serena wrenched her hand away, tucking it safely within her mantle. Her fingers burned, sending an ache up the length of her arm. She felt his disease reach out to corrupt her, creeping along her senses like black serpents that stretched and writhed in her blood.

Silas de Mortaine *was* in her blood, she reminded herself, sick with the thought that she could share any tie to him.

She backed away, a handful of steps to put him out of reach of her. He chuckled at her retreat as if her fear amused him, but then the taverner was speaking again, nattering on about the grand feast Silas would enjoy at Baron de Moulton's table, and Serena took the opportunity to flee into the crowd.

Now she praised heaven for the thick gathering of people. She let her hands glance off all she could, trying in vain to drown out the horror of de Mortaine's touch. And as she let the throng swallow her, she understood that even if Rand was there, the best way she could help him now was to keep Silas de Mortaine in Egremont as long as she could, so that Rand could make his escape to Scotland and retrieve the final piece of the Dragon Chalice.

The demons plaguing Draec les Nantes were no longer content to haunt him in his dreams. Now, more and more, even his waking hours were dogged by nightmare visions of fire and thunder, of seething dragons, molten rock, and an endless fall down a black and jagged chasm.

For all his life, Draec les Nantres had slept with the vision of his own death.

Now he smelled the brimstone while awake. He felt the beast's huge jaws rip into his flesh, fire devouring his skin and hair. Saw himself plummeting down into the hot, smoke-filled void.

Down, and down, and down . . .

He shook off the sudden disorientation with a curse, and focused hard on his surroundings. The docks below Egremont's town square were bustling. Boats carrying supplies or passengers filled the small port, most of the hubbub centered on the grand feast taking place in the castle high on the hill above town.

Draec and one of the shifter guards he had brought with him for reconnaissance watched from their position near all of the activity, searching for signs of Greycliff and the Chalice treasure. Draec was agitated, both from lack of sleep and the impatience he felt for his mission. Another boat had pulled in, and as a group of travelers began to disembark, Draec motioned for his companion to follow him.

But beside him on the dock, the shifter had paused. His big head went up, chin in the air. Wide nostrils flared as he turned his back to the ocean and sucked in a deep breath from the direction of town.

"What is it?" Draec asked.

The shifter's rough voice was thick with lust for the hunt. "Chalice gold." He sniffed again, then turned to Draec with a feral look in his eyes. "Part of the treasure is near. Up there, somewhere."

"Aye," Draec agreed, hardly trifling to hide his contempt for the Anavrin guard. "No doubt de Mortaine has Avosaar with him as he stuffs himself at the high table of Egremont's baron. I can practically smell the cup myself, without the benefit of your shifter magic."

The shaggy dark head shook in denial. "This is stronger than Avosaar. There is more than one piece of the Chalice on the wind," the shifter said, brows knitting on his swarthy forehead. "The cup I scent bears two of the Chalice stones, I'd say. Someone carries it."

So, Greycliff and his friend had indeed recovered another of the Chalice pieces, Draec mused. His thoughts spun back to a night some weeks past, when a flame-haired temptress with shifter blood had drugged him in an attempt to aid her mortal lover, Kenrick of Clairmont. Haven had been crafty with her deception; drunk on herbs and arrogance, Draec had practically handed her the key to recovering one of the hidden treasures.

He would not make that same mistake again. He would bide his time, and wait for opportunity to act. He had risked too much to fail in this now. The Dragon

Chalice would be his, by God. He would seize it for his own, or he would die trying.

Draec les Nantres pivoted to look up toward the busy street and center square of Egremont. Somewhere in the throng of travelers and folk, Randwulf of Greycliff carried one half of the Chalice's power. If Draec could get his hands on that, the odds were good that he could stand against de Mortaine and take Avosaar as well. Three pieces of the four would make Draec unstoppable in claiming the last.

Aye, he was very close to reaching his goal now.

"Lead me to it," he commanded the shifter.

The mercenary grinned a wolfish leer, then loped off ahead of Draec toward Egremont's town square.

❧ 26 ❧

SILAS DE MORTAINE reclined in his seat on the dais, feigning interest in his host's banal prattle about the bounty of his demesne's crops and the fine marriage he had recently procured for his middle daughter. The feast that night had been in celebration of the betrothal, a match that had brought many folk to the old fortress keep on Egremont's highest hill. Although he generally preferred inconspicuous travel, Silas was several days' sore from his ride north, and he found the offer of a true bed and a fine meal too great to resist. A pity those luxuries had to come at the cost of his infinite boredom.

"Ah, there's my lovely Sybilla now." The proud father gestured across the great hall with his raised cup of French wine. "Do you know I presented her at the royal court when she was just three years old. The king was dazzled, do I say so myself. She was a charmer even then, my girl."

Silas's disinterested grunt could hardly be heard over the spritely music pouring down from the grand gallery above the hall. He turned his indifferent gaze as directed, to where a group of country nobles attempted a dance that one of them was eager to announce he had learned in London. Young lords with too little sense and knights with overmuch ambition gleaming in their eyes vied for the attention of eight prim maidens. Sybilla de Moulton had her father's equine features, a long face and overlarge mouth that was at the moment dropped open in an unappealing twitter of girlish laughter as her betrothed whispered in her ear.

But where the daughter suffered her father's plain looks and manners, de Moulton's wife was nothing short of delicious. She sat demurely at his side, a petite beauty with golden hair and bold blue eyes. She caught Silas staring and held his gaze for a moment longer than was seemly. With a superior arch of her brow, she dismissed him with a cutting look of reproach.

"She is a prize, is she not, Lord de Mortaine?"

Silas kept his eyes trained on haughty Lady de Moulton, and bared his teeth in an indulgent smile. "Indeed. A prize, to be sure."

Oblivious to the insinuation, Baron de Moulton launched into yet another tiresome recollection, but Silas scarcely bothered to listen. He slowly drew his attention away from the man's cool, comely wife and watched the dancers fumble their graceless steps in the center of the lavish hall. Without a care for the blatancy of his assessing perusal, Silas took in the rich appointments of the keep. He settled into his chair and indulged in a pleasant imagining, supposing, merely for amusement, that he might take all of de Moulton's holdings for his own once he had the Dragon Chalice in his possession. When that moment came—and he was certain it would—nothing would be out of his grasp.

In truth, he could claim the place now, if he wanted. He was rich, he was powerful, and in the many long years of his life, he had met no steel strong enough to bar him from anything he desired. More than one fool had tried. Others would as well, but Silas would forever prevail.

Immortality, after all, had its distinct advantages.

But while he had no qualms about plundering for his

own gain, he had long grown bored with counting his coin and adding to his bulging coffers. Where a sip from the Dragon Chalice had given him unending life, it was the cup itself he craved. With it, he would rule this world and the next, a king of both the mortal and immortal. He would be a god.

Silas smiled, knowing the age of his reign was coming. How hard it was to be patient with so great a gift dangling before him, just waiting for him to grasp it.

His pleasant musing was disrupted by a vague disturbance near the door of the great hall. He heard a woman's voice, indistinct, yet urgent, followed by the low rumble of the door warden who guarded the entry to the sumptuous celebration within.

From over the rim of his goblet, Silas's gaze narrowed to hard slits.

There was a slight parting of the crowd, and in the space between the awkward bobs and twirls and curtsies of the continuing dance, Silas spied something peculiar. Something intriguing. He sat up in his seat and leaned forward on the table, his gaze piercing through the dancers' alternating movements. The woman who stood near the tall doors of the great hall, newly arrived and arguing entrance, seemed familiar to him somehow. He could not see her face for the damnable shifting of the crowd. He glimpsed only a glossy crown of sable dark hair framing a smooth brow.

The woman herself was a stranger to him, but the sight of her compelled him out of his chair.

"Is something amiss, Lord de Mortaine?" asked his host, staring up from beside him at the table.

"That woman," Silas murmured, "near the door . . . who is she?"

Baron de Moulton grunted, perplexed. "Why, it must be one of Sybilla's friends, I should think. Or mayhap a cousin. We've invited so many to our celebration, I've no idea—"

"I tell you I have urgent business here with your lord," she announced now in a clear, strong voice. "There is a man in this town who brings great danger to us all. His name is Silas de Mortaine."

Baron de Moulton turned a questioning sidelong look on his guest. Silas had gone quite still at the announcement, but it was curiosity more than concern that drew his mouth into the beginnings of a smile. He dismissed his host's uncertain glance with a vague shrug of his shoulder and resumed his place at the table.

"This should prove amusing," he murmured with droll humor, and deliberately lounged a bit deeper into his chair. "Please, bring the lady forward. Like everyone else in the room, I am intrigued to hear of this great danger she claims I pose."

With a smirk of noble camaraderie, de Moulton motioned for his sentries to permit the woman entry to the hall. Silas held his goblet in an easy grasp before him, lazily swirling the bloodred wine as the two armed guards escorted his accuser through the parting sea of revelers. Amid the crowd of country nobles, even in her simple, shapeless cloak, she stood apart like a shimmering dark pearl among a field of drab, common stones. Silas's mood stoked from mere curiosity to smoldering, lustful interest.

A note of surprise pricked him as she neared the dais.

It was the clumsy girl with the rose-petal lips who knocked into him in the town square. She had seemed shy then, but no more. Had he offended her somehow? he wondered, quirked into an amused sort of intrigue as he watched her approach, so serious now. The dark little dove seemed have found a hawk's tenacity, to attempt such a bold move as this.

"I am Silas de Mortaine," he declared, letting his voice ring out to the rafters. He took perverse satisfaction in the young woman's subtle flinch of trepidation as she was moved forward to stand before him below the dais. "Well, you have our attention, dear lady, so speak."

She licked her lips, glancing nervously to the armed guards who remained positioned at her sides. Waiting for the disruption to resolve, the rest of the gathered crowd approached in uncertain silence. The newly betrothed Sybilla stifled a sniffle behind a swatch of linen and lace, muttering over her ruined celebration.

The weight of silence pressed down on Silas's threadbare patience.

"Speak!" he barked, sending de Moulton's daughter into an earnest fit of sobbing.

The young woman before him lifted her gaze to his and held it, though it was clear she did so with not a little fear in her heart. In that, he found a speck of respect for her. But he would have no mercy.

"This man is evil," she began, directing her comment to the lord of the castle. "On his orders, a family was slain at a place called Greycliff. . . ."

Silas registered the name at once, and drew himself forward in his chair.

"A woman and her young son were killed in their keep some two months ago. This man seated beside you sent an army of demons to burn their home, to leave none living."

"Demons?" Baron de Moulton's question held a dubious tone. "What mean you, good woman?"

"Clearly, she's mad," Silas interjected, but it lacked conviction, and now that he was looking hard at the woman, he noted something disturbing about her.

Beneath her woolen cloak, she wore a bliaut that was

anything but common. His vision was teased with flashes of diaphanous silk, frosty blue, pale green, creamy pearl.

That gown.

By the sudden roil of his own seething blood, he knew that gown!

In a burst of furious action, Silas shoved his chair back and vaulted over the table, as agile as any stripling youth. His booted feet hit the floor of the dais with a heavy crack of sound, punctuating the flurry of gasps that went up from the lords and ladies who had since abandoned their feast of stuffed peacock. The woman took a fearful step back as he stalked up to her, but she did not flee.

"Who are you?" he demanded of her.

"My lord de Mortaine," cautioned the baron of the keep, "let the woman speak, if you will."

But Silas could not contain his growl of anger and disbelief. With a rough hand, he tossed the edge of her mantle over her shoulder, revealing more of the iridescent fabric beneath. He had seen the gown only once in his lifetime, but never would he forget it. The magic of its origin shimmered throughout each thread and bead. And as he stared at the royal Anavrin garment, a single name snarled through his recall.

Calandra.

"Where did you get this?" he hissed. "Answer me! Who the bloody hell are you?"

The young woman stared him down, defiant. "A better question might be, who are you—and how black is the magic at your command?"

"Witchcraft is a serious charge," de Moulton advised her. "You had best be certain, good woman, and have evidence to support your claim."

That she had gone suddenly mute pleased Silas de Mortaine. He saw the fear in her eyes and he reveled in it. The appearance of Calandra's gown was a vexation, however, and he would get to the bottom of that as soon as he dealt with this present inconvenience.

"Well. Evidently, the chit has reconsidered herself," Silas announced, pivoting back to the quiet dais in a flourish of charming bravado.

He started to walk away, confident that he had thwarted this unexpected trouble, for the moment at least. Before he could take the first step, he felt her lunge toward him.

The woman's sea-bright gaze locked on his. Then she reached out and wrapped her slender hand around his arm. Her fingers clamped down on him with uncanny strength and a queer warmth that seemed but a shade away from searing. But she was the one who winced as though stricken with sudden pain. Perspiration misted her forehead and put a sheen above her mouth. She looked like she might retch.

"This man . . ." Her voice trailed off, but she retrieved it, even squaring her shoulders when it seemed she might rather collapse. "This man is a criminal. He is a thief, and a liar. He is a murderer of innocent women and children. Most of all, he is a soulless creature who deals in the dark arts."

Silas chuckled, but his laughter was the only sound echoing in the suddenly silent great hall. He glanced around and saw worried faces, suspicious eyes, all of them fixed on him.

"My lord de Moulton," said the girl, "I have come to warn you—all of you here—that the devil walks among you tonight, and his name is Silas de Mortaine."

Serena knew not how she found the strength to speak. Touching Silas de Mortaine, feeling the depth of his wickedness seep into her through the Knowing, was to plunge into frigid, fathomless black waters. Wave after wave assaulted her, nausea engulfing her, threatening to buckle her legs beneath her. But Serena held fast—to de Mortaine and to her own resolve. She would condemn him here, publicly, and when he was taken into custody for his crimes, all the pain she felt now would be worth it.

Faces faded in and out of her mind's eye—countless lives snuffed at de Mortaine's command, many at his own hand. She saw hideous deaths, heard the screams of tortured souls made to suffer prolonged anguish, all for his delight.

Let the truth of his own evil deeds be testimony against him, Serena thought, ruthless now in her loathing of him. She clasped him tighter, feeling the burn of his evil in every fiber of her body. Amid the storm of agony that wrenched her very soul, the Knowing grew clearer, pitiless in its reading of de Mortaine's black heart.

Faster and faster the visions came, one after the other. Serena absorbed the record of every sin he had committed, every heinous crime, every evil dream that lurked in his dead heart, and she began to recite them each in detail for the noble folk gathered in the castle's great hall.

—*An elderly man called Delavet, garbed in white robes and sprawled on the tile floor of his church, his frail neck snapped by Silas's hands*—

—*Lara, shifter-born woman who dared betray Silas, paid with her life, consumed by a ball of otherworldly flame*—

—*A servile cleric ripped to bits by the gnashing teeth and brutal claws of two shifters, loosed on Silas's command*—

—*Silas himself, in a moonlit abbey courtyard, striding into the heart of a roaring blaze, only to emerge unscathed*—

There was further proof of the sorcery he employed, and countless other innocent lives smashed under the heel of Silas de Mortaine's black power. Serena told them all, until she could scarcely form the words. And still there were more.

"I have heard enough," Silas chuckled as she began to slump where she stood. He wrenched free of her loosened grasp and gestured to the gathering in the hall, his expression one of patronizing levity. "Have not we all heard enough of this filth and depravity?"

"Staggering accusations, sir," Baron de Moulton said from his place at the high table.

"Bald lies—delusions of a sickened mind," Silas countered hotly.

"Then you deny her claims?"

"Deny them? I reject them as madness! Nay, worse—this woman speaks of sorcery and evil like she knows it well. In truth, I am left to wonder if the actual danger might be here, in this pretty face."

He caught hold of her chin and squeezed his fingers deep into the flesh of her cheeks. Serena whimpered under his bruising hold, but she did not reach up to pry him off. She had no strength left beyond that which held her upright, and she could bear no more Knowing of the man whose rancid blood beat, even diluted through the generations, in her own veins.

"Look at her and tell me you do not scent the devil at work in her eyes. There is true evil here, and it can be found in this witch's heart!"

"Aye!" came a shout from somewhere in the hall. "Aye, I have seen it! I have witnessed the witch at work not a few days ago!"

Serena dragged her bleary gaze to where the call had issued. A man was standing on a bench at a trestle table, staring at her from across the wide expanse of the banquet hall.

"That woman came to my stall at the market. She cheated me out of a fair price for a bauble I'd have gotten thrice for had it not been for her witchery!"

The goldsmith, Serena recalled now, dimly recognizing him.

He pointed a finger at her in accusation. "She took my hand in a searing grip and looked into my mind! Took my thoughts, she did—and my profit as well! She's a witch, I've no doubt!"

Serena coughed, doubling over to hold her stomach, which roiled from Silas's lingering touch. He reached down and grabbed her by the edge of her cloak, hauling her back up beside him. He pulled her toward the dais, where Baron de Moulton and his wife sat in anxious silence.

"A witch," Silas said, loud enough for all to hear. "She has been witnessed exercising her black arts by that good man, and now all of us in this room have seen for ourselves her attempt to corrupt my mind with her spells and devilspeak. My lord, my friend, here is evil."

The baron was quiet for a moment, considering. His wife turned a pallid look on him, and from beneath her own drooping lashes, Serena saw the woman make the sign of the cross on her breast.

"No . . ." Serena's plea caught in her throat. "Do not . . . believe . . . him."

"There is but one way to purge such an abomination," Silas said, easily eclipsing her with the gravity of his silken voice. "The witch must die."

A gasp went up from the crowd, and very subtly, the baron gave an agreeing nod of his head.

"No!" Serena cried, panic swirling in her as the baron

and his wife turned away from her and the guards who
had shown her into the hall now advanced to seize her.

"Get her out of my sight," de Mortaine snarled to the
castle sentries. "My garrison awaits me in town. Place
her in their custody. I will deal with her anon, and in my
own way."

🐾 27 🐾

EGREMONT WAS CRAWLING with shifters. Rand had realized it nearly the instant he set foot on the road into town. He felt it more and more as he carried the cup bearing the Calasaar and Vorimasaar stones toward the docks, where he hoped to procure immediate transport up the coast to Scotland. He had just begun to head that way when he spied yet another hulking shifter and a familiar face he loathed.

Standing on the wharf, Draec les Nantres and the Anavrin guard at his side were carefully watching the arrivals from a boat recently docked and unloading. Rand saw the shaggy head of the shifter go up like a hound on the sudden scent of fresh blood. The big man then began to pivot toward him. The beast had sensed the presence of the treasure; Rand was certain of it. With a curse, he ducked back around to the street, only narrowly missing detection.

The docks were out of the question now. And he could not linger in town with les Nantres and the shifters in close proximity. Rand was willing to wager that Silas de Mortaine was not likely far away, either. He could be in Egremont as well, heading north, perhaps intending on much the same route as Rand himself. There was no time to waste. With part of the Chalice treasure on his person, Rand had to stay on the move or he was sure to be taken.

He switched back and walked with haste for the town stables. He had some coin now, what little he had taken in trade for Elspeth's pendant. Pray God it would be enough to procure a mount for the trek north. If not, he would hardly be the first in his line of scoundrel kin to thieve a horse from beneath a nobleman's arse, and for far lesser cause.

The stables were crammed, not surprisingly. Mounts of all qualities and colors filled the stalls. Those that had found no room stood in the center of the wide out-building, some being tended by four harried youths armed with brushes and blankets and buckets of water. Rand strode into the musty stables hardly noticed. He knew Draec and the shifter from the docks could be on him in little time; he would needs move quickly.

While the boys conversed about the celebration under way at the castle, grousing over added work for themselves when they weren't making ribald comparisons of some of the visiting maidens, Rand made a hasty appraisal of the horseflesh snuffling and stamping in the dust of the stable floor. He found a swift-looking palfrey— a messenger's mount, by the sleek lines of the beast— and was just about to bribe the lads into surrendering it when another boy skidded to a halt in the stable doorway.

"Hal! Jos! Where's Ned and Bren?" The last two lads came running with pitchforks in hand and reeking of dung and sweat. "All of ye, come—ye'll not believe what's happened!"

Rand's neck prickled with warning at the breathless alarm in the lad's voice. It did not bode well, and his hand immediately went to the linen-wrapped treasure beneath his cloak; the other hand drifted to the hilt of the shifter sword that rode at the ready on his hip. He hung back as the clamor of young male voices rose to an excited octave.

"I ran down as fast as I could to tell ye!"

"Out with it, Dag!"

"Aye, what's going on?"

"The castle! There was trouble at the feast. . . ."

Rand's gut clenched in dark anticipation. He expected to hear that a large black wolf had been spotted up the hill, or even that a man named Silas de Mortaine was wreaking havoc in some manner. But what he heard next made even those dread notions pale.

"I saw it all with mine own eyes," the first boy shouted wildly. "Come with me—I'll show ye! They've gaoled a black-haired witch up at the castle!"

Sharp fear jabbed Rand hard in the chest. He did not want to think it, but his heart clenched tight around a single thought. . . .

Serena.

With a combined whoop of boyish adventure, all four stable hands and the lad who had brought the news bolted from the building. Rand stood there for a moment, torn between the pressing matter of the Chalice he carried and the deadly shifters who would soon be on his trail, and the sudden sinking feeling that it was Serena and not some other hapless woman at the castle who had been captured and condemned as a witch as the boy reported.

He could not leave it to chance.

And he could not risk taking the Chalice up to the castle if Silas de Mortaine was there, as he fully suspected. He eyed the abandoned pitchforks, then the pile of dung the boys had raked up in the back of the stable. It seemed an unlikely place to look, and, as it was, his sole option.

Rand grabbed one of the forks and dug a deep hole in

the ripe pile. Working quickly, he unfastened the knotted strap that held the bundled Chalice on his person, then concealed the treasure beneath the stench of the stable refuse.

"God's love, it cannot be her out there," he said, tossing down the pitchfork and running back to free one of the mounts. He led the sleek messenger's gelding around, then leaped up onto its back. "Jesu, let me be wrong."

He gave the beast his heels and sped out of the stables toward the long road leading up to the castle on the hill. He was not alone on the trek; a large mob of folk from town was headed up the road as well, a few on horseback, some running on foot, still others walking with grim purpose. From within their ranks, a shout went out for a hanging in the square.

With a curse hurled into the wind, Rand broke away from the pack of advancing villagers and sent his mount into a gallop.

He spied the object of their morbid interest at once.

From out of the castle portcullis came a small retinue of guards bearing the colors of the manor's lord. Behind them, pulled by two brawny steeds, was a wheelhouse made of wood and iron. The cage was dark, but in its center was a figure that glowed like pale blue flame in the gathering twilight. Rand's heart sank like a stone.

It was indeed his beloved.

"Serena!" he called, driving his mount harder up the narrow track of road.

"Stand down," one of her guards advised as Rand approached with fury in his eyes.

"Serena! I am here!"

He saw her fingers curled around the bars, lily-fair skin holding fast to the black metal. She strained to see him, then he heard her voice cry out, "Rand!"

He rode around the escort, wheeling his horse about

to canter alongside the cage that held her. The castle guards gave up their warnings as more of the townfolk gathered at the sides of the wheelhouse, peering at Serena in leering curiosity.

"Good God," Rand exclaimed, wishing it were just an awful dream to find Serena like this. She looked so helpless behind the thick bars of the cart. So frightened. "What happened? Why did you come here? God's love, Serena, what were you thinking?"

He reached out to her, taking her fingers through the bars. Her skin was cold. Her ocean blue eyes were bright with unshed tears.

"I had to find you," she said, clutching his hand as though never to let go. "You left without a word. I just wanted to help you."

"I left so you would be safe!" Rand's skittish mount tried to sidle away from the rolling conveyance but he brought it back with a vicious jerk of the reins. "I will get you out of this, my love, I swear it. I'll get you back to the cottage, where you belong—"

"No." Serena shook her head, her black hair sifting around her in agitation. Her fingers loosened on his, then fell away. "I won't go back there. I cannot. Everything was a lie, Rand. She lied to me—all these years, I thought Calandra was my mother. I never dreamed those stories she told me as a child could have been real."

"The Chalice? What do you mean, you thought her your mother—what was a lie?"

"All of it!" she cried. "We are blood kin, Calandra and me, but she is not my mother. She is older than that. She is ageless, like him. Oh, Rand! You will hate me to know who I truly am—whose blood is in me."

"Tell me," he demanded, his mount startling near the

cart as the conveyance lurched over a rut in the road.
"Serena. There is no time—what is this about?"

"Silas de Mortaine," she whispered, her voice barely
discernible above the groan and creak of the cart and the
dull murmur of the trailing mob. "He was the man who
first stole the Dragon Chalice from Anavrin."

"What—" Rand swore an oath. "How do you know
this?"

"She told me. I started to put it together, but then she
told me all of it. He is the Outsider who breached the
veil between our world and Anavrin. And it was my
moth—it was Calandra who gave him the drink from
the sacred well that saved his life when he should have
died of his wounds. She gave him immortality, Rand.
She is the Anavrin princess who first gave Silas the Chalice so long ago."

"Jesu." Rand felt as if he had been struck with a
crushing fist to the chest. "That would have to have
been . . . hundreds of years ago."

"Yes."

A numb acceptance began to settle over him. "They
bore children together, the Outsider and the princess."

"Yes." Serena nodded, torment swimming in her
gaze. "I am the daughter of their daughters' daughters,
Rand. I am a part of them. Calandra of Anavrin . . . and
Silas de Mortaine as well."

He reeled back. He couldn't help it. The reaction was
gut-deep, an elemental need to deny what he was hearing. But Serena's gaze was too grim, too shamed, to take
this news as anything but the shattering, irrefutable
truth.

Sweet Serena, the woman who had come to rule his
heart, was the blood kin of his most hated enemy—a
monster that Rand intended to send to the depths of hell
at first chance.

"I'm sorry, Rand," she said, only she made no sound, merely mouthed the words as the driver snapped the whip at the horses and the wheelhouse lumbered on.

Rand's heart was pounding in his chest. He had two impossible choices now: continue his quest for the Dragon Chalice, or find a way to free Serena from the danger that awaited her.

Nay.

There was but one choice, he realized. He gave his mount a taste of his heels, ready to chase after the cart, but the beast reared up before it could take the first step. Two other riders had moved into his path, blocking him, while still others hemmed him in from all sides. He knew the one in the lead, although he'd never seen him face-to-face before this moment.

"Draec les Nantres," Rand growled, shaking off his astonishment over Serena's revelation in order to meet this new threat.

The raven-haired knight smiled, and gave a courtly incline of his head. "Randwulf of Greycliff. You have part of the Chalice. My thanks for delivering it to us. My employer will be well pleased to hear you saved us the effort of hunting you down to retrieve it."

"I don't have it. If I did, don't think for an instant I'd turn it over to you."

"Nay?" Les Nantres chuckled, turning a casual look at the departing wheelhouse that held Serena captive. His gaze came back to Rand, full of arrogance. "Well, we shall see about that. Guards, take him down. Remove his weapons and search him for the cup."

"Suit yourself," Rand drawled insolently.

Trapped on all sides by unwavering steel, at least one blade held by the deadly hand of a shifter, Rand knew the futility of a struggle. He could do nothing for Serena if he were dead. The weapons urged him to cooperate, and so he surrendered to de Mortaine's smug lieutenant.

As he was dragged off his mount and harshly shoved into a march toward the castle, Rand looked down the road, to where the wheeled cage rumbled on its way to town. Serena in her pale blue bliaut grew smaller and smaller, never more out of his reach.

❧ 28 ❧

SHE HAD BEEN in the wheelhouse cage for several hours. It was night now, and the town square was all but empty, save a few straggling revelers who paused to leer and hurl foul epithets at the witch imprisoned behind the bars. One old woman threw a rotting head of cabbage at the makeshift cell, cackling as she vanished into the shadows of the street.

Serena cared naught for their open condemnation. It was Rand's wordless rejection of her that had put a keen ache in her heart. Not that his reaction was unreasonable. She knew how deeply he despised Silas de Mortaine; Rand reviled him as the worst manner of beast, and so de Mortaine was. Why should Rand feel any differently toward his hated enemy's progeny?

Serena could not blame him for turning his back on her. In truth, part of her was glad, for she dearly prayed he would take the opportunity to leave Egremont far behind him while Silas and his minions were distracted with her. It might be Rand's only hope of beating de Mortaine in his deadly game. Now that Serena had seen with her own eyes—with her own Knowing—all the hideous things Silas had done in his quest for the Dragon Chalice, she understood how vital it was that the man be stopped, and soon.

If her life need be spent to aid Rand now, she would give it willingly.

"You know, I have often wondered what became of Calandra these many long years."

The voice issued from out of the dark, but Serena knew it instantly, and its cultured artifice chased a shiver of revulsion up her spine. She backed farther into her barred wooden cell and watched as Silas de Mortaine came out of the night shadows, materializing almost ghostlike in his gold-embroidered, white finery.

"That gown," he said, lifting his hand to point a finger at her, "came from a place very few have been. A place I intend to rule one day. The gown is Calandra's, and you, no doubt, are something of hers as well."

He approached the cage with easy, deliberate strides, sizing her up with his gaze, which pierced even through the dark. He reached through the bars as though to touch her, and Serena dodged his grasp, revolted to be so near him now.

He smiled too becoming a smile for the demon he was, then gave a mild shrug. "What, no embrace for your dear old grandpapa?" He chuckled, amused suddenly. "Or rather, your great, great, great . . . ah, well, no matter. You are kin, I can see that plainly enough to look at you now."

"Would that I were not," Serena replied. "I should rather be dead than live with the smallest drop of your blood in my veins."

Silas's smile became something cruel, twisting to an ugly sneer. "In due time, child. First I need you to take me to Calandra."

"I will do nothing for you. I don't care what you intend for me."

"You should," he answered casually. "The townsmen are pressing for a hanging. Superstitious lot, these northern folk. Some hunters claim they've seen you practicing your spells in the woods a few hours south of town. They say you and a white-haired crone share a cottage near a large cascade. I realized I know the falls they speak of, and I know the woman is no crone. If Calandra lives, as I do, and if she has remained near that forest waterfall—the very one that she and I crossed long ago, when we fled Anavrin with the Chalice in my hands—then she has a reason to be there. No doubt the conniving wench has been working against me all this time."

"I've no idea what you are talking about," Serena countered, terrified that he might turn his sights on Calandra as well.

"I will find her either way, girl. But you are going to take me to her, because I'm certain you've no wish to watch me torture her. She will long for the death I intend for you. Mark me."

Serena's breath stopped on his chilling words. There was no mistaking the sincerity of his threat, and although she tried to maintain her courage, she knew a real and growing fear.

"We leave within the hour. My guards will prepare you for the journey back to the grove."

The appointed time came far too quickly. Although Serena's confinement in the barred cart was a torture of its own, the idea of riding back to the cottage with de Mortaine and his retinue toward a confrontation on which she dared not speculate was far worse.

As hurt as she was that Calandra had deceived her all these years, she loved her dearly, nonetheless. That had not changed in light of Calandra's incredible revelations. Serena wished not the slightest ill or harm on the woman who had raised her, caring for her like her own child. She dreaded what Silas de Mortaine might do to Calandra if he thought she meant to thwart him from his villainous goals toward possessing the Dragon Chalice.

Serena knew she was as good as dead, whether or not she took Silas to the cottage as he had demanded. But to do so was to condemn Calandra to a similarly hideous fate—perhaps worse, given the look of loathing in de Mortaine's lifeless, ice blue eyes when he spoke her name. She would have to defy him, or lead him in a false direction and pray that Calandra would somehow be safe.

She was contemplating that very idea when the sound of spurred boots ticked hollowly toward her in the dark. Two men approached, both garbed in dark-colored mantles and clothing, both armed with deadly, gleaming swords. As they neared, the larger of them—a shaggy-haired man with massive shoulders and a squat, bulky neck put his face close to the bars and looked her up and down.

"A witch, are ye?" He sniffed at the air, startling Serena with the abrupt, animal-like mannerism. She backed away and he smiled, baring sharp overlong teeth. "Nay, just a human, I'd say."

"Time to let you out," said his companion without preamble. He jerked his chin at the leering giant in cool command. "Open the grate."

Under the dim light of a slim crescent moon, Serena watched in anxious silence as the big soldier stuck a key in the cage's lock. It sprang open with a metallic *snick*. The knight in charge gave a grim nod, and the other man opened the door of the cell.

Serena retreated to the back of the cramped space, her mind working frantically on every slight possibility she might have of escape in these few crucial moments. It seemed hopeless. The man now climbing into the cage to retrieve her was as big as an ox. The one waiting outside stared at her with cool, keen eyes that missed nothing. And both of them were outfitted for war.

"Now, where do you think you can run to in here?" chuckled the wolfish giant.

"Don't try to fight us," advised the commander. "You've nothing to fear, I promise you."

She did not believe him. The big man lunged at her, and made a swipe with his huge hand. Serena dodged, but he caught her arm and hauled her toward him with nary an effort. He pulled her out of the conveyance and set her down on the ground outside, still holding her in a bruising grip. She felt his fingers bite into her like claws.

"Easy," cautioned the knight in charge, a note of irritation hardening his previous smooth, intelligent tone.

"Let me go!"

Serena fought in earnest now, struggling with all she had to get loose. Her bare hands came down on a bristly-haired arm, and as the Knowing hissed of the danger that held her, it was all she could do to bite back her scream.

"Here's a rope," the commander said, withdrawing a coiled length of cord from a loop on his weapon belt. "Bind her hands for the ride."

The other man caught it in one beefy fist, his other holding both of Serena's wrists immobile. "It's full of knots," he groused, his gravelly voice blowing fetid air against her neck.

"Is it?" came the mild inquiry. "Let me have a look."

Serena heard a quick hiss of metal coming out of a sheath, but she had no chance to register what was happening until it was done. As she fought to break loose, the knight with the commanding air strode forth, and in one fluid, treacherous moment, sliced a dagger across the throat of the brute who held her.

"Shifters," spat the knight as the body collapsed in a twitching, gurgling heap at their feet. He threw her a look, the thin moonlight glinting in his dragon green eyes. "Loathsome bastards, one and all."

Confused, fearful, Serena flinched back. "Stay away from me."

The dagger dripped scarlet-black in the warrior's hand. He glanced down at it, then met her gaze once more. "There is little time, lady. And this blade is not for you."

He reached out to her, but she refused to accept his intimation of alliance so easily. "Who are you?"

"Your last hope," he replied, and there seemed no mercy in the statement, only cool opportunity and a confidence that bordered on arrogance. "We must go now. Your man awaits you with a ready mount."

"Rand?"

The dark knight nodded. "We have an agreement, Greycliff and I. Each of us holds something that the other dearly wants."

"And what have I to do with that?"

"You are the price he demanded in exchange for the cup bearing Calasaar and Vorimasaar."

"Rand would not surrender it to you. He cannot!"

"He can, and he has." The rogue's full lips lifted at the corner in a half smile. "Love makes a man do all manner of things, my lady."

"Love," Serena echoed. "Rand doesn't love me. Not after what I told him today."

"Aye, well . . . he wants you, and that is all that matters to me."

She glanced up at his shadowed features, the moonlight having softened the hard lines to a striking hand-someness. "Why should Rand or I trust you?"

The raven-haired knight's smile grew, a dazzling slash of white in his dark angel's face. "Because I just might be more desperate than either you or Greycliff—if not de Mortaine himself. And, dear lady, look around you. I'm all you've got."

"Silas will kill you if he finds out you have done this."

"He won't kill me," her deliverer countered without a speck of doubt. He shrugged. "I am most certainly dead already, but not by de Mortaine's hand."

His cryptic words drifting on the night wind, the mercenary hurried Serena toward a narrow corridor between two buildings and urged her to follow him into the waiting darkness.

Les Nantres was late.

Rand paced at his covert position near the bank of the River Ehen, two agile mounts gone missing from the town stables and now nickering behind him. They were itching for the road, and so was he. Rand held the horses' lines in a tight fist, cursing the fact he'd had to put his faith in a man whose only loyalty was to himself. Not two years past, Draec les Nantres had sold out a group of his closest friends, including Braedon le Chasseur, to Silas de Mortaine. Now Rand wondered if the devil intended a similar fate for Serena and him.

He wouldn't dare, Rand decided, not yet. Not so long as Rand held part of the Dragon Chalice. The cup bearing the Calasaar and Vorimasaar stones was strapped to his person in a saddle pack he had removed from one of the mounts. The treasure was all les Nantres wanted, and Rand cared not what drove him. Let him have the Chalice in full, if it meant Serena would be safe.

"Damnation, les Nantres. Where are you?"

The liquid rush of the river swallowed up his low growl, but it did not quite mask the sound of twigs snapping under heavy hooves in the brush nearby. Rand's free hand went to his sword in reflex, but then he glimpsed the horse and two riders. Seated behind Silas's lieutenant was the slender form of Serena, her long midnight-dark hair shining in the moonlight. She spied him there, and when he saw that she was hale, any anxiety he felt was swiftly washed away.

"Serena," he said, and opened his arms as she leaped off the horse's back and dashed toward him on a little cry of relief.

"Let's have done with this," les Nantres drawled with clear impatience, dismounting himself and now swaggering toward them while they embraced. "I've made good on my part of the deal. Now let us dispense with yours, Greycliff. You have the cup?"

Rand gave a single nod of his head.

When he reached within his mantle to retrieve the cup from the satchel, Serena, still clinging to him, lifted her worried gaze. "Don't do this, Rand. You cannot give it to them."

"I gave my word," he answered, then withdrew the golden goblet and held it out to les Nantres.

"My God," the mercenary gasped.

He took the cup in both hands, cradling the bowl in splayed fingers and holding it before him in rapt awe. The twisting form of a scaled dragon curled round on itself to form the cup's gilded stem. In its talons at the base of the bowl and glowing in the moonlight were two of the four sacred stones of the Dragon Chalice—Calasaar, pale as ice; Vorimasaar, like a red-gold ember.

"Well met, Greycliff," les Nantres said, finally tearing his gaze away from the splendor of his boon. "But we are even now. If our paths should cross again, expect no quarter from me."

"And to you as well," Rand returned with equal frankness.

He tossed him the satchel. With a final admiring look, Draec slipped the cup into the leather pocket and slung the long strap over his head.

"On to Scotland, then," les Nantres said with a grin. "There's but one piece left to this puzzle and I mean to have it."

Rand inclined his head in acknowledgment. "If your success means de Mortaine's defeat, then godspeed to you."

From within Rand's arms, Serena pivoted to face Draec while he stepped up into his saddle. "That is your plan? You intend to defeat Silas de Mortaine?"

"Aye, lady. That is my meaning."

"Then you should know that he does not ride for Scotland," Serena said in a rush.

Rand frowned down at the beauty in his arms. "What do you mean, love?"

"Silas plans to find Calandra instead. He told me so. He knows about the cottage in the woods, Rand. He lived there with her once—long ago. He says the cascade is the very place he and Calandra crossed when they left Anavrin with the Chalice. The cascade is a portal between our two realms."

"Jesu," Rand swore. "And Calandra?"

"I believe de Mortaine suspects she knows where the last of the Chalice stones is located."

Draec les Nantres turned a narrow look on her. "Is it possible?"

She gave a little shrug, then nodded. "I think she might know something about it, yes. And I know that if

Silas finds her, as he intends, he will find a way to kill her."

Rand glanced to les Nantres, whose grim gaze held like understanding.

"It seems our partnership is not yet ended," the mercenary remarked. "I have not come this far to gamble it all away now. Have you, Greycliff?"

❧ 29 ❧

THE TRIO RODE like hell itself were on their heels, for once Silas de Mortaine realized where they had gone, hell would indeed be snapping at their backs.

Serena held fast to the reins of her sleek palfrey, following Rand's lead over the black shadows of hills and vales, toward the heart of her forest home. It gave her comfort to know that Rand was there, never more than a half length ahead of her in the dark, frequently looking to make sure she kept pace. She dared not fall back. Everything she cared about had been brought into clear focus: Rand, Calandra, a peaceful life with both of them. It was all she needed, and she would fight at Rand's side to keep it.

In her heart, in the depths of her Knowing, she understood that the night would not pass without a battle. It was edging in like a storm, a metallic charge in the too-still air, the crescent moon peering down like a narrowed eye, waiting for the first shattering crack of thunder.

She could almost hear Silas de Mortaine's vicious roar as he discovered les Nantres had betrayed him. She could see him rounding up his cadre of shifters and soldiers, dispatching them with orders to kill all in their path. They were coming, she knew it. They could be no more than an hour behind.

At last, she began to recognize her surroundings. Her mount was huffing, sweating as it leaped the short rock boundary of the grove line. The trees became familiar, the patterned network of their trunks, the density of the area foliage. Rand must have known it, too. He navigated the paths as Serena herself would, and ably dodged his horse around hidden briars and treacherous bramble.

They rode deeper into the forest, and finally they neared the cottage at its heart. The little abode was dark she realized as the three of them brought their mounts to a halt in the small yard. Rand leaped down and ran to the door. He threw it open, calling for Calandra.

No answer came.

Serena slid off her horse and came up next to Rand in the doorway. "Mother!" she cried into the lightless chamber. She spun around, looking toward the darkened woods. "Calandra, where are you?"

But Serena was fairly certain she knew where to find her.

"The falls," she said.

With the two men close behind, she dashed for the little trail that would take them to the woodland cascade.

Calandra was there, seated at the edge of the cascade pool, her hair and clothing damp. Beside her was a sodden pouch, its contents partially spilled out onto the ground. Coins of varying sizes winked in the scant light, a veritable fortune, to be sure. Calandra must have been hoarding it for years, Serena guessed, astonished to discover it.

But the thought of unexpected earthly wealth paled next to Calandra herself, who sat very still on the flat slabs of granite, cradling an object in her lap. Serena approached her cautiously, sensing at once that something was very wrong.

"Mother," she said gently.

Even though her mind rejected it as untrue, Calandra was the only mother Serena had ever had. She was all the family she knew, and seeing her look so small, so withdrawn, squeezed her heart.

"Mother, it's me. I've come back for you."

Calandra slowly turned her head. She had been weeping. The moonlight was dim, but Serena could see the wet trails down the elder woman's cheeks, her bright blue eyes puffy and sad.

"What is it? Are you unwell?"

"Yes, child," she answered softly. "I am unwell. I am weary. So very weary."

Serena knelt down next to her on the cool stone. She saw the glint of gold in Calandra's lap and some of her breath left her on a gasp. "You did have part of the Chalice."

Calandra blinked slowly, then turned a wistful gaze back to the veil of the falls. "Do you know what lies on the other side of that water? A very long time ago, I was a foolish young girl who made a very grave mistake. Everything I once loved is on the other side of this waterfall, except for you, Serena. You are my joy here."

"The Chalice," Serena said again, aware of both Rand and les Nantres drawing near enough to see it as well. Clutched in the talons of the golden dragon stem was a stone of frosty blue. It reflected the moonglow, illuminating Calandra's sad expression. "Mother, how long have you had this? Where did you keep it—here in the cascade pool?"

Calandra gave a mild nod. "I knew he would not rest until he restored the Chalice. He was too mad to have it back. It was all he talked of, all he thought of. I had given him a gift, you see. And it could not be taken away from him. He would live forever, like me, and he would not rest until he possessed the Chalice again. I had to stop him somehow. I thought, if I could find just one piece of the treasure and hide it away, the Chalice would never be complete."

"Where did you find this?" Serena asked, bending forward to carefully remove the treasure from Calandra's slack fingers.

"A priest came through here . . . it was many, many years ago. He was from the north, a Scotsman. He said he thought me troubled. Mayhap I was. He told me of a small chapel across the marches, where pilgrims found peace and cures for their torments. He said I should go there, so I did. When I found this cup beneath the stones of the chapel well, I realized that perhaps there was a way for me to undo some of the ill I'd done to my kingdom. I could keep this cup out of Silas's reach for as long as I lived." Calandra laughed softly, ironically. "Do you know, that priest was right? After I visited his chapel, I did find some peace."

"The Stone of Peace," Serena replied. She pivoted and handed the cup to Rand.

"Serasaar," Calandra confirmed, her voice reverent with the Anavrin name. "But then, not a fortnight ago, another man arrived here and my tranquillity was gone. He brought the Outside with him, and two more parts of the Chalice treasure. That was too much power to hide away. That would surely bring Silas around in time."

"De Mortaine is coming now," les Nantres remarked grimly. "We've got trouble on the way, and riding hard."

Above the roar of the falls could now be heard the shouts of men and the crack of blades chewing through dense thicket.

"The cup," Rand said to him, his voice harsh with urgency. In his hand, Serasaar's pale blue stone had begun to glow, getting stronger. "Hand it over, Draec. Now!"

The mercenary threw him a mistrusting look.

"The cup, damn it!"

Les Nantres opened the leather satchel and withdrew the goblet containing Calasaar and Vorimasaar. It, too, was imbued with otherworldly light.

"Christ," he hissed, nearly dropping it. "The damned thing is pulsing. What is this? It feels alive in my hand."

"Bring it," Rand commanded.

As Draec came toward him, the cups they held sparked blinding light, throwing off rays brighter even than the sun. Serena shielded her eyes, turning her face into Calandra's shoulder. But the magic taking place was too extraordinary; she could not look away completely.

She could see Rand's strong arm shaking under the force of the Chalice's power. Les Nantres's as well. The light grew stronger. Neither strong warrior seemed able to control the will of the magic in their hands. The two pieces of the Dragon Chalice came together in a fierce, soundless crash. At once, a wave of incredible force blasted out in all directions, thumping in Serena's chest and ears, sending her hair flying as though caught in a gale.

It passed just as quickly, sucking the surrounding air back to the place where a single golden cup now lay in the grass between Rand and Draec les Nantres.

Serena felt Calandra stir, then slip out of her embrace. Before either man could move to retrieve the newly formed Chalice, Calandra had scooped it up.

And when she turned to carry it away, Silas de Mortaine and three shifter guards emerged from out of the forest to stand directly in her path.

"Why, Calandra," Silas snarled. "It has been a while."

He gave her no time to react. With a punishing swing

of his arm, de Mortaine struck the woman hard across her face. She flew to the ground, her head narrowly missing the sharp edge of a jutting slab of granite. The cup rolled out of her hands.

Rand lunged for it, but was brought up short by a length of shifter steel at his neck. In the periphery of his vision he saw that les Nantres had met with like greeting, scarcely able to draw his sword in defense. Silas's shifter guards made no move to retrieve the fallen Chalice; they would not, for none of the three wished to burn for touching the forbidden gold of the treasure they were bred to protect. The third shifter had apprehended both Serena and Calandra, one in each bruising hand, as he held them to face Silas de Mortaine.

"She has your eyes, Calandra," he remarked, casually strolling to where the Chalice lay on the ground. He picked it up, then pivoted back to the women. "She has your streak of stupidity as well. Did you really think you could elude me, girl?"

"Please, Silas," Calandra said, nary a trace of weariness in her voice now. "Let her go. She had naught to do with this. If you are angry, blame me."

"Oh, I do, Calandra. I most assuredly do blame you. And I'll see that you pay."

A fine white horse stood just inside the tree line, frothing from the ruthless run Silas had forced on it. De Mortaine walked there now, with the Chalice in hand. Rand could see that he struggled to hold it, and as he neared a bulging saddle pack, the three stones in the newly merged cup began to glow. Rand watched in seething fury as Silas withdrew the last of the four pieces.

"Jesu—we have to stop him!" Rand shouted, bucking forward, but he was held in check by the shifter guarding him.

De Mortaine turned to face them. "Behold, a new

dawn!" he crowed, his eyes wild, his golden hair standing nearly on end as he held the two cups out at his
sides. He tried to fight the pull of the Chalice's magic,
laughing maniacally. Then with a shout of victory, he
brought his hands together before him.

Rand expected another blinding explosion of light
and bone-jarring, otherworldly power. This time, as the
last of the Dragon Chalice merged into the whole, there
was light, but it was a climbing spiral of pure color and
heat. The power was there as well, spreading out to all
who stood in the glade. It lifted the hairs on Rand's arms
and scalp. It passed through him like fingers of some unseen being. It was beautiful, this power of the four.

Even de Mortaine seemed awestruck . . . for a moment.

"By the blood of Christ," he murmured, staring at the
treasure in his hands. "I had forgotten what this felt
like." He glanced to the pool of crystalline water behind
him. "I will never forget what a drink from this cup
tastes like, however. And long have I waited to taste it
again."

"The Chalice gave you life once," Calandra said, in-
terrupting his gloating delight. "It can give you nothing
more."

"You expect me to believe you?"

"It is the truth."

"The truth," he scoffed, looking at her with open de-
rision. "You would say anything to keep me from claiming my destiny—what is mine by rights!"

Smiling now, de Mortaine strode briskly to the edge
of the cascade pool. He crouched down, dipped the
shimmering Chalice into the water, and lifted it high into
the air for all of them to see.

"No!" Rand roared, a futile demand when the threatening edge of shifter steel still pressed meaningfully at his neck.

Silas de Mortaine laughed thinly. "This cup is mine. All its riches—all of Anavrin's awaiting power—mine at last!"

With that, he brought the Dragon Chalice to his lips and let the water pour down his throat.

❧ 30 ❧

NEVER HAD SILAS tasted anything so sweet. He had waited so long for this moment—his ultimate triumph. He was deserving of this greatness. By God, he was due.

He closed his eyes and savored each drop of the cool water that poured down his throat from the glittering, golden bowl of the Dragon Chalice. He felt it rush into his body, seeping into every sinew and bone, refreshing and sweet, so full of power.

All his. His destiny was at last fulfilled.

He would be king of this world and the next!

It was not until he lifted his heavy lids that he realized something was amiss.

His gaze settled on Calandra, on the clear blue eyes that peered at him through the chaos of the glade. She was smiling, content in her own private triumph as he brought the Chalice down from his lips.

The first sharp jolt stunned him.

Pain unlike any he had known ripped through his abdomen. His insides were on fire. Silas dropped to his knees on the grassy floor of the clearing, his breath robbed from his lungs. It was happening so fast.

Calandra's smile widened to a beatific, ageless grin.

"It can give you nothing more," she said, her promise again, only now he knew it for a woeful truth. Calandra's gaze was bright, never more entrancing than in her present fury.

"You—bitch!"

The words sprayed out of his mouth on a gasp of thick spittle. Silas held his stomach, which felt as if it were being rent asunder from within. He glanced down and saw that his fine silk tunic and mantle were turning a deep crimson, his blood soaking the white silk from an unseen wound in his torso. The stain grew and grew, and he realized he had, in fact, known a similar anguish once before—the very day Calandra had found him, stabbed from some transgression he no longer recalled, bleeding to death right here at this very cascade. He would have died if not for the drink she gave him from the Chalice.

Now he was once more, again.

Calandra laughed, content in his misery. "One sip from the Chalice to restore you . . . another to take it back."

Silas could no longer hold his own weight. The wound sapped him of his strength, but there was something more happening now. His skin was turning gray, wrinkling before his eyes. Shriveling. He cried out in horror as his fingers curled into stiff, ancient claws, his voice going rusty with the sudden onslaught of age. All the years the Chalice had given him were now stripping away, one after the other, faster and faster.

As death latched onto him and dust began to fill his mouth and eyes, Silas managed one final order.

"Kill them! Kill them all!"

The glade erupted in chaos on Silas's dying words.

The sword at Rand's throat bit hard into his flesh, just a small twitch of shifter muscle away from ending him then and there. As the blade moved, so did Rand. He tucked his fist into his chest and with a sharp jerk of his elbow, caught the shifter in the gut. A cough of sour breath wheezed past his ear—momentary reprieve from the pressure of cold steel at his neck.

With a roar, Rand snapped his head back, connecting with the shifter's close face. There was a crack of bone and cartilage, and the grip on him went slack for an instant. Rand seized his chance. He spun around, wrenching free the blade that bore the crimson tinge of his own blood on its length. He flipped it around, then drove it home with a curse, impaling the shifter in one swift blow.

"Serena!" he shouted, free to help her now and immediately looking to assess her position.

She and Calandra were trying to fight off the guard who held them, Serena struggling to pry away the cruel fingers that twisted Calandra's arm until she dropped, screaming, to her knees. Calandra kicked and scratched and gnashed her teeth, goading the shifter into giving her the worst of his animal rage. The beast began to change under the women's continued assault. Its shaggy head grew more bristly, its mouth stretching snoutlike, black lips peeling back over sharp, wolfish jaws.

"Jesu. Serena! Calandra!"

Rand leaped over the body of the shifter he had slain, sword raised, poised for attack. He brought the steel down on the beast's shoulder, recoiling as blood sprayed out from the wound. The shifter howled in anguish, and as it pivoted to face him—half man, half slavering wolf—it knocked Calandra aside with a furious swipe of its huge hand. The black talons sliced through her gown, ripping four long, bloody tracks across her stomach.

"Mother!" Serena cried, horror widening her eyes.

The shifter threw her down next to Calandra, its sights now fixed on bigger game. It stalked toward Rand with murder in its eyes.

Rand motioned the inhuman warrior to him. "Come on, cur. I'm ready for you."

The shifter leaped on him. Rand delivered one glancing blow of his sword before he was knocked to the ground. Deadly teeth snapped too close to his face, tearing his flesh. Animal claws held him like prey as the shifter rolled him over rough ground and into the thorny bracken nearby. Rand punched the terrible face above him, again and again, until his fist was slick with blood and spittle.

In periphery, he noted that les Nantres had his own hands full with the guard who held him. The mercenary was bloodied and panting, but giving as good as he was getting. In another time, on another field of battle, Rand might have been glad to have a warrior like Draec les Nantres at his side. He fought like a demon—all for the Dragon Chalice. But this hour had come down to just one thing in Rand's mind: protecting Serena.

Which was why, when he saw her scramble to retrieve the golden cup from the pile of ash that had once been Silas de Mortaine, Rand knew a bone-deep, sudden dread. She held it out before her like a weapon as she carried it toward the place where Rand and the shifter thrashed.

"Serena, do not!" he yelled at her. "Stay away!"

But he could see the ferocity in her smooth gait. Her aqua eyes had darkened to a stormy shade of determination. She came closer, and while the shifter bent its head to attack Rand again, Serena ran up behind it and pressed the Dragon Chalice to its spine.

A howl unlike anything Rand had heard before went up into the night sky.

Flesh hissed beneath the powerful touch of the Chalice, emitting foul smoke. The shifter recoiled at once, rearing up in agony. His animal face spasmed between

forms—wolf to man to wolf again—as he reached behind him, trying to beat at the fire that was eating him
alive.

To Rand's relief, Serena was well out of reach. She retreated with the Chalice back to where Calandra lay
near the edge of the cascade pool, while Rand sprang at
once to action. He came up off the ground, bringing his
weapon with him. One efficient, killing blow, and the
beast's terrible wailing ceased.

Not a few yards away, les Nantres had just ended the
last shifter's life as well. He gave Rand a reckless shrug,
his grin still arrogant even through a mouthful of blood.
The dark knight limped forward, haggard and wheez-
ing, looking like death itself.

"Oh, God!" Serena cried, racing into Rand's waiting
arms. "I was so frightened. Are you hurt? You're bleeding!"

Rand gathered her close and held her to him, never so
glad as he was to hear her little heart beating hard
against his chest. He wanted to scold her for putting herself in harm's way, but he had no words. All he had was
tender kisses, and a fierce need to never let her go.

He did not know what made him look up at that moment. Perhaps it was the thundering rush of the falls, or
the slow fade of night overhead as dawn began to wake
and rise. But when Rand lifted his head and saw Calandra, some of his peace fled on a hushed oath.

"Serena, love," he gently whispered into her glossy
hair.

But she already knew. Her hands on him, her touch
surely told her what he was witnessing.

Serena came out of his embrace, her gaze already tear-
filled and turning toward the cascade pool. Calandra
slumped at the edge of it, the Dragon Chalice tipped on
its side in her lap, wetting the front of her gown. Her

chin dripped water from the deadly drink she had just ingested.

"Mother?" Serena cried, her voice thick with emotion. "Oh, no. No!"

Serena felt as though she walked on wooden legs as she neared the place where Calandra—*nay, she was her mother, in all ways that mattered*—lay so small and quiet on the hard rock slabs that edged the cascade pool.

Serena knelt down beside her and lifted Calandra's hand into hers. A flood of sorrow filled her, but that emotion was hers alone. The Knowing showed her only weariness, and placid acceptance in Calandra's long-immortal heart.

"What have you done, Mother? Why this? Why now?"

"Oh, child." Calandra smiled, reaching up to place her palm against Serena's cheek. "I have lived too long. I have seen all my children and their children enter—and leave—this life. I am tired. Living here, on the Outside, is too hard."

"No," Serena argued. "We were happy, weren't we?"

"Yes, we were." Calandra nodded. "But it was wrong for me to keep you hidden away in these woods. I told myself it was to protect you, but in my heart, I knew that I did it selfishly. You were all I had left, and I couldn't bear to lose you."

"You haven't. You wouldn't have, Mother, not ever."

Rand strode up behind Serena. He put his hand on her shoulder, the warmth of his touch giving her strength as Calandra's fingers began to grow cold against her palm.

"You were an exceptional child, Serena. And you have grown into an extraordinary woman. I am . . . so proud of you."

"Then, why? Why are you leaving me now?"

"So you will be free, my dear child."

Serena felt a sob become entangled in her throat. "I will be lost without you, Mother."

"Oh," Calandra said, more sigh than answer, "you were never lost. You have known your own way all your life. And you have someone else who cares for you. Very deeply, I think."

"I love her," Rand said, crouching down to bring Serena into the circle of his arm. "I love her more than life itself."

Serena looked at his tender gaze beside her, so handsome and true. She felt such elation in that moment, yet at the same time her heart was breaking to have to say good-bye to Calandra.

She gazed down at the bloodless, beautiful face of the Anavrin princess who raised her, and saw that the time was near. Calandra's bright blue eyes were dimming, her lips gone thin and pale.

"I am ready," she whispered to Serena. The words were dry, a bare croak of sound. "Now go, child. Take the purse of coins I have saved for you, and go . . . live your life."

"I love you," Serena told her, bending down to kiss her fair brow. "I will miss you so."

Calandra drew her hand out of Serena's grasp. Death was coming, Serena realized, understanding that Calandra would spare her the Knowing of its chill touch. Calandra nodded, closing her eyes. Age began a swift march over her slender form. As it advanced toward dust, Rand lovingly cradled Serena's nape in his palm and brought her to him, holding her until it had passed.

"I'll have that cup now, Greycliff."

Draec les Nantres stood, battered and bloody, but an arm's length from them. The hem of his dark mantle sifted around his boots, deep crimson against black. He stretched out his hand, waiting for the Chalice.

"You would want it now, after what you've seen it do here?" Rand asked in clear disbelief. "That cup is cursed, do you ask me."

"Cursed or nay, it is mine. We had a deal."

"Aye, we had a deal," Rand agreed, and after a moment, he handed Draec the Chalice. "If that cup is worth so much to you, then have it and good riddance. But I don't think you'll live very long to enjoy it."

As les Nantres took the Dragon Chalice from Rand, he looked down at the grave wounds he had suffered in his skirmish with de Mortaine's men. He pivoted to the pool behind him and scooped up some of the crystalline water. "One sip from the Chalice to restore you," he said, quoting Calandra's own words to Silas as he had taken his fateful second drink.

Draec lifted the golden cup to his lips. As he did, a breeze off the falls caught the edge of his cloak and threw it open in a tempest of swirling fabric. Serena's eyes widened as she focused on the emblem the knight wore on his tunic. It was a black dragon, rampant and snarling over les Nantres's heart.

Serena stared at it, transfixed. All the times she heard the legend of the Dragon Chalice, the ending was forever the same: If the treasure came back to Anavrin by trickery, or carried there in a villain's hands, a great and terrible dragon would be unleashed on the land. The dark knight's insignia seemed to grin at her now, as did its wearer, les Nantres's green eyes bright with triumph.

"Oh, mercy," she whispered, suddenly fearing they might have made a grave mistake to bargain with the man. Could she be looking at the prophesied dragon that would rise to destroy Anavrin? "Rand, something is not right—"

But Draec was already tipping the Chalice up to his mouth, prepared to take the first swallow. He did not get that chance. There was a sudden whistle of disturbance in the air. Something flew past Serena and Rand, deadly fast.

It was a dagger, thrown from the first shifter Rand had fought in the glade. The slender knife struck with unerring aim, lodging into Draec les Nantres's chest. He stumbled back, a look of utter shock on his face.

Rand gave a sudden shout of rage. In a trice, he vaulted to his feet and drew a blade of his own, releasing it with lethal speed. The shifter went down at once, dead before his girth hit the ground, Rand's dagger protruding from its bulky forehead.

But it was too late for Draec les Nantres.

Roaring in pain, he tumbled backward into the cascade pool, the Dragon Chalice still clutched in his hand. Together, Serena and Rand dashed to the edge and peered in. The water churned as if it were boiling, white plumes of foam and swirling water nearly obscuring the mercenary and the gilded cup he had held as he fell. She did not think the bolt had killed him, for her vision teased with flashes of movement far below the surface of the pool.

"I've got to help him," Rand said, but as he started to move, Serena placed a warning hand on his arm.

A sudden cool breeze had rolled in off the falls. It sifted through the glade like a whisper, and then, silence. All had gone quiet, even the high cliff of rushing water.

"Good God," Rand gasped.

The cascade was as clear as glass before them. A transparent veil, it stood between the very real world of the glade and another, one of color and light and a beauty that defied description. And at the distant center of this other realm stood a castle—soaring towers, snapping pennons, and white bricks that glittered so bright they seemed to have been hewn from stars in the heavens.

"Anavrin," Serena breathed.

"Amazing," Rand agreed, equally reverent as he took her hand in his.

The illusion danced just out of their grasp, too distant to touch, yet neither moved to try. Although a part of her belonged to Anavrin, there was still much about this world Serena wanted to experience.

If only she could do so with Rand at her side.

As quickly as it appeared, the window on Anavrin was gone. The veil clouded over, then turned once more to the lacy rush of the falls. In the pool below, the water ceased its churning. It calmed, like the glade itself, as the new day stretched pale pink fingers through the trees.

Rand peered into the clear water of the pool. "God's blood. He's gone—les Nantres is not anywhere in there now."

Serena glanced around the quiet woods and saw nothing but summer foliage and dew-kissed grass. "They're all gone."

So they were. The ashes of de Mortaine and Calandra, the three dead shifters—all of them were vanished as if never there at all. Like a terrible nightmare chased away by the light, no traces remained of the confrontation that had occurred in this patch of forest. Serena took a step away from the edge of the pool, and the soft click of coins rang at her feet.

"Calandra's purse," she said, bending down to retrieve it. The satchel was heavy, more than a lifetime's worth of coin. Generations' worth, Serena acknowledged, accepting Calandra's gift with heartfelt gratitude.

"It's over," Rand said, wrapping his arm around her shoulders. "We survived it together. And it's over."

Serena nodded, but she could not dismiss the truth of

all she had discovered these past few days. Her blood ties to Silas de Mortaine were something that would never wash clean, nor would they disappear through any brand of Anavrin magic. She was, and would always be, part of the man who robbed Rand of so much. She would always be the child of his enemy.

"Rand," she began anxiously, "do you think you can ever forget . . . who I truly am?"

For a long moment, he said nothing. Then, finally, "No. I cannot ever forget that."

She slumped a bit, but nodded in silent acceptance. He smiled down at her bowed head, and gently lifted her chin until she was looking him full in the eyes.

"You," he said, "are Serena of the grove. My sweet dove, the angel who saved me when nothing else could have. You, Serena, are my hope."

"Then take me away from here now," she whispered, clutching him to her.

"My love, I would like nothing better." He brought her closer, reveling in the feel of her body pressed against his. "But I fear I have nothing to give you. I have nowhere to take you."

"That's not true." She pulled out of his embrace to look up at him, and he was moved to see the love shining so brightly in her gaze. "Show me the place where you say the sun lights the ocean to the color of my eyes. Show me the king's court in London, where we'll dine on fine food and rich wine. Or the highlands of Scotland, where we might meet some of your mother's kin. Show me all there is to see beyond the boundaries of this tiny grove, only take me with you."

Now he was smiling, unable to dim the glow of his own emotion when he was looking at the woman who so fully captured his heart. With Serena's head resting against his chest once more, Rand let himself imagine what might lay ahead of him—a wedding in a small highland chapel; a strong and beautiful bride who bewitched him completely; a deep, enduring love that he never thought he would know.

"It is a pretty dream," he said, letting his fingers roam over the velvet softness of her skin.

"Let us live it," she whispered. "Let's go and make it real, right now."

And as she twined her Knowing hands in his hair and brought him down for her kiss, Rand vowed he would make both their dreams come true. He would give Serena a lifetime of adventure . . . so long as he had the peace of loving her forever.

**If you enjoyed HEART OF THE DOVE,
you will love these spellbinding
books in the Dragon Chalice series
by Tina St. John**

A storm is brewing in
HEART OF THE HUNTER

Allied in a quest for a legendary treasure—a chalice that
brings its possessor ultimate dominion over mankind—
Ariana of Clairmont must join forces with Braedon le
Chasseur, a seductive knight with a mysterious past—
and a dark legacy he struggles to deny.

And a quest is beginning in
HEART OF THE FLAME

Kenrick of Clairmont is determined to find the hidden
Dragon Chalice. With the enemy ever encroaching, he
must rely on an enigmatic beauty called Haven, whose
shadowy past will threaten the quest and quite possibly
destroy their future.

Pillow Talk